MW01104978

Jillian Benson
31

ESPER'S DRAGON SONG

Book one in Pangaea series

Jillian Benson

authorHOUSE®

AuthorHouse™
1663 Liberty Drive
Bloomington, IN 47403
www.authorhouse.com
Phone: 1-800-839-8640

© 2015 Jillian Benson. All rights reserved.

No part of this book may be reproduced, stored in
a retrieval system, or transmitted by any means
without the written permission of the author.

Published by AuthorHouse   01/07/2015

ISBN: 978-1-4969-6268-3 (sc)
ISBN: 978-1-4969-6267-6 (e)

Library of Congress Control Number: 2015900151

Any people depicted in stock imagery provided by Thinkstock are models,
and such images are being used for illustrative purposes only.
Certain stock imagery © Thinkstock.

This book is printed on acid-free paper.

Because of the dynamic nature of the Internet, any web addresses or
links contained in this book may have changed since publication and
may no longer be valid. The views expressed in this work are solely those
of the author and do not necessarily reflect the views of the publisher,
and the publisher hereby disclaims any responsibility for them.

Contents

Introduction...,............vii

Present time xi

Chapter 1 1

Chapter 2 12

Chapter 3 51

Chapter 4 78

Chapter 5 98

Chapter 6 120

Chapter 7 144

Chapter 8 166

Chapter 9   172

Chapter 10 196

Chapter 11 223

Chapter 12 281

Chapter 13   340

Chapter 14 352

Chapter 15 361

Chapter 16 369

Chapter 17   400

Chapter 18   414

Chapter 19 433

Chapter 20 447

MAIN CHARACTER LIST 455

Introduction

One month earlier…

Zar paced the throne room, his gigantic feet eating up the distance, "*Zar, love, you must stop all this pacing and irritability. Everyone is afraid to even come close to the palace. We will never find his destined this way, I am just as anxious as you, but we must be patient,*" Averia counseled, brushing against me, nuzzling my cheek in support, her beautiful blue scales gleaming against her gold necklace.

"*It is unfair. Why should they do this to us? Wasn't it bad enough what that man did to Cigna, but must he now influence everyone else in his horrible ways? Enslaving others is bad enough of itself but to make our eggs unable to hatch just to get us to go to those monsters to fix the problem is despicable.*" I roar in frustration, the earth rumbles and move as wind whipped around us at high speeds. I pull myself together after a minute chest heaving, my gills opening to get more oxygen, and the room goes eerily quiet. "*Are you done yet? You are preaching to the choir. He is also my son that I may not be able to see hatched.*" She lashed her long webbed tail back and forth at wits end with keeping her temper. I could see myself reflected in her eyes in all my angry golden glory. The curse being a cruel curse that keeps our eggs in a deep slumber unable to hatch and when forced open unable to survive in the atmosphere.

"*Mate, the oracle did say there was hope without going to the slavers, finding his bonded,*" Averia went over to our swirl of dark blue/purple egg, stroking its surface, "*Love you know that we have already tried that; every year, every time a baby is born, and every summoning spell known to our caster!*" Zar felt another roar gathering, but choked back. "*Exactly, our casters know every well for our dimension, but maybe his bonded is no longer in this dimension. The person could've been among the poor creatures that were split! It would explain why a location spell for this dimension wouldn't work. We need someone who likes to dabble in more than our dimension for magic.*"

Zar exhaled, pushing her to their bed, "*I know who you speak of, but it might not even work. Their world is tremendously hard to get magic through. You remember the witch burning they did to those who were powerful enough to retain magic there, all those powerful casters burned, drowned, and stoned. They are not overly fond of it, who we would even get to go there to fetch his bonded I have no clue, we certainly cannot!*" Zar lowered himself and all his great bulk of dragon body next to her, comforted by her close presence.

"*We could send someone to make sure they would be willing to come the easy way or if we must force them! We only need them here for enough time to awake him from his enchanted sleep. It doesn't matter who we send. It could be anyone who looks humanoid. It is not as if we can't afford the caster's price. Zar you may be king here but I just gave you a customary warning, I am doing this with or without you! I would like to see my son hatched, if it means by any means necessary if it comes down to it, I will give myself to the slavers as an exchange, you can't stop me. I am still queen!*" Averia was worked up, near seething; there wasn't a doubt in my mind that she would do just that.

"*Averia, if it comes down to that. you wouldn't be the one doing the trade, I already would have. You would be needed to raise him. But how about we start with this plan you are working with, before we go to extremes, we know he breaks the curse.*" Zar would take his own life before he let her give hers up no matter how good the reason.

"*We shall send for the caster to do the spell, and send someone out to watch the bonded and in one month's time either willing or not bring them to us,*" Zar commanded, giving the last and final say to it, as Dragon King Zar of Pangaea.

*

Present time

The thunder sounds shaking the poorly built house. It is a minuscule one story house; with (maybe) three rooms. A tiny cramp kitchen and a room you can't even call a living room, and don't even get me started on the "bath room." It is a house from hell. You can go in a dictionary and look up hell and this would be the reference it took you to.

I have lived in a lot of places that are horrid but this, this one is the worst.

Our caretaker Mr. Johan is a despicable man who thinks is he was always right, and that even though, the government pays him money to take care of us, we are his slaves. The money that they give him is meant to be spent on us, instead spending on beer and the expensive gifts he gives to his "girlfriends." He likes to look richer and more sophisticated than he is, but only succeeds in looking like a middle aged, balding man.

The wind tears at the house making it creak ominously.

There are nine of us and not enough beds let alone rooms in the house that we have to be three to four to a room. I am the oldest at seventeen, and I feel responsible for all of us. I mean, we have spent two years together and you tend to get close. The youngest of us is about four. I'm Esper Collette; I'm five foot four inches, with amethyst eyes, a slight upturned nose, rosy lips, auburn hair, a curvy body, and a love for any and all knowledge.

Jenni, the youngest, cries out and runs into the room as the thunder booms closer than before. She jumps under the covers and crawls up to cling to my side.

"Esper," Jenni whimpers clutching to me.

I cuddle her to my chest, and pull her closer when she whimpers yet again. Another flash of lightning zips past the window close by.

Jenni has long curly copper hair, beautiful green eyes, and a plump youthfully round face. She is as cute as a button.

Garret and Dante, identical twins who are ten years old, come running in after, their shaggy black hair flying wildly in disarray, and blue eyes flashing in the white light. They try to act like the thunder and lightning hasn't scared them, and they were just there to check on us. "We thought you might be scared, would you like us to …. Uh guard you… yeah guard you!" It was a wonder that they hadn't got a home, but the same could pretty much be said about all of us. We seemed to be the ones that slipped through the cracks.

I motion for them to come over. Without any more prodding they dive for the bed, and curl up beside us. Toni rolls over from his "bed" and looks up at us, a sleepy smile moving across his face.

Toni is handsome for sixteen, with brown hair and eyes and a chiseled face. He is still growing into his body but he is looking a lot better than last year, kind of like Zac Efron in his younger years, paints a really bad picture. Things have to get ugly before it can become beautiful, I think.

My other roommate, Dash, looks up from his pillow and gives us a look like, "how-dare-you-wake-me-up-during-a-storm-for-some-mushy-moment" before dropping his head back onto his pillow once more.

Dash is part black and has that handsome mocha caramel skin, full lips, black hair, and big chocolate-brown, melt-me eyes. He is sixteen and going through The Faze of mushy, ick! The macho crap is getting annoying thou.

The rest of my 'siblings' look in from the door. Yanni, who is German, is fourteen and a half years old, with sandy blonde hair, all gangly limbs, bright blue eyes, and a love for playing the guitar. Raven, who is fifteen, with coal black hair, and grey eyes, is all about her makeup, fashion and herself. Then Lucan who is Raven's fraternal twin, with hazel eyes, and bleach blonde hair put like into a spiked Mohawk.

That just leaves me, I guess. I'm Esper Collette, seventeen years of age, five foot two inches in height. I have violet eyes, auburn hair, curvy enough to barely be called slim. I like my pretty things like the next girl but I just like knowing I can dress up if I want, rather not go through primping and prodding for hours only to have to take it off soon and start over the next day, to Raven's dismay. I can't speak for the others but I know myself enough to know I suck when it comes to others, I hate bugs, and if I make a promise I will come through no matter how long it takes me.

I stroke Jenni on her head and lift her, to clutch her up closer to my chest.

"Come on guys; let's get you tucked in and asleep in your own bed so Mr. Johan doesn't notice." Jenni shudders, and snuggles closer. "Esper, why hasn't anyone rescued us from him yet?" I just shake my head and repeat over and over I don't know, but some day one way or another we will get out. Not having the heart to force her back to her own room I let her sleep in my bed, trying to allow her some sense of safety.

1

The next day at school I have the strangest feeling, one I can't describe, almost like a change is in the air, or a thousand feathers running lightly barely there over my spine.

One thing you should know is that school is like the only place that almost rivaled home for the spot as hell. Kids here are cruel. I told Jenni if kids made fun of her she was to just smile and ignore them, and that they were just jealous. She was young enough to believe me.

When you have been in the system since you were six you tend to get used to either the pity or the kids who think they are better than you and you had better just fall into line.

I only have two friend at school, Luke, he is the kind of guy that if you told him not to do something he is going to do it. He is cute in the boy next door kind of way. I don't mind that we started off rocky because we became fast friends. Then there is Prisca, she is an odd sort, she appeared out of nowhere last month, but loyal and will defend anyone no matter who they are. She reminds me of one of those ethereal modal types with long white blonde hair with blue streaks and topaz eyes.

I am in second period when the inter com beeps and decrees "Esper Collette to the office." Like the children they are, the class does the little 'oooh you are in trouble' bit.

I walk through the hallways with the weird feeling, suppressing the need to shiver and check for spiders crawling on me or something. I thought my day might actually be somewhat okay spend it invisible, no waves, except the one person I have to walk into when I am not paying attention is Cara.

Cara is five foot four inches in height, with blonde hair, big boobs, good fashion sense (I guess), and she thinks she runs the school. She is also filthy rich and spoiled rotten but in my opinion I think her parents don't pay attention to her and that is why she seeks out attention, and when she doesn't get it she gets mean. I feel sorry for her, of course if I ever mention that were she could hear it she might throw an epic tantrum, a cliché in every way.

"Watch where you are going," Cara shrieks as if I have thrown something on her. "What you think you own this school; that you can just go around running into people!" She shrieks some more, not even lowering her voice when heads poke out of doors to see what all the commotion is about.

I give her a look that literally says it all, but add, "Well usually people spend more time in class then at the mirror, but I'm sure you know nothing about that." I walk around her. She screeches at me to come back here right this instant, but I disregard her and head to the office down the hall.

I walk in as the secretary looks out at the hall trying to see the commotion that Cara was making. I just smile as she looks at me questioningly. She's a nice older woman named Mrs. Lilla. She is small and pudgy, with curly white hair cut short like most old people do. She is easily near retirement but when asked she brushes it off, saying she is too young for that or she will have time to retire when she is dead, or no rest for the wicked. I may not know people well but even I can sense she is sweet she oozes it.

"What is all that noise about, Esper?" I shrug as if I have nothing to do with it, I don't need more drama my life is already the makings of a soap opera. "Just Cara trying to get attention; I was called here?" She nods slowly, about Cara, or me be called here, who knows.

"It's about your brother, Dash." She says it as if it explains everything, sadly it kind of does.

"What now?" I can't help getting exasperated. I mean, third time in a month and I don't need to ask why they came to me and not Mr. Johan. He was probably 'too busy'. Busy, my ass, he was probable off spending the government money that was supposed to be for our care. I sound old.

"Lead the way." I sweep my hands forward and bow.

She leads me back to one of the office rooms where Dash sits all alone. I also notice in another room a Goth punk kid who likes to play grab ass sitting moaning as he holds up an ice pack to his face were I can see what looks to be a black eye forming and a big fat lip.

"Dash this is the third time you have been in here. If this keeps up they are going to suspend you." I walk into the room. He doesn't look as bad as the other dude that is for sure. I know the only reason Michael isn't expelled is because we are orphans and they feel bad for us.

"He was trying to force himself on a girl. What was I supposed to do! Huh?" Dash stands, he is like Hulk, feeling that they need to protect the innocent.

I nod and the tension drains from his shoulders.

"No more, you hear me. You see that happen or anything similar you pull them off or go get help…. Ugh." My head falls forward. Now that I know the circumstances, I can't fault him. I probably would've done the same thing, can't even tell him to do differently.

He grins, I shake my finger at him, I doubt that even if we weren't orphans they wouldn't expel him, more like pin a medal on him.

The end of second period bell sounds.

"Let's get back to class before they decide to suspend the both of us for missing classes."

I shake my head, and head out the office room. The principle is talking to grab-ass and just nods as we headed out.

The day continues on and on, more boring classes with people I can barely tolerate. I spend most of the day indulging my romantic side with fancies about being taken away from this place, and half listening to my teachers.

*

The bell finally sounds letting us out of sixth period. I have a huge migraine and I can't wait to get out of there, I hug Luke before leaving to meet up with Dash.

Jenni is waiting for us out side of the elementary school. She is bouncing up and down and looks like she has something to say and if she doesn't say it she is going to burst.

"Esper, Esper, Esper, Esper!!!!!" She comes running towards us holding something in her arms. My heart sinks as she comes up with a tiny fluffy black kitten.

"Esper, look, look, look!" She holds up the kitten. It is so tiny, it meows in discomfort at being man handled, but cuddles back up to Jenni once she brings it back to her chest.

"Jenni…. You can't keep it." I make my voice soft, but she still starts tearing up, she clutches it closer.

"But… but… Mag was giving them away she said you wouldn't mind because if it didn't find a home they would have to send…. Send it to the big place in the sky." Her voice is coming out in hiccupping sobs.

"Jenni, Mr. Johan won't let you keep him." I try to sound comforting but she just keeps shaking her head. Dash stands to the side like a big lump obviously uncomfortable with this conversation and the possibility of tears.

We try for a while trying to let her down easy but she just starts bawling.

"Come on, Esper, at this rate we will never get home. Just let her take the cat back tomorrow. Her friend probably isn't even here anymore. It's also starting to rain again." Dash shifts from foot to foot, I finally concede, Jenni beams as if she has won the lottery.

Jenni runs up to Dash, curls bouncing. She hugs him tight, smashing the kitten between them until it gives out a cry in protest.

"If you met a dragon what would you do?" Jenni dances around us, twirling with her kitty. Dash hems and haws, "I would probable try and hide, with the teeth and such." Jenni glances at me, "I would hug it, if it's nice I made a friend if it plans on eating me then it's harder to eat me. What brings this up?"

Jenni pauses for a second to collect her thoughts. "We were doing what ifs." Dash motions to her, "What if you had wings…"

*

By the time we make it home Mr. Johan is sitting in front of the TV with his feet propped up. "Grab me a beer," he growls from the coach. "Go get it yourself." I mean to walk by him but he jumps up and grabs my arm. "Are you giving me lip girl?" Mr. Johan growls shaking me slightly, "What's that filthy creature the girl has!" I haven't had the best day so I probably should keep my mouth shut but of course…

"I'm sure you can get off your lazy ass for two seconds so you can get your own beer and get back to getting plastered, the *creature* is none of your business. Not like we planned on keeping it, your Lordship." I regret it as soon as the words leave my mouth, but I am just so fed up with him and his drunken stupors.

He turns five shades of red and purple, and I don't have a chance to cover my head before his fist smashes into my face. Knocking me into the wall, he is faster than he seems.

Dash runs in from outside, thrusting himself between me and Mr. Johan in the split second he assesses what is going on.

"Leave her alone or go through me." Mr. Johan just curses and goes to grab his own beer. Dash gives me a hand up, without turning all the way around, making sure to never turn his back on that coward.

"Let's go before he gets fake courage from the drink." Dash ushers us ahead of him into the bedroom so he doesn't have to take his eyes off our drunken guardian.

Toni gives a curious look at Jenni and the kitten, as we make our way into the bedroom. Raven, Lucan, and Yanni working on homework on the floor. I shake my head, to tell him to leave off until later.

I feel another tingle rush up my spine.

"We shouldn't talk here, let's go to the fort."

We make our way through the door and out the alleyway, walking for about two to three minutes before we reach the little shack, the twins catching us on our way out, and tagged along. The windows are broken, graffiti is all over the walls, and boards on the side are broken and have gaps, but it is a good place to get some privacy.

We don't bring any belongings here for fear of if we have to leave suddenly or our possessions being stolen. We sit down on buckets and chairs that we had scrounged up.

The rain is drizzling, so we have to worry about the house leaking on us a little. Thunder clouds form over the fort looking dark and angry. Thunder sounds close by nearly shaking the hut.

Toni pulls me aside, "Bad news Esper. I overheard Mr. Johan they are going to place Jenni…. with the Sherman's." The Shermans being awful people who collected kids, more after the check; I had been placed there once upon a time.

"God, if I could save her from that fate." I whisper my voice sounding hoarse, afraid the others will hear. My heart squeezes painfully for her, she is all soft and tiny five years old for crying out loud just isn't fair that she has to go through this.

When we settle down, Toni looks at Jenni, again.

"Hmm, there is something different about this little girl of ours." He walks around her and lifts her hair, acting as if he doesn't see.

Jenni giggles and shakes her head. He looks puzzled and circles some more before pretending to just notice the cute kitten as Jenni holds it up to him.

"Is it a rabbit?" Jenni giggles and shakes her head.

"Nooo," she giggles again.

"Is it a hamster?" she shakes her head again, looking about to burst.

"Nooo, it's a kitten!" Jenni squeals.

"Oh I see now." She giggles some more as he hoists her up.

Michael shakes his head, he isn't much for emotions and he knows that Jenni won't be able to keep it.

I catch Raven looking at Dash strangely but as soon as she sees me looking at her, she glances away. But I see the way she is looking at Dash. It isn't a healthy crush, that look just doesn't sit right, then again who am I to say what is okay, I mean he is just practically her brother.

"Esper, can I keep her, Pleasssssseeeeee!!!!!!" Jenni turns her big puppy dog eyes on me. I just don't have the heart to tell her no again, I glance at Toni.

"Jenni…we cannot keep this kitty, it has a great destiny away from this family she is meant to help some little girl elsewhere, who needs her very much." Toni hugs her to him as she whimpers.

The kitten leaps from Jenni's arms, just as there is a loud crashing noise from outside and the thunder rings once more…

Then there is another bang and I am thrown from where I was standing seeing only blue light and everything goes dark.

*

I awoke feeling hung over, couldn't have been that long that I was out. I might have tried alcohol once and knew what hung over felt like, I swore off anymore drinking after that And the taste who wants to drink dirty sweat socks!

I get up planning on checking on everyone but slowly I see a whole bunch of heads pop up around the little shack which is in shambles, and we are lucky not to have been crushed by the wreckage, little fires all around. I have two thoughts going through my head; *so glad everyone is okay* and *I am going to get blamed for this.*

I don't have time to think much else, I get to my feet as the bright blue light swamps over us again, it is a quick flash and then gone again, with it, so does my conscious mind.

*

Pain spasms through my frontal lobe, as I open my eyes to find blinding light shining into them. We are not in the remnants of our condemned little fort anymore. Instead we are in a forest bigger than anything I have ever seen, making me feel like I have shrunk. The forest isn't the only thing surrounding us, there are these things. They are like eight feet tall with dark brown leathery skin, and horns coming off their heads and almost every outward joint. Their faces are almost humanoid, but never would you associate them with humans besides, they have tiny horns along their jaw near their pointy ears, each monster a little fouler than the next.

I want to throw up just by looking at them or push myself into the small stream so I can't see their faces, and that was saying something.

Where are we? What are these things, how did we get here…. so many questions and no answers. Who could I even ask I certainly don't want to converse with these things more than I have to, I especially don't want them to

breathe on me. I feel something on my arm; just enough…
like a bug. I squeak swatting over my arm only to see
nothing and a sigh escapes me.

I am the only one conscious but Jenni chose
that moment to wake up, scream, and fall back into
unconsciousness. Jenni's screams awake everyone else, so
they come awake in a screaming fit when they lay eyes on
the horned monsters.

They finally calm down and the monster gives a grunt
and start speaking in what sort of sounds kind of like
English. But it also doesn't seem to sound like English,
maybe it's me.

"Send message back to his majesty that we have nine
humans under our coo may ar end." It could've been that
or command. What I can tell, it doesn't sound good.

A monster comes at us, speaking really slowly as if not
to startle a wild animal, Frankly I kind of feel like one.

"Who leads you? Where did you come from?" He - I
think it is a male either that or one horridly masculine
female– growls his R's in a deep gravelly voice. I stand
between him and the huddled people that are my family.
He nods, and motions toward the other monsters and they
come at us, a few staying back with their bows and arrows
pointed at us, and the forest.

The monsters wrench our arms behind our backs, a big
accomplishment with the back packs that four of us still

have, causing my shoulder to twinge at the strain. Then they bind our hands together with leather ropes. And push us forward to what looks like a deer trail. The monsters with the arrows bring up the rear and front, walking with a lope like one leg is shorter than the other. Not only do they look dreadful they smell a thousand times worse than like a pile of rotten fruit.

We blundered through the forest I feel a welling of helpless, these things are huge, and everything in this strange place is larger than life, I hate being this out of control.

The forest is a bit like that movie…with those blue people (?). The trees are huge, bigger than several people wrapping their arms linked; the forest is really beautiful. They have huge leaves and the most exotic flowers and colors.

By the time we stop the sun has started to set, in a wide clearing with dirt flooring. There is a raised platform, with an empty chair, and kind of stool with an empty pillow beside it. There are monsters with bows lining the side of the clearing. I once took archery in P.E. I was so bad at it they banded me from ever picking up another bow.

Where the trees lining the side were so closely woven together, they have grown to look impenetrable, not even a mouse would be able to escape through, except I see a hole maybe big enough for a person to slip through, it is covered in shadows and some shrubs, maybe that is their secret escape route.

There is a cage to the side made out of (gulp) what looks like bone. How did they get those…. I don't think the old owner of those bones gave permission.

The monsters lead us to the cage, pushing us into the cage and locking it behind us. One of the monsters stays nearby while the others head around the raised throne and out of sight. "Hey you know I am allergic to bone can I like get something a little more …I don't know humane?" Yanni calls tapping on the bone cage to get their attention.

Jenni sobs silently against Toni, while the others huddle around looking questioningly at me. Except Dash who stands like an avenging angel glaring out at the monsters. I feel shivers going up my spine, I don't know what to do, what I am supposed to do when you have no clue what planet you are on or what those things are, this is all just way weird.

"We need to just sit tight and find out more, for all we know they are just curious." Toni gives me a 'you got to be kidding me' look. "Hey! What are you? Why are we here?" I call over to them, only to also get the cold shoulder.

We sit there for what feels like hours, which is very hard when every five minutes I feel like a bug is crawling over me, sadly sometimes they are. The sun is almost done setting casting everything in a red and yellow glow, the heat of the day having beaten down at us until we are all hot and sweaty the evening winds coming as a blessed relief. Then the stranger stuff starts happening, believe it or not it seems things are still getting stranger.

The monsters come out arguing, another monster coming up behind with a rock… like thing… it looked too perfectly oval and too smooth to be a rock, and the colors it is a swirl of dark blues and purples.

"I don't care if we lost five warriors, we got what was important. We got the egg," Monster Number One growls; he is decked out in more extravagant furs and gold then the ot hers.

"Five warriors could have been saved if we had gone with my plan, and we still would've gotten the egg!" Monster Number Two grunts.

"Nothing will come of arguing, Argerith. You will only get yourself into trouble, go find some dogs for our dinner, I wish to eat good tonight." Monster Number Three grumbles to Number Two as he sneers back at him. Monster Number Two scowls hitting Number Three in the chest and ignoring him as he sputters back and indignant reply.

"We will have to hide the egg; we wouldn't want the parents to find us. With all those years of looking for ways to make it hatch only to have it stolen away, they will want it back. What do you boys think of giving it to the

Slavers? They would be very happy to get their hands on the egg, reward us very handsomely." Monster Number One suggests in his rumbling voice.

I look at the egg in question. It doesn't belong to them. Somewhere the parents of that egg are probable fretting their heads off. The fate they are talking of about selling it to traders seemed a far worse fate for the egg than being even with these monsters. I feel this insane urge to take it with us, I hate people who take stuff that doesn't belong to them and hate even more when people take when they know it hurt other people.

They bicker back and forth before Monster Number One sits on the raised throne and the monster with the egg sets it down on the pillow on the raised platform. The monster leader proceeds to bark orders at other monsters which stand to the side of the platform, not doing anything. These servants don't stand or hold weapons like the guards, but rather hold rags and trays for the whim of the leader.

An out of sight commotion draws the attention of the group of monsters, along with the attention of half the guards, sending everyone but three guards out of sight to investigate the commotion, shouts sound some turning into screams.

The three guards left in the clearing that shift uneasy, muttering amongst themselves.

The sounds of shouts and screams come from out of view. Two of the warriors glance at each other, one nods and the other heads over to see what is happening. I watch, having a bad feeling for the poor monsters. I watch him look past and gasp a strangle noise as an arrow lodges itself in his throat, and he falls back, dead before he hits the ground.

Don't get me wrong I have no love loss for the vile thing but he's something known and if something is scarring these monsters I don't think it's going to be a friend.

"Hey you let us out you can't just leave us in here to be slaughtered!" I plead; they don't even glance our way, I bang against the cage and call out louder.

The other two monsters exchange glances with each other, one raises his bow while the other unsheathe a strange sword, it was a graceful sweep of smooth sharp edges, no low guard would have a sword like that, and the blade is breath taking.

A leaner version of the monster bursts from where all the noise is coming from, shooting an arrow through the archer's chest before he flips the bow over his back and draws his sword to engage with the sword fighter, all with only a brief pause. Never one to miss a chance I go to work on the rope that they have tied as a lock. I pull the nail clippers that I keep in my back pocket of my back pack and set to work at the rope. I don't have much but the clippers will have to work.

Dash pushes me away and cuts through the rope with a big ass pocket knife. The cage door swings open and we spill out.

"Show off!" I tease. Dash gives me a smirk as he pockets his knife.

"Head for the hole, Toni you make sure it's safe first then the littlest." We all congregate around the hole. I watch the fight between our last surviving guard/capturer. The other monster slashes and bashes relentlessly at the guard. The guard monster trips up in the deadly dance and is cut down. He goes down bleeding heavily. It is all purple. The other monster heads towards the egg, I don't understand, I know this monster is no friend to that egg, call it women's intuition. I read about honor in all those knightly tales and I know that my honor will be stained if I leave that egg here.

Without thinking I leap from the group, my backpack thumping against my back, I pick up the fallen guard's magnificent sword; it seems to sing as I clutch it to my chest.

"Esper!!!!"

"Esper! Get back here."

"Esper! What are you doing? We have to go, now!"

"Go without me, I'll be through in a second." I call over my shoulder without pause.

I jump over the fallen warriors and dive for the podium, egged on by my honor and a weird force like a rope was pulling me. The other monster looks around to see what is going on and that is all I need to grab the egg and spin back toward the hole.

He snarls and makes for me, his hands coming forward as he frees his sword arm.

"Give me the egg, human."

I backed to the hole, but there was no way I was getting through that hole with this egg without a distraction. Someone must not like me because I hear calls from behind the platform, the monster smirks.

He doesn't know one thing though...... I'm an American!

I raise the egg as if to smash it, his eyes bug and he lunges forward.

It is a gamble, thankfully I haven't underestimated him. He gets to the egg in a major dive. It is what I am counting on so when he is right below me (having have dropped his sword in his haste) the sword I had taken from the other monster sings through the air and cutting his head off in a purple bloody splatter.

There is a pounding of footsteps, instead of standing there I work fast, I run to the two other dead monster and grab his sword belt for my new sword, but the supposed dead body grabs my ankle. I shriek and panic bringing his own sword down on his neck, flinching at as the warm purple blood splatters over me again.

I grab the egg from the first monster I have killed. I push the egg into the hole ahead of me and propel it through, as I wiggle my way after. I hear shouts from the monsters as they discover the carnage, they don't sound so happy. Everyone is waiting for me on the other side; I scramble up, strap on my new sword, and hoist the egg up onto my hip. I try not to process that I have taken two creatures lives. I shake my head to clear my muddled thoughts.

Dash looks at me as if I have lost my mind, I give him a shrug. Now just isn't the time to explain my actions partially when I have no clue what completely possessed me.

"We need to catch some air," I call, heading off into the woods. I glance over my shoulder to check on them.

Toni swings Jenni up onto his back, he jogs ahead by me, and the others straggle behind. Raven whining from the get go.

Dark comes fast and we stop in extreme shock, searching in apparent vain for the North Star only to see **six** moons; and no North Star anywhere in sight.

"We can't make camp just yet; we need to get as far away from here as possible… Oh, never mind, scratch that. Up this tree, everyone up these trees!" I start scrambling up the tree one hand wrapped around the egg.

The other's scramble up the trees following my example, I head for a high up branch, not worrying about it holding my weight because they are as thick as or thicker than my waste.

I empty my backpack of anything not useful, and shove the egg in, *that would have to do for now.*

"Find a place to rest for the night, were you won't fall out. Dash, Dante, Garrett, and Raven empty your bags of everything not useful; hide it in a nook or cranny in the tree. Keep papers, we might need them for a fire, I'm talking getting rid of makeup," sending a pointed look at Raven, "and things we can't use for our survival. We are now somewhere we don't know the terrain, the type of animals, people, or even if there is people, we can't afford for the monsters to find us."

Dash has already started but Raven cries and puts up stink about her precious makeup.

"But I just got it! It's an Avión special they don't make these anymore!" Raven wails more.

"Raven, Shut up! We are going to have to fight for our lives we don't – and you shouldn't – care!" Toni growls at her, stroking Jenni's head, she has already fallen asleep in his lap.

Raven looks pleadingly at Dash but he is also glaring at her, his look spoke volumes. She turns to her perch and starts hiding her makeup in a notch of the tree. I turn back to my own perch and curl up around the backpack, "Dash, you want to take first watch?" He nods and looking suspiciously out into the forest.

*

Dash calls over to me softly as to not wake the others. "Esper, your turn for watch, I need some sleep if we are to go on in the morning." Dash moves into a more comfortable position in the tree and rests his head back against the tree, soon he is out like a light.

I watch out at the forest. It is quiet except for the occasional rustle of the wildlife. This world for all of its primitive life forms is oddly beautiful. The moonlight casting the colossal trees to be edged in silver, neon flowers seem to glow an make the scene even more breath taking.

How did we get here? How will we get home? How am I going to get any damn answers? I wonder if anyone noticed we were gone? I honestly think Cara might be celebrating. What about Luke, I know he must be worried, we use to spend a lot of time together, and we work together he would notice us gone or me at least. Our teachers are bound to it's their job to take roll call.

Life wasn't simple at home, I have no doubts that here will also have its challenges, where ever here is. I pick a neon blue flower from a low hanging branch by my perch. I shall call it Luna, because I am pretty sure I didn't see this when it was light out which means probable a night flower, what better name then the Latin word for moon.

I can't help but muse silently to myself there isn't much to do when gazing out at the forest to keep me from not falling asleep…. Maybe when I get home I shall right my experience down and write a book about it…

I am up for about an hour when I am shocked from my musing to hear heavy footsteps and muttered curses from the monsters. I see Toni's eye below and Jenni stirs in his arms, I shake my head at him and he rubs his hand over Jenni's head, calming her until she lulls back into sleep.

I hold my breath trying to ignore the sudden thought that I have something on me.

The monsters traipse around under the trees looking for us, to no avail. They keep going, moving off into the forest. I let out a long breath that I didn't realize I am holding. I settle back into the tree hoping for a quiet watch.

*

The sun casts its sunny rays onto our faces bright and early, making it impossible to sleep. Toni starts climbing down the tree while Jenni still sleeps, that child could sleep through an apocalypse… maybe that's what's happening to us maybe our world ended and we were sucked into a black hole… nah. The others slowly shake the sleep from their eyes; I call a soft warning to the others so they won't fall out the trees. Garret and Dante nimbly climbing down, but then again those two are practically monkeys.

Dash is already down on the forest floor, looking around as if looking to for danger. I thought everything looks fine but at the last moment I hear Raven argue with Yanni on who is coming down first, and then an indignant yell as Yanni comes crashing from the tree.

He lands with a thud a few feet away as everyone comes over to see what happened. Raven hurries out of the tree, and lands a little away from Yanni. Her face is a mask of horror and guilt. "Yanni, Oh my Gosh, I'm sorry I just meant to push you back but you just lost balance!" She starts weeping crocodile tears as Yanni lets loose groan and rolls over. "Raven, stop, I'm fine."

He groans again, sitting up.

"Yanni, you sure you are okay?" I kneel down beside him when he can't manage to get up all the way.

"Yah, just a little bruised." He murmurs as he tries to get to his feet, but can't yet again, Dash finally takes pity and pushes him up.

I nod, glancing around again; I can't help it trying to making sure we don't have any unwanted onlookers. "Let's get going. We need to keep going hopefully we will run along a village or something, that doesn't like have those monster things." I'm pretty sure Raven did it on purpose if she wasn't my responsibility then… I can't finish that thought, she is and there is no changing it.

Toni tucks Jenni's hand safely in his, and we start down a deer trail (?), hoping it will lead us far away.

I bring up the rear with Yanni who limps after the group clutching his arm to his chest; Garret and Dante suspiciously try to put distance between themselves and the group only to bump into us. They have picked up rocks and sticks, and using their rubber band collection they had to pick on their teacher, they have made sling shots. Raven looks back at the tree where her make-up has been stashed, "Raven get up with the others." She glared but complied, but not without a parting shot.

"I want to go home." Then she runs up past the twins to get behind Toni. "Not like any of us have a choice about this!" Yanni screams after her.

Lucan being her fraternal twin runs up to un-ruffle her feathers. Dash falls into step beside me as I call to Garrett and Dante.

"You any good with those sling shots?" I ask Garrett who gives us a mischievous look. Dante and Garrett grab some fair size rocks and take aim. Each let loose a stone and they both hit the bird in the tree up about ten yards away. The bird falls from the branch stunned if not dead. They should be good for the amount of times I had to smooth things over with their teachers because of weird stones hitting them in the butt when they sat down.

"Go grab it, that's going to be lunch." Garrett lets loose a groan but Dante mutters cool and runs to go grab the bird, Garrett hard on his heels.

Dash shakes his head with a slight smile and we continue down the path. The path inclining even more until we are traveling up what I assume is a mountain. I probably should have checked the land scape from the tree. I move through the throng as everyone stops by a major slope. It is at a major incline and look as if it has had a couple mud slides last winter. The weather is hot but I want to put more space between the monsters and us. I really miss air conditioning.

I swing the sword up so it is resting on my back, so it will not hinder my hip movements; and I start up the hill. But by the time I reach the first tree roots (like two paces up the slope) I am traveling near where my knees are touching the ground, and it's more a scramble. I feel my feat sliding back making me scrape my hands and get mud up and down my pants. "Might want to avoid that spot, or you might go down harder than me."

I grab for the tree root wrapping my hand around it before I reach back for Toni's hand. I really hate mud and dirt and bugs why would anyone want to play in the dirt. If this wasn't essential I would not be scrambling a hill, nails breaking by the second, grouse.

Toni makes his way up until he has his hand wrapped around the roots alongside mine. I reached back once again and grab Jenni's hand. She slips half way up scraping her knees in the mud. "Esper!" she cries, but I don't let her hand go.

She scrambles up, her knees a big muddy mess. She has tears in her eyes, but she stays brave, sticks her tiny barely there chin out and preps herself for her next segment up. "I'm so proud of you my little trooper."

"Toni, you stay here and help the others up. Dash, you stay down until the last of us are up, and then follow, Lucan, you come up and you will be at the next post." I move up farther, sometimes using shrubs that are on the slope, and dig in for a purchase to help me get to the next tree. I am sweating and don't relish the last climb up but know we would be able to take a rest when we reach the top, making it all worth it.

I extend a hand to Lucan, my foot sliding down into an extra muddy patch, the mud seeping through my sneakers. Lucan has climbed to the last tree used as a hand hold in the meantime. Lucan gulps in ragged breaths then starts up the way I have come, taking my hand as soon as he can, since this climb is farther then my hand could make and actually a couple more paces up the slope. I pull him up so he is hanging on to the tree with me.

I pull myself then up to the top of the slope it seems to level out a lot so the rest of the climb isn't as rough as the stuff before. Then I prepare to repeat the process eight more times, pulling people up. How did I end up this way?

It takes about anther half an hour before everyone is up the hill. We rest in a concealed area behind shrubs just off from the edge to the slide we climbed up, since we don't have food we prepare our next journey in hope of finding something other than raw bird to eat hoping we decided not to start a fire to alert our new found enemies to our position.

We start back up the rest of the mountain. Feeling both dread and happiness that it isn't as steep of a hill as the one we had just gone up. Garrett and Dante practice shooting rocks from their sling shots, Raven trailing behind trying to comb her hair while she argues with Lucan. Jenni was spending her portion of the walk on Toni's back, exhausted beyond her limits. This time Dash brings up the back as I take the lead.

The sun shines hard down on us, but I head up along a new trail.

We stop again but this time to the discovery of what looks to be orange trees but the oranges are blue. I don't trust no blue fruit.

"Are they edible?" Toni asks me. I look at the fruit, we are all hungry and we need food, granted we don't know what will kill us, but if we keep eating nothing are going to die a slow and hungry death. I grab one of the fruit and using my nails to open it as if it is an orange. Only one way to find out if its edible, I can't exactly expect them to try one if I won't. Without bothering to individually peel apart each slice, I take a bite.

Everyone holds their breath as I swallow. Tastes…. Rather better than any orange I have ever eaten.

After a few minutes it registers that I am not dead or collapsing in a fit.

I nod and take another bite as everyone converges on the tree.

We each grab two, one for each hand and start eating away, I finish off the first blue fruit and grab some more. Soon we start shoving the fruit into Garrett, Dante, and Raven's bag until the bags are full, and about to burst. We are hopeful to find civilization before we run out but take no chances.

We spend some time eating and resting, before we set off again in a dull trudge up the mountain, the trail has not leveled out a lot and it is still steadily heading up but not as much as the incline. Garrett and Dante keep making jokes about how this hike was out of our world, and rubbing elbows, lifting everyone's spirits for least a while.

If this scenery was on Earth and the situation was different I might not actually have minded trekking up this hill.

We leave the forest soon after, the ground giving way to rocks. Toni (who has made himself Jenni's helper) often hefts her over rocks or onto his back, thankfully it never seems to slow him down.

Something whistles over us as if a jet flying low, our reflexes making us hit the ground faster than a flash. The air over us stirs, but by the time I look up all that is left of the thing that dived at us is a streak of red in the far off distance. That and what I assume is a piece of my hair that is no longer connected to my scalp. This place hasn't exactly shown me any advance technologies so why jets would be flying so low, I don't even think we had jets that fast.

Jillian Benson

We pick ourselves up, yet again, wiping off the dust and sweat, and keep going until we come across what seems to be a well-traveled path. I don't know if I like that, for all we know it is the monsters, Toni gives a long sigh, "Why yea sighing?" Jenni murmurs against his back.

"Good to see something familiar, sweet pea." He bounces her on his back until she starts giggling and wraps her arms more snugly around his back.

"I don't see anything familiar!" Jenni cries after a second glancing around and around. She smiles from ear to ear thou over him bouncing her. Her smile is infectious, everyone can't help but crack some sort of smile.

Raven sidles up to Dash, "do I get a piggy back ride too. Sweet pea?" she smiled coquettishly, and then slips her hand under his muscle shirt to pet his side. Dash gives her a look, pushing her hand out from under his shirt, and jogs up to me. "Do I need to ask?" I whisper over, giving him a side look, he scowls. How does she thinks that's okay?

I glance back at my little family and see Raven glaring daggers back at me, while Lucan walks beside her oblivious. She's going to be trouble.

Everyone has taken off their jackets and slung them over their shoulders in the hot sun, it seem so hot as if someone has pulled the sun a lot closer cause I can feel the sweat pooling on my skin. I sure hope this is summer because I will not be able to survive summer if it's hotter

32

than it is now! Guys have it so easy they can take off their shirts without breaching propriety, girls it would be oh my, what are you doing. I can't help my eyes look longingly

We follow the path up the mountain. The first person we see doesn't have horns and thankfully is fully human as far as I can see. It is an older man in his fifties, He takes a couple looks at us as if he isn't sure he is seeing right. I withdraw the sword and stand between him and my family, Dash stands beside me, giving off a united front.

The old dude looks surprised but points to the sword. "You know how to use that piece?"

"I can manage." I scowl back at the assumption I can't. Who is he to ask, just because I can't does that mean it's painted on my forehead?

"I plan no harm against you, or your friends." He drops his hands to his side.

"Is there a town near by not over run by those monsters things?" I tensely lower the sword point a smidge. He looks none threatening enough.

He nods, moving over off the path, under some of the few trees I have seen grow on the mountain once you broke the tree line. Grabbing some branches and he puts them in a pile, then lights them with a couple unknown motions that I can't see but he calls back over his shoulder. "Well, you may as well sit." I hesitate; everyone else waits to see what I will do. I shrug making my way over to the log across from the older man. I move to sit but trip over my own feet to land awkwardly on the log. I had planned on having a bit more grace...

The man pokes the fire stirring it to bigger heights. I leave the sword out of its sheath sitting across my lap, just in case.

My family moves hesitantly behind me, Dash choosing to sit down next to me, instead of peering around over my shoulder. "So you going to tell me where you're from?" he doesn't look up as he put rocks around and in the fire, starting to preparing dinner from what I can tell.

I feel the weight of the egg against my back comfortingly; I shrug out of the straps to my backpack setting it down so it is rests beside me, finally turning to look over this man. He is in his fifties; he has salt and pepper hair and the slightest amount of scruff on his grizzled face. He also has dark brown eyes, he is built rather stocky but also a lean waist, and he is fairly tall. He kind of reminds me of some actor I saw in Hollywood, beats me thou who.

"Nowhere would you know about." I shield my eyes with my lashes to not reveal anything too strange, leaning back, trying to look as if I am not interested in his response. Why should I tell him anything? For all I know it's open season on Americans in this place.

"Well, you must be fairly desperate to be walking off trail, uphill. But if you don't want to tell me, that's fine." He reaches into his bag and pulls out odd food items.

"I'm from Carrien, originally but I went to Glarician to get supplies for my school, come next fall, I teach youths how to protect themselves, usually around the age of seven, you never know if one day their kingdom might need them for the war." He keep working and pulls out a pot, I have no idea how he fit that into his bag. His bag is about the size of a women's purse, who could fit all that? He is still pulling things out!

What he says slowly sinks in.

"What's your name?" I asks, I know if this guy really wanted to hurt us he would've already done it but still he might be one of those people who like to toy with their prey first.

"Dragos, and you?" He glances up to look us over.

I clear my throat, we need help in this new world, who knows when we are getting home. We obviously can't wait around on our hands to be taken home.

"Where are we… I didn't think anything like this existed on earth." Something I say causes Dragos to scratch his head sending his already mussed chocolate hair with grey streaks in it.

"Well I don't know this Earth but this is Pangaea, kingdom of Anubis. I don't know why you wouldn't know that being that there are only five kingdoms and we aren't exactly close to any of them, at least twenty or more days ride no rest." Dragos's face showed his confusion like reading it off of a page.

"You mean Pangaea, as in the continent that shifted and Anubis as in the Egyptian god or something?" I feel thousands of questions that make it almost impossible to choose one to actually ask. Are we being pranked?

"I don't know what you are referring to… do you mean Egypt the kingdom practically all the way across the world?" With every question I feel just more and more confused. "What are the things here with the horns and leathery skin that seem so tall and gross?" I wave my hands pointing and making motions until I take notice and drop them beside me. I really need to work on talking with my hands less.

"Those would be the Drazarian, very vile things. Things to best avoid." Dragos's face contorts in a way like he could smell them from here.

"Could you… Possibly… teach us?" He glances up from his process of preparing dinner, seeming to take my serious face, and goes back to working, thinking it over.

"We are kind of new … here, and it might be good for us to know how to protect ourselves in this new place." He nods and keeps working. I want to know what's going through his head.

"Do you have any weapons?" He puts the last of the stuff in the giant pot, never once looking up as he stirs the soup.

"I have this." I had sheathed the beautiful sword while we have been talking, but I now unstrap the sheath and lean forward showing him the blade. He reaches out for her, but I jerk her back, I may want to trust him but trust to a stranger only goes so far and handing our only weapon over doesn't count.

He holds his hand out letting me decide to mull it over, with much reluctance I hand over my sword. If I am going to trust him to teach us then I need to trust him enough to hold a sword in our presence.

He unsheathes the sword and looks her over.

"Saphique," Dragos murmurs stroking his thumb over the hieroglyphs on her blade.

"What?" Dash asks, taking his persona as our guardian angel once again.

"Her name is Saphique. She has a long twisted history, if you ask me later I shall tell you what I know about her. I would love to know how you came to find this … beauty, Rajput Sosun pattern with flare nice enchantments, flame hand guard, nicely etched hieroglyphs… do you have any other weapons?" Asking as if he already knows the answer, he looks around at my family, his gaze stopping at each and every one (all neutral except for Michael and Tony).

Dash and I shake our heads but I stop, "Garrett and Dante are amazing with a slingshot!? Does that count?" I point out the twins who puff up, they deserve some praise, I know I forget sometimes that they are only ten.

Dragos chuckles and hands back Saphique.

"Some of you will probably not be much use, yet. But still you show some promise." Dragos mutters more to himself then to us, he has accepted that we aren't going to tell him about where we came from until we are good and comfortable.

The soup starts to bubble and he pulls ten eating bowls out of his bag (?) and passes them around. Setting his bowl beside himself and ladle soup into nine eager bowls.

"If we are to train you it might be in your best interest to head back to Carrien." He ladles out some soup into his own bowl, and pretends not to notice that all of us are watching him. As soon as he takes a bite, everyone start digging in, it tastes like gumbo.

Throughout the meal no one talks, except to saying the occasional thanks and praise for the meal.

I sit aside my second bowl of the soup and gaze at this man who has promised to help us. We don't have much choose but to trust this man, but I don't want to blunder in with a bag over my head. It could be like his magic one… endless.

"About this going to Carrien, What would that entail?" He looks over at me then gets the dishes and puts them back into his bag. "Your training," He disperses the fire and stands up. "We are wasting sunlight, let's get a move on." He leaves no question about it as he starts back the way he had come from, leaving us to follow.

I belt on Saphique, "Dash, take the rear, he may be helpful but we don't want to be left unaware." He nods and drops back without another word. Raven still sulks in the back and moves over trying to talk to Dash but he doesn't exactly help it along and tries to kill it any chance he can get.

I move to the left of Dragos so my arm won't be hindered if I need to draw Saphique. He nods as if to himself. Jenni is once more on Toni's back, giggling away in better spirits now that she has been fed. The bag with the egg is once again securely strapped to my back and it seems extra heavy in the intense heat and long exertion. Lucan herds the twins who have seen something that caught their attention, back onto the path before they could like run off after such things.

*

Us older kids take turns on who stays up at what times on watch, I had look to Dragos "why don't you stay up, so you can make sure we don't rob you blind?" he just chuckled and says. "I will leave all the watching to you young'uns." Then he just falls asleep. Now we are still tired and he looks five years younger and ready to run the rest of the way.

It seems to me like the days are long and the nights short because by the time we stops everyone is ready to pass out and by the time the sun comes up it feels as if we only got a couple of hours sleep. Jenni having Toni to carry her, sleeps as we start off at dawn.

*

The egg starts feeling heavier and heavier and a couple of times I swear I feel that thing moving in there. It makes me all jumpy to the point where I walk with my hand on Saphique and just about jump at the littlest things. I feel like a thousand spiders are crawling up my spine, which doesn't help at all, just reminds me I probable have an inch of dirt seeping into my skin.

The ground has leveled out, the trees now surrounding us on every side once again standing as tall as sky scrapers. Making me even edger, the egg is moving around nonstop like a rattle; it feels like a blistering heat against my back. A snap sounds off in the trees. I practically jump out of my skin looking wildly around for the source of the noise.

I notice my edginess was rubbing off on everyone except Jenni. Jenni has wandered off to the side skipping and twirling an odd shape of flower in neon blue, none the wiser.

RAAAAAAAAAAAARRRRRRRRRR!

The familiar dreaded roar doesn't make me jump... that much.

Raven's screams echo off the forest. She clings to Michael, who tries to round up everyone, as I unsheathe Saphique. Dragos takes the other side to defend my family an even weirder blade in his hands. The monsters burst out of the trees at a lower level.

"Run, we aren't that far from Carrien!" Dragos yells. Circling to the back where I meet up with him so we are protecting the rear, as the family ran for their promised salvation.

He motions for me to head up after them and I take off after them, I don't feel great about just leaving him but I'm more of a liability. I feel the wind become brisk against my face and my heart pounding so loud it's all I can hear. There is nothing to prepare me for this; his bravery is something I now have new respect for. Are they getting closer?

He engages with a couple of the monsters and within minutes he has killed one and run through the other. There's all about six of them, too many for Dragos to fight by himself. I am not in any shape to help. I will most likely get myself killed; and him along with me.

I'm ready for a time out? Who in this fantasy dubbed that we have to run so much?

I catch up with my family my breathing coming in deep gasps, I need to run more. We come into sight of the town, I want to stop my lungs are killing me, but I'm unwilling to get possible eaten by the monsters. Agape I run to the town, the town looks sort of like a medieval movie, but this one has a giant red old dragon sprawled on the outskirts.

He is a big red dragon he nearly dwarfed one story houses, but smaller than a two story house. But even from afar I can tell that he is old, he has big saggy leathery skin, that has patches of scales left barely hanging on him, a couple of his horns have broken off, but he still has major bulk. As we watch a scale falls off of his nose.

He looks as if someone has taken his skin and stretched it out, and now it just doesn't fit right.

At our fast approach the dragon looks up, "Fluke, you might give an old friend some assistance!" Dragos called forward, sounding out of breath. I don't dare look back, I think coupled with running i will probable fall flat on my face. Of course I look anyway.

Dragos is running as fast as he can with four angry monsters behind him. The dragon –Fluke – shrugs and fanning his wings, as he turns our way. With a mighty bellow he launches into the sky. With a few wing beats he is circling over us then lands a short distance from Dragos's flight path. Dragos makes a mad dash for behind Fluke. Fluke makes a rumbling sound as the monsters skid to a halt in front of him trying to back track as fast as possible. Serves them right, the tables have turned an I can **finally** breath. I stop to watch the scene play out... I must have an amazing imagination.

"It is very... irritating when someone tries to hurt my friends." Fluke looks at his claws as if sharpening them but they can't get much sharper. "I remember a time when this black dragon tried to kill,-" Fluke trails off thinking about once upon a time in his life. "Fluke, to the now, they are trying to kill us now," Dragos reminds urgently.

A crowd of people and animals are hovering at the edge of the town watching from a safe distance. The monsters start walking backwards, but trying to watch the dragon and walk is too much for them. One of the monsters trips, falling sideways, and into another monster that falls into the next. The four monsters fall down like bowling pins, and Fluke blows fire on them, I turn, grabbing Lucan and Dash so they turn away from the scene of carnage as Fluke incinerated the monsters into the dust they started as.

Toni meanwhile turns and covers Jenni's face to keep her from seeing such horrors, even as he grabs Dante. The others turn without prodding. Fluke lets out a belch and turns away from the ash.

"Old friend, I thought you had gone home?" His tail thumps down on the ash and it flutters up into the day's heat. "You always did know how to make an entrance. I could never seem to get it down as good as you." The dragon rambles on seeming to get a glazed look in his eye. Garrett and Dante who had snuck over to look at the ashes in fascination, get a mouth full and starting coughing and sneezing as the ash goes thick in the air.

Fluke looks over in amusement, "why you scamps." Dragos shakes his head and turns to Fluke, "much appreciated, Fluke. Wasn't looking to good, and I was heading home but…. Well I had some people who needed me here more than they needed me there." Fluke nods, looking over the family. "Well if you need any help I will be over at the forges." Fluke imparts before crouching as if to jump into air.

"Actually, buddy, I need these kids fitted for weapons." Dragos looks us over. "Couple of swords, daggers, maybe even a battle axe." He surveyed us again, and nodded. Fluke startles, as Garrett and Dante leaps away from him yelping, from the looks of it they have grabbed one of his horns at the base of his tail and it had cracked and broken almost all the way off. Fluke just laughs and reaches down to break the horn off handing it to the young boy closest, Dante.

"What about me!" Garrett coming closer, looking eager for his own horn.

"Okay, okay." Fluke reaches back to grab hold of one of his sagging horns and with a heave he ripped it off with scales attacked along with some leathery skin too.

"Oh dear…" he hands it to Garrett, but Garrett scrunched up his face and raises his hands to wave it away.

"Umm… I think I'm good." I Look at the bloody skin, I agree with him.

Fluke chuckles and just launches into the air, circling over us before leading the way towards a large forge where there is a section usable for dragons and the other part that has a couple of men scurrying about.

In the dragon section of the forge everything is enlarged, his was mostly fanning the flames and lighting the fires and items for the men from for their use. The men's section has a lowered ceiling and lots of hammering and metal is strewn all about, yet they move with efficient and seasoned craftsmanship. The forges themselves are really big one part of the wall is built into the mountain and the others aren't covered to keep them cool. I notice that they have a thick raw hide rolled up to the top so they can unroll it when it gets cold.

The men don't blink as the dragon that is bigger than a house sets down a little away.

They do look up though when Dragos leads us up to the forge, (which is a little ways farther up the side of the mountain from the town). Raven eyes the muscle forms of the men in the forge, then looks at Michael who also has his shirt off from the heat now, she sighs. I have to agree with her on this, nice form. There are about four men in the forge; three of them are older while one is around my age. Also a girl worked with metal off to the side looking a lot like the one young boy.

"Oldest to youngest now," Dragos pulls me to Fluke, who eyes Saphique at my side. Then he gives out a mighty whistle that sounds weird with his big muzzle, like someone has popped a whole in a balloon. "Maybe a couple of daggers don't need much else with one already legendary sword." Fluke surprise us by knowing who the blade is, but Dragos isn't surprised and just nods along.

"I think I could think up another legendary blade but you know what they say it's not the blade it's the person who wears them, but you need no second." Dragos nods silently, what is with these people/ dragons and nodding? "Quinn! Come give me a hand, you too, Delan." The young guy and gal make their way over from the smaller forge.

"Quinn, please take Esper and the others get fitted for some clothing, instead of this weird garb." Dragos instructs, pinching my ripped up blouse between his fingers, his nose wrinkling in distaste.

"Yes sir." The young girl and guy who could be twins say in unison as they lead the way down to the village. Everyone is dressed similarly; in loose fitting pants that flow with their movements, loose shirts, and big laced up heavy boots, men and women alike. A couple of women are in dresses, with tight fitting tops with long flowing skirts.

All the villagers give us weird looks. I am wearing jeans, a rocker band t-shirt with lace woven at the hem and a swooping neckline. Wearing also sneakers, and of course underwear. It feels not good enough, especially with all the rips and tears in them. The others are all in similar garb, except the shirts differ.

Most women have their hair pulled back in braids, or ponytails, but a few have them done up in intricate stylish ways I haven't seen before, wish I could learn that. The guys mostly have their hair cut short in crew cuts, some have their hair long and hung in a ponytail at the back of their heads, most have scruff or no beard at all but a very few have mustaches.

Animals of all kinds mill about under eves and doorways, staying out of the summer heat. The animals are also doing manual tasks that you would usually see people doing.

I look at our guide, Quinn, she has black hair, blue eyes, and her hair is short and cropped. Quinn is built lean and with slight but noticeable muscles probable from working in the forge. I envy her and the muscles, I'm rather soft compared.

Delan had left in search of something, never really saying as he muttered under his breath.

The shop we stop at is little and quaint, with big windows, with which to display the clothing. The house itself reminds me of an old shop in one of those movies you see about mythical time like knights and the round table. The inside smells like leather and fabric. I could see me spending time in here just to enjoy the feel it seems to just throw off.

The tailor is an old man who you would *usually* think of as a friendly jolly sort of man from his look.

"Yes, yes, what is it?!" He bustles through the shop, a tape measure - with strange lettering - around his neck and he has scraps of cloth in his hands. The man peers at us, pushing up his round wire glasses to see better, I don't know how he sees over that nose thou… it is huge.

"Selvester, we have nine new … costumers." Quinn calls to the shopkeeper as she ushers us into the shop.

"And exactly how do they tend to make restitution?" The old man looked up from his work squinting harder.

"I have some money," I pull out my wallet showing them the bills, I get strange looks from the shop keep.

"Oh, you can put that under Dragos tab I guess, since he has taken them under his wing." Selvester nods a couple of times, and then bustles over.

"Reliable man, that one, always pays his tab, never bothers me with stupid things," the man Selvester mutters. Selvester waddles to his books behind his huge cherry wood desk that is bigger than him. Selvester ignores us as he writes some stuff in a big leather bound book. Garrett and Dante edge away as if to look about the store... seems harmless enough.

"Humph, now how shall we go about this, a lot to work with, and I doubt you will give me much time." Selvester edges around the desk his pot belly seems to get in his way a little, causing snickers from Yanni who leans over as to whisper something to someone who isn't there. I smile biting back any urge to picture what would happen if he tried to actually get out of somewhere while being stuck... I fail.

He grabs Dash's arm, and starts skimming his hands over his body. Dash looks extremely uncomfortable and looks to be debating either to be angry or embarrassed. "If you planning on going any lower I wish you would at least buy me dinner first." Dash fills the silence, jumping as Selvester slaps his low back; the twins reappear.

"Don't worry, sonny, just getting measurements," Selvester chuckles.

Garrett and Dante exchange looks and push Yanni closer to Selvester before moving off away. Selvester doesn't notice until something hit him in the rear when he turns to grab something from the table.

He twirls around and looked at Dash who is behind him, "Sonny. It's my job to run my hands over you!" Dash looks so uncomfortable, he sputters for an answer.

"I… I … I didn't….. But..." Selvester raises his hand waiving Dash's complaints off.

He moves on taking each person's measurements.

"I thought there were nine of you?" Selvester looks around seeming to count our heads, I follow his eyes doing my own mental count… and coming up two short, once more.

"Never mind, let's just keep going." Selvester says, even as I look off around trying to locate the two devils.

"That is a puzzler, where are those two."

3

Garrett and Dante had wandered off in the store, probable doing things I don't want to know about, but none the less it is their time to get fitted. Jenni is the last person to get fitted, though before I have to worry about them and their trouble. Jenni takes the most time, she won't stop giggling and squirming thinking Selvester was trying to tickle her, if only I had a camera.

"Okay little girl, I think you're done." Selvester gets up off his knees, I can hear them creak and pop. Just how old is this guy?

"So young'un's, I have a couple of already done stuff that can work for now and some that can be taken in." He scurries off in the back.

"While I find the clothes how about you find the other two? I still need-" He cuts off with a cry and a ….

CRASH!

CLANG!!!!

BASH!!!!

There is dust flying everywhere, followed by major cursing, and then Garrett and Dante come running from the back, with guilty looks.

The Tailor comes running out after them waving his fist covered in.... a substance. A rabbit hops after him covered in the same green slime.

I grab Dante by the shirt collar; Dash grabs Garrett practically taking out some hair. I shake him hard, "What did you do!" It isn't so much a question in need of an answer.

I thrust him aside to Dash, who grabs him by the scruff of his neck, witch probable ended up being his hair but they have it coming.

"I am so sorry, Selvester! They... Well... it's inexcusable." The old man waggles his finger at them then goes as if to go to the back, but stops short.

"There isn't any more surprises for me are there!" He looks at the boys again, this time Lucan is standing behind them as Toni and Dash start arguing, Yanni is trying to get between the two boys, even if his arm wasn't hurt he wouldn't have been much to keep them from pushing each other, now he is kind of bouncing in-between them. Boys, come on who said they have to always be with the pushing and such.

"There shouldn't be any more unwanted surprises... just don't open the container with the thimbles." They exchange conspiratorial looks. The old man looks at them then shakes his head and moves to the back.

Toni's and Dash's conversation is getting more heated; Yanni looks as if he is going to be sick being pushed in-between the two. I grab Yanni, pulling him out, and unable to stop the two grown 'men' before Selvester pulls me into the backroom, pushing me into one of the dressing room.

"Put these on!" He hands me breaches, a top, underwear, a trench coat, and some combat boots.

"But why do we need trench coats?" I look over the dark brown trench coat with multiple pockets.

"This here coat, shall probable save your life one day. These here breaches shall help with your movement, especially if you are hanging around the likes of Dragos."

I hear the old man bring in Raven and Toni as I pull the screen back to close off the little changing room. I swing the backpack down onto the bench so I can change into my new clothes. New stuff and I don't even have to pay for it what person wouldn't love that? Taking off my old cloths is a smelly dusty experience, who knew a person could get so dirty.

The new breaches fit pretty nicely in a nice dark brown and loose feeling all soft like pajamas. Pulling on the new bra seems more strips that cross and take a while to figure out. Be a great spot for a how many people does it take to put on a bra joke, right? Next comes a dark red corset with black laces up the front and at the ends of the long sleeves. The trench coat goes all the way down to my ankles if not a little farther, but just right so I won't be stepping on it. Just wearing the trench coat makes me feel bad ass like some old western hero.

When I step out swinging the bag onto my shoulder, Raven is at it again, "I need makeup! Why does Esper get the corset! These pants are too loose! It doesn't even show my figure............." She goes on and on. Her hair is pulled back in a braid, and she looks different without her makeup. They kept Toni in his shirt but changed his jeans to breaches and gave him a regular old leather coat, kind of like an aviator from some old war if you ask me. None of the clothing seems to have zippers.

Selvester ushers us out, and brings in Dash, Lucan, and Yanni. I wait out with the others; it doesn't take them more than ten minutes to come out.

Selvester finally takes in the twins and Jenni, who looks giddy to be getting her new clothes. We really should have split the twins up... I really hope they don't burn down the building while back there this time.

All of us are dressed similarly: combat boots, loose pants (he calls them breaches), and an assortment of leather type of coat ranging from just jackets or trench coats like me and Toni, we kept our shirts if they are suitable which only two of them are.

Jenni is the only one who isn't dressed like us, she has on a little pink sundress with intricate spirals curling around it, and some tiny combat boots, and she is the cutest little vision. If I have kids someday this would be the like perfect one, all sweet and what not.

Narock herds us out of the shop we are followed out by, "Come back again, so long as you don't have those pester some twins with you!"

*

We still draw curious looks from the people who live in this mountain village, but not as many as before. Dragos, Fluke, and Quinn's brother have been hard at work and have more than two dozen daggers, some swords, a staff, and a big battle axe awaiting us. Fluke is off to the side working on something, and Quinn's brother sets more weapons down on the table. Now if Quinn and her family keep giving me goodies I just might have to find a way to join the family.

Dragos looks up from the forge, "well now you don't look so odd, how about we get you armed like people who are being hunted." He thrusts about five daggers to Dash, when Dash doesn't immediately start putting them on,

Dragos curses and grabs them back putting them on the table. What did he expect Dash to do with them? I didn't think he needs a haircut with one of those, just doesn't have the right edge.

He grabs a smaller one and pushes Dash into a wooden chair. Grabbing his foot he opens a little slot in the sole of the boot where he puts the dagger, and then closes it again before proceeding to the next.

Everyone is slightly stunned at this new development, but it doesn't take Garrett and Dante but a second to jump up yelling "COOL!" Then they proceed to trying to check their boots. Quinn grabs some daggers and starts getting Toni decked out. Delan moves over to help me.

Delan has short dark chocolate hair, ice blue eyes like his sister, with muscles all over, and towers over me.

He puts a dagger in each boot and three more in the stitching of the jacket, that cause of the padding you wouldn't be able to guess can hold all the daggers he's putting in it. Next he grabs a strap and pushes up my pant leg up strapping it to my thigh. "Usually I don't let a guy run his hands all over me until the second date." I joke, but he seems horrified by the joke.

"Hopefully not the second date! A beautiful girl like you should at least wait to the third date!" Dash snickers, "more like the first! Oooff." Dragos elbows him in the gut, "You don't make jokes about a ladies virtue." Dash rubs at the sore spot. "Looks like you pups will need more training then just weaponry, like manors." Dragos goes into a little huff.

Yanni comes running from the back. "There's a wolf in the forge!" Quinn just waves him off. She oddly doesn't look panicked…

Yanni seems to deflate even as he pants and gasps for air, pointing back the way he came, trying to get everyone to heed his warning. He gets no attention the others have completely dismissed it, I look questioning but shrug, they probable have their reasons.

The other daggers go onto Saphique's belt that Delan hands back to me. Now it has three sheaths added to the belt. Two of them are dagger sheaths and the second is a slightly shorter than Saphique and sheaths similar, except Saphique's has little jewels on the base.

"Has anyone shown you five the Nursery?" Delan stands back up, and moves over to Raven to start helping her put the daggers in place, she blushes as he put the one on her thigh. "What's the Nursery?" I ask going over to Jenni who looks wide eyes at the weapons on the table.

"Do I get to come?" she looks up pleadingly.

"You don't even know where that is, or what it is?" I ask teasing her, she smiles serenely.

"It's a nursery means there will be cute baby things, so can I?" Jenni turns puppy dog eyes on Dragos who just chuckles far stronger then I am when faced with her cute little face all sad.

"No, ladybug, you're not old enough yet." I take the dagger she has picked up away, grabbing another and go to Dante and Garrett who have been wandering around the forge. They look stunned, "you promise not to play around with these?" I hand one to each of the boys. They nod and stick them on their belts that they have taken from the table, looping their sling shots through the loops on the belts.

"Esper, we promise we won't let you down! Can we get some more pouches to keep our better ammo in?" They look so serious.

"Ask Dragos," Dragos looks up from his spot sharpening some swords at the sound of his name. "Sure, Quinn, run down to Selvester... don't take the twins with you he left a message on the wand to never let them back in."

I walk back to Delan and Quinn, "So back to our conversation, what is this Nursery?" Quinn holds up a finger and goes off to the smaller forge to grab some stuff then head back to Selvester's tailor shop. "Well I figured that since you aren't bonded you didn't match with any at your last Nursery." Delan pipes in for his brother.

"That tells me nothing about what this Nursery is!"

Delan looks shocked, and slightly suspicious. "You don't know what a Nursery is?!....... And you don't know how to fight….. Or have any weapons….. Where did you say you're from?"

Dragos steps in, "The Nursery you shall be visiting tomorrow, and you can find out for yourself. Also, Delan, you need only to know they aren't from around here."

*

Once everyone is fitted Dragos shows us back down into the village, the sun is almost set. He leaves us halfway through town, to an inn where everyone seemed to know Dragos pretty well, calling out and embracing him like family. "Dragos, I heard you were back! You couldn't live without our pot pie now could you?" An older woman about his age, very attractive for an older woman calls over. She has greying brown hair and brown eyes, her face round, with a tiny nose. Awe they would be such a cute couple, I wonder if she is his wife, if not how can I help make her his.

I hear a squawk and drop to the ground on instinct. For over my head a big bird swoops down from the rafters and alights upon Dragos's arm. It is a huge bald eagle.

"Taren, how have you been, bud?" Dragos doesn't use a patronizing voice. He talks as he would to a friend.

"I have been good, Friend, so has Carmen. Have you brought me something?" The eagle telepathically answers back, preening under all the eyes on him. I think there is enough air released from his head someone could've floated a dozen paper airplanes on the air waves, "Cool" the twins chant. They close in on Taren, who flutters his wings and preens on the attentions, "Can I hold him?" Dragos laughs and instructs Dante on how to hold his arm and Taren hops over.

Dragos rummages through his pack, pulling out a bloody piece of meat that he holds out to Taren who picks it out of his hand with care not to bite him. *"What brings you back so soon? You only left a few days ago?"* Taren preens more as Dante and Garrett stares at him in wide eyed amazement. He is a beautiful creature, a bald eagle, but he seem not like an animal but almost human.

Dragos makes hand motions, "well I ran into these kids who needed me more here. Carmen, this is Esper, Dash, Yanni, Raven, Lucan, Garrett, Dante, Toni, and Jenni." He gestures to each of us making a big show of saying them fast till he is out of breath. We shake hands with Carmen and nodding to Taren each in turn. Jenni can't stop giggling and I look away for one second to find her petting Taren. He seems to be enjoying himself thou. I want one, even though birds are kind of freaky, they just never seem to like me.

Lucan is looking around the place the same as Raven who is looking around like it was something disgusting on her shoe. It is like one of those saloons you see in one of those old westerns.

Carmen starts shaking her head but stops, she looks angry at the look Raven has been giving the place. "Something you got a problem with?" Carmen put her hands on her hips and glares. Raven looks her over, "Oh, just getting a feel for this…. Place. It's so ….like its owner." She gives it in a way you know it isn't a complement. The few patrons that are here at this time gave her a glare then get up to leave with friendly goodbyes to Carmen.

I just can't take this girl anywhere, we are in some dream thing and she still can't make friends.

"Girly, mind how you speak to your elders, Carmen is letting you stay here for free so do not disrespect her!" Dragos glares at her defending Carmen's honor, and so is everyone else including Michael.

"I'll show you to your rooms, I'm just giving you two rooms, guys in one, girls in another." Dragos leans down whispering something in her ear, but she goes tromping up the stairs seconds later. Onto the upper level of the inn and all the way down the hall out of view of the floor, while we stand watching on at the bottom of the stairs.

Jenni tugs on my coat, "Esper I think we are supposed to follow her."

We hurrying after her, Taren taking flight after her, landing in the rafters, checking things out before moving back down to manage the floor, which is now almost empty.

The rooms have three beds and a basin and mirror, a large window looking back towards the woods and horses playing in the field as the sun sets. The three beds are more than we had at the halfway house. We split up, into our rooms.

"We get up at dawn for weapons training and then after lunch we shall head to the Nursery for you five," he points to me, Lucan, Dash, Raven, and Toni, "to see if any of your bondeds reside here, there are occasionally those who aren't." Dragos then heads into the guys room, Dash is the only one that doesn't follow. Earlier then school but you have to do whatever to survive... and all that I guess.

"Esper I'll bunk with you, it's kind of crowded in there." I nod and head into the room. I end up sleeping with Jenni, letting Dash have his own bed. I fall asleep before my head hits the pillow.

*

Dragos storms into the room pulling off blankets as he makes his way through the room yelling "up and at them." Raven moans and looks up to see Dash getting out of bed, her scream reverberates off the walls as she rolls pulling her blanket over her head, which lands her as a heap on the opposite side of the bed on the floor.

He is going to make no friends this way, I certainly like him less.

"Don't look, Dash, being in a bed for the first time in a long time has made my hair into like a rats nest!" Raven yells.

Raven pulls the blanket over her head more hiding behind it, as she runs about the room, trying to keep covered and find either something to cover herself or something to brush her hair with. I really wish we were on Earth I would have found some way to record that!

"Talk about sleeping beauty!" Jenni giggles at Raven, as she trips her way out of the blankets and reveals her major bed head. Raven glares, and grabs a comb that is sitting by the basin. I roll out of bed which kind of takes Jenni to the floor. Who cares what Dash thinks about my hair it's not like I'm into him, then it would be a whole other story.

"You do know we have all seen your bed head we did share the ground together on our way here." I push by her to sip a glass of water that sits on the night stand next to the mirror she sits at.

"Raven you have ten minutes to get ready get down and eat breakfast." Dragos pointedly looks at her, because the rest of us are already pulling on our leather jackets; I grab the backpack with the egg in it along with an extra comb sitting on the night stand, and head for the door, Jenni scrambling after Dash and me.

We decide to sit at one of the empty tables near the back. I start running a comb through Jenni's matted locks.

"Can I do yours next?" Jenni leans back to ask, I chuckle combing her hair till it shines. I really wish I could remember my mother doing this for me... did she? I honestly can't remember anything but a picture. She had long red hair, button nose, big blue eyes, and graceful features. I use to try an imagine stuff she would say or do for me when I was little... it was a long time ago I sense I last did that.

"Okay, my turn." Jenni moves behind me, swiping the comb through my hair, she uses all her leverage in her body to get the snarls out of my long hair, it kind of hurts but I don't want to disappoint her.

Carmen brings us out bowls of porridge and something purple shaped like toast. Raven comes grumbling down, interrupting our conversation about our journey here. The others in our group have already come down and already on their second bowl of porridge. Raven picks at it, with a loathing look. "You better eat up; you're going to need your strength it's going to be a hard training." Dragos commands never once looking up from his food.

She ignores him. "Can I have eggs over easy with side of bacon and hash browns?" She pushes her plate away and looks to Carmen expectantly.

"You do know that my bonded is a bird and you are asking for a baby bird to eat." Carmen's face is a mask of horror, Talon letting out a shriek; everyone stops what they are doing to stare at her.

"Whatever." She leans back with a pout.

This girl needs to learn friends are better than enemies.

*

Dragos takes us out into a little valley speckled with wild flowers, a nice place for our coming torture. He starts us with a long run, Jenni staying with Dragos as he watches us. She giggles every time someone trips, not even deterred by the glare whoever shoots back at her. Then he gives us wooden practice swords and axes, he shows us basic technique and then lunch comes around. We finally head for the inn for lunch, where Carmen has sandwiches waiting for us. Even only being here for such a short time I already know that Carmen can cook better than anything I have ever tasted on Earth. I wonder if when we get back if everything will taste bland.

"Carmen I'm take the older ones to the Nursery, can you take the others back to the glen and have them run through the routines I showed them? Jenni can help," Carmen nods. After lunch she leads the younger kids out the back heading for the glen, the twins and Yanni plodding after her, Jenni skips and sings ahead of them all. I have never seen Jenni this happy; I don't think she ever wants to go back.

Dragos lead us in silence through the dirt streets in the opposite directions, passing the people of Carrien going about their day. We come to a building with big windows that seem to be one way, (not our way). I can see around the building, where horses of all species are grazing while the new colts and fillies frisk down by their hooves. Some of the horses have big wings and some with the two toe hooves, or spikes instead of mane and tail. I can feel my mouth gape open and I kind of want to giggle and clap my hands at the beautiful creatures. The others wear similar looks of awe and wonder, if Jenni ever sees them there is no way I am going to unglue her from a Pegasus baby. I can't blame her, I want one too!

We enter through a big barn door to a warm homey stable. All around the room there are soft fuzzy baby animals like ponies, horses, spiked horses (horses with manes and tails of spikes), Pegasus, goats, and sheep.

"This is the stable room, each room is fit for each species, later if you still haven't found your bonded then we shall go out to the fields where they play."

Most of the babies don't spare us a second look but, Dash seems to be headed for a fuzzy blue eyed Pegasus in the corner who is looking at him. She is around two years old, very pretty, so pure white that she is almost tinted blue. "See that is a bond…" Dragos gestures to where Dash leans down resting his head against the Pegasus. Dragos's gestures overlooking rather proud of Dash, "So unusual…" Dragos whispers. I feel tears well up, it's just so beautiful.

A sucked in a breath alerts us to a woman in the room that we hadn't noticed. I hastily brush away my tears. She rushes over to Dragos and they start conspiring leaning their heads together. I walk over to Dash, "When two creatures bond it is like a friendship that is soul deep and that is more, lasting forever. You will be able to communicate through normal speech like what you experience with Taren. The connection has been made between you now. Dash meet Sheena." Dragos says but he might as well have not have been talking. We gather around Sheena petting her as she looks at Dash. "Hello," he whispers to her, "*took you long enough to get here!*" Sheena butts her head up against Dash softly, nearly knocking him over. She seems small for a two year old almost like a baby, then again I've never been around horses or Pegasus's before.

He just smiles. "Let's let the new bondeds get acquainted better, moving on." Dragos leads us out of the room and into another with all different types of two headed creatures. This one isn't as quaint it is more a pig sty, more couches and soft bedding then straw. Weirdly thou there is a pig with tiny wings over in the corner suckling her babies, who also has little white, wings all flapping wildly. Guess pigs are flying I think Luke owes me some cash.

"What are they?" I point over to the pig thing. "That is Pork's; they must have not felt comfortable in the stables." He waves them off, and when no one starts hypnotically walking over to anyone, he walks us through the room. A tiny little green reptilian thing with two heads hisses at us, trying to bite us with its multiple heads. Nearly getting bitten by the Hydra, Dragos gives up and leads us out of the room.

The next room is cozy and has a fire place going, there are different types of birds in this one – including a phoenix egg according to Dragos, and wolves.

"The phoenix egg was found with Delan's bonded Radiva, it had been just laid so it still has incubation time. We saved it from the poachers, but it's just too far along to return the egg to The Phoenix Mountains." Dragos explains, stroking the egg that a mother wolf is sleeping around, two tiny puppies curled around it.

Toni walks over hypnotically to a male silver wolf pup that is playing with the other pups. He projects an aura confidence sort of like Toni, huh. I would have thought Toni would have a herbivore and Dash the man eater.

The little male pup has cobalt on his ear and dark black eyes. *"My name is Cobalt."* I hear his voice echo through our heads. "Hello, Cobalt, my name is Toni." Dragos grabs me and Lucan's arm and pulls us to the next room looking proud, Raven trailing after us.

"Dragos, where is your bonded?" His face got really dark; I hadn't meant to be insensitive, damn my inability to read people well. "He's taken and as far as I know killed." He doesn't say anything else. This new room also has a fire going but it has baby snakes curled up on the mantle and big cats littered all over the furniture like where there isn't a cat there are snakes, sometimes three giant cats to a chair. All the creatures in the room are fairly young looking like babies that have been super-sized a bit, or are the parents nursing the babies. We look around and I get this weird feeling that makes me scan harder.

Lucan lets out a yelp as a snake winds its way up his leg. Winding up his body to curl around his ribs, the snake is about less than three feet in length…. and a python! The python holds itself before Lucan, looking him in the eye, and hisses. Lucan gulps, than hisses back, "My names Lucan." The python loosens his hold on Lucan's chest. *"Shar,"* even his telepathic voice hisses his S's.

"Sheesh, these kids work fast and aim high!" Dragos mutters under his breath.

"What?" I look over at him. I can't find whatever is giving me this feeling.

"Nothing, God dam elephant eared youths." I snicker behind his back. I don't think he meant for me to hear that.

"Why do they stay here?" I ask.

"This is just kind of a resting place they can stay until they find their bonded then they go live with their bonded. They chose, if they wanted they could go live somewhere else but it would be much harder. They are by no means forced. Usually though the mothers like to bring their babies here when they get old enough for the choosing, some though just have them here, but it is all up to the mother."

Something lands behind me. I look back over my shoulder and feel as if I have been hit by a brick wall. A female big cat knocks me over, and growls in my face. If I wasn't already freaked out, something slams into her. Another leopard tackles her, a young male that even thou he is younger – I can tell she is older by her muscles and size – he is about her size (about the size of an actual full grown leopard on Earth). He is just a cub, he still has the soft baby fur, and the extra wrinkles on his nape. Why would the female leopard attack me? I am so confused.

He knocks her off me and they go flying to the side, fur flying, he growls as he moves over me.

The she cat backs off, the male waits making sure she doesn't try anything. I kneel beside him not really in control of my movement. He has a spot shaped like a little dragon on his shoulder, it is so cute, and he projects an aura of power, hence him taking down that she-cat. He purrs as I run my hands down his back stroking him, "Esper." I whisper feeling like it's more a rasp, so thick with emotions. His fur is so soft if any hunters on Earth heard of this they would hunt these odd baby adult leopards to extinction like they did with the regular ones.

"*Flare.*" His telepathic voice is like warm honey, probable because he is purring.

I see Dragos throw his hands up into the air in the corner of my eye. People tell you, you talk telepathic with your bonded like they talk telepathic with everyone, what they don't tell you are the quiet conversation that you have with them. I feel stronger, I feel peaceful, and I <u>almost</u> feel whole for the first time in my life, it's like I just seem to be get warm after being in the cold for a very long time. The reason the she cat attacked me being inconsequential.

It isn't so much a conversation as his memories became my memories and mine became his. I can feel the bond forming, like he gets a piece of me and I got a piece of him, like a puzzle. Flare rubs up against me; I don't even realize

I am stroking him. I'm too busy noticing the new feelings and the egg that is so warm, comforting, like sitting by a cozy fire.

I can feel Flares feelings they are also peaceful, he also agrees with me about finding the parents of the egg, strengthening my resolve.

I'm finally not so alone.

*

I don't know how long we sit like that, but after a while, we head outside where the others were patiently waiting. With our new editions to our family, all except Raven, everyone has a bonded with them.

"It's sad but she was unable to obtain a connection with any of the youngsters." Dragos whispers beside me almost talking under his breath.

Cobalt sniffs Flare who gives him a baleful look.

"*Go chew on a bone, pooch.*" Flare growls shouldering by him to sit at my feet.

Shar was wrapped around Lucan's neck and chest, apparently loose enough to let him breathe.

We all have found our bondeds or gone through the bondeds before dinner, Dragos still mutters under his breath. I notice whole bunch different animals running about doing chores and such. Such as carrying baskets and beating the sheets and putting a sort of paint like thing on houses, those only being a few of the menial task that they accomplish without thumbs.

If I mention any of this when I get home I am going to be committed… what if this is a dream? I could've hit my head when the shed collapsed and maybe I'm in a coma… do coma people dream? The thought of this being a dream fills me with disgust; I don't want it to be. I don't think I could even have imagined any of this… this is even beyond me.

I feel mean calling them animals but I know no other word for them. Flare reassures me that it is ok, but still…

When we get back to the inn Jenni comes running to meet us at the door. She practically lunges for Flare and Cobalt. She squeezes them so hard they are calling foul. *"Make it stop!"* They echo, Jenni leaps back, "they are like Taren! When do I get one, I want one?!" She turns her pleading eyes to Dragos, "Lady bug, you don't get one till your fifteen you got a while to go, but sometimes people bond early, we just prefer fifteen so they can help take care of their bonded, cause it is seemed as a grownup decision."

Dash calls from outside, "Dragos, I'm stay out in the barn with Sheena."

"Who's Sheena?" before we can answer, Jenni, Dante, Garrett, and Yanni go running outside. Flare shakes his fur out, and jumps onto the bar. *"What now I'm not good enough? I get trumped for a pony with wings.*" He snorts all aghast at the audacity.

Taren flies down from the rafters to check out our bondeds. Cobalt jumps up next to Flare, it seems they are going to be best of friends. Weird cat vs. dog no more.

Shar slithers done Lucan to rest beside them, "*I promise not to eat you.*" He hisses when Taren shies away, deciding to not risk sitting by the python.

Flare jumps down rather done with the bonding moment with the other bondeds. I understand being around all these people makes me long for me time, or in the case me and Flare I doubt me time would be any rejuvenating if it was just me now.

We head outside, I hear Dragos explaining to Dash. "Carmen has rooms specially made for those with the hooved variety; they should accommodate you two rather nicely."

Sheena butts her head against his back in thanks, she only comes up to a little past his waste.

Flare jumps up into my arms so he can climb up over my shoulder and peak into the back pack, giving a rumbling purr as he gazes at our egg. My thoughts stop at that... ours? This isn't ours its some worried mother dragons somewhere, who am I kidding? I feel like it's mine.

This kitty's is heavy he needs to lay off the mice. Quinn comes bounding over with a young black she-panther on her heels from the forges.

"I heard that you guys got your bonded's!" She stops in front of us, grinning as her eyes survey the group

"Oh, this is Asland; she was busy yesterday that's why she wasn't there." I set Flare down beside the she cat, he is getting rather heavy on my arms. She sniffs him, flicking her tail about, and then goes to sit beside Quinn. Flare copies until we stand across from each other with our bondeds sitting on our feet.

"Yeah, Quinn this is Flare." The others shuffle out of the inn, and I point to each new bonded, "Shar, Cobalt, and Sheena." Quinn seems surprised. I turn towards Dragos, "Dragos, I am ready for a long hot shower or bath so please lead the way to whatever bath house you have." Quinn looks incredulous. "You smell fine!" mutters Toni while blushing down to his roots, "I didn't... I mean it's not as if ... I smelled you!" he stammers, Dash and about every guy within hearing distance shakes their heads.

"Come this way before he starts writing ballads about your hair." Carmen calls from the steps of the inn. "So Carmen how big will Flare get he is already about the size of a full grown leopard from where I am from?" I call up, trying to imagine Flare at full growth he is also about to my waist.

Carmen glances back, "Uh, well about the size of a horse I suppose."

Flare close at my heels, as Carmen leads us around the inn and to a shed that looks like an old western out house. She leads us into the shed but instead of anything in it, is stairs that go far into the earth. Flare hums in my head, he likes the feel, it was pleasantly warm and the air feels slightly damp. It was dim as we walk farther down lanterns with balls of light floating in them lighting the cave walls. The underground path gives way into an underground hot spring. "There is a door over there with linens, and all sorts of body lotion, shampoos, and pretty much anything you can want." She opens the cabinet up to show me the many bottles and linens in it before heading to the door to leave.

When she pauses, pushing Flare back away towards the stairs. As soon as Carmen is gone he closes the secondary door. I undress and grabbing some strawberry smelling shampoos and lotions. I smell one of the purple lotions, it smells like nothing else I have ever smelled before. Imagine the most beautiful smelling thing and times that by like ten, it has something written on the top.

Flarian

Seems rather fitting to use the lotion since Flarian is Flare's full name.

I grab the bottle and all others with the same label on the top, saying Flarian. I put the bottle next to the pool along with a couple of towels. I glance over at Flare who sat looking at the door, like a guard, then look back to the steaming pool, practically shivering from the thought of relaxing in it.

I soak for hours after I had soaped my hair and washed every nook and cranny. Flare comes over and sits with me, while we quietly talk. I stroke his soft fur, knowing he takes as much pleasure as I do just from the radiating heat. After a while I hear a soft knock on the door, "Esper, can I come in, I want to take a quick bath?!" Lucan asks through the door. I jump out reaching for a towel and dry off. Flare growls at the door to tell him he can't come in yet. I grab my clothes, and am about to put them on but I notice something, the label.

67% Cotton

33% leather hide

100% magic washable

With a promise to never get dirty

"*Odd,*" I send to Flare. He just shrugs '*I don't wear clothes'*. He stops growling when I finally get my shirt over my head. I open the door to not only Lucan (with Shar), but also; Toni (with Cobalt), Yanni, Garrett, and Dante. No Dash thou, I guess he didn't want to leave Sheena yet.

I nod moving past them to the steps, letting them file in, making my own way back.

*

Carmen had a hot meal ready of fried something covered in gravy, with mash potatoes, blue beans (She had a garden out back by the shed), and a tall glass of milk. For the bonded's she gives them bloody sides of animals, or whatever they usually eat, I see a scrap of fur as Flare gulps his meal up… it's… green.

"Carmen what do you guys eat if you are bonded to animals? Cause like I can't see you eating some one's bonded." Carman looks kind of horrified by the prospect. "We eat cattle." Plain and simple, "but the fur, Flare was eating was …. green?" Carmen looks puzzled, "well of course the valleys cattle are green, aren't yours from where you are from green?" oh yah, they don't know we aren't from this place.

"Umm… yeah," I drop the subject. Dash comes running in the doors.

I grab my dishes and head for the kitchen, I watch Dash from the corner of my eye as he moves into my recently vacated seat, gulp down the meal Carmen sets in front of him in record time. He puts the dishes in the sink and run back outside, barely saying two words in the process.

"Well that boy seems to get odder and odder." I say sitting back down in my seat.

Jenni looks about ready to pass out from her long day, bobbing and weaving in her seat, I agree with her. My muscles scream at me, needing some heat and like a billion years of sleep.

"I think it's time to get to bed, Toni would you mind carrying Jenni to her room?" I declare, for if I didn't every one of us would be asleep on these very tables.

"Sure," Toni stoops picking up Jenni, letting out a groan at having to get that low; Jenni's eyes are already closed. I follow them up the stairs, everyone else plodding after mixing with a whole bunch of 'ohs' and 'uhs' and any other type of groan they could think of.

The bed seems extra cozy, as Toni puts the sleeping child on it; I lie down next to her, a deep sigh escaping as my muscles spasm and relax. I feel Flare jump up beside me. Within minutes I fall asleep, my mind ignoring the sound of weeping - coming from the next bed over - in my drained and exhausted phase.

*

Dragos wakes us again for breakfast and weapon training, making us run over and over for hours. A form of cruel and unusual punishment, I felt like I died a thousand deaths from sour muscles.

When we start tripping and falling he lets us stop. Instructing us with how to wield our new weapons; including the daggers. He has us training until the sun is almost gone and the six moons start to show in the night sky. My body feels so battered, like I have worked muscle I have never before used, I'm sure everyone else feels like wise.

The bondeds have joined us in our runs and training, so in a fight we can fight as bonded's should, together.

Carmen awaits us, having a sixth sense for when we are going to be there, and has dinner waiting. Not having much energy we stumble up the stairs after dinner and fall into bed. I have a feeling I am going to feel like death warmed over for a while.

*

Seven days later….

Our days start the same for a week. Our workouts for muscle strengthening gets worse making us feel like someone has put us through Willy Wanka's taffy puller. While our simple weapon maneuvers get easier as Dragos slowly progresses us to harder ones. None too soon one week turns to two weeks, our muscles slowly stop screaming with the slightest movements, but not by much.

*

Seven days later...

On our thirteenth day in training Dragos gives us the evening off, telling us to go and enjoy. "Dash, would you like to, uh ... go for a walk ... I found this little lake about a mile from here. With lots of apple trees or their equivalent, Sheena would just love it." Raven lures, with a coquettish grin.

"*Yes we shall go that sounds fun doesn't it Dash?*" Sheena forces Dash's hand. "I guess ... how about you Esper, you want to go, safety in numbers and stuff." Dash mutters the second half to himself, but I'm close enough to hear it. I mask my laughter with the back of my hand and turn it into a cough.

"I want to go!" Jenni cries pulling on my coat, "please Esper, please, won't be fun if you don't go." She turns her big green puppy dog eyes on me, leaning in to whisper conspiratorially, "they are too quiet to be too much fun."

"Yeah I guess it will be fun." Raven scowls but says nothing about us butting in on her date.

"Anyone else want to take a trip to a small lake?" I look around but the others wave us off already dispersing for whatever plans they have for the night. The twins share exterritorial looks as they jog towards town and the town people who already labeled them as trouble makers. I don't look forward to this, it's just going to be tedious.

"What are we standing about for?" Jenni squeals twirling around, already running ahead, we follow behind her, enjoying the summer sun, with a light breeze. This certainly makes up for the promising to be annoying conversation.

"Esper, do I have to walk all the way?" Jenni asks after five minutes, Flare moves next to her, lying down on the ground at her feet. *"Hop on,"* Jenni squeals with delight. Jenni found riding a teen leopard more enjoyable than walking all the way to the lake.

"Dash, I was thinking that maybe we could like do more stuff together." Raven starts, kicking a rock through the grass. Dash looks like he's floundering for an answer, sweeping back willow branches from my path. Flare, bored with the weird romance, runs ahead. Jenni's squeals and giggles of delight follow behind in their wake.

"What you think, Esper, you up to more group stuff?" Dash hedges, I nearly trip but right myself at the last second.

"Uh, depends." I like how he flounders for a reply. Dash is saved as we top the rise to see a picture perfect lake nestled around by willow trees.

A shriek sounds behind me. I turn expecting the worse, like the Drazarian or some mutant squirrel sense everything are bigger here.

I turn around, drawing a dagger from my coat.

I see Raven flat on her back with a baby Capuchin monkey sitting on her stomach. I stop running towards her, seeing the hypnotic look exchanged between the baby monkey and Raven.

"I think Raven just found her bonded." I state to Dash who stands beside me. "Maybe that will distract her enough to keep her hands off me." A shudder works up Dash's spine at the thought of such a fate.

"That girl is not going to stop, you need to grow a spine and tell her to keep to herself, unless you don't want her to... it's like you are actually siblings." Dash's face scrunches up, "don't even you know how I feel, it's just I figured she would grow out of it but now it seems it has only gotten worse." Dash sighs looking towards the lake, "I have a feeling this was a bad idea."

*

We spend a couple hours at the lake, enjoying the sun, and water. Making it back to the village as the sun turns orange and pink, expecting business as usual. As soon as the villagers see us though, a collective gasp goes through. They all stop what they are doing to gape. I realize not at us but at Raven and her new bonded, Verico; pronounced, 'Vare-ic-o.' Talk about weird I feel a blush creeping up my face from all this attention, why are they staring at the monkey.

"What is she doing with that thing?" Dragos rages, running from the inn. "Do you have any idea what you have done? Come in side before you make more of a scene." Dragos seizes Raven's arm, jerking her into the inn, not stopping until they reach our upstairs rooms. I follow rather curious as to what all this was about, what could possibly be so bad as to warrant this reaction?

"OF ALL THE CREATURES TO BOND WITH YOU CHOSE THAT!" This is the first time any of us have had Dragos raise his voice. I slip into the room closing the door behind me, so we aren't over heard. They need at least one rational voice in this.

"What do you mean? I think he is rather cute." Raven goes on the defensive scratching Verico's head as he curls around her neck. Dragos's chest heaves, he takes calming breaths before continuing. "There are certain creatures in this world that always bond with those who turn … bad, such as Monkeys, Crows, flying pigs, and Hydras."

"Then why are they in your nursery?" I pipe in; thinking of the room Lucan had found Shar in.

"They are in the nursery because they weed out the bad seeds, and such. Of course there are some that have other bondeds that turn evil, but *every* one of them who are bonded to those species goes bad." Dragos eyes the monkey with distaste. "You will have to leave or the people here might run you off." Dragos turns lost in thought, and plans.

"Raven, would you please step out for a minute I need to talk to Dragos." She sputters for a second. "It's my life I should be a part of the decision!" I give her a look not to argue, after a second she huffs and exits the room. I don't need that girl to hate the world more then she already does. I wait for a second then start counting to thirty before I begin.

"Things may work that way here, where you kick them out because of someone once upon a time said that those bondeds are no good. We aren't from your dimension, as I see it, they don't apply, if you have to that's what you will say. But as long as I live we will not cast her out, because believe me, that's the surest way for her to fall in with the wrong crowd." I feel like throwing punches or breaking something, it's unfair Raven wasn't always moody. Raven may not be my favorite but she is family, and I <u>will</u> fight to the death to protect her.

"Esper, no one will accept her, you think it's fair to allow her to be alienated?" Dragos whispers, placing his hand on my shoulder, trying to make me see his view.

"Yeah, so I should allow you to cast her out without a friend in the world? I won't do it and neither will you. That's the last of it." I don't give our friend and teacher a chance to reply, I throw the door open and leave. I head to where Raven sits hunched against the wall. I feel shaken because I may say she can and will stay but is he right will she eventually want to leave because people won't treat her like she's worth anything?

"You're staying, now let's go eat dinner, we probable have another long day tomorrow."

*

One day later...

On the fourteenth day things change, Dragos takes us to the stables after lunch. The stables are warm and have a feel about them unlike any stable. The stables has soft mat flooring as to not hurt hooved feet, and soft red walls aesthetically pleasing to the eye. Dragos sends us each to a stall that has different climates fitting the designated species of horse in them. All non-bonded horses we are sent to, of course.

The horse I am sent to is a fire horse, named Vala. She's jet black with orange streaks in her black mane, her feet and most of her body burst into flames but still has fur. But some magic keeps the rider safe while her body lights up like a roman candle at will. Most everyone else's horses are as weird and different as Vala is.

We mount our rides and meet in the paddock.

Raven was on a Unicorn, named 'Dalia', who is as white as snow, with hair that has rainbow coloring. Toni's on a thoroughbred colored as a blue roan, named 'Philip', Jenni sitting on his lap, content. Lucan rides on a coal black horse that leaks shadows. When he passes by shadows he seems to mold with them as if she isn't even there almost as if they are drawn to her, named 'Davidia'. Dante and Garrett on twin water horses that are white dappled grey, with a blue tinting, named 'Arachnid' and 'Navi'. Yanni rides a blood red horse that is part cannibal, stronger, faster, bigger, and meaner than most horses; his name, 'Red Feather'. Dragos also has a horse, but his is normal, just a buckskin, named 'Taryalla'.

We set out for a long run – bondeds beside us, running by themselves or on our saddles. Running over the hills, down a gully, the horses running faster than most horses, but I can't really say from past experience. We travel to a lake on the other side of the mountain. We stop at the lake to let the horses rest and graze on the banks. I beside the shore enjoying the day off, soon we leave the shore to play in the lake.

"This is the life! Nice rides, lovely ladies, cute little kid laughter, and a nice big ... packed lunch!" Lucan yawns, Shar sunning himself on top of Lucan's lap. Guess those two have a lot in common.

I just moan, leaning back onto Flare as I stretch out on the grass pleasantly damp, Flare content to let me use him as a pillow. I have always been waiting for this.

"You know the army, in the capital has divisions made up of certain species and their bondeds. It is quite breathe taking to be a shadow rider, beyond a dream come true." Dragos sighs pausing in his musing, "Vis was the head of a his own divisions, We road before the army or apart from it when they thought to dissuade the slavers, we were the guerilla tactics. Many battles… one to many." Dragos pauses his mind lost to us as he thinks about, probable how he lost his bonded.

"Dragos, what happened to your bonded?" I whisper having a bad feeling. "It was our last mission that was supposed to end things with the slavers, but everything went wrong. They were expecting us and when we broke the trees to get at them, they had measures in place, netting and such, I was thrown from Vis and he went under, I was forced to flee by another of our comrades, leaving him behind. When our bond went cold… well I knew what happened to him." Dragos voice sounds so strangled and alone i want to comfort him, because he seems like a lost child, I can't imagine life without Flare. If Flare was to die…

"The group we had assumed would be easily eradicated spread, becoming something worse than your Earths Plague. The capital still fight a war against them, I am surprised that our young men have not been wait listed already." Dragos finishes self-conscious, trying to shift his sad story into a history lesson.

We sit for a long time just relaxing, then for some reason the egg – still in the backpack beside me – started shaking so much so that the bag is quaking and nearly bouncing up and down. "What the hell is in your bag Esper?" Toni jumped out of his skin, only to end up getting wacked in the head with a rock, as Dante's hand jerks back, letting his sling shot go wild.

Bursting from the trees, a horde of those monstrous creatures come upon us like a pack of devils. They spook the 'horses' until they skitter around to the other side of the lake, taking most of our weapons with them. I draw Saphique, having taken Dragos's advice and kept her with me, or close by at all times. Red Feather stays and attacks them with his razor sharp teeth and hooves, soon the other horse species come in to help.

Share hisses in front of Lucan, protecting him. Dante and Garrett are beside Dash and Sheena. Ever one seemed to be covered…. I hear something that makes my blood run cold.

Jenni shrieks.

I turn, looking…

A monster bears down on her; both Toni and I run for her, but ……

Neither of us makes it.

*

Jenni screams as the monster grab her by the back of her dress, and hoists her onto the saddle. I run after them, trying in vain to get to them before they get to the trees. I can't lose her, she's my favorite.

I feel my heart break as the monster disappears into the underbrush. Another monster swipes his sword at Toni's unprotected back as we run after Jenni. I won't give up she is counting on me.

"Toni!"

He drops in time to keep from having the sword sever his spine. Instead the sword scrapes over his shoulder as he ducks. Dash is closer to Toni, so he hurries over to our fallen family member, so I continue after Jenni. I whistle to Vala who comes cantering over to me.

I swing into the saddle mid run.

"Esper don't leave you don't know what you are getting into!" Dragos called. "*Stay and guard the egg don't let anyone near it I don't care who it is.*" I send to Flare, Valla and I race off after the monsters that have Jenni, her strides eating up the ground. We can't lose them we can't, she's only five!

They haven't slackened once leaving the lake making it harder for us to catch up. Valla races faster and faster, her feet burning the grass because she's worked up. She runs until we are farther away from the lake, and keeps running on for hours long past the sun sinking and way into the night. I'm not even sure how long she has been running.

As the first rays of the sun peak up again Valla slows, "*I'm sorry Esper, I just can't go any longer, I lost the trail too, I'm so sorry, they just seemed to vanish.*" She looks back at me before hanging her head, her sides lathered as she pants for breath. We turn back with heavy hearts... we have only been here a couple of weeks and I have already failed Jenni, she's gone and I don't know if I will ever see her again, at least alive.

*

Being that we had ridden so hard for so long we don't bother to head back to the lake, spending the next day on our trek back to the village. As soon as everyone sees us come empty handed, I can see the hopeful faces change to something worse than anguish. Toni opens his mouth to speak but I just shake my head at him, and he closes his mouth again not asking the one question everyone wants to know, and the hardest one I don't want to answer.

"They are getting really curious about this egg." Flare growls at Cobalt who comes to close trying to sniff the bag. Dismounting I walk over and retrieve the bag. Even with all the fur Flare looks as somber as I feel, he knows how I feel. I also know he will be there for me when I have to sleep in that bed tonight without Jenni and when I have to answer the heart wrenching questions of how I failed her.

He brushes up against me, "I know I disobeyed you but I would've hated myself for not at least trying." Dragos nods then looks over at Valla, "you will be okay?" Valla gave him a baleful look, and just heads back towards the stables. Normally I would find humor in Valla's temperament but... the world seems just shades of grey.

*

Carmen and Taren had brought the first-aid stuff out before I returned preparing for anything. Dragos had stopped Toni's bleeding but he still had needed stitches. I finally reach the bed I have shared with Jenni, by the time the sixth moon has reached its tallest point. We are a sorry bunch, anyone with eyes – maybe even without – can see that someone has killed our puppy. I burst out weeping at the thought, crying myself to sleep.

*

The next day Dragos gives it to us to mourn, but the morning after Dragos wakes us as normal, and letting us have the morning to ourselves, to pull ourselves together. Before Dragos demands our presence in the valley for sword training at noon. You would think that we would be out of it after… but it is the opposite we are all steaming mad, and practice becomes more intense, as we take our aggression out on each other. Flare stands to the side guarding the egg, *"there seems to be something different about the egg, it's starting to worry me, Esper."*

"Not much we can do Flare, but just keep watching it." Toni had originally been excused but by the end of the practice he had somehow gotten Dragos to show him some moves that won't stretch his shoulder. I watch as he hacks a dummy try to take his anguish out on it, after a minute he falls to the ground, sobbing into his hands.

"Toni, we all miss her, we will get her back one day." I whisper kneel beside him pulling his head against me and let him cry.

"Why would they take her she was only five years old?" Toni clutches to me, much like how Jenni would when she was upset. I feel two pairs of arms being wrapped around us. I glance to the side seeing Dante and Garrett. Dash soon joins in on the group hug, following soon by everyone else.

*

"Esper, we are going to eat at Marin's would you like to join us?" Dash asks as we finish up the drills Dragos had wanted. Marin being a lovely older lady, mother to our good friends Delan and Quinn. I've never had such a good girl friend. Marin though, is like even sweeter then Carmen, if you could believe it, I think it's just something in the water here. I don't think we would have made Jenni's kidnapping without her, I'm pretty sure half of us would have done something stupid like race willy dilly into the woods in hope of finding her. If I ever knew my mother I wish she would have been something like Marin.

Dante and Garrett shift from foot to foot eager to eat dinner at Marin with her amazing food and cute daughters. Marin actually had seven daughters and Delan being the only boy, though Quinn did try to be the second son, when she wasn't being the most girl-girl I have ever known.

I Shake my head trying to think about their question and stop with all my wander thoughts… that seems to be happening a lot.

"No, Flare and I have plans; see you back at the inn. I would love if you could bring me back some of her Clin." Clin is soft chocolate sponge bread with a slight peanut butter taste, it is to die for.

I grab the backpack and head into the woods a little away from town with Flare. We look over the egg, trying to gage what is different. Flare sniffs, *"seems as if no one's around, safe."* I set down the bag and pull the egg out it; the bag now snug fit, big darn egg.

"The dragon egg seems to be growing warmer and bigger." I sit down, pulling the egg into my lap. Flare stands over us like a protector. The egg does seem slightly warmer.

"You're sure it's a dragon egg?" Flare nods, nuzzling the egg with his snout, *"this is defiantly a dragon egg, Shar's egg would've been about the size on a full man's fist. A dragon egg is almost as tall as a baby pony. Dragons don't usually bond, and they are creatures that prefer themselves not tied to another. They also have their own towns and such, only people who go to trade with usually stay. Humans usually disconcerted about living around creatures that live for a very long time, never stop growing until they are a dragon story high and can stomp on them. A dragon hasn't been hatched in almost….. Fifteen years, yes, they have eggs, but none have hatched, they have a prophecy about the reason why, but no one but the dragons really knows it besides that it resides around one egg. Actually that's wrong there are an occasional rare egg that hatches, but it takes an extraordinary dragon to get through the curse they suppose has been put over them."*

"Flare, you seem to know a lot about this? If these creatures think this egg is so important, important enough to slaughter the creatures that had captured us to get it and then a whole lot of other people. Does that mean this is the egg with all dragon kind are relying on it so that their kind can live on?"

Flare just gives me a look *"I live in this world, you don't, this is supposed to be common knowledge, and I suppose it's possible but the possibilities are minimal."*

"We gotta find this babies parents, Flare."

Two months later...

Dragos's training goes on for almost two more months, the moons constantly shifting. On the second month I finally plan on putting my foot down, and plan on asking Dragos about the egg. Flare and I trust him... He hasn't steered us wrong yet. We are walking back from the field, when I pull him aside.

"Do you think we are ready to face the world?" He mulls it over, Flare looking at him with keen eyes.

"I think you guys have gotten really good, but well there's always someone who is going to be better." Dragos thinks it over; we are getting better than expected for studying for almost three months.

"We need to find the dragons." That gets his attention; he looks up from his sword he had taken to sharpening. "Why would you need to find the dragons?" I look at Flare, now or never.

"When the monsters had us... I might have taken something from them that they want back. Something that before you get all 'what' about, it didn't belong to them and I wasn't going to let them harm it." I can't help but wring my hands at confessing to having something valuable that could have possible been why they took Jenni. Guilt has already been eating me alive to hear him accuse me of it I think I might just die.

"Is this something like Saphique?" He now searches my face for answers, "is this what you and Flare have been guarding in that bag of yours?" Pointedly look at the bag slung once again over my shoulders.

"Yes and yes. It's a dragon egg." I open the bag to let him peak inside.

"And you keep it in this unsafe rag!" He gets up coming towards me, pinching the bag. Then grabs my arm and starts hauling me back off to town. "Where are you taking us?" I ask trying to keep pace so he doesn't drag me behind him.

We turn a couple of heads on our way through town; he brings us to a stop outside of Sylvester's. Flare pushes on ahead of me to greet Selvester. I feel kind of exposed, holding the bag in front of me like a barrier, I don't know why. I just don't like letting the cat out the bag, but I also feel kind of good, I can trust Dragos…. right?

Well what's done is done; I can't take it back now.

"Flare, Esper, Dragos, good to see you, you don't have those little monsters with you do you?" Selvester brought up his sowing knife he uses to cut off extra pieces of cloth, as if to ward them off, while looking to and fro. "No, no, I thought we would spare you the trouble," Dragos says in a halfhearted effort, pushing in behind me and into the store. Dante and Garrett had taken to tormenting the poor old man, along with a couple of people that they had run into that hadn't been too nice to them.

"We need one of your endless bags, the ones with the secret pocket please." Sylvester grumbles and heads in the back, I cover my eyes hearing......

Crash

Bang

Clang.

Sylvester comes screeching out of the back, he is covered in paste and other horrible substances. *"Uh, not again, Flare; I am totally letting you eat them this time!"*

"If I see those boys again they are dead!" He shakes his hand at me, I rush to assure him it won't happen again, but he just waves his hand and grabs a bag from the back. He thrusts the bag at Dragos; he all but pushes us out of the door, happy to be rid of us. I see him hobble back to the back room with cleaning rags piled high in his arms. At least he is starting to get how to clean up after them, and to have that on hand... I really need to straighten them out. Dragos tries to do it constantly we all do maybe next time it will stick.

Dragos sighs and grabs the egg's bag walking away from the store. We duck into an alley where he puts the egg in the magic bag. "Tomorrow we start training on horses." He jerks the bag into my hands, bouncing it up and down until it jerks and caves in on itself, "What are you doing you are going to hurt it!" The bag morphs into the size of one of those Indian medicine bags. "You want it open just pull the string and jerk it a few times." It even kind of looks like an Indian medicine bag, fawn color with hieroglyphs on the side.

He pushes the pouch over my head, "It won't hurt the baby just keep him safe, and it will warn you if anything changes about the egg, and so be sure to listen. I know that will be hard for you." He pretends a serious tone… I am totally going with pretending. "Hey," I protest, but chuckle anyway.

When we walk back to the inn we bombard Dragos with question after question until we make it back inside.

"We saved you a couple Clin but… well we ate two of them. There are still one thou." Dash calls from a back table, playing cards with a couple of men, and Talon.

"One will have to do not like I can cut you open for them," I greedily snatch the towel wrapped pastry and wolf it down not feeling the slightest bit guilty about not asking if anyone else wants some. Quinn comes bouncing in so full of energy. "You ready for our girl night?" I nod making a basket by throwing the napkin into their wall garbage's.

*

The next day Flare joins me at Quinn's. Marin is rather plump from having seven kids, one of the kids still only a year old and giggling happily from a high chair in the kitchen. Marin's kitchen is like rustic interior from American settler's time, with modern appliances, and magic. Back to Marin she has soft blonde hair streaked almost completely blonde, with blue eyes that twinkle, and she just oozes motherly love. I swear this woman doesn't care if you are her child or a chinchilla she will treat you like her child and shower you with all the love you could want. For an orphan she is the biggest and one of the best treasures we could find here.

"Hey Marin sorry we didn't come over yesterday, just had some things that needed to be done." I call walking into the kitchen. Marin sets down her plate and engulfs me in a big hug, even though I just spent the night in like the next room. I lean in burying my face in her hair, she smells like cookies. "Well you missed Gregory's latest display of inventions but nothing to major this morning." Gregory being her bear of a black smith husband. I smile… it's like impossible not to when you are around Marin.

"*Well I think with all the nights we are here Carmen is starting to get left out, she might get the impression we don't appreciate her food.*" Flare pipes in from the floor rubbing his body against her like an over grown house cat.

"Esper, hey I need your help!" Quinn races into the room hair curlers half way put into her hair. "I can't get the back curlers in? Could you?" Quinn doesn't wait for a reply just sits at the dinette and turns her back to me. I put my hand over her head to get her to give me the curler. She hands over the pink bedazzled curlers which I begin working into her hair. I like how everything here is a lot like Earth in some ways it doesn't make me feel to alien.

"Where is Asland?" I ask, glancing over at Marin, as Shanti her bunny, the size of a large dog is now curling herself up on a … bunny bed?

"Oh, she is on my bed, she fell asleep when I was contemplating putting streaks into my hair, and which colors would go good with my nice dress to visit …" She leans in close, "Me and Spencer are visiting the temple tomorrow… I think he is going to ask me to mate with him." She giggles looking super excited, her cheeks red with excitement. Mating is not having sex but more of marriage that is more intimate, forever, and soul deep, like bondeds.

"Oh my gosh!" I squeal, surprising even myself, but she shushes me and glances at Marin who glances over at our odd behavior. "I kind of feel bad for Spencer he may be a big boy but you know Gregory and Delan are going to go all macho on his ass." I smile at the image, Quinn gives me a look.

"Now why would they do that?" Quinn asks oblivious, "You know they just seem the kind to be all 'if you do anything to hurt my daughter I going to castrate you'!" I deepen my voice an wave my finger, I am pretty sure Marin knows cause I hear a slight chuckle from behind us.

"Now why would they do that? Cheating is physically impossible for mated pair." Quinn chuckles slapping my arm and turns back around so I can finish her hair.

*

Three weeks later

Over the time we had stayed in the little mountain village we saw Delan and Quinn almost every day. Quinn even invited me to her small mating ceremony with Spencer being a small family thing... which included the whole village. Sometimes Delan, Quinn, and Spencer would join us during our work outs or just come to join us for a meal at Carmen's inn, or Marian's.

Spenser being a strapping young man with blonde hair and big blue eyes, he is just shy of being a six and half foot tall giant but still falls short on her father. From the times we have hung out he seems to be the perfect half to Quinn. I'm glad for her, I do find it weird though that I'm not jealous but would want to settle down when you are put in a new world and you could be exploring it!?

Most of the Villagers seem to like us, and we pretty much know everyone by their name. We manage on without Jenni, it is hard but we had agreed that we wouldn't be leaving this world until we know what happened to Jenni... But I know if we had an option to go back, some of us would go, most likely Raven. Summer is half way over according to Dragos. Fluke sometimes oversaw some of our practices, giving us pieces of his vast history. But he is no longer in Carrien; he had left a couple of days ago, for some dragon thing, in another city.

The day is beautiful and we had decided to go on a ride, all the 'horses' seem to enjoy stretching their legs.

We spend the evening running exploring down and around the mountain, finding things never before on seen Earth. Every day we spend here is like another day that my eyes are open to miracles, as sappy as that sounds. Dragos has made a promise to us that he would take us to Phoenix Mountains, a place where phoenixes go to roost and give birth but they are the only ones that live there. Anything from griffins to dragons to pretty much anything that hatches, goes there to roost in the cliff and piers that are guarded by a lake and mountains surrounding them. In the meantime thou we enjoy practicing our riding and exploring the surrounding territory for stranger things.

The third moon has cast its glow by the time we get close to the village, but the moons aren't what cast the orange glow that covers the country side.

My mouth goes dry, Flare keens from beside me, along with all the other bonded's, Vala increases her speed worrying over her mate Nathanial. What's going on, we left just a while ago, I hope every ones okay they are like family!

We round the bend to see the village up in flames. Being that everything is mostly made of wood and stone, it hadn't been flame-retardant. All the houses are all on fire except for a couple that are farther away than the rest ... or had been made from stone.

But that isn't what caught my eye.

We move in through the streets, the horror is everywhere people run screaming or clutching their loved ones. More people litter the ground from many different wounds marking their bodies. I feel like someone is sticking a poker down my throat as I look at the nursery. The woman who runs the place is sprawled in front, her throat slashed, and the door is wide open. A couple of the older animals are piled in the door, arrows littering their pelts; one has an axe stuck in it. It's was a massacre, who would have done this!

"Toni, Dash, go into the houses on the other side of the street and look for survivors, call out if you find someone, I don't care just look for them. Twins, Lucan, take this side work your way from the south over. Yanni, Raven, go work from the south on the other side of the streets also. Esper, you come with me, we will check in the nursery, and the outlying buildings, any people found we offer asylum, don't harm them, they might be in shock." I see them off before stepping over a dead boar and tiger, to follow Dragos.

The room isn't as grizzly as on the street. Only a few bodies are inside, the next room only has one, after that the rooms were empty.

The last room, Flare bolts in. I didn't know what to expect.

Flare kneels down nuzzling some other leopards who look to be his littermates. A young eagle is up in the rafters hunched in on itself, he also has two young owls sitting next to him. We find a baby wolf about Cobalt's age and two Thunder tails – kind of like fox but they have multi colors and can control lightning with their moods - hiding in the back shrouded in shrubbery.

Dragos takes us out the back so we can look through the pastures and head to the little shack behind. We find the shack empty but hiding just in the woods is a family of Pegasus's we had seen on the day we got our bonded.

We next head for the inn, checking from room to room finding only bodies and a whole lot of nothing, including no sign of Carmen or Taren. We even go so far as to check down in the bathing pools hoping to find them hidden away down there, no luck. We have to find them, so many people Quinn, Spencer, Talon, Carmen, and Marin. So many people I can't even list them all.

Next we check the forges, the good weapons are gone and the work shop has been worked over, it is in total disarray, sacrilege. I check the back of the forge, hoping I find nothing as I step around and over turned work bench. Blood splattered the walls and floor. Flare crouches low inching towards a corner of the back forge. I look not knowing what to expect. Finding Asland slumped in the corner, her fur matted with blood and she doesn't look like she has long, she has a gouge in her shoulder and an arrow in her hip. Flare nuzzles her, getting her to look at him, *"Where are Quinn and the others?"*

She's too week to answer, except in images. She shows us images of Quinn fighting the Drazarian along with Delan. Quinn soon fights clear, herding some survivors away; she calls silently to Asland who hears a cry from the back of the forge. Promising to be back soon, Asland runs off to investigate. She had made it to the forge but the baby raven was already dead along with a human child. Asland was then attacked, were she was injured. She shows us an image of a cave farther up on the mountain where they had agreed to meet. A tear tracks down my face, watching and seeing such things. I'm from a peaceful enough place that people aren't murdered in front of your eyes you don't see carnage unless you enlist in the army. Now I've seen so many friends dead before me Asland can't be another one.

She is so week… I scoop Asland up, grunting under her weight, which isn't easy; she is like as big as a Great Dane still growing. Flare precedes us out of the forge, Dragos a waits us, having already backed out of the Forge to let us speak in private.

He looks her over anguish contorting his face, "we need to get her to the horses, I can bind and treat the wound, but it will probably be touch and go." I feel unfathomable sorrow, I know if Flare was the one injured I would be worried sick but to not even know if he was alive… to have to part with him and not know he if was even hurt. We have to get Asland back to Quinn, any means necessary.

"They are staying at a cave up the mountain we can take her there that's where we will find Quinn, first we must get the others." I stroke Asland's head crooning softly to her to make her feel better.

Dragos takes Asland form me and we set off for the horses and my family.

On our way back we see Dash and Toni heading into another house, Dash breaks off from Toni and comes our way. Dash has a little boy – only a toddler draped over his shoulder. "We found him hiding… his parents had been killed in the street." The boy's aqua eyes are the sizes of saucers from shock and he looks off into the distance as if seeing nothing thou. "Hey… what's your name?" I speak softly and lightly tap him on the arm trying to get his attention; the boy doesn't even look at me, doesn't even look like he notices me talking to him.

"Here I got to help Toni, can you take him?" He tries to hand him to me but the boy screams clutching at Dash. "Hey, little man, I will be right back, Esper is going to take care of you." The little boy looks like he is going cry but he nods anyway. I take him into my arms as he looks beseechingly after Dash. Dash runs over to Toni, and then they disappear into yet another house, continuing their search. The horses are waiting in front of the nursery; the parade of un-bonded's and bonded's sit down with a thump in front of the horses.

Dragos sets Asland down on a horse blanket I have lain down for him, she whimpers but stays still. Dragos bustles over to the saddle bag of his horse, pulling out some bottles, ointments, needles and threads, and some bandages. I feel as if I am going to hurl if I watch, so instead Flare and me go through the refugees, passing out spare blankets and passing out the water skins we have taken with us on our riding trip.

*

Dragos lays his hand on my shoulder a while later, "I've done as much as I can, it's up to her but it will do her a lot better if we can get her to Quinn." I nod feeling far more drained then I ever had in my life, I need a nap or a weekend in Hawaii. "As soon as the others get here, they should be coming soon." As if summoned by me, Yanni and Raven come in empty handed, Raven looking as if she is going to throw up.

"We had to hurry up because Miss Thing here wasn't feeling so well…" he raises his hand, "don't worry we went through just not as thorough as I wanted. I hope we didn't miss anyone because she couldn't keep her lunch down." Yanni drags his hand through his semi-short hair a sign of agitation.

I close my mouth and nod, not really wanting to just drop her making short our search for survivors in favor of her stomach, then again she is who she is. Flare sniffs Verico, and then growls when Verico tries to land on his back.

Lucan and the twins come in next; they are carrying a wolf cub.

A little while later Dash and Toni come in empty handed.

I nod taking count, "everyone helps the refugees." Dragos picks up Asland, and I slip my hand into the toddlers as a gesture of support, he squeezes it back, and I sling him up onto my hip. Our little precession heads out, me in the lead to find the cave, with the other survivors.

*

It takes a while for us to find the cave. I keep getting turned around, and by the time we come into sight of the cave the sun is a couple hours from coming up. Quinn peeks out of the cave at the sound of our approach; I let out a sigh of relief. Even from here I can hear her shouting orders to someone in the cave. She disappears for a second, and then runs out of the cave. Quinn stops short at the sight of Asland being carried by Dragos, it takes her all of two seconds to get over it and be by her side. Spencer running up for support, worry marring his face for his mate and his mate's bonded.

I can tell that they are talking privately, because she isn't asking what happened she just takes Asland from Dragos and heads towards the cave. *"Flare why wouldn't she know?"* I send softly through the bond feeling warmth through the bond from him. *"Asland didn't want her to feel that when she had no way to get to her without risking more than herself."*

There are about thirty people in the cave, most huddles around a fire that is in towards the back. The young unbonded's warily trudge over to the fire, taking comfort with the other refugees, glancing around as if to find their families. The Pegasus's and Sheena go to lie down In the back, where no one will step on their wings, "Toni, Dash, can you please take care of the horses."

"Delan, what happened?" Delan and his bonded – a Phoenix named Radiva – weaves among the new and old refugees, taking account of everyone. "They came upon us a couple hours after you left; we had been in the forge, when we noticed the fires. Radiva had gone to check things out, when she came back she told me about what was going on, we went in the back getting as many people as we could out. Quinn goes in the front trying to get to anyone still alive." He gives water to the wolf pup, another wolf coming to snuggle and give comfort to the pup.

Quinn was crouches beside Asland, with the assistant doctor to look Asland over– the doctor having died.

"Is she going to be okay?" Quinn frets like a mother hen, stroking her head and cooing softly to her.

Delan crouches beside him, Radiva hobbles over.

"I don't know, her injuries are indeed grievous maybe even life threatening," Quinn all but sobs, Radiva moves to Asland's side, a tear slowly trickling down her face to fall onto Asland, light surrounding Radiva till she radiates red and orange light. A hush falls as the light surrounds Asland and I can see her skin nit together, her rapid pants slow to even calm breathing, almost as if a great weight was lifted off her body. It's the most beautiful things I have ever seen, spell binding, and I don't even know what's going on.

Quinn all but jumps Radiva, she gives a squawk and moves away preening and fixing her feathers. She is deep shades of red and oranges but what sets her apart from the few phoenix's that are out here (according to Dragos or Delan) is her black feather tips, going from light to dark.

A refugee stands up and storms over, a man who is beside the woman tries holding her back but she shakes him off.

"You did this to us! You brought them here! First, they stole that girl after you came and now they have come again! All a couple months after you guys showed up here! All these good people dead! Leave before we are all dead! Leave! My son and my brother! All gone!" she sobs openly. T

Oh shut up Sie, they are just kids." Marin calls from somewhere out of sight, never showing herself... is she even okay? A man beside the sobbing woman finally manages to turn her around and lead her back to the fire.

The twins look about ready to burst into tears, none of the rest of us is better off from her words either. Its hard hearing from people that you have come to love and respect telling you to leave, at least we will always have Marin and Carmen on our side.

"Esper, she didn't mean that." Quinn whispers from over with Asland, her head in Quinn's lap. I look around at the desolate face, all because of us. We can't keep doing this to them, they don't have enough people, and I won't ask them to lose more by harboring us.

"Yes she did and she has every right to." I start turning back to my family who happen to be covered in soot. "Guys I think it's about time we head out." I face towards the cave mouth, but notice Dragos hasn't moved from beside the villagers.

"Are you coming with us?" I call over motioning to the horses, Dragos shakes his head, "I have to find Carmen." We lock eyes, I may not be able to read most motions but I know from Flare too... there is no way I could sway him from finding the woman he has been in love with for a long time.

"When you find her, find a way to get a message to us. I would like to know that she is safe." I soften my voice to let him know we are okay.

"Esper," he pulls me aside, "if you plan to go, how about you find the parents to the egg, maybe along the way you will be able to find a way home." I nod, and turn to go, but Dragos pulls me back hugging me tight. "Be safe."

"Esper, wait!" Delan stands, "we are coming with you."

"Why would you do that?" Radiva alights on Sheena looking like that's where she plans to ride the trip out. Sheena gives her a look, *"what do I look like a perch, take a hike."* She glares back at the pesky bird. *"Yes"* Radiva snorts and settles more comfortably on her.

"We have our reasons, one being that we want to see more, of well, everything." I don't get a chance to answer, Dash cuts in.

"Of course I mean we do need someone who knows how to work their way around even if they haven't been that far." Michael claps him on the back and walks out but stops when a small cry sounds from the back… I guess that's the end of it.

"You aren't leaving me are you?" The tiny toddler runs to Dash, tripping a few times on the way to fall into his waiting arms.

"I want to be like you I want to stay outside in the sun till I'm also as brown and stay with you! You found me you can't leave me." The baby toddler cries out, Dash wipes his tears with a chuckle.

"Your place is here, you'll be fine, but the road is no place for someone so young we learned that the hard way." Dash ruffles his hair, as the child's eyes get big and round, near breaking my heart with the puppy dog eyes.

"Now don't give me those eyes, you have to be strong these people here need you to help put the village back together, look me up in fifteen years okay?" Dash ruffles the little boy's hair once more and scoots him off to the back of the cave before exiting. "Goodbye." Quinn calls softly tears trailing silently down her face.

Garrett and Dante run for the horses, each hurrying to saddle as many as they can. We all join them; the hooved creatures – horses and such - are in a portion of a cave that has a blue grass growing in it. Vala gives me a baleful look *"who says I want to go?"* She snorts but allows herself to be tacked once more. "I know you we ride together you forget how many times do you tell me you want to go farther eventually. What else do you have here?" I say softly against her feeling her great black body shudder but she says nothing.

We walk out with the horses and mount up. Flare jumps onto my lap too tired to walk. God, even though he is still a cub, he weighs like a ton.

"I've run enough today." He settles in even after Vala gives him another malignant look.

Beside me Dante is having a hard time mounting his water horse. The horse kept skidding away.

"What is going on?" Garrett was nearly falling off his horse in laughter, *"I don't want to! I have run enough today can't we just wait until morning!"*

"Cause Esper said!" the Navi snorts but holds still none the less, Toni taps Philip forward. "That is a good question. Why are we leaving in the middle of the night?"

"We need to get past the barren stretch of land while it's dark, and into the woods. Otherwise we might run into trouble and get shot down by archers, or staying could cause more danger to these people. We will take it slow, for the horses."

Toni just nods and heads back to ride beside the twins – they are the youngest now. Dash being well... Dash falls back to ride in the rear. I take up the front with Delan and Radiva, the others – being Yanni, Raven, and Lucan, filing into the middle. We may be tired and stressed like hell but we manage to ride over the barren hills – only rocks on those long hills – and into the trees, before I finally let us stop.

"Take care of your mounts and then you may get some sleep." I trail Valla over to a place in a quiet meadow with a little stream.

"Why didn't we ask for food or water?" Raven whines walking over with Verico, leaving her mount to itself still tacked in its soft leather saddle.

"Because they had nothing to give, Raven, those people just lost their homes and a lot of family! If anything, if we had anything to give we would be giving it to them." She harrumphs but shuts up for once, instead of going on and on and on, on one of her rants.

"Toni what supplies do we have left?" I call quietly stroking Valla's soft fur. I hope we don't have to sleep on the ground who knows what kind of bugs are on the ground? Shudders work up my spine, so gross I can't stand it the ants and the spiders all crawling over me.

"We have the sleeping bags that were already packed for our trip we came back from, maybe food for a few days, and water shouldn't be hard to come by and we have about four skins." Toni calls I watch as he takes his own blanket and prepares to drape it over Cobalt. Flare has made a nice little nest out of the tall grass and is already fast asleep, so are the other bonded's except for Radiva who perches in a tree standing watch. *"Flare you sure that's as good as our sleeping arrangement will get?"* He peaks open an eye, *"Just lay down no soft bug free bed tonight get used to it E."*

"Dash? You want to take first watch with Radiva?" I look to Dash, who has settled with Sheena at his back.

"Sure, so long as Toni takes the second." He calls from behind me somewhere.

"Works for me, Toni you hear?" He calls an affirmative then I hear the sound of flesh hitting flesh. "Owww! Esper, he hit me!" That's Dash; this is going to be a long night one very long night. "Owww! Esper, he hit me." There's Toni.

6

The moons had been high in the sky by the time we have gone to bed so we sleep well into dawn before setting out once again. The twins are so tired that they nearly fall out of their saddles but manage somehow without complaint. We find the tree with the strange blue fruit again a couple hours after noon; I put a couple dozen of them in with the egg, and some in the saddle bags until they brim who knows when we will come across food again. Toni is partially asleep in his saddle, managing to keep from falling off to my bewilderment, until I notice ropes tying him to his horse and saddle. Everyone else passes the long ride with idle chitchat, mostly about what the other world must think about our sudden disappearance.

"Do you think they are even looking for us? Or wondering what happened, I don't think Mr. Johan even noticed." Garrett tosses a large rock to Dante and Dante passes it back soon after.

"I agree, but I think at least our friends would have noticed and called the cops after like over three months."

Raven mutters. "Has it even been three months there?" I wonder out loud but more to myself.

"Esper, where are we going?" Yanni brings Red Feather alongside Valla.

"I have something that needs to be returned." As if sensing it is the point of the conversation, the medicine bag bounces against my chest, shaking and vibrating until it feel like it has left a bruise. The familiar sway of being in the saddle keeps me from freaking at the strong pulse.

"What do we need to return, ourselves? Other than that we have never been anywhere else so we couldn't have borrowed anything that needs to be returned!" Yanni looks so puzzled and kind of flustered. I take the medicine bag off my neck and pull the string. The bag expands in a slight whoosh that feels like a strong breeze buffets my face. I reach into the bag trying to pull out the egg but it bounces and starts shaking. "What the hell!" I reach in for it again but stop at the sound of a crack. A long crack appears along the egg, webbing out, then it stops.

Thoughts of the worse run through my head, it is best not to move it, so I lean over and let him look inside the bag. "It's cracked. What is it?" I nod gravely for this little guy or gal, seemed they aren't going to be staying in that egg for too much longer. "Dragon egg, from what Dragos says." I clutch the egg, I hate not knowing if the baby is ok but it isn't like I have an ultrasound machine in my pocket that works on eggs….. Do they work on eggs?

Michael has been listening intently along with Toni and the others, and leans over my other shoulder to look into the bag. "hmh." He gallops ahead, lost in his own thoughts.

We ride on in a playful companionship, won by long hard practices with each other. It seems very odd that in all our time here it may have been hard but I am not as home sick as you would think. I have always loved reading mythology I have had dreams of dragons and knight, it is hard to think that I am now living in a place that is like a cross between the move Eragon and Avitar and well any other medieval or mythological movie or book you can think of.

The scenery is striking, trees three times superior to those on earth, more lifelike in some ways. The people here have tales about how the trees used to be alive but now they just send off a sort of hum. The trees are draped in moss and vines, the foliage on the ground is about the size of the stuff on earth but more vibrant. It is just like earth with its seasons, but only in winter did it really rain and other than that it only drizzled in autumn(from what Dragos told us). I wish I was someone who painted because this would be like the ultimate chance to paint unseen art.

So far we have come in summer, as of now it is winding down into autumn, of course they have different words for it but in the end it mainly means the same thing. Like any civilization they have many dialects. I'm just thankful that the main one is so similar to English .. I think, I understand them like its English but for all I know when I came here something happened and like messed with my brain... things to ponder.

*

If given the possibility would I want to go home? Here may not be perfect but neither was earth, here I at least had ties. Would I want to leave Flare?

I am so lost in thought that I nearly fall out of my saddle when the egg starts to rapidly shake in the medicine bag. Toni had been riding beside me and manages to keep me in the saddle thou and out of the dirt.

"That was close, what are you thinking about that has you so lost in thought you're falling out of your saddle?" He glances around tracking any movement in the nearby vicinity.

"Do you find it odd that we aren't trying our damnedest to get home?" It was sort of what I was thinking about.

"No, this is kind of…. I don't know I guess here seems a lot better than there. Here I have Cobalt and it's like a fairytale; there we had nothing and after what… a year… A month… hell maybe even a few days, we might have been split up. Here I don't know why it just feels rights."

I totally got where he was coming from. "You know the real fairy tales were also kind always grim."

"Could you even see us going home when Jenni's out there somewhere?" Toni looks out in the distance like if he tried hard enough he would be able to see her.

Flare was waiting around the bend with Cobalt, *'If I had known you were so slow I would've stopped for a nap.'*

"Slow and steady always wins the race." I chuckled, when he sent baffled emotional waves through the bond. *'That is untrue if the faster one happens to get there first the slow and steady one would still be very far behind!'*

Toni having apparently heard him chuckled, *'I don't get it either?'* Cobalt appears to the side of Philip startling him into Vala who lunges to the side nipping him in the shoulder for the slight, which starts them into a big bickering fest. Dash chuckles from over on Sheena, which lead to the twins to try and find out what was going on. Sheena flutters her wings, when Valla and Philip look over her way. *"Come this way and I will be forced to take you down."* Valla snorts not thinking highly of the threat.

"*Want to bet?*" Off they go again this time with Sheena in on the arguing, Family.

*

The day passes rather fast in a sense of purpose, well except for the shaking of the egg; it hadn't crack anymore, but Flare and I still worry for it.

We are making good speed down the mountains and is well away from the village, following the road down which followed a small creek or ravine, I'm not good with those dang names is it a river is it a creek who knows… I don't really care. It is such a pretty ride that I could forget about the extremely sore butt.

*

Three Days later…

Three days later the Phoenix Mountains rise like avenging angels ahead of us. As we get closer we angle so we can travel between mountains down the gulley. They are more beautiful than I had ever thought they could be the mountains are covered in green foliage and trees until the tippy top before giving way to snowcapped tips. We get closer and closer the trees obstructing our view for a while before we break the tree line and make or way down the rocky gulley.

Wind ruffles us as we go through the gulley, like it was just any other day and we are taking a nice long ride. The crevice between the mountains gives way opening up to the lake that is cradled by fourteen mountains. The lake is large, bigger than most I've seen, going on as far as the eye could see. In the middle of the lake are many stone piers standing two to three stories high up over the water.

I can see from the closer ones brimming full with eggs of all sizes. Some of the piers are just lumps of rock others look hand carved and ornate. Griffins lay on their broods, some flying away or branching down, Other creatures of course were in a couple of the piers but they are mainly griffins. Other creatures that lay eggs seem to have also migrated over because seems all kinds could be seen on cliffs or pretty much any place big enough to hold a nest.

We follow along the shore, looking in shock amazement at the beautiful creatures, not even realizing they are also watching us. I look up as a griffin sails ahead, only to see that up in the tree we are passing under it must have housed about three different full nests. Bald eagles the size of ponies gaze down with suspicion.

We continue on, everything all good, until we start noticing how all the creatures stop what they are doing to glare or look at us suspiciously, unsure on our motives. The vibes we are getting are kind of crushing my child like excitement from seeing a bird big enough to ride.

"*Why do I have a feeling if we make one move they don't like we are going to end up lunch? I think as a show of good faith we feed them the dog, only fair. We are crossing their territory during the hatching.*" Flare states looking up as a golden eagle swoops down softly raking his claws through Flare's fur without actually hurting him. Cobalt growls shaking out his silver pelt, as if shaking off the unwanted staring, "*well I vote we feed them the cat?*"

"*Why, I do more for them, I can climb trees and do everything you can, also I'm related to the griffins like way distant cousins. You're kind are enemies of both.*" Flare argues back, his tail twitching rather happy that he had verbally bested Cobalt as the wolf fails to retort.

"No one is feeding anyone, anyone; if we do it will be those yummy blue oranges or whatever they are." I call up ahead trying to let Cobalt bow out gracefully sense; I knew he didn't have a way to counter Flare's. Valla plods on flicking her tail in annoyance at her audience but, doesn't argue as we follow the lake through the mountains.

Eventually the natives of the mountains loose interest with us and go back to their everyday lives. The sun slowly sinks and we finally stop for the night on the shore of the lake.

We set up camp in a sort of peacefulness that seemed to surround the mountains like nothing bad could penetrate this area of peace and tranquility where eggs hatch.

Sitting around the fire we all talk quietly about nothing of consequence just enjoying the company and reminiscing, telling Delan about past things that happened on earth.

"You have no clue how many times I had to go out of school to go pick these two up from school. Those two and their shenanigans left two teachers with blue hair, one with a clown face, and three with their rooms covered in toilet paper, paper towels, or paper shavings. Those are just some of the highlights; they almost destroyed a freaking museum." I laugh ruffling one of the hellion's hair as he sits between my legs and back against the log I'm sitting on. Our fire making it cozy even with the dying light. I really do love them like a brother; I would die for any of them.

"How did the teacher end up looking like a clown?" Delan asks, leaning forward on the log. "She was asleep and she well had been mean to this one kid unneeded, so we might have used the sharpie in her purse to... draw stuff on her. She walked around the whole day like that."

I tune them out for a second watching out over the water of the lake as the parents set down for the night. One catches my attention as instead of setting down it falls from one of the more ornate pier. It was tinier then the others, about the size of a pony as I watch the baby griffin flaps and flaps but it doesn't look good for the little tyke. I watch with my heart in my throat as the baby griffin tries to catch air, but only succeeds in slowing his fall. At the last minute as I focus on the baby, my heart in my throat, the baby finally manages to take his or hers first wing beat forward, stopping his down ward fall.

Having watched the baby griffin take its first flight was one of those most beautiful most hearts stopping thing I had ever seen. "Did you see that?" I ask, my eyes glued out on the lake as more baby griffins jump from the same pier. Everyone glances over, and look again, rather taken away at the sight of the baby griffins.

"What you think their mother is thinking letting them fall out of the nest?" Garrett whispers in total an utter awe.

"*Probable the only way to get them to behave… who knows maybe she can babysit some time.*" Flare gives them a Cheshire grin like he was seriously thinking it through.

"Hm, definitely if they keep causing trouble everywhere we go." I agree sharing an evil grin with the older kids.

Dante and Garrett's eyes bug out to the size of saucers, maybe that will scare them to the good side for a while. "Maybe we should hit the sack; we have a long day tomorrow." My mouth splits in a loud yawn, as I climb into my sleeping bag.

*

I awake before the others, grabbing the soap I had gotten from Carmen and sneak off to take a private bath. The air holds the morning crispness that promises a semi cold bath. Phoenix's look down at me every once in a while from their nests, as I head towards a secluded peace of the lake shore I had seen earlier, I doubt it will be completely private but as good as it will get. I stop as the reeds grow tall enough that I can strip, heading into the icy water.

I shiver as my body begins to adjust, *"keep down the cold thought I can feel them from here."* I can see Flare shiver and flips back over into sleep, from the bond. I grab the soap but otherwise ignore him as I clean the dirt from my skin and wash my hair.

"The others are stirring." Flare sends to me, so I climb out of the water to lay on the pebbles, *"Okay, tell them I'll be back for lunch, these warming pebbles feel too good to give up to come baby sit."* I joke back, I feel drowsy from the warm sun and rocks that dry my body, maybe I'll just close my eyes for a second.....

*

"Hmmm stop that Flare…" I mumble trying to shake off Flare, who apparently is nibbling on my fingers while I'm trying to sleep. Doesn't this cat know I was sleeping? I flick my fingers trying to push the irritating cat off my fingers. I feel a similar nibbling sensation on my ear, I try to flick off whatever it is. A squawk shocks me up, my eyes fly open to find…. Two baby dragons gathered around me. They all about the size of a big house cat, with wings bigger than they are. The two dragons are covered with little horns, scales, and spikes, and big round eyes, both rather earthy colors of autumn an earth. They kind of look like they swallowed a bowling ball from their pudgy bellies.

I hear a squawk from the reeds, turning to see a little gold head peeking out of the reads, half in his shell. The other two climb into my lap, giving a slight hum from their chest and totally melting my heart, who wouldn't be melted from their big brown eyes?

I'm startled from petting the cute little things from a roar coming from the lake. I jump up a little, the baby dragons take a running hopping start and head out to their mother who flies on the lake waiting. The mother was as big as Fluke and a mix of colors that show in her babies.

I don't get a good look, she flies off doing swoops and games with her three young hatchlings. I have to admit one of the cutest things I could ever imagine… I think if I ever went back to earth I would hate it for its lack of… everything.

*

We continue on the next morning following the mountains northwest, to go around the lake and out of the mountains to get back onto the course, a heading north. We know all this by following a map that Delan had the foresight to pack. Sheena sometimes flies out over the water to play on the lake as we ride along the shore.

The next day is mainly going around the lake, and by the end of the day we had managed to go around most of the lake. We decided to stay the night at the lake to stay near the relative protection of the griffins, fairly certain that they would attack any hostile people. Also it is hard to leave; Radiva is so at peace, even gaining the eye of some male phoenix's that followed us all the way around the lake.

*

"Esper, can I have a word?" Delan lightly grabs my arm, leading me away from the families hearing. "What's up?" Curiosity niggling at my brain, speaking softly, thou as to not awake the other kids who are still asleep in their sleeping bags. "Yeah, well I was just wondering, not like we need to hurry to much, sense you are the unofficial leader, I was wondering if we may stay here another day. I haven't seen Radiva this happy for a long time.

"Yeah, it is great here; I don't think anyone else would mind because after we leave here I don't think we will be slowing down for a while. So I see no need to deny you this." I'm rather happy myself about staying a bit longer it's so nice here.

I move towards the others but another thought pops in so I turn back around, "let them sleep, how about we go for a walk." Delan smiles showing cute boyish dimples, and laugh lines, "I would love too." Delan and I stroll off onto the pebbles that surround the lake, when we reach the sand we slip off our boots and leave them there, and roll up our pant legs. With the heat I had left my trench coat with my stuff and just left me in my butter soft leather pants and shirt that was woven together at the front. Delan is in a shirt with a lace up collar and similar pants.

"So I we never got a chance to like talk before, how about you tell me a little about life growing up in Pangaea?" I kick a rock, interested in the topic for more than one reason.

"Well, I was born a twin as you know, Grew up in Carrien. We have our advanced gadgets and stuff, but we also weight the cons to it and world to decide if it's safe, the stuff we can't have through technology we make through magic without harm to the environment. Things were like any civilizations unique, being that we are so far from the capital we have freer rein to run ourselves, with the occasional checkup, of course.

"Life was sort of like how you described just different I guess, like any place, me and my sister were a step between Dante and Garrett and well normal nice kids. People say we grew out of the worst of it, which I find rather offending. I have never been this far from Quinn, we do everything together. But lately I just need more space need to know I am more than my sister, more than that small town, I just need space... I think I got off topic." Delan chuckles, shuffling his feet, he seemed rather awkward now that he had spoken aloud his reasons for wanting to leave home. Angle between him and the view thinking if I ever lived somewhere small I might want to get out too, claustrophobic an all.

"I think that's admirable, lots of people have wander lust, and the need to make something of themselves, how do you think they manage to make armies?" I squeeze his shoulder to show him support. Delan smiles his thanks, seeming at least a little less homesick for his twin.

"Why is it that you never see ferrets or bugs or rodents or rabbits or stuff like that as bonded?" I look out over the lake again at nests that are just waking up, finally remembering what I have been wanting to ask for a long time.

"I don't know, they just never do, got to respect their wishes. I think we should go back we have been out for a while." Delan suggests seeming happier, I nod searching his face; it wasn't too late for him to go home. "You can still turn back you know, help your sister and the town pick up the pieces." He looks at me and back at the lake that stretches so far, "They may need me but I need to do this, Quinn understands." He nods more to himself.

Everyone is either up by the time we got back or wiping the sleep from their eyes. "Great news you get a day off, we are going to enjoy the day." Everyone smiles seeming to like the idea to enjoy the day at the lake. "Last one in the water is a rotten egg." Yanni calls, already ripping off his shirt and working on his shoes as he hops towards the pristine water. All the boys start running after, also throwing off their clothing on their way towards the lake, I'm right after them.

*

The day passed in a sort of bliss, like a bubble had been placed over the lake. We put up such a clamor that soon the griffin babies joined us in our play. But none the less we set out again the next day leaving the phoenix mountains way behind us, setting out once more for the capital better known as Quincenia, but always referred to as the capital.

*

Five days later….

Five days later we see the first sign of the next town, we see it over the horizon which kind of tells me that the village we had stayed in wasn't a very well-traveled place. Delan tells us the place is 'Anasazi'; it is a nice sized town. This place is also like a medieval met western town, specially the buildings they are extremely big and could with maybe a little room handle Fluke to walk thru their halls.

People are going about their lives as if they didn't notice the Clydesdale size dragon, maybe bigger than a Clydesdale that is roaming around with some sort of bags slung over his shoulder – pretty sure it's a him. The bag is filled to the brim with scrolls of all sizes and an old time stamp on them, like past royalties seals. He is a blend of colors looking like the dawn; he has spikes going down his back, and a sleek aerodynamic body, and no fur what's so ever on him, just how I imagined a perfect dragon.

The dragon was talking to a man in a cloak; they look pretty into it, the man hands over a scroll to the dragon, who tucks it away into the bag. "Delan, why is that dragon taking a scroll, from that man?" I ask bringing Valla next to his mount.

"He is a courier dragon, I think that is Xavier; he sometimes makes his way to come see Fluke or bring my father a message, usually a request for weapons." Delan waves to Xavier, who nods his head, saying a parting goodbye to the robed man before heading over this way. "Hey Xavier, how are things in dragon court?" Delan calls kind of craning his neck to look at the dragon.

*"A big hub has been going on, but still Dragon's being Dragons. We have their issues, like another family is trying to run for the crown because they are still in possession of their egg. Just one big mess that the royal family is trying to scramble to fix, another fire hatchling was found with the Cutanions. Dran has been … well Dran …"*Xavier moves on rambling about the things happening in court, who was doing who, who was sleeping with who, actually not the same thing.

Everyone in our group starts wandering off losing interest in the conversation. Dash heads for a group of Pegasus and some men and women who were standing off by a trough. A male Pegasus sidles up beside Sheena chatting her up, oddest thing to see, not even I could have dreamt this. The street has a lot of weird creatures, one of which stole my attention. It was a grown leopard except he had big fangs coming down from his jaw, like a Saber tooth tiger that are now extinct on Earth. "Flare, will you get those when you get bigger?" Flare looked over at the bigger leopard, and then curls his lips to show me two teeth already poking out his jaw that were much bigger than the others.

"*Of course, don't they have them were you are from?*" I just shake my head and keep looking around, "at least not in my time period. A lot of species have been killed over the years, it's just tragic." Flare looks sick, "*who kills whole species!?*"

"Sometimes it was our thoughtlessness or it was the world evolving or others times just people killing for food and over hunting. I imagine if some creatures hadn't been over hunted and stuff and they might have evolved with the world it would be really different...." I end with a long sigh, because I'm not a vegetarian I get the natural order like the people in this world, but still sad to see rare beautiful creatures disappear from the world over greed or sport. "*Do you miss your world?*" Flare sounds worried, like I might want to leave him, but in all the time I have been here I hadn't really thought of Earth with the want to go back. "No."

He seems reassured. A female with petite fangs comes over to sniff him. Flare doesn't seem to like it. "*Who you think you are sniffing,*" He growls baring his teeth and shows his fangs that are still growing and just about to pass his lips. The girl Leopard sniffs – kind of like you see women when they have been dissed but turn it around like 'I wasn't interested in you anyway' - and she ambles off.

"Xavier, is it even safe for the egg if it was able to make its way back to the courts? How did it get stolen in the first place?" Delan asks, I focus back into their conversation, could they be talking about my egg? Radiva perches on Xavier's shoulders fluttering her wings, Xavier flutters his own wings in response to her. "*I can't say I just know that it's not like it's any safer then out by itself or worse with those monsters.*"

Delan nods and shoots me a glance, he didn't have to I was hanging on every word.

Delan and Xavier start walking thru the streets, Flare, Valla and me slowly following after.

The town is very odd as I looked around people aren't all human, I realized that of course bondeds but there are humans who don't look human. A woman is talking to a man, but that wasn't what was weird, they both have heads that have multiple snakes coming off of them, some ranging in color, slithering around on their head. But thankfully they don't follow the Medusa lore and turn people to stone. I should know I accidently caught the eye of the man as he looked around, I felt like I might have jumped a couple feet, until I noticed I wasn't stone. The woman looks over her shoulder to a regular women passing by and they exchanged greetings, eye contact and everything.

They aren't the only thing that are weird a young girl had a hole in her pants ... so her tail could stick out. The women beside her – probable her mother – not only had a tail …. She had eight or maybe nine.

I can go on and on about the strange people I see but well they are odd, there were Elves, medusas, Centaurs……. The list went on and on, I am so glad I paid attention when they talked about mythology in class. Most have an animal beside them of some sort, a most were extremely beautiful, I kind of made me start wondering was this were our lore came from? Have our worlds once connected? Flare looks at me curiously when I keep staring at the man centaur's ass. *"Don't they have other races were you are from? You said they have no dragons but certainly you have Elves, they are so closely related to you humans."* He glances to and fro, looking at the people around to see what I thought so weird.

"No, or at least not anymore, we might have at one point not that stuffy scientists would admit it. But we might have, they are talked about in our lore." I have to jog to catch up with Delan and Xavier.

Xavier looks puzzled, *"where did you find a human who seems to know nothing about our world?"* Delan seemed a little taken aback, "You know mountain people, no one of other races ever visits so we tend to be rather….

uneducated." Delan shoots me a glance to shut up and he draws Xavier away from me and further through town.

"What did I say?!" Flare just sighed at me, *"Your lack of knowledge is very…. unsatisfying."* Flare bumped up against me in reassurance. *"We should round up the others. It would seem that a male Pegasus has taken a liking to Sheena, and a Medusa's snakes have taken a very bad disliking to Shar. When we get to the capital I will look into this dilemma more."*

I look over to see what he is talking about, but it wasn't that which caught my attention. It was how Raven and Verico are being avoided like the plague. Anytime they come near someone would give a startled gasp and move away. A woman went so far as to hit at Raven. Lucan comes to her rescuing her from the woman and pulling her back to the horses. My heart went out to her it seemed even here in another world she couldn't find a home.

Dash meanwhile with Toni's help had persuaded Sheena to move away from the big black Pegasus. Yanni and the twins are suspiciously standing near a building trying to act like they are up to nothing.

I was going to interrogate them…. I mean talk to them when I hear the ominous sound of something breaking and someone cursing.

A man comes running out of his shop followed by a big cloud of stuff…. Did I mention the man was painted

green?! Surprisingly it was just Yanni he was chasing…
but I don't doubt the twins had something to do with it.

"Garrett! Dante! Yanni! Get your butts onto those
horses right this minute, OR ELSE!!!!!" Toni screeches.
I mount Valla in a hurry, grabbing the horses reigns and
head to the group, feeling a little bumpier than normal.
The man is yelling his head off at them cursing in many
different languages, I'm sure if he wasn't painted green
his face would be purple, they chose the wrong color. I'm
a bad person. Flare grabs Dante's pants and pulls him to
the horse, baring his fangs when Dante would've turned
around.

The man has proceeded to hitting Yanni with a …
Stick. Garrett takes one look at the heavy blunt object
Yanni was being hit with and high tails it over to Navi.
Sighing I get off Valla again and walk to the poor man,
"sorry for my … inconsiderate family, I'm just glad they
didn't seriously hurt you." The man finally stops hitting
Yanni to curse me, giving Yanni sufficient time to duck
away and run over to Red, like someone lit a fire under
him. I hand the little green man a gold coin, "I'm sorry for
the inconvenience." It was a good thing Delan was smart
enough to foresee the need for cash. If I wasn't getting a
headache I would find his similarity to a leprechaun funny,
ok maybe I find it a touch funny still.

Sheena and Dash force our little delinquents to head back towards Delan, Raven, and Lucan. Toni makes his own way back, damn, sometimes there is just too many people to keep track of!

Making my way back I nearly trip over my own feet, the egg gave a soft tremor, I look into the medicine bag to see the egg all safe in the bag/pouch, it looks different though. Worry forms like a rock in my stomach, I reached inside lightly brushing my fingers against it, afraid I may break it if I pet it too hard. "You all right little one? We are going to find your parent." The egg seems almost…… Harder thou… Flare bumps up against my legs, I jerk the bag closed, and set Valla at a lope out of town, my family following me like a circus act. I can see the similarity's being from the whole town watching us go.

7

Two and half days later....

We had creep back into the city as it gets dark to an inn on the outside of town, unwilling to face the residents. We spend the night in the city enjoying a somewhat soft bed, before leaving first thing in the morning. I feel as if we are some big caravan, with nine humans, five bonded's, and nine horses. Delan often tells us about how we are maybe two and a half days ride from the ocean. Which we would then cross to the shores follow that for about a month before renting a boat to take us to the palace of the dragons, and the egg's parents. He also mentioned that it wasn't going to be an easy trip we would face rapids, waterfalls, etc. Etc. I get tired just thinking about it why couldn't it be oh yeah its next door just go knock?

We all pretty much knew each other real well so the next two and half days weren't quiet, instead filled with sibling bickering and such.

We have just finished the noon meal, (I sound like people from here, yay) and we are just sitting around the fire we had used to cook. The twins conspiring, when the first feelings of unease made their way up my spine- the egg helps too sending heat and vibrations. So imagine the most beautiful forest you could ever imagine and triple that and add some big trees and you get the scenery, but with all the big trees you get really good hiding places, making me much too uneasy.

Radiva came swooping in, *"We have some monsters coming in from the back, you need to move and you need to move now!"* We all move for our horses as the first few monsters move towards us. Panic claws at my throat but I move anyway.

I unsheathe Saphique, Toni, Delan, and Dash also unsheathing their weapons so as to let the littler ones to get on their horses. Within seconds the beasts charge us, one heading for me. He raises his battle axe over his head and brings it down at my head. I react on my new instincts sweeping Saphique up and to the side, so that the blow was swept down and away from me. The monster readjusts bringing the axe up again and again. Each time I dodge and sweep away the blow, knowing blocking wasn't possible against an axe. Until finally he makes a mistake and I run him thru. I breathe through the nausea as blood splatters a bit on me.

The others have been doing well with their own battles and have managed to mount their horses just waiting for me to join them. "Go," I scream ahead of me. I merely throw myself half on Valla, and we take off like a shot fired from cannon, all the while trying to right myself. You know if I went back to Earth I could become a trick rider, Toni would get a kick out of that.

Yanni and Red cover my back, protecting me with a long staff topped with a knife, but in the effort of getting away a monster grabs his arm, jerking him out of his saddle.

I pull up with all my might on the reins, like I would a normal Earth horse, wheeling Valla around to go back to Yanni. I am the closest one, which means it's up to me to help him.

"Stop," I scream even though I know the monster won't listen, why would they?

The monster sweeps his sword around and plunges it into Yanni's stomach. I feel myself screaming 'No' but I almost can't feel anything but extreme anger as I lunge to the side of Valla decapitating the monster in a broad stroke that he didn't see coming.

Jumping down from Valla I wedge myself under Yanni's arm and manage to prop him up. With a great big heave I surprise myself with; I get him up onto Red, who bends his knees in an effort to help me. Dash and Toni finally getting over here and protect us as I tie Yanni to his horse. I jump on after, unwilling to leave him for a second, and kick Red onwards. I feel so numb world war three could be going on and I would have no clue.

"*I don't appreciate the kicking!*" Red calls back but proceeds none the less.

"Valla follow, Red shut up, and just keep going, don't stop until you see water!" I leaning low over Red and Yanni.

I am in no position to coddle him. We have to get far enough away so we can get Yanni help. He isn't doing to good, I can tell just from sitting leaned over him on the horse. Yanni is sweaty and he is bleeding profusely, I just hope and pray he will make it through the ride.

I apply more pressure to the wound, "you're gonna be okay, Yanni! You're gonna be okay!" I say giving him the empty promise even though he has already drenched my hands. "Don't lie Esper, we both know it's bad." His voice is weak and has an ominous rattle to it.

"Red we need to go faster!" Flare and Cobalt are racing beside us, covering us.

Red speeds up, taking us as fast as he can after the others.

"*Esper, I can smell all the blood, it shall attract more predators and the monsters, with all the blood I can smell…. Esper, he will not be making it much longer… I'm sorry, even with the pressure.*" I can't answer back to Flare, my throat is closed all I can do is shake my head unwilling to give up

147

on him. How can I give up on family when there could be a slight chance?

The monster's stench still seems to be around me even with the high powered wind blowing over us. Toni has hung back to guard us also, and is taken by surprise as a monster grabs him by the hair and tries to yank him from the saddle.

Dash pulls back beside him never stopping as he yanks a sword out of the monsters belt and plunges it through the monster's ribcages. The monster convulses, let's go of Toni's hair, and falls out of his saddle, dead before he hit the ground. If I hadn't been numb before it would have shocked me to see Dash and Sheena take a few crow hops and jump into the air. Her big wings that are normally pressed to her side draw out and proceed to pump the air up and down, until they are air born. I want to sit an gape but even the magnificent display can't get rid of the rock lodged in my throat.

I do as much as I can do for Yanni, but I can barely detect his pulse by the time the coast is clear, once more.

*

"We are Miles off course. Esper, Yanni, and Toni are nowhere to be seen! All we know is that Yanni went down by a monster and Esper got him out, they could have been taken after you left!" Delan is super ticked off I could hear him even before we came into sight.

"Help, he needs help!!!!" I scream as soon as Red has come to a complete stop in the grove. I fall out of the saddle and move back towards Red. With shaking fingers I untie the knots holding Yanni on the saddle, sliding him off the horse and into my arms. My arms strain and I fight going to one knee under his weight. Delan stops his blustering and comes running to help me ease Yanni down to the ground.

"Can Radiva help him?!" I haven't even noticed I was in tears until I feel them pass over my lips or fall onto my hands. Gosh why do I have to cry I need to be strong not a baby in tears, I look to the twins who look worried and tears stream from their eyes too.

"She can't." He starts in a hushed voice broken up.

"Why can't she? He's only a fourteen year old German boy who was afraid to come out and play guitar in front of people!" I am rambling on trying to convince Delan to heal him. It is also the only thing playing through my head, just a boy who wanted to be a rock star but never would admit it. I once caught him sneaking out to go to a poetry club back on Earth. He never knew I saw him sitting at the café scribbling down note after notes as some cheesy poet went on and on. I never got to tell him I loved the music he would sometimes hum to or sing in the shower, it was hard not to listen from the other side of the door.

"Esper, Esper!" He shakes me trying to get me to shut-up. "If Radiva could she would, you should know that! She can't, a phoenix after healing once with tears her magic it is totally depleted, she needs longer before it's a possibility. We both wish we could… but it's just not possible." Delan ends in a whisper and clutches me to his chest as I start weeping, I don't care how childish or how much they need me, I am only a girl I need to cry!

After a moment I manage to pull myself together and duck out of his arms. I move over to Yanni, "He's not gone yet! You can still help him!" I can feel Yanni's shallow breath against my cheek as I lean over him trying to see if he is still there. *"There is a town about a half of days ride, he might have a chance if we get him there, but we need to stop the bleeding."* Radiva perches on Red's back, she had flown off to get an aerial view of the area to look for help or the enemy. "In the meantime we need to stop the bleeding or it won't matter where the town is." Toni all but pulls me away and I let him as I watch Delan hunch over Yanni doing his thing to stop the profuse bleeding.

"Dash, watch what he's doing, it never hurts to have someone else who knows how to help others." My voice isn't very strong and I feel as if my heart is in a panic but I can't freak again right now, Yanni needs me calm. "We can't be caught unaware again, I want when we are stopped people practicing their weaponry and I want one or all our bondeds on watch of our surroundings." My voice is a bit stronger as I resolve to be better for them. Flare takes it to heart and goes over to sit facing the woods by Yanni and Delan. Cobalt takes a position on the other side of the camp facing out into the woods.

Dash steers me away from the huddle and over to the fire the twins have made in case we need anything warmed up. Dash maneuvered me onto a log facing the fire and hands over some fruit. The night is crisp and clean and the birds are starting to come out again. Sometimes I don't get how some animals can communicate but others can't or maybe they just choose not to take a bonded and to talk to people, it's all confusing.

The egg gives a little hum against my chest in the bag; I think that the hum might be a sign that the egg is going to hatch soon. I am not an expert on dragon eggs, but it seems to me like the hatchling is going to be big. The egg is like a good forty-five pounds maybe, light for how big it seems.

The egg is like a foot and a half maybe more in height. The egg has grown a bit since I had found it in the monsters lair. The colors of blue and purple have seemed to have gotten more vibrant. The crack running along the side seems a little wider, yet not enough to bust open on a little bump, thankfully.

"Hold on little one." I whisper under my breath, skimming my fingers over the smooth egg; the egg almost seems to hum back.

It is un-usually cold for this dimension at least since we have been here. Everyone is huddled together, trying to keep warm. Delan looks drawn and I can read all over his face that he doesn't see Yanni surviving, but he forges on trying to keep him alive with no medicine and the beginning of Vay.

Vay is the equivalent of autumn; we learned really early here that most of this dimension is similar to the Greek stuff. I once asked Delan about it and he said that once the veils between the dimensions are thinner and the dimensions used to comingle, and that is why the Greek culture is so similar to theirs. I think on anything and everything to keep me distracted as we wait.

*

We had thought that the morning would bring some relief and maybe warmer weather.

We wake to Radiva swooping into the camp calling out the alarm. *"They seem to have gone far around us doubling back until we have been completely surrounded,"* She sighs,

I know the but she is about to give I am not going to like. *"Except for a way …that would require us leaving behind Yanni."* She breaks the news in a sad tone.

"Dash, twins go saddle the horses. Lucan and Raven break camp." I order as Delan tugs on my arm pulling me away from the bustle and towards where Yanni was bundled up protected from the cold.

"Esper it's the only way…" I know exactly what he was suggesting; I won't have any of it, he is one of ours!

"How could you suggest that, he's your friend we can't just leave him to die?" My voice sounds shrill even to me with all the outrage I feel coursing through my body.

"Esper, you don't know the ways here. The Drazarian's are a slave based people, if he is not beyond saving they will heal him to work for them or be strong enough to sell. You need to think of what's best for him! This could be his only hope, and our only hope, because we can only take that path they are counting on us not because of our wounded. If we leave him here there is always the chance that we may get him back." Delan looks rather convinced and I know him, if there was any other possibility then he would have never suggest us leaving Yanni, even as possibility, but still its betrayal to even contemplate it or is it? I search Delan's eyes for the answers and I know this is the only solution he knows.

"If we do, that's a big if, when we get this egg back to its family we would go find him, Promise me!" I look him in the eyes, right up in face. My hands grip his collar tugging him closer.

"I promise." He whispers softly, he grabs my hands and squeezes to cement his promise. My stomach revolts and I feel like puking... how can I even entertain the idea? If I did would we see him again? How would we even know he is alive?

"Mount up." I yell again to the others, tugging Dash away from Yanni, and grab Red's reigns and tie it to Valla's saddle. I move over to Yanni knowing I have seconds to make a decision. How am I supposed to choose? It's us living and him possible dying or sold into slavery or its us all being sold into slavery or dead... there is no chose.

"But..." Dash tries to protest but stops thinking I had something else in mind. Delan mounts and starts off towards a trail to the east, forcing the others to follow. All of them thinking that Yanni had already been put on a horse or something similar... never in a million years would they think that I would let him be left behind.....
Even though that is exactly what I am doing.

I ride just out of sight but still able to hear. I know I should ride hard and put space between us but I can't leave without knowing he is at least alive.

I hear the explanations behind us as the Drazarians come upon our camp only to find Yanni and some hastily put out fires. The animals have fallen silent, and the only to be heard are birds alarming each other, thundering horse hooves, and the call of our enemy. I turn Valla racing away from one of my charges in order to save the others. I have wasted time, I waited and I don't know if he is or isn't alive.

The path Delan led the others is along, a steep embankment going straight up, and along a cliff. I catch up at the bottom, and we follow a ledge down that was probable created by some nimble footed animal that probable wasn't a horse. The ledge continues up, unnerving because the horses nearly slips a couple of times. We reach a cliff top up high, following another ledge down until like five feet off the ground, sinking down into a bank.

I am going to be sick, I now know I do not like being on a horse climbing up a cliff because I feel like I might lose my lunch.

The horses launch themselves off the bank, and down into the dirt embankment before a raging river, I clutch to the saddle for dear life. This was all done at a brisk hurried speed making my nausea worse.

I manage to glance back up and I can see the first of the monsters coming along the cliff top. Their steads were much more bulky and not meant to go down the ledge at a fast speed. Valla and Red plunge into the river following down the river after Delan – who was following Radiva – who is heading down stream. Flare leapt onto Red's back, Cobalt following as far along the embankment as possible before plunging into the frigid water after us (not being a snake or a monkey to be able to just cling to the horse's necks.) Why hasn't Flare said anything about what I did? Isn't he supposed to help me with stuff like this?

"Esper, this was something you needed to decide, if I had said leave him you would have got defensive." Flare lets his presence of listening to my thoughts known, and gives me a long look that is almost a balm for my soul.

"Stupid mutt; not so smug now are you, that you aren't nimble enough to hitch a ride like me." Flare mocks friendly breaking the moment, from astride Red, Cobalt just snorts and concentrates on keeping his head above water; the river is as high as Valla's withers, going part way up my thighs.

Delan Leads us to the other side of the river and onto rocky pebbles and over overturned trees, some requiring to be jumped over. We watch as the shaggy horse/goat like creatures the monsters ride, refuse to take them over into the river, some going to far as to rear and throw their monsters onto the pebbly ground.

I let out a sigh releasing the breath I didn't know I was holding.

Delan doesn't stop and neither do we, Radiva leads everyone threw the twist and turns, until eventually the sixth moon has made its way to its peak.

*

We finally stop when the horses can't run anymore, Phillip finally trips after caring Toni's weight and new found muscle. Everyone dismounts and starts loosening the saddles to the horses could also get some rest. "Wait! Where is Yanni? Esper, didn't you put him on Red? Where is he!!!" Lucan had gone to help Yanni only to discover the empty saddle.

"We couldn't have taken him with us, he never would have survived." My reply comes strangled and pained. I have to face the music for my choice.

"So you left him to those monsters so he could die anyways, just because it would be harder to take him with us?" Lucan looks horror filled and is getting hysterical. Our conversation has attracted the attention of the others they look over frowns marring their faces.

"I did what I had to do! If he had come with us he never would have made it and by leaving him behind the Drazarian will take care of him so they can sell him and give us a chance to get him back!" Lucan moves back as if I had hit him, he looks like he might strike me his face saying what he really thinks, and moves back to taking the saddles off of Davidia in angry jerking motions.

Delan moves up behind me, "you did what you had to do, they will see eventually. I made you a promise we will get him back." Delan rubs my back for reassurance. I move away, it isn't the time; I can't take comfort when Yanni is all alone in enemy hands.

The fire that night is quiet as everyone is lost in their own personal thoughts. They probable see me as the bad guy for having to do what needed to be done... hell I see myself as the bad guy.

*

The next village, along the coast, was a couple days ride; we spent those days in stone silence. Because of the hard ride Delan checks us into the local inn, were we were given warm baths, stable for the horses, and beds that aren't made up of dirt and rocks. We make plans to spend a few days here at Gizmo sense we have been riding none stop for the last three days. We have a new system we avoid the conversation of those we lost, and so far it works, Lucan no longer wants to stab me in my sleep that I can see.

After long nights sleep, Dash and I head out to explore the village – which was more of a town but not as big as the last one. The village has venders along the street kind of like a brazier an Arabian village on earth, and Dash and i wander from stall to stall looking at the wares. I stop at one that has silks scarves and dresses, the vender pushes a pretty purple dress with beads and fancy patterns towards me, "matches your eyes."

"How about for your pretty girl, *Ναι?*" The vender looks at Dash and puts the silk sari up to my face. Dash turns bright red, "She's not…. I'm not…. She's like….." He sputters and tries to find the right words. "*Ναι?*" He pushed it up again to my face. "Esper, you should try it on." He finally comes up with his response seeming unsure in this position the man has put him in. "I don't know…. okay." I turn to the vender, "How do I put it on?" He repeats the Va….. Word again and starts wrapping me around with the sarong or sari as he puts it.

"You look like one of those women from India or something; it looks good on you." Dash nods before handing the vender some gold coins he has earned in the mountain village. "Dash you shouldn't be spending your money on me, you earned it!" I try shoving his hand away from the vender.

"Exactly, this means that I can spend the money as I see fit." He drops the money into the vender's hands that reach forward to make a cup to make sure none of the coins fall to the ground. "If anything you can use the silk to protect the egg." We move on to another stall, this one has jewelry. It is so beautiful that women would have wept with how beautiful the jewelry has been formed. I shove the silk into the pouch that holds the egg, but before tucking the pouch into my shirt, a women bumps into me sending me reeling into Dash.

She mutters an apology and hurries off, I shove off laughing. "Well, thanks for being my wall, I think I might have fallen if it wasn't for you." I reach back up to tuck the pouch back into my shirt...

It isn't there; I search around trying to find it. Where did it go!? Flare! "Egg!!!!"

I move to searching the ground.

"Ma'am the lady took your pouch!" The person beside me calls overly loud, "conmen thing you must be careful." Before he even finishes speaking I run after the lady who is barely visible weaving her way through the crowd. "Come back you thief!" I scream giving her a warning, because one way or another I will get the egg back.

The women weaves through, going under stuff and barely visible to me. I jump over and try to not crash into people but most people see me coming before I hit them and move out of the way in time, some aren't so lucky. I am gaining ground running on pure adrenaline. I continue until I am a little bit behind her, then I duck behind the stalls, giving her the feel like she isn't being chased and stocked her from out of view.

The woman looks behind her, not seeing me she slows and walks at a brisk pace into the crowd. I catch up to her and when I come alongside her I jump towards her grabbing her wrists and push her to the ground. I ignore my need to sneeze, more important things then too much dust.

Landing on her back I pin her with my full weight, "Where is it! Give it back!" She cries out and babbles, but I ignore her and start patting her down, panic wells up when I can't find it immediately. I discover the pouch in a seam in her belt, a place I know to check from my interesting friendship with Quinn. "Be hopeful it didn't break!" still sitting on her I open the pouch to see the egg safely nestled inside the crack seeming to have gotten longer.

"Be thankful, if anything had happened to what's in this pouch I would kill you!" it kind of shocks me that I meant it with my whole heart.

Dash has caught up; he gives me a hand up, while grabbing the arm of the women. The women's demeanor completely changes, seeing Dash as a young gullible man she pushes her body up into his side. "Honey, if I had known that she is your girlfriend, I would have resisted the urge." She practically purrs, as she wraps herself around him.

"She's not my girlfriend!" He tries to move away, trying to move one hand between their bodies to push her away. He really isn't the touchiest feely person.

"Even better, now I don't have to steal you away!" The woman just pulls him closer.

"Get off me! We shall turn you into whatever authority is in this town!" She pulls back acting as if he burned her.

"No need to bring them into this!" She shrieks and her demeanor changes to that of a victim.

"Yes there is a need because this world if you don't have enough all you need is to but ask and somehow someway it will be provided, which means you have no reason to steal." With all the commotion everyone has looked on not bothering to intervene. Until finally the authorities -which is a dragon and a dude in light weight chainmail-, make an appearance. The dragon is a blue grey with lots of horns and is maybe the size of a draft horse.

"We will take it from here, and thank you miss, without you tackling her we might never have caught the women who was stealing from people. It has not been a common thing until recently." The man spoke, with purpose as they takes the women from them and doesn't even bother with us anymore as he turns and leaves with their prize.

"Maybe we should go back to the inn?" Dash helps me brush off the dirt off my cloths.

"Why would we do that when we still have another half of the bazar to look at?" I twirl around, reaching into the egg to pull out the sari and wrap it around me. I just want to forget that Pangaea is still has flaws like Earth. Why should one hiccup cause us to go hide?

*

The next couple of days are bliss. We spend the time exploring the town and just relaxing at the inn. When it is time to go we leave with extra grumbling, but the bridge in our little family that has become strained because of the chose I made with Yanni has been somewhat mended. They expect that we will get him back … one day. It is a promise I refuse to break, with the help of the capital hopefully.

Delan leads us through town to the docks, our horses following diligently behind, as we weave through the Brazier once more. "From here we will rent a boat to take us across were we will follow the coast to Cape Venn, to the town of Vennis. From there we shall take another boat to the Capital." Delan heads off to talk to the skipper. I glance over my shoulder seeming to take account of everyone, buts stops short.

"Where's Raven?" Radiva swoops down from the clouds searching for our missing family member. Dalia,

Raven's mount looks shocked around, looking for her wayward rider. "Esper, you need to see this." Dash calls, having on a hunch looked through Ravens stuff for clues. He pulls a piece of paper that had been jammed into a place on her saddle.

Dear Dash,
If you are reading this, I have left. I just can't take being
an outcast with people who are 'destined' to be 'heroes'.
Verico and I aren't welcome here; we have gone to seek
out others of our kind who have been out cast from
society. If we meet again may it be with us both happy
about who we are and maybe able to see each other
through different eyes. Tell the others I will be okay
wherever I am, I hope you will live well and prosper.
Till we meet again.
Raven Ren

"How could she do this? Just up and leave, disappear into the crowd with some stupid note. She may have been a pain but she is family, this is not how you say good bye to family." Lucan seethes his face a mix of emotions, from his fraternal twin's sudden and impersonal departure. He seems livid; I have never seen him this mad even when he found out about Yanni. I watch him in somewhat shock, Lucan whirls around and slams his fist into a pole standing next to him. The pole wobbles but stands firm as he clutches his fist and curse.

"Feeling better?" Toni asks but gets promptly ignored.

"Let's spread out we can still find her she couldn't have gotten far." I call, about to mount but Lucan stops me. He raises his hand in a move to show me to just stop. "She made her choice, now she can live with it." Delan returns, curious about the commotion, Lucan takes him by his arm and pulls him back towards the skipper. "Let us board, you look happy so I assume that you found a captain." I look back towards town unsure for the hundredth time sense we got here of what to do. "Esper, you heard Lucan, Raven knows where we are going she will catch up." Michael tugs my arm, before heading off to a somewhat normal boat. Valla and our other mounts start loading on to the below deck, the remnants of my family straggling on after. How did we go from a whole family to only a half? How have I failed so totally?

*

Being on the oceans is breath taking, like a colder version of the Caribbean. The boat we have commissioned to take us to Pleesh - the next city, cuts through the water easily, faster than any boat on earth.

Three days later…

We make camp on the beach, in better moods now that we are closer to our destination and on dry land once more. Delan says that from here we will go to one of the coastal villages, we will follow the coast on horseback, until Vennis where we will get a water transport to the dragon capital, our destination.

To everyone it sounds like a lot of steps but Delan says it would be a four day to a week ride whereas we just spent almost two weeks riding from the little mountain village to here. I think why he said it would take a week because we stop every night early and just kind of play in the sand. Life is too short Jenni, Yanni, and Raven has just proved that.

One night we stop just to play in the water and enjoy the sun as it starts to fade. Sometimes we just need the time to reflect that we are just in our teens, I don't even know if I am eighteen yet. When we left Earth it was winter but we got here in summer so there is no way for me to tell.

Delan plays in the surf with the twins who have upset the horses into getting off their high horse and joining them in them fun… horse get it? Lucan sulks for his sister's departure off by the tree line with Dash to keep him company. I move over sitting down beside them. "Hey," I start lamely, curiosity niggling at my brain about his thoughts, on a matter I seem to love to turn over by myself. "Hey yourself," Dash smiles at me, before turning his attention to the other's playing farther down the beach in the frothing waves.

"If we could find a way back to Earth would you go?" I turn to him, giving him my full attention as he mulls over the question. "I don't know, I guess never felt so at home on Earth as I do here, I have Shar here and well I don't think I could leave with Yanni and Jenni still here." He looks over at me for a second to see if I agree before petting Shar who had curled up in his lap. "My thoughts exactly, but I want you to know if we get a chance I wouldn't think less of any of you if you decided to go back. Not like we actually have a home here, we are sort of running for our life and going on an adventure." I chuckle, "now that I think of it that way it doesn't sound so good, more like a nightmare, but somehow still feels right." Flare appears seeming out of nowhere from the forests and settles against my side, letting lose a comforting purr.

"Esper, I know you say that but, well if you don't actually mean that, just know we won't think less of you if you go back. You have had a rough time here... with having to make the decision of leaving behind Yanni and not being able to save Jenni." Lucan looks down at his hands, but then looks over to me after a second. I look to Dash and he also holds my gaze, seeming to say he believes the same.

"I just want you to know I am sorry for the way I reacted." He finishes still looking at his hands.

"Thanks, but I would never leave Flare or you guys, you are my family. How about we stop with all this mushiness and go show these suckers how you really do a water fight." I stand up, shaking the sand from my clothing. I give Lucan a hand up and we head down to the water's edge, sometimes you just have to forge on.

*

The coastal village is booming, with lots of dragons, weird people, and lots of animals. We stop for an hour to pick up supplies before moving on out of the village. By now the freakiness doesn't surprise me so much, its actually soothing, in some weird way.

We see no signs of the monsters and I don't think we would survive a sneak attack at our vulnerable time, everyone is so happy. We have seemed to have retreated into a bubble. The village of Vennis is big it has dragons taking off from many points, serpents playing in the bay where normal ships stay docked. But these are different they have chains hanging from the front where I assume they attach to a serpents. Delan puts everyone up in an inn, while Dash, Delan, and I go to the docks to talk about more transportation this time to our final destination, the capital.

We stop at a captain who is a medusa; his snakes staring back at us as Delan barters for our passage to the capital. In the end we get what we want and the medusa gets his, for us it included passage for Sheena, food, water, quarters to sleep in, and above all safe passage. The captain gets three elegantly carved swords Delan has brought to barter with, it isn't the only swords, he brought with him from Carrien. We agree with the captain that we will meet again in the morning to board. The horses plan to make their own way to the capital.

The inn is in full swing when we get back, jam packed with people, serving women flirting and trying to avoid long conversations. What surprises me is dancing on the dance floor was Lucan. Well he is until Dash pulls him away from him seducing one of the pretty serving wenches as she bumps and grinds against him. Lucan yells something and waved his hands, Dash whispers something in Lucan's ear that makes him laugh before he turns back to his pretty friend. "Maybe you want to dance with a real man, beautiful?" Dash teases sweeping the girls hand up to his lips, like a gentleman.

"Maybe the lady doesn't want a brute like you." Lucan pulls her closer to him, she sputters turning red in the face, over both ... attractive men's attention (I guess most girls would consider them attractive). "I think I shall stick to this nice young man, maybe another time." She giggles behind her hand. Dash shakes his head mockingly and heads into the throng looking for his own beautiful lady. I raised lady kills! I shake my head I have the rest of the next twenty years to enjoy players.

*

The boat isn't that bad for most of us, except seems Dash doesn't like boats so much, spending most the time below decks with Sheena. Most of us chose to help out but he politely excludes himself from it. The serpents apparently make great time according to the captain, but not like I know anything to compare it by... none of us do.

The boat is rather large, having the captain's quarters and three barracks, one for the sailor's one for servant and another for passengers, sense we have no servants they have made it into another sleeping area where Sheena and

Dash sleep. The boat also has the mess hall, kitchen, and the store rooms.

We have finished dinner when I feel the quake of the egg in the pouch around my neck, I have learned by now I need to know what's going on. I silently excuse myself and leave the mess hall and head into our barrack. It would be awhile before the others turned in, Flare follows on my heels to find out what's wrong. I untie the sting holding together the pouch and reached in, pulling out the dragon egg. It is so smooth and perfect, it shines with a blend of dark blues and purples, it has grown even more so now it is as high as an average dog and as wide as a foot. The egg hasn't seemed to weigh all that much thou, almost like the weight of a small child… like Jenni.

The crack that runs along the egg is worse, it now runs all the way down the egg and I feel the little shudder again. The egg cracks more until a small fragment falls off.

9

I can see what looks to be leathery blue purple in the egg but not much else. I feel curiosity and excitement so much I feel like jumping up and down or helping it out. I hear a slight deep chirp coming from the egg. The egg shakes again as another piece falls off and another, the little hatchling burst from the shell with squawks of offense. The hatchling is … breathtaking…. Beautiful… it has deep rich colors of blue and purple along his body, but his eyes are snapping amber with green flecks in them.

The Dragonet tumbles out all the way, it has five fingers and toes covered in soft leathery scales I assume would become hard like Flukes. Its tail is a prominent feature, it is much too big for his body, and it is mostly because at the end it has seven spikes that jut out with tough webbing in between. It also has big wings that are nearly twice his body and seem rather gangly. The hatchling hisses at the egg for encumbering it, but when he goes to take its first steps his balance is off and he tumbles over his head. I notice its talons are huge for the little thing it is only the size of full grown beagle.

Flare and I exchange looks, I can hear that awe inspiring music that you hear right when something dramatic happens, also a mix of what's going to happen, is it hungry? I also feel like squealing awe cute again.

Most people at this point – at least in the dimension I am from – would run screaming, me I feel curiosity. I reach out, slowly putting my hand on his head. The dragonet watches me with wide amber-green eyes. I slowly pet it, its scales are super soft, like a human baby soft, I don't know why I do it, but my hand slowly make its way to down to cover the dragonets heart.

It is like the connection to flare, I feel like I am seeing into him. With one exception I feel like a hundred watts of electricity are traveling through my body. While he is in the shell he had heard the people around him, he knows that I was protecting him, and he knows that his mother was going to name him Raja. Raja seems to connect with Flare and me, like a trio, best friends forever.

Raja turns from me to look at Flare, "*He may be a wee thing right now but I feel that our new friend shall be very big.*" Flare gives a little purr of his approval. "Stay with Raja, Flare, I am going to go get some pure milk from the kitchen." I don't pass anyone on the way to the kitchen but

Dash is the kitchen rummaging through the fridge, before moving over to the counter to cut some stuff up.

I pull him close, "the egg has hatched." Dash glances around, "what? Where is the hatchling?" Dash is never to mince words.

"He is in the room with Flare. I just came to get him some food...Dash, he bonded with me." Dash let himself think about it for a minute then nods. I grab the thick un-watered down milk; Dash goes to Pangaea's type of freezer and grabs some meat. "You know he might want meat instead of milk, like I remember Fluke speaking of how he was raised on milk and small pieces of meat. Makes sense that you would bond with him, I mean you have been a mother hen over the egg."

We head for the room again to find Flare tucked up under Raja's big oversized wings. Raja isn't as big as Flare even with Flare still growing but he makes up for it in wing and tail size. Raja gives a cute little chirp, when I put down the milk I had brought for him, "hold your horses, mi amor." I put the bowl down, sitting next to him, and start stroking Flare as Raja laps up milk with his forked tongue.

*

I am down below when I hear the alarm. Flare and I head up to the deck to check things out while Raja sleeps soundly below. The sailors are all about scrambling about grabbing weapons. I next notice the dragons flying rapidly at us from the distance shore. I expect the serpents to quicken their pace but instead we sit bobbing up and down in the water. I look over the side for them; they were thrashing in the water the fighting of some unseen foe.

I don't have much time to find out what's going on before the dragons descending on us. There are three of them, snatching men from the deck, one red and black dragon grabs one of the masts on the boat and wrenches it from the deck to cast it off to sea. The medusa captain grabs a bow and sends arrow after arrow off at the green dragon, they sails true and hits the dragon in between one of its massive scales in a whole where a scale has been ripped from its body. I think a resounding yes at the small victory.

The captain goes to reload his bow when the ship pitches under us and throws everyone to the side.

I look over the railing and can see the ocean have been stained red from a serpent's blood, they lay slaughtered. I can just see the colors of a serpent or possible dragon under the water attacking the boat.

"Esper, what's going on?" Toni and Dash yell from near the door that leads to the below decks. "Dash, grab Sheena and the younger kids and take to the air, Toni it doesn't look as if we will be able to keep the ship. Get anything that can float and cast it out, and grab our stuff from below decks." Toni runs off with all due haste Cobalt on his heels, just as Dash comes out on Sheena, the twins holding on tightly from her back. They take to the air in a few strides, circling over the boat and avoiding the attacking dragons. Lucan stays by the railing, with Shar looking very uncertain.

Cobalt meanwhile has run down with Flare and to get Raja. The ship groans again and starts tipping forward till I feel like I need to grab onto something or slide. The boat groans again and with a jerk splashes back with a spray of water. Raja gives a little growling chirp that might one day be ferocious but now is just adorable. I watch from the side standing guard by the archers as they fire volleys at the dragons. Why couldn't I go to a normal work one with no villains trying to kill us or whatever they want?

The green dragon zeroes in on Raja. The dragon stops picking off sailors, and zooms towards my dragon. I dive for Raja using the boats momentum to push us out of the path of the dragon. The dragon growls when he sweeps by harmlessly and without his quarry. The green dragon turns around for another pass at Raja. I grab for raja again but we don't have anywhere else to run. The ship gives a mighty heave and starts tipping forward like in the movies of the Titanic.

So I go the only way that seems to be an option, over the side. Who do I think I am James Bond? I shouldn't... but I have to, but ...

I clutch the baby dragon closer to my chest and hold my breath as I jump over the edge.

Hitting the ocean about five feet off the water isn't as bad as jumping from very high diving board, but still smarts a bit. Everything turns dark around us as we are pushed farther under the water as the green dragon lunges into the water with his talons the sizes of people! Raja squawks but kept swimming down, he takes to the water like a fish to water, breathing thru.... Little slits under scales on his neck. He uses his tail as a fin to push us farther away from the flailing legs and arms of the grasping green dragon.

It's getting cold... why did I think this was a good idea? I need air is the dragon gone?

After about a minute and a half my lungs are burning and if I don't get any air I feel like I will lose consciousness. I can feel Flare's worry for me, and that he has also been forced to jump into the water, along with everyone else.

I am going to pass out; I see dark spots flooding my vision. This is how I am going to die, I'm drowning. This is it. This is it.... I'm going to die.... I am going to die surrounded by crystal blue water... so pretty...I am going to die.

I have no air left, my body inhales in the hope beyond hope… that I might actually get air. It was a stupid hope but I still inhale.

Only what I get is …….. air? Can it really…. Am I going crazy?

Raja gives me this funny look. *"Mother use to tell me in the shell that when you have the affinity for water the person you bond with will inherit it, actually each affinity has special ability inherited to the bonded."*

"So does that mean that serpent's can have bonded's?" Even as I am surrounded by water I can't help asking because, it makes me wonder if the serpents pulling the ship were bonded to someone; maybe even the ship's medusa captain.

"Yes, but she said it is rare cause most serpent eggs are laid under the see or hidden in caves." He looks up when the big dragon's claws rake through the water again. *"When will it stop, Esper?"* his voice is all soft reminding me of Jenni's earlier plea for Mr. Johan to stop, *"Why is it after us?"*

"I don't know Raja; I think we just have wait out."

*

After an hour Flare sends that the dragons have left with their dinner (or hostages). Little has survived the dragons furry but somehow we haven't lost anyone from our group.

Breathing fresh air is strange after somehow turning into a fish. I kind of panicked for a bit what if I hadn't been able to surface, Forced to swim the watery depths for the rest of my life.

"You're alive! You have been under for a while!" Toni treads water towards Raja and me, most everyone has found some floating part of the ship that is scattered and taken hold of the pieces to keep afloat. "If help does not come we will drown here."

A sailor bemoans from his board. "What will my wife say? She never wanted me to take jobs sailing this course with all the dragon raids!" The scruffy sailor looks about to just give up and let himself just drown, "well she sounds like a formidable woman, I wouldn't give up for fear of her following me to the afterlife to make me pay." I point out in hope of giving the man some hope, or at least a healthy dose of fear, giving up is stupid.

"Your right… might be more trouble to give up then to actually fight." The man chuckles, clutching his board, "I've met your wife Harry I'm afraid for her coming after me if I die on Celia!" Another sailor laughs from a few boards over.

"I think I might like this woman she sounds formidable." I call over treading water to grab onto a board. My limbs are feeling sore from all the swimming.

"What ways shore?" Toni calls from a large piece of gang plank that he and Cobalt are sitting on. The sailor looks over, pointing to in a direction. I really suck at the compass stuff so I couldn't tell you north, east, west or south, unless told first.

"Well we had better start swimming that way." Garrett pipes in from the side trying to be helpful and come up with a good idea on his own. Raja tires easy, being that he is only a day out of the egg, so I push him up onto Cobalt and Toni's raft of sorts. Others swim over and help push it while using it to stay afloat and we head the way we assume shore is.

*

I am so cold, I can feel Flare tiring and everyone is starting to swim slower and slower. Every once in a while we would trade off for being propped up more on the drift wood, due to some of the crew starting to sink below the surface.

I think I see a speck on the horizon; it can either mean our savior or our doom, because I don't think we can keep swimming for much longer.

When the three dragons finally make it to us we are exhausted and icy cold unable to do anything other than climb aboard the out stretched talons. A big red one picks up Raja and me. It cradles us against his body as if we are precious to the dragon. It honestly doesn't matter if they are friend or foe, its death or a chance at life.

Raja curls up against me to let me have some of his excessive amount of heat. Flare has been picked up by another dragon but reporting that there are men on the dragons and they aren't acting hostile, but that is doesn't mean they aren't. I know I shouldn't rush to judgment but I think I have the right to be suspicious.

The dragons fly for a while back to land away from the boats course and off into the trees and mountains. Sheena hovers at the edge of sight unsure of if they are friend or foe. Sheena looks plum tuckered out, her wings seem to droop an she keeps dropping to then beat her wings up, so as not to fall into the ocean.

The dragons finally stop after a while in a small valley just off of the ocean maybe a mile or two inland. Mainly because of us survivors from the attack are frozen solid and risk a higher chance of getting hypothermia from the high altitude at such a fast speed.

The valley is surrounded by trees and barely fits the three dragons but it works when they drop the people off and two leave 'to go find water'. With two of the three dragons gone we are left to look at our 'saviors'. I am unsure of what to make of these people and their intentions.

"Where are you going?" A man from our sailor's stops, he had been heading for the woods probable to go take a leak. A man from the dragons is glaring at him, while two other of the dragon men stand in front of the sailor pointing weapons to turn him back to where the rest of us huddle. Another of the dragon men steps closer gaining our attention.

"We are so glad we found you, before you drowned." I don't like them. "Sit, sit, while we light a fire, we don't want you to catch a cold." The man speaking is bedecked in gold, more so then the others, obviously a dragon bonded. I should know because over the day I have been with Raja, he has given me any shiny objects that he can find. This man thou is handsome in a scraggily shaggy sort of windblown look, but not hideous for an older dude, of like his thirties. His words are forceful and made less friendly by the dragon men standing guard around the valley… except they are turned towards us instead of out into the woods.

I nod an head over to the fire.

I have been kept warm tucked under the dragon with my own little space heater in scales, but I still sit with the others who huddle close to the growing fire. The twins move closer to Raja trying to keep warm, I wouldn't be surprised if the squash the poor baby.

Sense I have gotten dry by Raja my hair has fluffed up like some pissed off cat, that's just what I get for flying and drying, I wonder if I look as silly as Toni. Toni's hair and pretty much everyone else's hair stands up like halos.

Sheena settles down at the edge of the clearing so tired she lies down so she can eat grass and falls asleep within minutes. Dash joins us by the fire and makes a face at my hair.

"You say anything and I will make you live to regret it." I threaten with a smile twitching at my lips, Dash just throws his hands up and laughs. "I didn't say anything…. yet." I punch him in the arm and he rubs and rubs like I have hit him a lot harder.

Cobalt, Flare and Shar are curled up by the fire as close as they dare, snoring soundly. "How do we know we can trust these men? They could be associated with the dragon's that attacked us!" Toni worries from across the fire, looking about at the strangers, who mill about setting things up for the night; if they hear us they don't show it.

"Hope you guys are feeling warmer. Now, would you guys like to tell me how you ended up in the ocean far from shore with no ship, with a new hatchling too young to have even bonded yet? Where is his mother?" The dragon man struts over after commiserating with some of the other dragon men. He keeps looking at Raja with fascinated glances and spending the most time looking over his spiked tail, too much time for my liking.

"We were attacked." I don't offer anything else, even when he gestures for me to keep going. "Was the baby dragon's screened bonded killed? Because none of you look fit enough to be chosen to be a bonded to a hatchling. Why is he away from his mother... wait has the royal egg hatched I thought no more would hatch until it did?!" The man seems to talk himself in circles. When we don't say anything he gets a tick in his jaw and I can see the vein in his forehead throb.

"Eh." I pet Flare as he sidles up to me and Raja.

"Before you ask us more questions why don't you tell us who you are, and why you were flying so far into the ocean?" I keep my voice sweet so it doesn't come out too suspicious. Raja cracks his eye and looked at him suspiciously, seeming only to become suspicious after it was pointed out.

"I am Torge, and my partner in mind is Tafetas, and you should be thankful that we were out there you mouthy Dane!" Torge is turning red and I can't tell if it is from rage or something else. Something green catches my eye, I glance over seeing a green dragon circling the camp.... *'Flare is it just me or is that the dragon from the boat? Big ... what's that word.... Hood that flares out when agitated, he's*

the first I have seen with it, is it common or something?' The
dragon in question looks as if he landed nearby.

Are they working with that dragon? That would mean
they shipwrecked us and then came in to play hero… *"It
is not a common thing; it is a genetic thing of certain family
lines."* Flare's hackles seem to rise a bit more, I can feel his
mistrust. I believe cats are an excellent judge of character.

"Answer the question!" I stand and face him off.
If he was so innocent they why would he be getting all
defensive? Raja meanwhile puffs up like an offended cat
and gives a cute yet outraged growl. *"Do not call my bonded
names that I don't know what they mean yet know you are
insulting her!"* Flare joins Raja growling at Torge. Tafetas
gives a warning growl and opens one giant luminescent eye
to glare at us; but that doesn't seem to make Raja cower it
actually made him madder.

The other dragons swoop down into the valley, taking
in the scene of everyone about to jump down everyone's
throat. "Now, now, Torge, no need to call name's," one
of the other Dragon bonded calls. "Answer the question
Torge!" I snap ignoring the man trying to make peace; I
want answers not diplomatic answers. You know what they
say about diplomat's answers….

"You ungrateful little-, Maybe we should have left you
out there and just taken the hatchling with us!" Raja gives
another chirping growl from beside me. "I would like to

see you try! Why is it you are avoiding the question, unless you have something to hide!?" I am working myself up into a fine temper so much so that I poke Torge in the chest. Maybe I can justify my thoughts of wanting to kill this dude as seeing red from both my anger, Flare's anger, and Raja's anger, but it all comes down to I flat out don't like this guy and he is the enemy. Call its women's intuition and mounting weird an somewhat threatening behavior.

I move away from him pacing until he make a sound in the back of his throat, like a fake laugh, "so like a women to retreat!" I spin on my heels and move threatening towards him with Raja and Flare flanking me. There aren't that many rules for trying to intimidate people but here is one; DON'T TRIP!

Raja's big clumsy tail lashes to and fro in aggression and in one of his passes he knocks into me with his tail taking my knees out from under me. I go down into Flare who barely gets out of the way in time to keep from being crushed.

To add insult to injury Torge hovers over me when I finally look up. "You have a lot to learn petulant Dane; apparently one being how to walk." Torge laughs and turns away intending to make his dramatic exit. "*THAT TEARS IT!*" Flare snarls and launching himself at the pompous windbag, only to have Cobalt knock him out of the line of pounce. Bothe being the size of full grown Earth leopard and wolf on earth at half growth on Pangaea it is horrifying as Flare turns on Cobalt, ripping at him.

I watch this from my peripheral vision on the ground trying to fend off Raja and his long serpent tongue. He tries to use his tongue like a dog and lick my face in apology. "*Sorry! Sorry! Sorry!*" Michael gives me a hand up, as I try to get up, pushing Raja lightly back, and wipe dirt off my butt.

Now there is a lot going on. People trying to get Flare and Cobalt to stop fighting before they hurt someone and there are something's you don't have time for, one being the twins.

Meanwhile Garrett and Dante have gone over beside the snoring Green dragon with some sort of herb in their hand. The twins exchange looks, and being an idiot with a riot on her hands I ignore them till a soldier runs that way screaming bloody murder. Garrett is ticking the dragon's nostrils with the plant and Dante shoves the rest into the green dragons mouth. Why couldn't I have an easy normal family with well-behaved twins? I'm starting to think I am cursed.

The twins jump back as the dragons roars an sits back on his haunches making the sound people make before they sneeze like a-a-a-a-and of course then most of the time that follows by the achoo. The dragon sneezes right at the twins who are almost lost in the nasty stuff that leaks from the dragon, I am just thankful it only comes out his mouth and that it isn't fire. Well maybe I am a little bit more thankful that I am not standing next to them, who wants to be coved in dragon snot?

"EWWWW,"

"COOOL!"

The twins scream brushing off the guck as best as they can but it keeps getting stuck to their fingers. The hysterical Bonded is fussing over the giant bigger than a house dragon, he can't help himself an rails at us, "You didn't even know if it could hurt him!"

"Over by Sheena, NOW," I yell at them turning red in the face. Swallowing my pride I turn to the rider, snubbing Torge, "I extend my apologies." Least I could do, I just wish I wouldn't have to constantly be apologizing for things I didn't do.

Without another word I move to the others waving them to Sheena. Michael is already shouting at the twins while Sheena rest behind them, seeming not interested in listening. I couldn't blame her, their trouble never ends, I wish I could nap through it. "I don't trust these men they… do not want to give a straight answer. It would be smart to leave now." Delan looks first at me and then moves around until he is sure everyone is in agreement. "We should leave tonight that way they can't call in anyone or get us to farther away from the ocean." I answer back.

"We must be careful I feel we are supposed to be guests either willing or not." I can't help but add gazing at the guards around the camp who watch us.

"If we are we must wait until everyone is asleep and someone should stay up so they can wake everyone else up. I volunteer to be that person." Dash strokes Sheena. I can just see the wheels turning in his head. "If we bring the sailors in, we risk the possibility of one of them betraying us but also we can't leave them, I mean we did get their boat sunk." The sailors being about twenty in numbers minus their main medusa captain who had gone down with his ship and bonded.

Sheena nickers softly and speaks into or heads. *"Best be that you get some sleep so that you won't be too tired when we must leave."*

Cobalt moves in beside Sheena, being almost as big as her, almost at full growth. Flare - being almost as big - joins him but on her other side. Flare thumps his tail down in an invitation and I join him down by them, Raja cuddling up to us so that it reminds me of a dog pile. The rest of the group cuddles up around us taking in the warmth from being huddled together. I like it I can see why animals huddle in groups feels safe.

"Delan, do you know where we are?" I whisper as quietly as possible with him able to hear. "I think so but it's not a perfect coordinate or what not. I think we will be ok." Delan whispers back, I drift off feeling a bit better.

*

Dash shakes me awake holding his hand to his lips, telling me to be silent. He doesn't say anything just moves on to wake the others and we each fan out waking the sailors, filling them in on our escape plan. The sailors decide to head to the ocean, instead of joining us, partly because some have left their bonded back at sea and feel the need to hurry back. I think they also plan to head back to Vennis, instead of heading to the capital but they don't confirm and we don't mention where we are going to head either. I'd rather if they are recapture they don't know for sure where we are going or them us.

Since Cobalt and Flare are the size of small horses, yet they are stronger and lighter on their feet. We put Dante and Garrett on Cobalt and Lucan, Shar, and Raja on Flare. While the sailors make their way directly to the ocean we head inland the way the dragons have been carrying us. After about five hours Cobalt lets out a blood curdling howl.

"Toni, what the hell is he doing?" The call is taken up by other wolves from far and wide, and before we know it big horse size wolves come bounding over fallen trees to surround us. Okay I have a sudden need to scream and run the way we came, its stupid weird things happen in Pangaea like it's the normal yet it still unnerves me.

Cobalt walks over to a smaller silver female and starts mind speaking to her.

"We request your help, to hide our tracks and divert attention from our path, there is also another larger party making their way to sea, we request you do the same for them." Best that they don't find us so easily by just following our tracks, we have to make it a little harder for them, it is a good plan. I am being out thought by a dog.

"Why should we help you?" The silver female lets out a snarl, which the wolves around us echo.

"Because you haven't found your mate and I can give you a pup that will bring new blood into your pack…" Toni clears his throat, he seems to hear something we can't something very uncomfortable. Apparently this answers if Cobalt is sexually mature yet, maybe it's like human they become sexually mature before they are finished growing. I really need to pay attention more and stop thinking so much!

The silver wolf gets a gleam in her eyes and circles Cobalt, taking in his silver pelt with blue black ears.

"Where are you from?" The silver female sniffs him near his shoulder.

"A small town in the mountains, we wolves from the mountains are very hearty, can take extreme cold, very good

endurance, and have I stayed, I would be Alfa." Cobalt boastfully tells her puffing up his chest and preens a little.

The female lets out a rumble and nods her head slowly in agreement. She turns towards the other wolves and gives a sharp command to the wolves. They don't question, but streak off the way we have come. The female leads us on the way until we reach the wolf camp. I really need to get better endurance, these bondeds an kids are running me ragged.

"This is a good place for us to take to the air and not have to worry, any animal with a nose can scent that this is the wolves' valley and means death to trespassers." Toni walks beside Cobalt and listens to them speak often turning colors over their… monolog. I only pick up bits and pieces from Flare, their… puppy love is adorable.

From here Sheena is going to fly us around, back the way we have come but at an angle so we will be heading in the direction we would have been going from sea; so we can get back on track.

Sense Sheena is only one Pegasus, we are taking turns. Sheena will fly us to the same spot and return for another load. Dash, Raja, and Shar make the first trip, then Lucan, and Dante. Flare being so big decided to take the ground route and ran over land be himself going wide and climbing trees, and other animal paths so they won't associate him with us.

Sheena seems to be tiring but still chugging along taking next Delan and Garrett. Radiva having gone off to look over the dragons and warn us if they get on our winding trail makes sure to say all clear before Delan heads to the others. Toni is near green when it is our turn, from listening to Cobalt and the silver female – Aroura – talk. Meanwhile the couple are cuddling up together, Cobalt about has her purring and she is butting her head up under his chin almost like a big cat, and licking his chin.

Cobalt stays behind, saying he will catch up, he has a deal to finish, I really don't see where he drew the short stick, he actually seems to have gotten lucky.

*

Sheena pants and drops heavily to earth as soon as the others come into sight. Dash moves to comfort her telling her she did well.

Toni grunts, "Cobalt, will be staying for a while and he will make his own way, we are not to wait for him."

"Delan, call to Radiva, make sure she flies closer so we know what's around." I touch him on his shoulder as I pace over to check on Raja, who is curled under a tree fast asleep.

"Let's walk for a couple more hours then we will make camp and hunt. We should sleep during the day, it would be the safest." Delan recommends, already moving forward.

Flare joins us after walking for a little bit, seeming pleased and has a little bit of blood splattered across his pelt.

Once the sun is at its highest Delan calls for a stop, and Raja takes the opportunity to plop down in some shade. Sheena all but collapses beside a tree too tired to stand. "Dash, Dante, and Garrett, I want you to go look for berries and food for Sheena. Toni and Delan I want you guys to go hunt with Flare, you can draw them out he will go for the kill… Lucan you can take Shar and go find some fire wood."

Once everyone else had left off doing what they will, I moved to make a makeshift fire from scraps around, that would last till Lucan and Shar got back; we needed a fire to cook the meat.

Lucan sets his pile of sticks on the ground and starts collecting the strewn grass.

I head to sit by Raja kind of wishing I had some of the technology from home, like a lighter.

Everyone soon returns with the meat and food, in good spirits livening up the place. We cook the meat there and sit around the fire, falling soon asleep. If only we could stay this way, so peaceful… even though we are sort of on the run but what's new about that?

*

Cobalt joins us around the time everyone is waking up; he is quick to anger and seems to be angry at everyone including Toni.

"Toni, what's going on with Cobalt?" I pull him aside, after the tenth time Cobalt snaps at someone.

"He just misses Aroura… Esper…. if we make it through this, and if we can't make it home…. I think me and Cobalt will come back here, that's even if we want to go home I mean do you really want to go back to foster care and Mr. Johan …. leave Raja and Flare?" He pauses looking around; he knows I know that he is right. "This is as good of place as any to make our home, wolves for Cobalt, peace and a beach. Maybe not right here but around this area." Toni's eyes are shining with wicked ideas of what his future might be.

"Anyways let's let the others rest Cobalt will like some rest before he's ready to go he's been running for a while." We settle back down to go to sleep, needing no extra warmth being that the sun blazes down in all its glory.

*

When going to sleep there are a lot of ways that I thought I was going to be woken up to… actually I didn't put much thought into it; but this is the last thing I expected.

"FIRE!" Toni pulls me from the ground; he has a cloth over his nose and is hunched over. Everyone else is scrambling to grab our things and run away from the fire that fills our sleeping place with smoke and gives it an eerie feel to the tall huge trees as they are engulfed in flames. Cobalt goes crazy everyone can hear him he as he goes in a fit running up and down by the flames.

"Aroura! She is back there! She could be in trouble got to get to her!"

I cover my face and push myself away from Toni so I'm not dead weight. *"How could it bare down on us without us knowing? Who was keeping watch?"* I call to Flare but to no answer. What is the point of a bonded if they don't answer!

Sheena leaves with the twins and Raja to get them out of harm's way. Lucan mounts Flare, like a horse… except

Flare bows down for us, we try to calm Cobalt, but he is going crazy; he won't listen. If one of my family was back there I would be going crazy that's just love.

With a final growl Cobalt is preparing himself to leap into the flames to go in search of his mate. Toni, Dash, Delan, and I grab onto him hoping to drag him away, but when dealing with a wolf the size of a small horse it is like fighting a losing battle.

"What have you been feeding him, people!?" I cry jerking hard on Cobalt's leg which only succeeds in slowing him down.

"Says the girl with a Leopard, the same size of a horse that can carry people," Toni growls back, pulling against Cobalt's other leg.

You know when those books say stuff slows down when bad things happen, the world actually kind of does. Because one minute we are fighting a battle of strength and the next Cobalt is jerked backwards, barreled over by a figure that has leapt out of the flames.

Poor Delan happens to be under the giant wolves. Around us a couple more wolves flee the flames, only to disappear from sight a second later.

"Get up, you are crushing him!" I scream pathetically pulling on Aroura's legs trying to pull her away.

Cobalt and Aroura jump up as fast as they can leaving a frazzled looking Delan smashed into the ground.

"You okay?" I help him up he has this supper weird look on his face like he has been knocked over the head instead of sitting on by giant wolves. I guess his head could've taken a few hits also with lack of oxygen.

"I think so but I don't think for much longer if we stay any longer!" Delan points at the fire that is now breathing down my neck.

The smoke is thick almost too thick to see. Dash helps Delan onto Aroura and I join him letting the others - weighing more - take Cobalt. The mated wolves with their extra passenger's race after the others trying to out run the fast encroaching forest fire.

My head feels funny with all the smoke and I crouch lower on the wolf's back and thread my fingers through her fur to stay on. With the lack of oxygen my gills try an come out to help me breath but I resist, I'm pretty sure that will kill me. I urge Aroura on; slow deep breaths aren't helping much anymore.

"Flare head for the ocean its probable our only chance now it's amazing that we weren't burned alive while we slept." I speak to him through the bond. I doubt I can get enough breath let alone speak aloud. I feel slight annoyance through the bond as if to say 'no duh'. I can't help it if I have an idea I am going to say it, because who knows if the others have thought of it or not.

Aroura gives another surge forward to keep up with the well-rested leopard. Flare swerves to the left heading toward the beach.

"Esper, Delan told me to tell you that this might be their plan to force us to the beach where we will be easy pickings." Radiva sends to me as she circles above the trees, flying high enough to keep out of the smoke. *"I know, but we have no chose we have to get to the beach."*

"We shall meet you there, Esper that way I can come back and get more people it will go faster." Sheena calls as she flies at a faster pace than what we are going. *"Just make sure Raja is safe we will get there soon after you."*

"I will be fine Esper, just stay safe." Raja's voice is soothing as of that second I am mind linked with both him and Flare, but the sensation is fleeting as they withdraw to concentrate.

Aroura is going strong even with her weariness from running to escape the forest fire. Every once in a while we will find a pocket without smoke and greedily gulp in the clean air before racing through.

Cobalt keeps near Aroura but she trips over a log barely visible from the brush on one of her downward strides. Aroura moves to correct but calculates too late and instead trips tumbling over the large log. Dash and I go tumbling off of Aroura thrown almost inches from the flames, my hair getting slightly singed. The hot breath of the fire against my face, makes me long for ice cold winters on Earth.

Aroura moves to get up but howls in pain as her paw refuses to take her weight and she falls back down, the ground quaking at the impact.

Cobalt comes rushing back to his mate's side, even against the protest of his bonded.

"Cobalt, you must go take the others so that you can come back and help until then I can limp along." Aroura nuzzles his face, before giving him another soft push off towards the edge of the clearing. He lets out a long whine but turns and leaves.

"Dash you gotta get up, we need to help Aroura and keep moving." I grab his arm and help him sit up even though he looking even more dazed then he did when hit over the head.

We move as fast as we can and I know that by doing so we are causing Aroura a lot of pain but we don't have much choice, it is either walk fast or die… not that death is off the table yet. "Come one Aroura you are tougher than this you got to push back the pain and increase your pace." I cough, more as I urgently pull her forward, having to stop mid-sentence to cough again.

She manages to increase her pace a little but it isn't going to be enough. "Come on girl laugh through the pain get some adrenaline pumping." I try to encourage, i laugh myself when in pain it's like wires are all crossed in my head but it helps to tolerate pain.

The flames are closing the distance, raging unchecked. Aroura yelps as her tail is singed and increases a bit more. Flare comes bounding out of the flames coming to our rescue. Without protest Flare bends down so Aroura could drape herself across his shoulders. Sense we no longer have to help a struggling wolf we take off alongside him at a faster rate, our lungs clogging with all the smoke making it harder to breathe, so we stay low to the ground. Flare is strong and Aroura is a small wolf so he is able to run what is to a human is full speed.

Breaking from the trees and into fresh air is like being socked in the gut but in a good way, Raja is waiting for me and comes to butt up against my legs.

Cobalt hurtles himself at Flare and Aroura, letting her lean on him as she gets off of Flare and moves slowly towards the water. "Any sign of the other dragons?" I move down by Lucan. "None yet, but if the forest fire is a trap they won't be far." Lucan puts out there what we are all thinking. Meanwhile Shar slithers around to hover over Aurora's leg, looking on curiously.

Toni moves over to Cobalt and Aroura. "How is she?" I ask over their shoulders.

"She sprained her paw, she should stay off it." Delan is hovering over her, lightly holding her paw and examining it. "Cobalt says he will carry her." Toni pets Aroura's head in slow long strokes, he tries to sooth her but she still winces every time Delan moves the paw.

"That may not be needed, if we can get some wood from the trees not on fire we can make her a raft and pull her along in the water that way whoever pulls it can go faster by having her float." My brain starts working over time trying to think up ideas.

"Esper, I don't think that will happen." Garrett tugs on my arm and points out at the forest which is completely engulfed in flames. "We need to get away before the water dragons come to put out the fire." Delan suggests already moving down the beach before anyone even agrees to. I know we need to get moving but I also need a breather, but none the less I start on. Flare comes along side, *"Hop on E, we need to keep going faster."* I don't argue, who would it's a free ride.

Sheena nudges Dash from the side towards her back. Dash climbs up seeming kind of shaky but still manages to make it on. The autumn breeze makes the fire grow bigger, also managing to keep us feeling cool even thou there is a raging inferno to our right.

*

We stop when we get away from the fire and are far enough away for the water dragons not to see us. The twins look as if they are about to fall over from adrenaline and exhaustion. Raja has for the past hour been tripping over his own tail as he tries to keep up with Flare, he tells me he was sooo nervous cause he could have lost me, but stayed strong none the less. Flare keeps up with the group fine and the only one who seems to have any energy is Radiva and it is because she has just flown away from the fire she doesn't have to bother running like a scared animal.

We don't have the energy to build a fire and don't really feel like it we need a fire after running from a raging inferno so we just huddle together in a pile like a pride of lions.

*

The next morning we continue our forward march down the beach, I feel like every bone aches but I still trudge onwards, if they can do it then so can I. By noon Sheena has a passed out Raja on her back, looking none too happy to have to carry the growing dragon. Raja is now the size of a Doberman who ate the mail man. His claws and tail still are bigger than he is. Delan said his wings will always be bigger than him, so as to carry his weight; he just has to get adjusted in proportions.

A couple of hours later we see our first sign of civilization, it is a well-traveled path that swerves into the woods but also continues off down the beach. Delan leads us along the beach so that we head in the same direction we have been traveling over water.

The first person we see we wave him down, he is a shifty little man with a raggedy beard and smells like he hasn't taken a bath in like years. Usually when you see people like him they also smell of licker but I don't get that smell he just smells like a used port-potty. His hair was dark grey and his beard goes all the way to his knees, he is also wearing some sort of brown colored cloak.

"Excuse me, Sir, we are on our way to the Palace can you tell us if we are on the right path?" Delan asks him, the man shifts from foot to foot and looks at suspiciously at Delan. "Yup, yup, the palace couple miles down, miles down." He gives us the thumbs up as he kind of sings the words.

"Thank you kind Sir, can you tell us if anyone was sent after the forest fire down a ways?" Toni puts in when the man looks as if to scuttle away. "Yup, you, big group of water dragons looking none too pleased to be leaving to take care of earths mess, earths mess, none too pleased." The man nods his head so hard I think he might hurt himself but the next second his head snaps up when Raja huffs and shifts around in his sleep.

"Goddess blesses me, you have a… you have a… a …"
He gulps hard, I can see his Adams apple move, "I want
no trouble kind people, kind people." He looks from each
person to the dragon huffing in his sleep, before the man
turn tail and runs off towards the woods, looking terrified.

"I never even caught his name." I sighs this could be
bad. "People in your world are very odd." I look at Delan
who put his hands up in an 'I surrender' pose; and we
watch the man run out of sight.

We don't wait and ponder the strange man but forge
on. After a while Raja joins me up at the front so that when
we reach his home city we can see it together.

*

From a long ways away we can see the capital city and
within a couple of miles it looks almost as big as a human
palace. But when we get close I can see it is way bigger
than any puny plain human palace. This palace and city
are breath taking; one floor is equal to eight human floors,
so that it can accommodate dragons at their biggest size
comfortable. The palace is eight to nine dragon stories
high and is like a medieval palace met technology that
met Egyptian and all those other cultures on earth that
had big beautiful palaces.

It is also about a mile out on the ocean with a pearly bridge leading out to the palace with arches cast over it, so it is shaded; I also think for effect. The city is round and has a wall around it that is one and a half of dragon stories and has a blue light glowing faintly along the top. There are also smaller islands floating a little ways off from the palace.

The palace has high pearly glass arches, some of them have dragon statues made of gems and glass and other sparkle things like that. Each gem dragon statue is a little different in either color or appearance and a couple has humans standing below and next to the dragons head or heart. I can see some from here the guard gate is made out of like opal or pearl or one of those beautiful gems, but I'm guessing this is some hard stuff for them to use it as there wall and gate. The materials are not so shiny that you can't live around them and be blinded.

The palace has lots of flat places and no towers probable because any tower I'm guessing would have to be huge to accommodate a dragon. Actually that's a lie there is a giant tower just big enough apparently because dragons fly in open doors to plop down and sleep is my guess, its somewhat shrouded in fog. As we get closer and come to stand on the beach in front of the bridge I can see large spikes coming off of the buildings in random places. One building that is rather large and has an amphitheater next to it has hundreds of the spikes coming off it, and young looking dragons are weaving in and out of the spikes. We start down the bridge in wide eyed awe.

Every once in a while I can see one of the young dragons do a one eighty and launch itself at a dragon behind him. Next to the amphitheater a mountain rose that has buildings built into it, and the city itself is built around the mountain on the island. I can see faintly, dragons flying around the mountain and some perching on the tip keeping watch.

As we get closer to the magnificent gate, I can see the curious looks from the guards, they aren't exactly hostile thou. Even before we reach the gate one guards runs over to the pocket in the side of the arch under the wall. Speaking into a glowing purple orb that is perched against the column almost like a low hanging torch. The other guard rushes over to the others on the other side of the gate and commands them to open the gate before hurrying towards us.

"Goddess blesses! It is the lost prince; we did not know what had happened to you! And you bring a bonded and an entourage!" The guard gushes as he kneels. The guard is soon joined by the rest of the guards and some people who are near the gate peer out at us. Why would they know exactly who he is? Raja was just an egg when he was stolen. I get know answers.

We are push through the pearly gates… kind of weird because the inside looks amazing… like what I imagine heaven would. The men try to lead Raja away from me but he growls, snapping at them, and did his run where he trips over all his gangly limbs back over to me; his tail seeming to impede him the most.

I was going to lean down and offer him some comfort at least a reassuring rub on the head; but an earth shaking roar that shatters some of the windows stops me. Big doors from the palace boom open and a breathtaking blue-green dragon burst forth from the giant doors of the palace entrance. The blue-green dragon is closely followed by an even bigger brighter metallic dragon, who looks as if he is dipped in gold.

I also notice the blue-green dragon has the fin on her tail like Raja, but hers doesn't have two horns at the base and a lot more webbing. The big gold dragon also seems to have little stuff about him that reminds me of Raja. The two dragons hurtle themselves down the steps partially flying over the steps. They do take flight over the busy streets heading straight for us.

Almost in passing I notice more dragons spilling out of the palace and dragons in the street looking up at the palace dragons flying and bow showing respect. The blue female dragon gets here first – I guess she is female, she is a smaller and just something about her says female – but the gold male isn't far behind.

"My baby, Goddess bless you are safe and hatched!" She lunges forward scooping Raja up in her talons and cradles him to her giant chest.

Raja lets out a little purr and nuzzles her, and when the big gold dragon comes over n wraps his body around them, Raja in turn leans over n nuzzle the big golden dragon's muzzle.

Flare comes up beside me and starts purring as I stroke his head, tears welling up over the family moment.

It seems to be going good, with the heart felt embrace, and what not. Even the bowing and scraping doesn't detract from the beautiful moment.

The mother dragon is breathtaking up close, she seems to look a darker shade off of the bluest water on Earth, and her scales shimmer to a blue green. She has lots of webbing up and down her body. She is obviously important she has gold and jewels all over her body, but only enough to look regal.

The… father (I'm guessing) has enough gold on him being the color gold, and instead has bronze and silver with jewels – some of the jewels not like anything on earth. He is bigger than most all the dragons present but a few; and only two are bigger, both clearly male. The mother flutters her large wings as if to take flight, but before she can, Raja wiggles so he falls out of her arms. Raja runs tripping to stand on the other side of me; so without thinking I start to stroke his soft head, you would think that his scales wouldn't be soft but u have never felt anything softer... sort of like a babies skin.

"*What is the meaning of this!*" the mother's melodic voice thunders, she peers down at me with her silver eyes.

"He's fine ma'am." I pull out my best manners for her, because you see how politely you want to be facing down an angry mother dragon.

"*Come Raja, back to your home, your entourage may leave.*" Her tail thumping in agitation, whereas the father just listens with interest and a curious gaze etched into his features.

"*She is mine.*" Raja growls stepping fully in front of me all pint size he is.

"*She is yours...*" Both parents echo in stunned voices, taking a second look at us, then at each other, dragons have the market on poker faces.

"*Of course... then she and her friends are... welcome...*" She seems to look at us differently almost contemplative.

"I... apologize for being so rude. I am Queen Averia and this is King Zarom." She leans closer to me, her razor sharp teeth as big as my arm.

"*But being that you are family now, you may call me Zar.*" They sound nice, and because they are Raja's parents I want to believe the best in them and of them.

"*How about you tell us your story inside, we have already eaten but we shall call for some food for you and your party, along with a healer. Others of the court shall carry the rest of you.*" She moves over and put her hands… (are they called hands?) Out to let Raja, Flare, and me letting us climb in to her paw, she doesn't say anything about Flare, and she just gives us an odd look.

Being carried by her with so little other passengers, like our 'rescue' dragon, is a lot more pleasurable and preferable. I can see that her skin while looks sort of like scales is more leathery. Raja sticks his head through a gap in her claws and watches as she flies over the city.

When we land Raja hurries to pull his head up before she opens her claws and we step out. Raja doesn't manage to right himself and tumbles out. Flare chuffs his cat laugh and lazily jumps over Raja; only to have his paws swept out from under him from a long skinny tail.

Averia's musical laugh echoed off the immaculate columns and doors. The door is so huge I feel like an ant for the millionth time since coming to Pangaea. The door is actually wood, but carved like nothing I have seen before and it has the tiniest almost none seeable glow to it. Two dragons are stationed outside and two more stationed inside. The door is so big it can fit three of the fighting giant dragons standing a breast easily. The hall is wider it can fit four to five and goes on until it opens up into a gigantic throne room.

That's where Raja's father leads us. This hall is not like any normal medieval hall. This one has columns that lead to two gigantic pillows on a raised dais, with two empty pedestals set to either side of the pillows.

Be the wall every couple of feet there is holes in the floor that lead to the ocean. I nearly get startled out of my skin when a serpent like dragon pokes his head out of one of the holes.

The serpent perches up on the stone half in half out of the water, regarding us with big silver eyes. Zar nods to him, as everyone files into the great hall. *"Cali, would you please go fetch Victor, and some food for our guests."* Zar moves to sit himself nicely on one of the big pillows. Averia moves to sit beside Zar, as the hall fills up with people. Servants move to pull a table into the room and some chairs for us to sit and enjoy our meal.

Cali turns out to be a very pretty woman, she looks to be a few years older than me and has dish water blonde hair, and brown eyes set in a very lovely face. She looks normal enough until she brushes back her hair; she has pointy tipped ears and this pink think coming from the base of her skull and is pulled over her shoulder. It has this feeler thing at the bottom that seems to be moving and other weird things.

Cali smiles as she sits down some plates of some sort of meat and bread with what looks to be green beans. A couple other servants set some food in front of the others, giving our bondeds each their own type of food, they don't even seem to mind Sheena, but she looks kind of uncomfortable.

Sheena looks over to Dash before she follows behind a servant out of the hall.

We were sitting beside the small pool of water and as we eat Zar and Averia leaves us in peace letting us eat while they talk quietly to a couple of the warrior dragons. While I eat I look over to study the pool of water next to me that is like the one the serpent came out of. Around the edges of the pool there is scripture something like hieroglyphs. I look deep into the pool but can see no end. I am leaning almost into the pool, when something jumped out of it.

I leap back as I get soaked in salt water, a beautiful girl looks up at me giggling her head off an splashing me some more. She has long cyan blue hair, and hazel eyes with giant pupils, she looks like the picture of perfection. She has this blue green webbing that looks like vines covering her breasts and wound up around her neck. A couple of the vine like webbing wound down across her stomach towards her... tail? I can see it that the webbing changes into blue green scales that narrow only a little all the way down for three to four feet; At the bottom I could see it flare out. She was perfect making me feel all frumpy, the only thing looking to be weird with her is her legs grow a tail.

She and I stare at each other before she chuckles and ducks under the water only to pop back up and spit water in my face. I nearly fall out of my chair from surprise but manage to keep my butt partly on the chair.

"You okay, Esper?" Dash grabs my arm and is helping me into my seat when something else burst from the water again.

This time it is like the picture of maleness, he has blonde hair with brown highlights, shaved close on the sides and high on the top formed into a Mohawk. He has broad shoulders, and a tapered waist of a swimmer. To begin with he doesn't have legs but as he bursts from the water – the shock sending me actually tumbling from my chair - he has a purple green tail.

He has vines snaking up from the start of his waist/start of his tail and traveled up broadening out to cling around his torso like a clingy lover. The vines thin out as they wove their way up, only to stop short of the underside of his arms. What surprises me thou he doesn't just jump up out of the water and back in, he jumps all the way out and onto the hard concrete but he doesn't flop like a fish he lands on legs encased in jeans. On two feet he is tall like over six foot.

"Ray! You are startling the poor thing!" she titters, "Oh, look at that I think she likes you, she's blushing." The mermaid snickers again poking at me as I blush five shades of scarlet. The merman named Ray looks over to me giving me a lopsided grin that displays laugh lines.

"I guess I will just have to startle her more often, I think it's cute." Ray grins again and moves over to sit on a stone bench on the other side of the pool to chit chat with another merman who had popped up on the other side of the pool.

As I finish my dinner Cali and some other servants clear away the dishes they even take away the tables. Zar's rumble echoes through the hall as he calls for silence.

"Far ones tell us how you came about our precious Raja." Zar doesn't seem to state anything as a question more as statements… guess being dragon king he can't afford showing any weakness even if it is a question.

I tell them how we came from a totally different dimension and Zar and the other dragons seem fascinated by our dimension, by the time we get to our escape from the monster camp Dante and Garret have taken over the retelling and are on top of the table acting it out for them.

"Esper drew her blade Saphique out of its sheath and in both hands but her whole upper body behind the blow as she swung her sword around to decapitate the monster that had wounded our brother Yanni, all while holding on to her horse with her legs…" Garret trailed off in a dramatic pause, only for Dante to pick up where he left off.

As Dante brings it to a close, everyone even the people who have lived through it are listening and watching in rapt attention. Dante makes sure not to disappoint and ends in a rather dramatic ending everyone applauds and whistle, so much so that Zar has to call for silence again. *"Well it would seem you have had quite an adventure and we will get some people right on to searching for your sister and brother, but I must tell you that the chances of finding them are slim. Rarely anyone is found after getting taken, when we go in to get them the owners who participated in buying them tend to try and dispose of them to get rid of the evidence."* Zar ends gravely. The news that I might be already doomed at the promise to find Jenni and Yanni hits me like an explosion.

"But can't your like do something, you are the king!" Toni cries and throws his hands in the air, Jenni having been closer to him then pretty much anyone. Zar looks at him with silver eyes that seem to hold sympathy for the still grieving boy.

"We shall go off to sleep on this and talk more in private, tomorrow." Zar dismisses everyone, everyone seems to be

used to it, and files out of the hall. I get up to stretch, feeling tranquil after a warm meal.

"Hey, so is that story your brother's told real?" I turned hearing a warm masculine voice, to see Ray the merman. He was still shirtless and I could see his vines on his chest.

"Uh ...yea maybe a little exaggerated but they got bulk of it." I stutter a little edgy about talking to attractive guy after months of not talking to any... well besides my brothers. "Wow, then you are a very brave girl." Ray doesn't pose it as a question and he looks at me as if he knows me already.

"I can't say that I try, trying to be brave would be stupid... not that if you do that means you're stupid... even if that's what I just said and believe. Wow I am confusing even me." I gave an anxious laugh forcing myself to stop babbling, and rub my palms over me trench coat.

"Well then you are very courageous when put in compromising positions." Ray chuckles, "I would like to ask you to breakfast, oh courageous one?" Ray seems to bore into me with those hazel eyes.

"I... um...I" I look around looking for some cue. "I... I would like that."

I give Ray a half smile and he startles a little squeak from me as he grabs my hand and leans down as if to bow. Ray kisses my hand first on the back side and then turns it over as he straightens, and kissed it again on the palm and the wrist over the veins. Ray gives a big grin before going into a big dramatic flourish and releasing my hand while backing away. Ray gives another grin before doing a sort of jump diving thing and dives into the salt water pool.

Toni laughs startling me out of my thoughts, "I guess we don't need to know if you are having breakfast with us, should we push our meeting with Zar back till the day after?"

I punch him in the arm, and make my way towards Averia whose talking to Raja.

"I so wish I could've been there for you. When your egg was stolen from the palace it broke our hearts, we searched high and low, being that we went to such great lengths to bring your bonded to you then only to lose you." A shudder works through Averia's great lithe body, she sounds so heartbroken if I could have wrapped my arms around her I would've.

"Averia, how did Raja's egg get stolen?" I look her over imagining what it must have taken to get Raja's egg away from her. *"Raja's eggs place was on the podium in front of our beds and while we slept a platoon of Drazarian snuck into the palace and got it, before we discovered them they had already gotten the egg out."* She sighs looking off to the stairs. Raja brushes up against her in comfort, I can feel how he doesn't hold it against her, for it brought him to me.

"*Your friends shall be staying in the human section of the palace while you and Raja will be put in a dragon sweat so that as he grows you will not have to be constantly changed.*" Averia glances fondly at Raja before leading us down a hall way off to the side of throne pillows. If I live here for a million years I doubt I would be able to get over how breath taking everything is.

This hall is slightly smaller but still roomy enough for Averia to walk thru with Zar beside her. They lead us through corridor after corridor and up a whole bunch of stairs. I'm starting to get the image that Averia is the one who does most of the talking.

"*We had a couple of quarters made up for our human or littler guests, so that they would feel more comfortable in them without feeling so small.*" Averia explained as we go down a corridor that is different; the doors are smaller and have numbers and letters on it. "*Toni, yours and Cobalt's room has been set to better suit you and it is set to have everything you need. You can ask a servant to bring you up some food, there is a wand on the table to allow you to send waves down, and they will answer and bring it right away, also a list of foods next to it. Your number is 96B.*" Averia says as she looks over at them, we are all content to just walk behind her and listen.

Averia waves them over to the door we have come to a stop, Toni and Cobalt break from the group to enter through the hand carved door. I can hear the gasps but Averia moves on, leaving Toni and Cobalt to explore on their own. I am so curious as to what is in there, it's just some unanswered question, what was so amazing?

"Lucan and Shar, you shall be sharing an adjoining room to both Garret and Dante, this is your room." She waves them to the next room over 97B with her big talons, and leaves them to it as she drops the twins off at 98B.

"A very smart move on your part, with putting the twins next to Lucan and Shar," I laugh to Averia, I knew I liked her for a reason.

"I am queen for a reason." The she dragon winks swishing her large tail out of the way for a passing servant.

Next she drops Delan and Radiva off a couple rooms down and on the other side of the hall. After getting rid of the rest of them she lead us out of the smaller rooms and back to the giant rooms and down. As we keep going I can see doors getting fancier and fancier. She stops when we reach the last four at the end of the hall, 4A. It isn't on the first floor thou, it's the top floor.

"We shall take our leave of you so that you may look over your rooms." Zar says, following Averia down the hall to 1A, which makes me curious who lives in the other two rooms.

"So shall we go in?" I looked to and from Raja and Flare. They nod enthusiastically Raja hops from foot to foot I'm kind of afraid he might need to use the bathroom and I don't want to clean that up.

I push open the double doors, for a more dramatic entrance, and am stunned. The room is absolutely huge I can see in the main walk is a living room with a normal size couch and has a coffee table in front of it with neon flowers sitting atop it in a basket. The wall across from the door large arches lead to the balcony overlooking part of the city and the ocean were you can see in the distance the bridge and mainland.

A cloth hangs over an arch next to the main door, I push back the magenta fabric with sparkles and mirrors on it like some Indian cloth. To a normal size closet filled with games and other means to entertain myself. A juice bar sits in the corner facing the balcony and nice living area. Flare relays that it is all juice and water as he sniffs around rubbing up occasionally on things to put his scent on things. Next I head for the other hidden entry way that is much bigger than the other doors, like dragon bigger. This arch is covered by a royal blue Indian cloth, the mirrors sparkling from where the sun shines on them.

Behind the fabric and drapes a bed that is set into the floor part way and is massive, as if to let a dragon sleep on it. The room is all silks and looks kind of like a huge version of an Indian palace room. It is draped in colorful fabrics and has large windows and a terrace with railing and part of it without. The windows are like so big that a full dragon and half could pass through.

Raja looks it over with wide eyes, "*this beats the ship I hatched in.*" With a big yip Raja runs towards the bed and throws himself in the middle of the bed and rolling around. "*Come join me the bed is sooo soft.*" I give Flare a look before taking a running leap onto the bed beside Raja. "*Am I the only one here that is not a child?*" Flare gives us a look as he sits pretty on the floor. "Live a little, try being a cub again, I dare you." Flare gives me a glare before he gives out a howl and launched himself onto the bed next to us.

I grabbed him when he makes contact with the bed and rolls over on him, kind of like a wrestle…. Except it's not so easy to wrestle a leopard and he is two times more weight than me. After about a minute – that's my story and I'm sticking to it – Flare has me pinned to the silky soft mattress.

Flare gives me a long rough cat lick on the face, then rolls off me and bats his paws in the air. "*Okay maybe I can be a little more like a cub now that we aren't running for our lives.*"

"*About time,*" Raja declares with a big yawn. I look over at him from my position on my bed. Raja looks so tiny on the end of the bed so I pat my side and he creeps over the bed to rest at the crook of my arm.

"You know you want to, Flare." I pat my other side and he takes up residence on my other arm….

When morning comes I am a mess, I can't believe I accepted that invitation from Ray. I don't have any clean clothes or a hair curler or ...or ... who am I kidding if I had that stuff I would still be freaking out. Flare nudges me awake an hour before Ray is going to come get me for breakfast. *"Averia had some servants put some gowns and a vast selection of cloths so you may try to find what style you like."* I yawn wanting to roll back over and go to sleep, *"If you don't get up then when Ray gets here you will have bed head and rumpled close!"* Flare persists, nudging my side.

That gets me up, I launch myself so fast out of the bed that I half roll and half fall until I am in a crouched position where I hit the floor. "Well you obviously know your way around here, show me to the bathroom and closet." Flare sends me a look, before leading me beside the bed to an excellently carved door, lined with gold and other gems, beside it there is another door just like it. He first takes me into the bathroom where there is another door in there leading to what I'm guessing is the closet.

I take a shower in record time. The shower has an assortment of fragrances each one I smell before I settle on the one that smells sort of like strawberries. Then I brush all the tangles out of my long hair and put on a little of what looks like eye liner; that I had found on the vanity. This is what I need Raven for, she was the girl who showed me what goes where. I make my way to the closet…. I can hear a drum roll and a mix of angels singing.

I open the door and it leads to a cubby that has a digital pad attached to the wall. I tap the screen and a digital image of me appears. A female voice sounds from the side, "Tap on the buttons saying, casual, dressy, nightwear, pool wear, and dress-casual. Then tap on the parts you would like to change colors will also appear at the bottom for the assorted choices highlighted." I tap on random ones to just catch the drift. I just need to know what each button does it's like getting a new toy.

The closet is amazing it has anything from the style of outfit I came in, to long ball gowns, I like the princess dresses best. My favorite is where they cling to my curves and then drop into a simple long skirt. The sleeves are long and when at the bottom they trail down just like a foot from the ground. No one can say I don't have a soft side, I like the pretty things. I sometimes wish though I had a mom to teach me. I muse while skimming through more choices.

One of my favorites from the princess style is light blue and has a dark blue sash around the waist, and has a pattern not to unlike the vines that had traveled up Ray's torso. I press the purple button at the top and wait for something to happen; of course I am not disappointed. A side panel opens and my chose item rotates out of it.

I grab the dress off of the hanger and step into it but it is almost impossible to tie up the back and I have to make some fancy foot working and stuff to get it tied. I might have tripped and fallen a few times.

Then I scroll through the pad to find some shoes and find the most beautiful pale cream gladiator slippers; along with about like hundreds of types of shoes and colors and styles too many to look through. Below the cloths an accessory button is located and I find jewelry and bracelets, what I like the best there is some that are claws that slip over my fingers sort of like cat women except those were shorter, these go all the way to my hand and have joints. Raven used to always say always take off the last item you put on, but come on its claws! What she doesn't know won't hurt her. Jenni probable would spend house playing dress up in my closet if she was here.

I can't help it the claws are just so cool, I put them on am about to walk out of the closet when my eye falls on a silver head band crown. It is just a silver band that goes around the head, the others are more jeweled and stuff.

I dawn that too, and make my way through the room. Emerging from the closet to the sleeping area where Flare and an inquisitive Raja still lay. "Slug-a-beds, always in bed," Flare snorts knowing how ridiculous that is coming from me.

"*It took you awhile to dress for breakfast with that fish man.*" Raja jumps down and circles me. "*You look nice, but why is it so important?*" I shrug feeling self-conscious; I scratch him behind a scale on his soft head. "I don't know, I guess I just like him, and I don't know Raja can we leave it at that?" Raja nods and heads over to settle on the bed with his head on Flare's back. "*Well I am just glad that he has you dressing like the princess you are in jewels and shiny stuff, those drab cloths were not pleasing to the eye. I must talk to momma about getting a pile of treasure in here that is if we are not immediately shipped off to the academy, I guess we shall find out after breakfast.*" Raja yawns his eyes getting unfocused. Boy am I going to have a tough time if his mother lets him have everything he asks for.

There is a knock on the door...

*

I open the door to see Ray in a crisp button down white shirt that is slightly see through so that I can see the pattern of his green and purple vines. His spiked

Mohawk has slight purple-green died tips, that bring out some flecks of green in his hazel eyes. "Wow…Esper, you look… wow… Are you ready to go?" I feel my heart leap at his praise. "Yeah, where are we going?" I close the door behind me and step into the hall. He tugs my hand, "well it is a surprise." He leads me down the hallway to a plain door hidden by some curtains. "Wow pulling out all the castle secrets for me?" I tease following him, I move so I'm not walking behind him. I always did have that habit of stepping on people's feet.

He chuckles and leads me up what looks to be a normal human stair case. I bet those are rare sense we are in a dragon palace.

I follow him farther up, until we come to another door. He opens it to pull me into a room that is breathtaking it is made all of glass and has flowers and vines creeping along the edges in an array of color some of them neon. In the middle of the room there is a small table set for two with a serving tray next to it that has two covered dishes.

"What do you think? Is this a good first date? Or should we like go out or something? Did I get it wrong? You aren't afraid of heights are you? No you are bonded with a dragon of course not, so stupid!" Ray rambles on sounding extremely nervous. "Ray! Take a breath! I love it." I grab his hand so I can get his attention and look him straight in the eyes… even thou he is really tall.

Just to prove the point I kiss him on the cheek… yup all about making people feel better… totally selfless… shut up. I quickly move away from him to stand by the windows and look at the view, not because I am blushing.

"I like your way of telling me to shut up. So am I going to be able to get to know you?" He says as he sits down at the table and pats the chair next to him as he sets out our breakfast. "Well that depends do you have a year because in the last few months alone it has made me much more complicated." I smile at him, showing dimples.

"You should know I made this all myself, I wanted it to be special." He smiles at me and we take a seat, "well what do you want to know about me… uh sorry I know how that annoys me when someone does that. Um okay… I'm originally from Earth twenty-fourteen, I'm pretty sure my eighteenth birthday has passed; I am bonded with two souls, Raja and Flare. I'm not biologically related to my siblings, and two of them have already been lost to the Drazarian's… and another left us because she needed to find her own way, oh and my favorite colors purple." Ray chuckles nodding his hands up in defense. "Wow," He thinks for a moment.

"Do you have any family… boyfriend… real siblings on earth?" Ray asks, "Um, no to all three as far as I know." His smile spreads until he has a Cheshire grin. "Same questions," I say leaning forward giving him all my attention. "Well, only fair, I am currently unattached, who you think I am? The kind of guy to ask you out while dating another gal?!" he acts in mock horror, clutching his chest as though mortally wounded.

"Good, so what's to eat…"

*

During the date I learned a lot about Ray, he's a fun and attractive guy. Turns out the males in the Merr people prefer being called water nymphs, something about mermaid being offensive. Ray has three siblings, a brother, two sister, and loving parents. Which kind of led me to the question of how? Do water nymphs like have a special mating thing with the tale or do they go on land…. Wow very bad images there, thankfully I didn't ask it. We had a peaceful breakfast and rather enjoyed ourselves before a servant comes in to tell us that Zar and Averia are going to give us a tour and would like us to meet them outside the palace doors in ten minutes.

On our way down we head through the great hall to meet up with the others, nearly got drenched when water spouts up out of one of the pools. Water creatures need to work on their landing, this wet look isn't good for me.

Following the spout is something worse, an angry mermaid. Out of instinct I grab for Saphique but Ray just sighs and waves it away. I inspect the mermaid and nearly fall on my ass from shock. She has long blonde hair and is Cara, as in mean girl Cara from Earth. She is also dressed rather like she did at school, all slut. She doesn't exactly have cloths on she has red vines - I use this loosely – covering her. Her vines are barely a couple fingers down from her butt and they only cover practically her nipples.

"Ray! How could you!" Cara storms to us, only leaving a second to pause and let her feet turn into feet instead of a tail. "I saw you! How could you go on a date with this troll, especially when you are going out with me?" She sounds angry but Ray just calmly gave her a look that spoke volumes.

Obviously not getting the reaction she wants by the long silence she takes a few breaths and changes tactic. "I'm sorry, I'm so sorry I just get so jealous seeing you with others, I've miss you, I want you back. I was wrong I made a mistake, give me another shot, you use to love me!" She throws her body against him, rubbing all along him enough to let her vines push up and show… way too much, more than I ever wanted to see of her!

It leaves a bad taste in my mouth to bow out to Cara but Ray and i have only just now been on one date, so I pat Ray on the arm, "Ray, I'll let do whatever you need to, see you later." I turn to leave, "Esper, wait! Cara leave me alone!" Ray pushes her away, and runs after me. "Sorry about that she does that to chase off other girls, sadly it works."

"So you aren't with her?" I ask as the guard dragon's pushes open the doors for us. "NO! She is too much in love with herself, and every guy who she thinks is worthy of her."

Averia and Zar wait for us outside the doors with the gang.

"You guys ready to get the grand tour?" Averia gives what I guess was the equivalent of a dragon grin, I nod. Ray walks beside me as we wind our way down the slope of the palace to the town and market. People respectfully nod their heads to Zar and Averia and call greetings, some even stopping to have a word with them.

I pull up beside Toni, "How's Aroura? Cobalt must be ecstatic now that she can be treated." Toni glances briefly at me before gazing back at our surroundings. "Yeah, those two are off in some cave somewhere… the images I get at random could scare what chest hair I have off." Toni shudders, "Oh, so no problem then." I tease, he scowls but it cracks and he lets out a laugh. "Guess I opened myself to that, just wait until Raja an Flare are mated, then we shall see who is laughing."

"Oh, lordy!" Just the thought of the stuff I might be subjected to at random due to mated bondeds has shudders working through me.

*

The market is open and huge in each stall it is big enough to fit multiple dragons browsing the wares and still has extra room. Each store space has a giant pool in it to let the water creatures also have a chance at the wares. I also see some of the merchants are smaller dragons, I watched as a dragons land and start stalking one of the stalls with the wares from his back.

The market is stocked with anything and everything you can imagine, there is every day things that you can find on earth but made so that they are better for you, to what I can guess are some magic shops. From what I can see is the market goes on for a long time; "Zar, why is it you guys have some stuff from earth like technology and some foods but not like others?" Zar glances down at me from watching the others look in awe at some of the things in the market.

"We do not plan on killing our planet as you have been killing yours with your gasses and pollution. Our researchers would try a product in a contained area and see if the effects will hurt our planet." Zar hisses at Dante when he let loose a fire work that nearly singed Zar's scales. Another firework goes off nearly hitting a griffin. Averia looks over to the people who are trailed behind us, and one of the people hands the angry merchant a gem.

"I don't get this system that you people have?" Zar takes a moment to think on how to word it before he goes on.

"Let me explain; so when a person choses their bonded they also chose what work they are going to train in, of course they will be trained in other things, but it's like they chose the one as their dream job that they will do for their life. Of course there are some who will chose more than one that is fine, each field of job has a delegate who trains them. Each delegate will only take the amount of people they need for the job, and only the people who excel at it.

"Each person does something that will better the community, if someone does not wish to do any of the jobs we know they may leave or talk to me and the queen about it. Each person does there job for wages as I believe they do on earth, when they graduate from the academy they are given a house or all the stuff they need to make a house and the land. If a person needs anything they need but ask for it; our researches make new products to see if it would better our society, like in your world I believe they partake in alcohol, here we do not or at least do not condone it. But you can't tell people no and expect everyone to follow so few places carry it and it's closely monitored to a respectable limit.

"Now I have gotten off topic, so in all, sometimes they get extra materials left over at work and will trade it or make it into something that's usually not needed… are you getting what I am telling you?" Zar sighs and looks down at me. I think I get it, I am no dumb bunny but it is slightly confusing.

"Let's move on." He calls to the others, and leads us out of the trading post and off into a street that meanders away from the bustle and off into the less busy streets. The streets are quiet, until after a long walk a small object tumbles at us from the sky.

Zar catches the falling young dragons with amazing reflexes as if it is nothing. "With how old Raja is he will have to immediately be put into flight school and should have already been. With your travel thou he has put on extra muscles that pampered hatchlings have not yet gotten."

One of the dragons Zar doesn't immediately release, it is a rather scrawny thing, all limbs, which I am starting to get most dragons look like as hatchlings. The little dragon seems male in all his hard lines and bulky appearance. He has white with edges of black, and a few speckles sporadically placed over his body. The little dragon thanks Zar and acts as if to launch into the air. Zar stops him with a gigantic claw on his shoulders.

"Remidus, would you stay for a second." Zar makes it sound like a question but in no one's mind do they take it as one. "Remidus, this is my youngest son Raja, and his bonded Esper." Zar tilts his head towards each of us, he sounds so proud. "Nice to meet you," He chirps sounding a little anxious to get back to the sky and whatever that had thrown him out of it.

"Why did you fall out of the sky?" Raja sounds rather befuddled by the very notion of anything throwing a dragon out of the sky. "I was going through flying practice and Amorvious decided to show me a battle move. Soon I to will be able to throw people out of the sky too!" Remidus puffs up his chest. He has this barbed ball on his tail that is too big for his tail, and the beginnings of spikes growing up his back and big gangly wings; this guy will be a ferocious fighter one day. With that Raja is lost to us as he and Remidus start conspiring, what about I do not know.

"Being that Raja is heir apparent and you are his bonded, you both shall be staying at the academy, it makes much more sense, or it will to you as soon as you finish your first day and drop into bed I do not think either of you would want to make the trek to the palace. Raja and you shall learn every position not just one, of course you will not devote your life to just one skill as some do but in doing so you shall better understand the people. You and he shall also be learning and working your way through the military portion, but more in depth so that you shall know how to move your armies, and when the time comes you and he shall be a force like none other." I widen my eyes, wider and wider, whose wouldn't after hearing that one moment you are just helping a baby find its way home an another you were gonna inherit a kingdom.

"Raja and you shall be trained with the other hatchlings that have hatched sense you got a hold of Raja's egg, the few dragons that hatched in the last fifty years… which only a rare few will be your mentors. Of course some older dragons shall help with some cause of the severe lack of dragons born. Your mentors shall be Liam and his bonded Veevia, they are third years here, a rare wonderful thing, also because of the experience they have they are also very… fun." Zar rough voice ends in a chuckle like rumble. "Liam's father is a close friend of the family also."

"Ray, would you be as kind as to show Esper to Liam? Esper I think it wise you wait meet up with Raja after Liam has gotten you settled, I think he would enjoy it more." Averia glances over at Remidus pulling Raja off onto the field of writhing hatchlings learning to fly and fight. Remidus is imparting everything the teacher had taught him about how to fly, every other step he flaps his wings in example.

"Yeah, best to let him enjoy, Ray, come on we got a person to find in this vast academy." Ray nods and hurries me around the edge of the field as best to avoid falling babies.

The school is enormous it has nothing modern like on earth it seems more Greek with high white columns and statues, I could almost swear that it stepped out of one of those pictures people make up of what Greece. Looking like when people still worshiped the gods and Caesar was in reign. It became abundantly clear when a bell tolled and classes let out for the younger kids how much different it is from Earth. Animal babies and small children run through the halls and Ray pushes us into a corner so we aren't stampeded.

After three minutes they all disappear and we venture out of our corner. "So even... animals go to school?" I still feel weird calling them animal, because these ones have some major stuff going up stairs.

"Of course," Ray looks at me like I am nuts to even ask. I am still unclear on weather I have or have not gone nuts, and if this is a hallucination.

"This game of hide and go seek is rather not fun! I do not appreciate being forgotten for the flying lizard." Flare grumbles, as he came up behind me shocking me, I know instinctively that he doesn't mean any bad will towards Raja just a point proven.

Ray takes us through the school until the ceiling changes into a cave that has been carved into intricate columns and high ceilings also big enough to hold two giant dragons walking a breast. We pass a couple people who are making their way to the school with a tiny leather book in their hands. "These rooms are your fellow students, when you turn twelve and your classes increase and then at fourteen you get your bonded and they increase more, it is optional for them thou. Each room is designed to hold multiple people with their different type of bonded, whether hooved or other."

We pass the rooms he points out and farther and farther into the labyrinth I could get lost in here easy. "How am I supposed to remember the turns?" I ask as we take another left and then a right. "You will get used to it also one of the things that Liam will be helping you with is learning how to make your way around here and the city."

Ray finally turns at the end of the hall which opens into a large cavern that has large pillows for dragons of all different sizes, each with its own ornate staircase to let the smaller bondeds who share the bed be able to get on it. On some of the beds wounded and sleeping dragons of all sizes lounge most empty thou.

"Here comes Liam now." Ray says with a pout. I look to where he gestures, Ray motioning for the descending dragon to make its way over here. This dragon is a smaller then the warrior dragons, and something about the dragon said female, just something about the curves and lines. She is a mix of greens and blues, her body seems sleek and has no protruding scales, and she seems more built for speed.

She does have some spikes at the base of her tale, and webbing all over her body. She moves her neck to another angle and I can see air slits on her neck but they look as if they are mainly covered and hidden.

I look farther up her neck to the young man sitting at the juncture of her neck and wings. Liam appears to be huge, not like unfit, more body builder, wide shoulders... he could have snapped me in half in a second, like a twig. Liam has Jet black hair framing his broad jaw, and dark green eyes, with a crooked nose to top it off and make him look ruggedly handsome. Liam Leaps off the beautiful dragon and onto the cave floor with a thump, as he stands up in front of me, he towers over me at over six foot.

Ray snorts and moves towards the hulk, "Liam, I would like you to meet, Esper, you are to be Raja's and Esper's mentor." Ray doesn't exactly introduce us with a smile, more a scowl. "You can go Ray, thanks for bringing me my way ward apprentice to me, she is several hours late!" Liam may seem big and intimidating but he also appears to be a big goofball, even flashing his dimples and laugh lines. Ray lets out a strangled laugh and kisses me on the cheek before leaving me to Liam. I don't think I like that he did it to somehow mark his territory on me.

"Esper I would like to introduce you to Veevia. Just to get it out of the way, we have been bonded for two years. Veevia was a rare case of an egg hatching, as some strong spirited dragons did during the fifty years of the curse. Enough with the boring stuff let's go get your school stuff!" Liam strokes Veevia's nose dotingly before kissing her on the nose. Veevia bumps him back and then takes a mighty leap to fly into the cave ceiling where there is a huge tunnel, leading up and out. I guess she is a woman of few words.

"You will need your book, some padding, and the physicians need to look you over. Along with a visit to the blacksmith and anywhere else I remember you are supposed to go too." Liam teases already heading for the maze they call hallways.

*

It turns out the Physician was a twenty year old looking young lady named Kyly, with honey color hair, and dark green eyes, with some padding on her. Kyly was super nice, making me feel instantly at ease. She pronounces me fit after about thirty minutes and then sending us out the door with a demand that I have lunch with her tomorrow.

Our next stop was the blacksmith, which turns out to be another hidden away spot in this giant school it is wicked. It has multiple stations and five to ten blacksmiths making swords, armor, and gadgets I have no means of knowing what they did. The forge is medieval like but also has modern type of creations, and technology like the one in my room. The Liam takes me to his longtime friend, Jacques, who us a big strapping man that kind of makes Liam seem small, he is also as smooth as his name. He has chestnut hair with silver blue eyes that seem to claim you with a glance. When Liam introduced us I thought I was going to get crushed from his hug but he stops just in time his attention diverted to the blade hanging at my waist.

"Oh, my heavenly goddess, can it be I have fallen in love and she is taken! Wow, is me my heart shall shatter and lay on this floor for her love to walk over it! Let me see thy fair lady in return I shall not hug you till you burst." Jacques threatens. Now it might have been more flattering if he hadn't been talking about Saphique. I hand her over with a smile; in return he hurries around the forge giving Liam and me weapon upon weapon. I just love it, it's like Christmas.

One I rather like is a five pronged spear like a trident but instead on it in a row like a fork with one in the middle lower than the others to finish off anything that slipped in-between. Liam told me it was used for water fighting and for when needing a spear to throw in the air to maximize damage to a dragon's wings or other soft parts.

"So, Jacques is there anything I need to know about my new mentor? Serial killer whose gonna murder me when we are alone? Or mama's boy who has three dozen cats?"

Jacques bellows a laugh when Liam gives an indignant huff. "Hmm... so far Liam hasn't killed me when we were alone, definite momma's boy and I don't think he could keep any cats, what cat could stand to be around him."

"Definitely not I," Flare jokes moving around his feet, *"You smell like a hellhound!"* Flare accuses Jacques jumping back and arches his spine hissing at him, also making this formidable growl in the back of his throat. The hellhound in question comes trotting in, looking like he hasn't a care in the world. "Ceribi, come meet some friends." Flare growls again and moves back till he is in front of me, most cats only reach their humans knees at most, and mine is to my forehead.

Ceribi's three heads all swivel over to look at the hissing leopard. The hellhound is about the same size as Flare except maybe a little bigger, he has three heads, and is obviously a mix of wolf, pit-bull, and Rottweiler. He is black with brown and grey markings and a long tail, he also has had three pairs of three different colors of eyes, one pair is red, one golden, and the last bright blue.

Flare watches the hellhound with narrowed eyes but relaxes marginally when Ceribi doesn't make any threatening move towards us. "So how does the three head thing work, does he like have one mind or like three separate minds?" I move slightly around Flare to look more closely at the three headed hellhound. *"We can assure you that we are not of one mind!"* Thunders three rather indignant voices, Liam chuckles, "if they were of one mine they would not be always giving me a head ache with their sibling squabble." Liam's reply comes back as three voices yell that they do not squabble and then one saying they did and their yelling keeps going.

"So Liam how about we get those text books, so I can get back to Raja?" I turn away from Ceribi who then starts in on another tirade about being ignored and dismissed. I know its slightly rude but the tree voices hurt with their pitch.

"Yeah, come on I'll take you before Ceribi starts lathering at the mouth." Liam grabs my arm and pulls me from the forage fast with a wave to Jacques. Next he takes us to the main school building which Ray has taken me through, this time it must have been lunch because the younger ones are roaming the halls and gaping at Liam, Flare, and me. Liam takes us to a room that is just off the main door, which has a receptionist and birds flying around filing stuff. Liam brings us before a Hawk who is writing something with his talon.

"Flir, we need to get Esper her text book." Flir glares before wiping his ink stained talon on a cloth before flying to the back. Then we hear…

CLANG

BANG

BOOM….

Flir burst forth covered in paint with papers sticking to him chasing… who you would guess Dante and Garrett.

"Dante and Garrett Virose, get over here right this freaking second, this cannot be happening what were you thinking! What is the damage?" I can literally feel the steam rising from my head, they aren't here even three days and they have already managed to wreak havoc. Dante and Garrett take one look at my furious face and turn and ran into the angry receptionist. "Zar said we had some hellions starting here but not even signed up for class yet and they have already destroyed one room!" The plump older lady scowls before she sighs and chuckles.

"It was an accident, we were just looking for a pen and I tripped and it took out some weird orb thing…" Dante tries but the receptionist interrupts.

"Well you certainly are going to be making this school more interesting… I'll have Zar have this all fixed anyway, and I am sure with all your free time you shall be instead working to give back to the school as in cleaning it!"

"Oh yeah, I forget that they are footing the bill." I mumble almost to myself. "And they most certainly will be helping out."

"Yes well the crown isn't heartless they give us more than we need and add other stuff along with perks from the job we have more than we need to live on, and they have taken responsibility for these two." The older woman says patting down her skirt.

"Yeah sounds a little too good to be true." I glare harder at the twin boys who shuffle from foot to foot under my stare, their black shaggy hair moving to cover their eyes. "That is it... what to do what to do... I can't take away T.V., Liam any ideas?" Liam watches from the side with a slight grin.

"So these boys like to slip away do they, my advice is we put them to having an escort; Ceribi." Liam grins evilly showing a dimple and laugh lines, "He doesn't have much to do and I'm sure that these little hellions shall not be too much for him." Out of the corner of my eye I can see the twins exchange contempt grins thinking they could get away from the person really easy, boy are they in for a surprise.

"How about we introduce the hellions to Ceribi?" Liam has an evil grin on his face that gives the twins pause.

"Yes... yes, we should," I grab them each by the ear, and with lots of 'owes' following us we head back to the forge. Ceribi isn't there at first, but Jacques is; "Jacques, can we borrow Ceribi for a month or two?" Liam asks following me and the screaming twins. "You shouldn't have-" Jacques gets interrupted by three indignant voices, *"Hey what do we look like a book!"*

"Yeah, what he said."

"We aren't a milking goat!"

"You think you can just loan us from person to person, we have a job... had a job! What does a goat have to do with it?"

"You know people buy and sell them."

"That is stupid it still has nothing to do with being loaned out!"

"Sorry, but this will be fun!" Ceribi grunts falling silent to listen. "These two need a strong cunning watchful guardian to keep them out of mischief, but when thinking over these lists of traits we only came up with one name, Ceribi, along with more amazingly needed traits." I lay it on thick, letting go of the twins ears so I can stroke each of the three heads, making sure to get behind the ears.

"No need to beg..."

"Am I supposed to beg?"

"No Dumbo, Esper is! Beg, beg, beg for your life! ..... oh I mean uh yeah I guess we could do that."

"Why not after we got fired from cattle herding, we need something to do,"

"Oh that was a good job it had some pretty good meals."

"That wasn't lunch Dumbo, apparently we weren't meant to eat them, even though no one said such."

"What else did they expect us to eat dog chow? What do we look like, dogs?"

"Hey, stop calling me Dumbo!"

The hellhound seem to be having a miniature little battle in everyone's head, soon they start in on how they end up with three heads and on and on.

"So our mother she was a hellhound and fell for a-"

"Ceribi! Will you? I am sure Garrett and Dante would love to hear all of your stories, but Liam and I need to go get some school stuff." It is amusing in a way that leaves you with a sudden need for a nap or maybe a quiet place.

The hellhound only nods. That is all Liam needs thou, he nearly jerks my arm out of its socket trying to leave fast as we can, to not hear how their mother fell for a hydria and had a wicked affair.

Liam lets out so much air that I think he is going pass out, "now that is what I call a punishment, let's see if they act up after a couple months with those three. One more stop till you can be reunited with Raja!" Liam chuckles, Flare growls beside me, *"about time."* We move into the office once more, it looks a little like they had cleaned up.

"So Flir, about that book…" Flir glared before once again wiping off his talons and heading to the back room, this time more warily. Flir returns still looking around every corner, with a small book clutched in his talons and indignantly drops it in front of us with a thud. "Now you don't mind him girl, he just hates untidiness. You think after four-hundred summers with me he would get use to the world being untidy!" The plump receptionist says, she doesn't look a day over fifty-five, it is hard to believe she is four-hundred and above; impossible.

"UM… Just by a chance how long do people usually live here?" Flare snorts at my apparently dumb question. "Oh to about five hundred summers, why didn't you just ask Flare?" She laughs showing pearly white teeth. "Oh, well sometimes I forget that I have someone who knows all this stuff." It makes me feel silly but for some reason her pointing out my forgetfulness makes me feel bashful.

"Well if you're going to rule with Raja you need to learn. How rude of you Liam, you never introduced us to Esper! If you are not I most certainly will, I am Mrs. Dubai." Mrs. Dubai preens a lot like her four hundred year old bird. "What a lucky man, I am Esper, and this is Flare." This older women gives off a warm and loving feel and I can feel it in my gut she is a trustworthy loyal person… either that or those eggs I had for breakfast with Ray were expired.

"Sorry ma'am, I had no intention of being rude, I hope you can forgive me?" Liam gives her big puppy dog eyes until she laughs and nods then he rewards her with a winning smile. "Now Liam I am much too old for you to be turning those charms on me." She scolds shaking her speckled finger at him. "You are not to old you barely look like you could be older than thirty Mrs. D. You are also beautiful to boot." Liam grabs her hand that she had shook towards him and kisses the back of it giving her cheeky grin that makes her blush.

"You young man could charm the stripes off of a tiger, a fish from a bear. I won't have you sway me from my husband. He is a ferocious man," She titters acting as if he was actually hitting on her, it's so cute. "Uh, yes that is a bad thing to consider I could never sway your fierce loving heart." He sighs as if giving up and clutches his heart for dramatics. "Liam, stop trying to sway the lady, her husband might get jealous." I laugh pulling him out of the office.

*

Liam leads me thorough a tour as we search the grounds for Raja and Remidus. We eventually find them back in the dragon's cave, fast asleep on their pillows, which are side by side. We stand gazing over them, "Liam, I forgot to ask what you are studying?"

Raja is almost the size of Flare, who is the size of a small horse. Where has the time gone? I feel like it is just yesterday that he was a tiny little hatchling spilling from his egg and soon we will be taking to the skies together. Raja looks to be swallowed up by the giant pillow they had given to us. It is the most adorable thing you could ever see, if you put aside that he is a baby that bristles with spikes and scales, I find it too cute.

"Battle instructor, I have had to complete three years of warrior training top of my class here, and then I need four years in the army. I'm actually finishing up my last year I should be shipping out soon. I will be here though for your assessments soon to see if you will be going on with your age group into the army." Liam gets a slight furrow between his eyebrows. I pat him on the shoulder, and move to the soft welcoming bed, "You will be a good battle teacher."

"Night, Esper." Liam whispers softly.

"Sweet dreams Liam." I call softly, fighting back my yawn as I crawl over to Raja to snuggle into his soft belly.

Flare curls up against my head and I lift it so that Flare can settle under my head and I can use him as a pillow. He starts purring and soon I feel everything slip away on a field of soft leopard fur.

*

I awake with the shock of my life, to a frigid splash of water, which also splashes Raja and Flare. Flare produces a mighty roar and comes up spitting and hissing. Being on a pillow with a wet dragon and leapord is not the smartest idea, stuffing and paws flying everywhere.

"Rise and shine, sunshine, if you sleep any longer you might have to go to classes as is. I would dress warmly because half your classes are outside, and don't forget your book." Liam chuckles and leaves with his offending bucket, to go wait with Veevia at the mouth of the cave.

The female dragon has a smug look as she inspects us as we try to dry off. Behind the pillow there is a door with a plaque with my name on it. Through the door I find a bathroom that is exactly like the one in the palace having everything I could want and a closet attached with some of my more durable cloths - including the set I arrived in - probable brought while I was sent on a wild search for Raja.

*

It takes me about ten minutes to take a shower and get dressed I even remembered to grab the tiny little pocket book.

Liam takes me and Flare through the tunnel, while Veevia leads Raja out of the tunnel at the top of the cave, his excited voice echoes through Flare's and my head.

First we go to the cafeteria to grab breakfast, everyone seems friendly enough and I can see that it isn't odd for some students to be studying at the table. Unlike Earth cafeterias this dimension's cafeterias food is heavenly, and everyone seems to get along with most people, not really formed into clicks. There are always exceptions to the rules and apparently Cara was one to it, she and her –what I am guessing is – mermaids, all are exceedingly beautiful and all could have been movie stars or models, and all seem to laugh when Cara makes fun of someone.

End up sitting with Liam and this one girl Ace who is like a punk rock girl from Earth, all brown hair with a purple streak. I honestly forgot what she was wearing though right after I saw it. It might have had something to do with us goofing off with her hypnotizing section in our book…. It's really foggy.

Our first class turned out to be less 'our' and more 'my'. It would seem Flare has his own classes which Liam tells me will be determined by a placement test that he shall take him to.

On our way to class we pass Garrett and Dante in the hall with their chaperone. One twin has his hands over his head to cease the endless chatter from Ceribi and the other is banging his head into a locker "How's it going Ceribi?" The hellhound pauses in his story to start retelling every tiny thing that has happened sense we departed them yesterday.

"So we had some fun when they started throwing food at breakfast for us! We caught every bite." The hell hound boasts, *"But they seemed rather put out! Also they wanted to*

*play hide and seek but they are rather poor at it, it would seem
they were never taught how to cover their scent!*" Ceribi Starts
rambling off again, nothing in order so it is rather hard
to follow. Ceribi sounds really excited about spending the
next couple months with their new found friends. Dante
grabs my arm though and turns his big blue eyes into
puppy dog mode, "Esper we are super sorry! We swear that
we will never misbehave again, just make it stop!" I smile,
sweetly but shake my head.

"You know I would but I have to go to class, so enjoy it,
because you will have to deal for a very long time." Dante
clutches my arm and won't let go until I am almost to class
and I am finally able to wrench my arm from him. I pat
Liam's cheek as I reach the class door, "best plan ever I
doubt they will misbehave ever again after a couple months
with the hellhound." We exchange evil grins before I enter
the class and my first day in a different dimension school,
wow in a different dimension and I still have to go to
school.

*

The first class of the day is a kind of everything
about this dimension. I find this class fascinating while
everyone else in it is doesn't find it interesting and sleeps
through it I guess all schools are the same. It is a little

awkward that everyone in this class is ten or under. I learn so much just from five minutes, like Pangaea is only one of many kingdoms. The others being, Knoff, Atlantis, and Petania, there is one more but due to how it has evolved into a separate group they do not acknowledge it as what they call it they just call it Slaver's territory. They only acknowledge it now that it is a threat having conquered Pangaea's neighbors the Ignanian's. Their Earth is called Pangaea because it was the first kingdom. Wow, so much information my head is going to burst.

Through it I get updates periodically from both Flare and Raja, both excelling in their classes, Flare being put in advanced or higher up classes. They also keep me up to date on how the rest of my family is doing; Flare even tells me Dash is doing so good he has a group of girls following him and Toni around.

*

My schedule includes increasingly more fun stuff to do. My classes include; Pangaea 101, hunting, battle, tactic, gymnastics, and finally a two hour period on flying with Raja. Liam informs that we won't actually fly for another couple weeks until Raja is big enough to carry a passenger. I find each class more fascinating then the next, most of the teachers liking to take a hands on method of teaching, less of a 'do what I say and not as I do' kind and more of leading by example. I am not any good at some of them and in other rather good. Throughout the day I am called from a lumbering bear, a great shot, and about mediocre with a sword.

I feel like I like the battle teacher the most thou he seems to take everything I learned from the others and put them into something very useful. I got the impression that if he had wanted he probably could have taught any of those classes.

I am already feeling tired by the time I finally make it to class I spend with Raja, but still manage to listen diligently to the dragon who is teaching us, as he goes over the best way to care and provide for your bonded either it the scaly one or the human ones. He tells us that the best way for a dragon to stay clean would be of course a bath in a lake but if we aren't around one a soft towel under the scales will help, otherwise they can get stuff growing under them. After the time is almost up, Professor Quinavar lets the hatchlings finish it off by letting them show their bondeds or flying partner what they have learned thus far.

I learned a flying partner is a person assigned to a dragon in the place of a bonded when the dragon has yet to find their soul friend.

Raja seems to take to the air rather easily, as if he was born flying, especially compared to the other hatchlings; even with and none proportioned body.

"*I do not suggest flight together just yet it would be best if you all waited until you were at least the size about one eighths of a floor, but alas I know you are all eager to start flying, so you shall only have to wait about four days. Until then you shall mount your dragons and we shall be trying mock battle… tomorrow.*" Our teacher's assistant says, also a dragon, he is on the small size and a mix of green and gold.

*

Three days later…

Raja and Flare move forward with their classes quickly and each gain praise from their teachers left and right. On our third day at the academy Zar made a visit at the cafeteria…. Yeah.

"Esper, HOW MUCH LONGER!" Dante repeats for the twentieth time since I have sat down with my dinner. "Maybe next time you won't destroy everything you see." I say instead as Garret looks at me pleadingly several seats down next to Ceribi who chatters on and on about how when they were a pup….

Ace sits across from me and chuckles, "I wish I had thought of that for my twin sisters they are always into mischief they just love messing with Flir." She tosses a roll to Toni, while getting out her wand to show me pictures of her sisters.

"*Ah-hmm*" A booming voice cleared behind me. "*Daddy*," Raja crows and barrels into Zar's waiting arms. "*Hello son, I just came to bring your mothers greetings and to tell you how proud I am that I seem to have teachers coming to me every night to relate how well my son is doing.*" Zar puffs his chest up with pride and strokes his claw over Raja.

"*They tell me you shall be a flier like none other!*" Zar speaks so loudly that others around us drop into silence to hear what he has to say, and cheer with him as he declares his son's destiny.

The hall falls silent to listen as he looks at his heir, "*You have made an old dragon proud… after Dran… well you are everything we could've wished from you.*" Zar looks like he is going to start crying and closes his eyes for a second. "*Father I have not even done anything to make you proud.*" Raja whispers in his father's head unwilling to hear his father take it back in front of everyone.

"*Son you shall never have to worry about disappointing me, you cannot possible be a disappointment.*" Zar whispers back stroking his sons head.

"*Raja come look at this!*" Remidus calls from across the room, sending Raja bounding after his friend. I wait for a full two minutes before moving over to Raja's father.

"Zar, I need to talk to you about the search you are mounting for Yanni and Jenni." Zar glances up from watching his son, seeming to take in me and the dead silent quiet lunchroom. *"How about we go for a walk, we need to talk and I'll get you informed."* Zar says nearly bonking his head on his way through the door. I follow behind Zar, as we get out of ear shot he finally acknowledges us.

"We have been searching for your friends far and wide but if it is what we believe, or rumors are the Drazarian have been selling off all their prisoners to the slavers. This is not good news; barely anyone is ever recovered from the slavers, unless they live in outlying villages or captured during war. But to find a four year old and a fifteen year old the possibilities aren't good." Zar's voice goes deeper in sympathy, stopping momentarily in his stride to give us a pitying look.

"So there is no way to go get them?" Tears form in my eyes slightly, as I speak in but a whisper. *"No, there is nothing we can do, until we win the war."* It is an arrogant statement to make, but he makes it sound like it is a for sure.

*

Ten days later...

We work it out with Zar that we will come for dinner with them at the palace every couple of days, that way we will have time for other stuff, and Averia still gets family dinners. Over such time I have been too busy to ponder over the conundrum of how Zar thinks so little of his first son that his second could be anything even a major disappointment and he would still be proud.

Over the ten days Toni finally points out something I am totally ashamed to say I didn't notice. So on Earth a person an there animal tend to have certain similarities like hair and clothing and such. On Pangaea it is kind of like that but we notice it more as we seem to change to fit those. Dash's hair now has a faint blue glow like Sheena. Toni's brown eyes seem to have gotten darker, so has his hair so it's more chocolate brown. Lucan I swear in some lights I can see the ripping of scales, and his muscles look like with one squeeze he could strangle you. I look in the mirror to see what has changed about that started this revelation that Toni told me about and I see purple and yellow sometimes swirling in my hair. I knew that my hair was becoming lighter in color but I thought it was just because I was in Pangaea not because I am bonded to a yellow leopard. The purple and blue tones though are new.

I am a big enough person to say I panic slightly at seeing this in the mirror and Flare found me on the floor of our bathroom with Pangaea's version of a hair dye that I had got some science based kids to make for me. It worked but needs to be reapplied every few months. Averia clued me in that when both my bonded's are full growth it is most likely that my hair will be completely yellow with blue and purple highlights, sense I have to bondeds.

Another revelation was when Flare happened to let it slip I have leopard spots climbing my spine, faint but there. Raja then commenced telling me that when he was a grown up that I would most likely have spikes going up to. How wonderful if I ever go to Earth I shall be a science experiment at worst and freak at best.

All in all week and a half pass and Raja has grown to the size of about a giant elephant, and it is finally time Quinavar declared to take to the sky. The others have finally reached size, and Raja has been waiting for them to catch up. I may or may not look in the mirror every night he gets bigger to check for spikes.

Raja has to place me on his back because he has grown far over the size where I could be able to climb on without a pickaxe. Raja settles me nestled on his neck before giving a dragon smile to Remidus and his assigned man.

Remidus hasn't bonded with anyone so he has been assigned a person of his own choosing to fly with. Her name is Lolane; she's rather a diva and likes to hang with Cara so I stick clear of her. Remidus thought she was okay but hopes to one day find his true bonded and that he or she won't be offended over being replaced for the time being.

During class I found out that even when you are older you can still bond with someone, it is like best friends for life, not like soul mates or anything. You can still have a bonded and soul mate similar but just different types of love here.

Raja snaps me out of my musings when he leans back before I have totally strapped my legs into the saddle. Like a racing saddle for thoroughbreds on Earth, but the straps being the softest yet toughest fabric they have here. The straps go around his neck placed strategically under the scales to avoid in battle being cut and around his front legs under his belly, the saddle also having straps on the side to go around the legs, to give the rider a better safer flight by being strapped on.

I barely keep myself on his back with all the weaving Raja is doing. I lunge for his spike that is above me on his long neck as big as my forearm. "Raja, Hold!" I grab on harder, *"sorry, why you are taking so long?"* Raja's booming voice has a slight whine from his impatience take to the sky. His wings flap up and down nearly hitting Remidus in his excitement.

I hurry to strap my legs into the saddle harness and stroke his scales. "I'm ready," I call up to him as he shuffles from foot to foot, *"Let it rip!"* Quinavar calls out, it is less than two seconds and Raja leans back on his haunches, flaring his long giant wings out more, nearly overlapping

the bulky Remidus's wings. "*I can barely feel your weight!*"
Raja boasts, and flaps harder and harder until I feel the air
whip my hair all around.

We soar higher and higher than the other dragons,
who are still struggling with the vertical takeoff. I can
feel the wind blowing through my cloths and I watch
with fascination as clouds flit by my face. After a minute
Raja changes directions and heads in another direction I
can only see clouds and more clouds, I can also see stars
peeking through some. "Raja are we supposed to stay with
the others?" I call but its only halfhearted I don't want it
to end.

I lose track of time and how far we fly but it must have
been a long time because after a while Raja wavers and
drops about ten feat. "Raja, maybe we should head back I
can feel your strength fleeing." Raja seems to snap out of
a trance his joy had put him in. he weaves his head up and
down in a way of clearing it, coming to a stop hovering
over the large forest. "*I think that would be an amazing
idea, I feel rather tired-*" Raja's voice wavers as his right
wing seems to collapse on him.

We fall.

"*Raja you need to pull your wings, or they will get
crushed!*" I scream in my mind and vocal to be sure he
hears me, I can see in my mind a vision of Raja landing on
his wings and the damage that could happen if he does.

"*What about you! If I do you will be unprotected… Esper, unbuckle your legs now!*" I don't know what he is thinking but I try to unbuckle as fast as I can. I tug and tug on the buckle but it won't give, I grab one of my daggers and start cutting them off. Raja choses that moment to hit a tree thou and I grip onto the saddle having to let go of the dagger, the dagger's thrown away from me.

I try to hang on but my hands are sweating and they just slip on the leather. I am thrown away from Raja. "Raja," I feel a scream well up, I can see tree branches and other awful stuff rushing towards me. Raja lunges towards me wrapping his claws around my middle, and pulls me towards his body.

Raja gathered his wings around his body; I can see in his mind how they overlap a long ways. Raja lunges repeatedly with his back legs trying to grab onto branches as they rush past us, each thou going by too fast and he's unable to keep a hold.

This managed to slow us down but the ground still pulls at Raja's great body down, about twenty feet from the ground Raja tucks his head under his wing and sends a silent prayer to his goddess. I feel like I was getting whiplash when we make impact on the ground I can feel my neck jerk and I can feel through the bond how hard Raja hits; and then everything goes pitch black, even the bond.

*

A major crick in my neck brings me awake with its insistent pain to the feel of a weight around my body. I groan low out of my throat; I can't help but rub my neck, trying to relieve the horrible ache. Why can't this dragon get I don't like to be held like I am his favorite doll. Ever since he has become as big as an elephant he likes to his hold me close to his chest like a child's toy, especially while we sleep. I laugh hysterically, unable to stop my pain from my neck causing it to just bubble up. I can't wait to see him try to do that with Flare who is the size of a horse.

"Raja, let go," I poke him hard in the stomach but he doesn't move. I pry at his claws trying to pull them away from my stomach, where they seem to have left imprints. What is new is he usually doesn't like sleeping with his wings tucked over us like this because Flare likes me to use him as a pillow. Speaking of Flare where is my wayward bonded? I finally manage to pry Raja's claws away from my middle and his claws fall limp on the ground, having been released from their death grip.

"Flare where are you? What's wrong with Raja? Why won't he wake up?" I call softly out in both mind and voice, I know I probable sound like a scared kid, but I am. I push Raja's top wing off so I can get to his head easier and get

some light. I scramble over to his still head. I pick his head up and move under him so he can rest in my lap.

He doesn't even stir.

"*Are you going crazy on me? Thank the goddess you are okay! I hadn't felt your mental waves for a while, I could feel you guys crash, but then nothing, and you had me so scared.*" Flare's panicked voice echoes through my head loudly, and lonely I feel like I have a slight hangover, and his voice is so loud.

We had crashed…. My mind whirls painfully trying to think about those ghastly minutes before we crashed to earth… or Pangaea… whatever. "*Flare we need some help, I don't know where we are, Raja won't wake up, I'm scared, I'm sure that if Raja was awake he wouldn't be able to fly he hit so many branches, and I think something happened before we fell to his wing. You need to bring help to us by using the bond, I believe in you Flare.*" I stroke Raja's soft nose over and over finding it soothing as I watch in Flare's head as he gets help from Zar and Averia. I honestly didn't know I could do that, things just seem to keep evolving as time goes on.

"*Esper, you have to snap out of it. Dark will be falling soon, you need to find fire wood to keep warm it's been getting colder and colder as our version of autumn approaches and you aren't wearing anything made for cold.*" I waver; I don't want to leave Raja all alone, even if it is only for a minute to go get firewood. *"Esper, you aren't any good to him frozen and if you get moving I will distract you and I'll tell you why Earth's dimension is no longer connected to ours."* I nod only because I know Flare is watching to make sure I am okay.

I try to move fast but manly focusing on Flare's story so I don't become catatonic with worry for Raja.

"So way back when both our dimensions were interconnected, considered to be a whole dimension rather than two, people enjoyed being bondeds. But there always some who consider themselves superior to everything, like they work it around in their heads that they were superior." I shuffle forward picking up anything that might be good for a fire. *"There was a woman named Morgona Lee Fay who was bonded to a baby dragon. The dragon grew so that he was malformed due to a mentally unstable person chaining them in a tiny well. We do have the rare cases of psychotic people you have in droves on your Earth. Morgona and her bonded believed they were above everyone else. On the new moon her bonded killed someone trying to protect himself, but the person's friends didn't see it as self-defense. Her bonded was murdered by the person's friends before her eyes while she was too far to do anything but run in vain to help. She already felt contempt for everyone, and this made her became even bitterer towards people, especially those who had a bond with another, be it soul mates or just bondeds.*

"She consulted the greatest sorcerer that was known at the time under a different face so as not to reveal her identity. You know him as Merlin. He was a mighty dragon who protected King Arthur, who was King Uther's human bonded. Morgona tried first to demand Merlin give her the spell to help her with her nefarious means. Merlin turned Morgona away, enraged with this she hatched a plan and so later that night she snuck into Merlin's cave and slew the him as he slept, stealing his spell book. She burned his cave and body as a means to make sure that nothing could be found inside that could undo her plan.

"Morgona took many captives, those that she wanted to take with her to her new world she was to create. She did such so she could rule over them. Morgona had hundreds of cells created in a castle set on a hill and bided her time until she had enough people to start her new world. Anyone she believed deserved to live under her in her new world and partake in the numbness it would cause to the soul and magic.

"Then Morgona cast Merlin's spell on the New Year, King Arthur tried valiantly to get there in time to stop Morgona and save the captives, but alas he did not make it in time and the dimensions were split. Interweaving the spell so that she had her own dimension and that the people who went would never be able to or maintain or feel a bond on what they now call Earth. What she didn't seem to take into account was that many things changed as they changed dimensions, including *how long their life would be and that magic couldn't exist on Earth, consequently any of the beings that needed Magic to survive died a slow painful death. Some shrank or changed sizes having different gravities and such. Somehow thou Morgona was not able to erase all memory of Pangaea from the unwilling inhabitants of earth. They remember it as when the continents shifted, instead of the splitting of dimensions and their history."*

When Flare finishes his story I have already collected the firewood, lit the fire, and settled under Raja's head again trying to console myself knowing that I can faintly feel air coming out of Raja's nostrils.

"Flare why didn't King Arthur try and fuse the dimensions back together?" I say going back to stroking Raja's head.

"He couldn't the one magician who might have been able to stop her or reverse it she slew. You know what they say we must learn from our history." Flare finishes, I can feel him waiting impatiently for Zar and his guards. Soon he leaps into Zar's claws and they take flight. I think of many things to reply but I just don't have the heart to voice them when Raja is hurt and won't wake up. Flare understands my sentiment and he doesn't push.

I keep tabs on Flare's progress and Raja's breathing, as Flare tells me the folklore of Pangaea. The stories were a lot like Earth's just changed to fit Pangaea's culture. In earths we have fairy tales about how we can find true love with another person, in Pangaea the heroine might already have hers. One story he told me was of a girl who lived in a valley village and her soul mate had been taken by the slavers. The girl hunted the party of slavers using any and all resources she had to track them down and free her true love, nearly not escaping, only to return to the village together once more. Their stories are sometimes even about Earth, us being the unbelievable story to them. Flare goes on to tell me that all of their stories are actually true, that what is the point of telling untrue stories to learn from.

Not long after I have settled down to wait it gets colder, and I can hear some rustling in the brushes. I move my hand closer to Saphique, clutching the hilt when I hear a huge snap and what sounds like someone cursing.

"Call in to the dragon's I think we are getting closer to the prince and his bonded." I gulp extracting myself out from under Raja, and drawing Saphique as quietly as I can. I don't know how I can hear… its almost like I am using Flare's super hearing.

"Don't worry Raja I will protect you, they won't get us I just got to hold them off until help arrives." I move away from Raja into the tree line. I shadow from tree to tree following the sounds of the lowered voices.

They are slinking through the woods making hand motions and such as they combed the woods for us. I can't tell how many they are they are too far spread out.

I quickly and quietly as possible run back to Raja. I hold Saphique and wait, having decided that it is smarter to not mess with them and have them clue in on that they are getting closer to us.

It takes them about half an hour to an hour to make their way to us.

"Over here! AHHHHHH" The first man who sees us charges at me with a war cry, raising his sword above his head. He brings it down on me with a lot of might behind it, our blades clash with more noise than my probably concussed head likes. He pulls away to try a side swipe, I bring around Saphique to deflect it and he goes stumbling. I swing my blade up again this time to bash the hilt into the base of his spine as he stumbles. He drops like a sack of potatoes.

Another man charges out of the woods but stops short, holding back two other men, "let's talk this out, your bonded needs care, no one knows you are out here, we can help you. Just put down the weapon and surrender peacefully and Raja can get some help, he will live." The man holds his hand forward nonthreateningly; three more men come to stand behind him.

I want Raja better but my gut is screaming that this man is no good and might mean death to both me and Raja.

"Go to hell." I snarl and take a ready stance that in my time being on Pangaea has been drilled into me like breathing.

With a cry one of the men behind the placating man jumps past and attacks.

I let out a war cry that could've woken the dead and hold my worry, frustration, and helplessness in a tight ball preparing to use it to come out swinging. I have decided I will survive this one way or another. It's me or them.

*

Flare and the Calvary arrive before the attacker's dragons do and scare away the small contingent of the enemy fighters after I had already taken down a couple and am about to be over run. Zar ignores them and keeps his attention on Raja. Raja still hasn't awoken and I can't help but become even more worried. Help consists of Zar, Quinavar, and three of his big bulky dragon guards. *"Are you okay, Esper?"* Flare nudges my shoulder reassuringly, "I'll survive, let us just help him and get home."

Zar delicately picked up Raja being extremely larger, it doesn't seem very hard for him.

Zar cradles Raja's body to his chest muttering something over him, *"Mahigo la rovan ian vas."* Zar let loose a long breathy sign of relief. *"He still lives, we must make haste thou we do not know what damage he has sustained."* Quinavar lifts me up onto his back and Flare takes up a position in one of the guard dragon's claws. I wish I could be with Flare, but I don't argue. Even if feeling Flare beside me his big body rumbling in a reassuring purr would be the best thing next to it being Raja.

"What happened, girl, it was supposed to be a short flight not a freaking race to the mountains!" Quinavar tries to lighten the mood; I can tell by his tone that he doesn't mean much by it. "I don't know he was just so excited and we didn't even notice the time or distance until we were a long ways away, and then something happened to his wings before we could turn back." I feel so small on Quinavar. My eyes track Zar and one of the guards as they increase their speed, Zar still whispers something against him but the words are stolen by the wind. I feel our bond, I try to get any reading but only coming up cold. Shivers rack my body, soul deep along with the biting wind I just now seem to notice.

"You were very brave to protect Raja even though you were outnumbered five to one. It is not uncommon thou that a dragon on his first flight with his bonded to get excited and work himself into a trance like state. I have a hunch

though that these mercenaries had something to do with your falling out of the sky." Quinavar falls into silence thinking things through in his head and I just don't have it in me to conspire with him. Shudders seem to take over my body as exhaustion and the cold seem to have both caught up to me.

The flight back to the capital seems to go on forever. I can't stop fidgeting and looking over to where Raja is clutched to Zar's chest.

*

Averia meets us just inside the dome and starts fretting over Raja but makes sure to keep out of the way and lets us make due haste to the palace where Vector and his other physicians await. Zar speeds up, leaving us to follow behind. By the time we get to the palace he has placed Raja on the cold marble and the doctors are already clamoring over him. "Can you tell us what happened to make you guys fall out of the sky?" Vector approaches me as the others are already binding together some of the soft scales that have been hurt during the fall.

"We were just about to turn back and he just seems to be drained of all his strength but not like just from fatigue and his wings wouldn't work so he tried to break our fall by grabbing onto one of those thick branches but he couldn't seem to catch and hold one for long enough. Then we made impact." My voice breaks, "and then he wouldn't wake up." My voice is all but a whisper and I'm not sure if he hears or not, I don't really care.

Vector nods and moves back over to take care of Raja, I move over to his head picking it up and placing it in my lap. I stroke his muzzle and whisper soothing words even praying to the goddess to make him better. The goddess that all in Pangaea worship, she goes by no name, but apparently has been worshiped since the beginning of Pangaea, I hope she hears me.

*

After a while what is left to do is only to wait. Flare joins me in my vigil, I can feel his worry but I can also feel he has more optimism then me, he just didn't know how hard we hit the ground.

*

I don't know what happened one minute I am stroking Raja's nose and the next I am on our pillow in the dragon caves and Raja is lying next to me, along with Flare. I can feel the allure to sleep but I need to know if Raja is going to be okay.

I push myself up and head to the platform and stairs and trip over a long scaly tail. Unlike Raja this tail has hard sharp scales. I land with a thud on… Liam.

"What are you doing on our pillow?" I try to be quiet my voice so as not to awake anyone. "I was here to make sure no one had an aneurism or something in their sleep, doctors words not mine." Liam replies sleepily moving his arms around my waste as if to use me for his pillow or something. "Liam! Now is not the time for cuddling I need to go talk to the healers!" I push off him, which if he hadn't let go I would't have even made any head way. "Are you hurt?" He starts running his hands over my body trying to find wounds other than the ones that have already been patched up by the healer.

With all the adrenaline that had been running through my body I hadn't even noticed when during the battle with those mercenaries that I had got a long cut on my right arm, a stab wound on my right hip, and what feels like thousands of cuts from the fall and hitting all those trees on my way down.

"Liam, if you are going to be feeling me up, I would like to at least have dinner first? I'm fine I just need to know what the doctors think on Raja, is he going to wake up?" I try to keep it humorous but I sound like a lost child by the end. I'm just not one of those people who always have a well thought out come back line.

"Esper calm down they looked him over and they say he should wake up soon, just go about your day. Of course your teachers have been notified that you have sustained injury and will be taking it light for the next couple of days. So instead of opening your stitches with all this tripping you need to go back over to your bondeds." Liam strokes my hair soothingly until I nod my head and rub my eyes on my way back to Raja and Flare.

"Thanks Liam." I whisper already asleep. What would I do without my boys?

*

The next day isn't easy the adrenaline has completely worn off and I can feel ever spot the knife had broken the skin. Raja wakes up briefly before I leave for classes and breakfast. Raja being awake makes it worth all the pains I am suffering to know he is going to be okay.

"Esper Collette! What the hell happened! We leave you alone for like two days and you manage to get yourselves lost, attacked, and injured!" Dash thunders trying to act like he was the big dog this time but he cracks and gives me a relieved smile. "Seriously though, what happened?" Toni cut in, fingering the bandage on my arm, Dash moves up beside me to pull lightly on my mussed auburn hair. "Oh that's not the worse one, I have two more. I was flying with

Raja and something happened, and his wings wouldn't work and we fell. Then we were attacked, with a lot more detail but I don't have the energy or heart to go detail by detail for you." Toni and Dash look horrified as they seem to take me in from head to toe.

They both seemed to have adapted to life in Pangaea rather well, Toni has filled out so that he has the body of a lean muscular young man, a little taller than Dash. But Dash has more muscles even at his younger age. Both seem to move and breath as if they had been born to this world meant for its exciting adventures and unpolluted air.

Cara decides to join the party with extra wiggle in her hips for the boys and a sneer for me. "So Esper, got your attention last night didn't you? Having all those people fawn over you, being the center of their attentions." Cara throws her blonde hair over her shoulder and links her arm through Dash's even though he has sour look on his face. "I mean is your ego so big you can't share the lime light with us more humble people." She glares when Toni snorts.

"Cara, I think you are getting you mixed up with me because I know for a fact there has never been a humble thing about you and if you are done trying to molest Dash I would like to go get some breakfast." Cara sputters when I walk away from her and I sadly thought it reminded me of Raven. Was that what she would have turned into?

Today is bacon and eggs, synthetic of course because it would be tragic to eat something that you can have a conversation with that was more than one sided. "You never answered Esper where else where you injured." Toni slams his hand onto the table to get my attention. "Fine," I stand up and undoing the bottom of the corset to show him the slightly bled through bandage and point to my other hip and draw a line above it where I could feel my skin radiate with heat.

"God damn, Esper, you let yourself get injured three times! What were you doing, daring them?"

"I didn't do it on purpose I had just been in a dragon crash." The explanation seems to mollify Toni but Dash still mutters under his breath. The twins and about everyone else seem to be just staring uncertain of what to think.

"So Lucan, how are your classes going?" I change the topic to them trying to in the same breath find out what I hadn't been paying attention to. Dash starts swearing like a sailor... where did he learn that language? But he lets me change the subject.

"They are going okay, except like I just couldn't seem to get some of the thing about their political system. It's just so different from ours." Lucan shrugs going on, "and like apparently when give a girl a rose, you are dating them. So like I was trying to give this girl Simone a neon pink rose and ask her to the dance, she's like older and more sophisticated and turned me down. But she gave me the rose back so I happen to give it to another girl so it doesn't go to waste but now she thinks we are dating. What will Simone think?" Lucan rambles.

"Simone … I think I know her she's in half my classes and way too old for you." I say arching my brow and shake my finger at him.

"Whatever when have you ever heard of an age limit on love." Lucan scowls, but Dash chuckles next to him ruffling his hair. "In other words that aren't crazy, and out of this world, I have a date for said dance, Simone." Dash declares giving Lucan a smug glance, leaning back in his chair pretty proud of himself. "Oh, no you didn't, you know that I can call you to a duel!" Lucan leaps to his feet indignation etched over his face.

"For one, man, if Simone found out about that she would kick both of our asses. Two, she doesn't want a possible sixteen year old boy, she wants someone her own age." Lucan face falls as he thinks it over, sitting down with far less energy than he had leapt out of it.

"So Esper who are you going to ask?" Toni leans on the table looking at me with his head in his hands.

"Are you kidding me I could barely do the strict regimen without having holes in me. There is no way I am going to be able to do anything after a day of that." So on and so forth it starts.

*

My day seems to be pain on top of pain. I still have to walk with the class or help out I just am not doing the more straining things, such as sword fighting or balance beam. Sadly my favorite time of the day is the time I have in Tactic and History and I have to sit on the sidelines. When the time comes for my two hours of flying with Raja Quinavar has me go up on his back instead of Raja who is still fast sleep off in the dragon caves.

It feels different to be on Quinavar far more intimidating. As he instructs the others he has me run through routine that I would be doing on Raja, the ones I can do without breaking more of my stitching of course. Left, right, weave left, butterfly sweep, duck low. Each one hurts like a !@#$ but I still work through, telling myself it will get easier, duck left, bring trident right block. I don't think Quinavar gets that I don't have scales and of such rip more easy.

By the end of the class I am exhausted, I look at the mess hall with all the pushing people and small talk and keep walking. Skipping dinner probable isn't smart... but like I'm exhausted and am exchanging it for a long sleep next to Raja. That makes it worth it right? I barely even notice when Flare joins us in our snuggle fest.

12

One week later…

I start to feel my strength improving as the week passes better. I stand in line enjoying the warm air and light refreshments Quinavar was passing out for our excellent work in class. I don't know why but it seems the summer goes on and on. "Esper, hey I've been meaning to talk to you for a while, I'm Simone." I turn to see a long haired brunette, with porcelain skin, perfect features, and blue eyes. This must be the Simone that both Lucan and Dash have been arguing over.

"Uh, yeah I know, we have a lot of classes together." She waves her manicured hand in the air, brushing aside the fact, and giving me a smile. I don't see her slanted pupils or feathers to show if she has a bonded.

"Yeah, well now I have, I don't think I need to tell *you* how hard our work load is here." She giggles, actually giggles, do girls actually do that without flirting? "Anyway I was hoping you could like talk to your brother Lucan for me." My face twists up, did this chick my age actually have a thing for my fifteen year old brother. Is he fifteen still? Wow my brain is going everywhere.

"Oh, not like your face says, gosh he is way too young for me; I need you to talk to him about leaving me and Dash alone." She leans closer, whispering the rest in my ear. "See I like Dash and ever sense the dance we have been trying to be alone but everywhere we turn Lucan is there." I chuckle but nod. Every time I see the cute couple together I also see Lucan right next to them. "Yeah, I noticed… what do you expect me to do?"

We grab our lemonade and ice cream before she draws me to the side, "well you are like the leader of your family. I mean a blind person could see that just from the stories Dash tells about your journey. I just want you to talk to him or distract him when you see him our way. I really like Dash but I don't know if our new relationship will survive your brother. Please." Her blue eyes plead with me for help but I already meddled in Dash's life I don't want to do it again. I open my mouth to say no but a change goes over her face.

Her eyes get bigger, her bottom lip pops out and starts trembling, and her eyes tear up. I close my eyes and open my mouth again but I can still see it even with my eyes closed, "fine." I all but yell it, I throw my hands in defeat and her sad face immediately transforming into a happy smile. "Thank you, we need to hang out more." Simone kisses my cheek and leaves in a whirl wind.

I watch her run over to Dash, jumping into his arms and kissing his cheek. "Flare I think I just got played. Why can't I do that? I think I need to enlist some help from our little delinquents." How did I get played like that? I'm not even a guy but I now know there pain of a few tears and big eyes. Talk about painful.

*

I find the twins head in their hands listening to their wand music up so loud that they can't hear the incessant chatter of Ceribi. "Ceribi would you give us a minute." The three headed dog looks over shutting up for two seconds.

"I think we are being dismissed."

"I don't want to be dismissed, it feels rather belittling."

Arguing follows them out of the room. I turn back to the two rather relieved faces. "How would you like to get out of your punishment and on probation?" Dante and Garrett leap from their seat in rapt attention. "What do we have to do?" I bet I could say knock over a bank and they would probable do it. "Just follow around Lucan between classes and keep him away from Dash and Simone." Both heads start nodding even before I'm finish talking. New experiences all day I guess, this one much better. "Dance my little puppets."

*

I meet up with Simone and Dash after a few days. They are such a cute couple, like an Oreo. That sounds bad but they so adorable, the perfect couple. They lounge in a love seat in the library, her part way on his lap as they work on something together. Every few seconds they stop and laugh or smile at each other. I make my way over to the couple, around desks and people doing book work. I see Lucan making a be-line over to them, only to be diverted by one of the twins, while the other one takes aim at the back of Lucan's head. Lucan curses as the egg size rock hits him before taking off after the other twin, in revenge. You know I should probable make sure the twins try to minimize harm… but I am a teenager too why do I always have to be the face of reason, Zar said he would look after them.

I chuckle finally throwing myself into the love seat next to them. "Well, the twins seem to have Lucan under wraps and I didn't even have to be the bad guy."

"Uh, it has been perfect. I really hope it stays this way." I stretch out my legs throwing my hand out to wave the comment away. The soft black leather pants feeling nice matching my red long sleeved corset. I just woke up an felt like I wanted to be a girl and dress nice, yet badass.

"Oh, my word, I am starting to miss earth flip flops, these boots are so stuffy." Simone looks puzzled. "What are flip flops. "They are like sandals with only a band between the big toe and across your foot." Dash speaks against her hair.

She leans forward to show me her gladiator sandals. "Get some of these; they are so easy to move in when you just doing school stuff."

I look over her black gladiator sandals, "I think I actually have a whole bunch of those in my room at the palace. I have a closet there that is like a wet dream, shoes, bags, and cloths as far as the eye can see." Simone's eyes widen and get all dreamy as she sighs and leans back into Dash.

"Well I shall leave you love birds and go see if I can track down Liam and Flare." I get up from the cushy couch, finding it rather hard get up out of the love seat.

Before I have even left the library Flare appears beside me, rather sneaky for a horse size leopard. "You scared me you big over grown house cat." Flare snorts finding no insult. Then again house cats are waited on hand and foot. Doesn't seem like a bad deal. "*Who is the one who is waited on left and right, E?*" I ruffle his hair on the top of his head even thou he is taller than me, he gives me a baleful look but just twitches his tail.

"I am trying to track down Liam, any ideas?" We weave our way through people and out into the paddock the dragons like to use for sunning themselves. Raja, Veevia, and all the other dragons spend their free day soaking up the sun in random piles, we walk over to them. Veevia pops open a sleepy blue eye, unwilling to say anything she just stares at us expectantly. "Veevia, do you know where Liam is we wanted to ask him some things?" Raja grumbles and turns over in his sleep. He is getting as big as Veevia already. My baby dragon is going to be all grown up soon, I don't even have pictures.

"*He went down to the closest tavern with some buddies; they felt like celebrating, they shall be full knights in a couple months. Free to choose either to join the army or we shall travel around searching for adventure. I rather think that we shall join the army in a means to vanquish those evil sons of a …. Sorry I forget my manners."* Veevia gets worked up for a second but calms down to resituate herself into a better sunning spot and go back to her drowsing. When she gets agitated little webbed spines pop up on her rather like one of the lion fishes on Earth.

"Well thanks for the information." I call over my shoulder already heading down the path. We walk through the arches leading either through to the second paddock that houses the wishing well. Or you can follow under the arches to either the office that leads to other places in the campus or go the opposite way to the school. The well is set in a garden. The well has a legend surrounding it, that if your heart is true a wish will be granted, I rather chose that path as much as possible just to walk by it.

We pick our way across the garden to the hidden entrance we had uncovered a couple days before, when enjoying ourselves. We leave the academy behind and make the short walk to the small tavern right by the academy. Why anyone would put a tavern by a school is beyond me, but apparently it still made good business.

The tavern is a simple building nothing fancy, sort of like a medieval tavern, at least in my opinion. Liam and his buddies sit in the back enjoying cold ale, which has like point two percent alcohol in it, and more just amazing taste. "Liam, did you save me one?" I call ahead weaving my way through the room around tables. "Well what good would that be when you took so long? It wouldn't be cold by the time you got here." Liam stands and pushes the other guys over to make room; Flare settles on a pillow in the corner a big bowl in front of him. "Tavern keeper, another round pleases," Liam waves his hand indicating the table. I move to sit beside Liam's friend Jeremy, but Liam waves me to sit by him.

The inn/ tavern keeper makes his way over with an empty glass and a huge pitcher of ale. He sets the glance down in front of me, filling the empty glass to brimming and goes around pores the ale into each glass around the table. I watch as he heads to the back only to get waylaid by a clearing throat on the ground. Flare glares from the ground and then looks to the empty bowl. The man chuckles nodding as he goes for another pitcher.

The man hurries out a second later to fill Flare's bowl, and he contently starts lapping at the sweet goodness. Liam clears his throat and I turn back to the table and three very handsome men sitting at it with a sweet wafer thin girl. They are all nice and all but I feel kind of bad I like them but there is one small problem... I can't remember their names, except Jeremy. I am probable the worst person when it comes to names and I couldn't be worse at remembering these people. They have a slight problem of never saying their names to each other. I mean they call each other nicknames like Skid, Ace and Rev but I mean come on cant they say their names once in a while so I don't look like a food for calling them the wrong one? I do think Rev is the girl's nickname, could also be Skid, don't ask me. I am also pretty sure that she was the girl I spent a meal with on my first day at the academy.

Rev has short brown hair kept up in a messy pony tail; she has a rounded face and full lips. Her big brown eyes bright and her face covered in a splay of freckles. Rav was thin and looks about fifteen and very much a tom boy. She is a very easy girl to get along with. I wish our paths would cross more.

"So what is up that you had to track me down to the tavern?" Liam knows I have been trying to ask him something for a while I just forget it sometimes or get waylaid.

"A couple reasons… have you heard what happened to Ray?" I feel lame for asking but we had a great date I thought and I haven't heard anything since.

"He was shipped out weeks ago. The aquatic platoons were dispatched pretty hush-hush but my brother was visiting when their orders came in. It was very sudden some new threat." Ace interrupts Liam to jump in. I nod my head mulling it over, I get it, moving on.

"What do you know about Raja's older brother?" I feel Raja sit up in my head eager to hear the answer. His parents never talk about his other siblings, for all we know he could have another sibling we didn't know about other than the brother.

"Uh, you go for the hard stuff, don't you? Um, that's a very touchy subject that not a lot know the whole of. I only know because my dad's one of Zar's confidants and I heard him telling mother." Liam looks around beckoning us closer, the other guys lean forward just as eager as me.

"Keep going," I urge, this has been nagging at me for some time.

"Well Dran of Creel was the oldest son he originally was to be heir to the kingdom. Zar and Averia also had another child, a girl her name was Joan, Joan of Arc to be exact. Joan was to be soul bonded to a prince of Atlantis-"

"Wait Joan of Arc really? There is one on earth she was tried as a witch for hearing voices, after she helped turn the tide in the... French war, I think it was the French." I feel a thousand questions egging to be asked and he hadn't even gotten to the good part like what happened to Raja's brother and sister.

"Yes, Joan liked to meddle in human lives, she spoke to the young girl, told her what to do, she was the voices. She had the girl use her name as a symbol that she was here. I can't remember what Joan told me the girls name was. She was an amazing person, and Atlantis is on the other side of the world, but Joan had made a connection with the prince and it would benefit the kingdom. Zar only agreed to let his little girl go because she swore she felt the beginnings of a soul mate bond." He pauses for a second his smile he had slips to one of sadness.

"What happened to Joan? Did she go to Atlantis? Is she living with her prince?" I have a bad feeling but I can't help but want a better ending for the name sake Joan of Arc then the girl who used the name in Earth's history.

I am so curious but I also don't want to hear it. I would rather cover my ears and pretend she got her happily ever after.

"Joan isn't in Atlantis, she never made it. It was only I think two years ago that it happened. She and Dran had been arguing, always arguing. Joan had a level head and would have made an amazing queen, but they were like fire and Greek fire. She and Dran never saw eye to eye, he was too self-important, always thinking of his own comfort before the kingdom he was to inherit. Joan never approved of her brother but he was first born, so she went along with her parents plan. A servant overheard it all. Joan and Dran were once more at each other's throats. The servant told Zar that it was different this time she yelled at him that he wouldn't get away with it this time that she wasn't going to keep his secret now that she had proof.

"Dran became enraged with his sister and their fighting became more heated, he threw her through a window and she took off to get away from him. The servant, being winged took off after having a bad feeling for the princess. He followed them to the other side of the mountain were she had thought she lost him so she alighted upon the cliffs. Dran dropped on her from the clouds ripping her wings near off and making them useless. If you haven't seen the other side of the islands cliffs then I shall describe it. The cliffs are a shear jagged drop onto rocks that can kill anything that falls on them. Joan was grounded with her wings in shreds and almost ripped out." Liam's breathing becomes labored as he seems to be taken back to the night he had overheard this. Or even right there watching it.

"The servant being too small to interfere and hope to live against Dran in his killing rage sent a plea for help back to Zar and anyone who would help. Unwilling to let the princess's story get covered up by her brother if something happened to her he stayed and watched. The small dove watched in horror as Dran moved towards his sister. She fought him tearing at him as best as she could but he had her wounded and backed up against the cliff, and he pushed her. Zar arrived too late. Joan literally slipped through his talons and crashed onto the jagged rocks below. Zar was distraught and nearly killed Dran in his haze only having Averia to pull him off his only child left. Raja still in his egg they couldn't allow Dran to die, now or let the truth to come out. Either way would see the kingdom in a suction cup of destruction.

"So, Zar sentenced Dran to fight the war never to be welcomed among the capital as a citizen until he had redeemed himself. I have no clue what Zar thought could ever allow Dran to redeem himself, but he must have some idea. It was for the best no one knows Dran killed his sister. Heir apparent passes on to Raja. Dran works to better the kingdom on the defense against the slavers. People aren't totally dumb they know there was more to Joan's death then what was told to them, and I don't think anyone would be surprised if the truth came out, that Dran killed his sister. The kingdom is better off thou now that he will never be king." Liam takes a long pull from his mug as he finishes the equally if not more tragic story of the real Joan of Arc.

I can feel sorrow ebbing in awful waves from Raja as he grieves for the sister he never met. "I see why Zar doesn't expect or need much from Raja to be proud of him. I just can't believe that Zar or anyone would stand to let Dran run the war when he did something so heinous to Joan." I feel warm fur against my side, and I grip Flare's fur for support. It's just so unfair when the just die for a something they believe in. I know I should cast judgment yet but who couldn't if they knew the real story.

"Yeah, that is not the story I was told." Jeremy pipes seeming shocked to hear the truth behind Princess Joan of Arc's tragic death, I didn't even know her and I feel a great loss. "No one knows." Liam waves the inn keeper over to fill the tankards. "I wish I could've met her, she sounded amazing." I stretch feeling a yawn build, "Flare you ready to go back to the campus?" I move to get up but the guy's wave me away. "Well instead of going home and doing nothing. How about you go to the games with us?" Ace stands chugging the rest of the ale. Ace is such a tom boy, like I don't believe I have ever seen her without her hair pulled in a pony and slacks with baggy shirt.

I finish my also and look between the four men.

"Where are these games? I haven't heard about anything?" I look around in puzzlement like I can see the arena or whatever it is.

"You have been here two weeks and apparently you haven't gone to the amphitheater. Well come on you are coming with us then." Liam tugs my upper arm and weaves our way through the tables. I make sure to leave a couple silver coins on the table.

The amphitheater is on the other side of the city. We seem to follow the flow of people making their way there. Soon we pass the market place going through, passing a church and the other tavern. The amphitheater is huge building. It looks like the Roman coliseum in its full glory. With long pillars set in a donut shape. They wrap all around, and have intricate carvings and symbols etched into them. As we come closer, the coliseum looms over larger than life and certainly larger than the one in Rome.

People flood in, taking their places. Somehow Liam manages to get us close seats. We watch dragons and other creatures with wings descend into their seats instead of go through the masses, Zar and Averia among them.

They wave a greeting before settling in a raised platform evidently set aside for them.

Everyone sits down. Quiet descends as a hologram appears out of nothing in the middle of the arena. **Welcome, to the games of Joan,** broadcasts across in vivid clarity. Next a magnificent creature appears in the illusion. He is a big lion with a full main, but that is where normal ends. He has big tawny wings spread out behind him and big black horns rising high.

"*Now these were Joan's idea as a way to let our hot blooded fellows get the violence they need without doing something stupid, this is the third game of Joan. There are but two rules, no killing and no permanent damage such as eye gouging or severing of parts.*" The illusion of the lion beast says then he disappears in a shower of sparks. I look around expecting to see projections in places or beams of light but nothing. Everyone breaks out in a mighty roar of clapping, only to fall silent as a gate creaks open in the arena. I lean forward practically leaning across Flare's back in order to get a better view.

A guy emerges in full battle gear. A helmet with blue plume on top like a Roman soldier covers his face. He also had on a leather padding that seems to have been molded to his chest, leaving his arms bare. He has on a kilt, carrying only a sword in his hand and a single dagger on his belt.

The man throws his arms into the air and **Michael,** appears over the warriors head. The crowd cheers for him almost more than half. That changes though as the portcullis goes up on an adjacent arch. This warrior is in similar regalia but he seems a little bigger then Michael. Both also seem tan like they spend a lot of time outside. Above the warrior, **Laden** appears and the other half of the crowd goes in an uproar.

The lion creature appears again but smaller and between the two squaring off opponents. *"Now boys you know the rules, remember no eye gouging, killing, or severing of limbs. Now shake hands and…. Begin."* His final word echoes through the coliseum and the two warriors face off. After they shake hands Michael explodes in action, his sword whistling for Laden's head. Laden ducks at the last minute. Michael's blade whistles inches from Laden's head. Laden seems to bring his blade about in an ark as if to land a blow against Michael's head only to misdirect and block the blow that Michael had aimed at his gut. All the action displayed by a hologram up above our heads so everyone can see.

Laden brushes the sword aside and twirls his body out of range. Michael follows to keep the offense. Michael swings again. Laden avoids the next close encounter by throwing his body to the side. Laden rolls away, coming up with some ninja move. Laden comes up swinging, parrying

Michael's side cut to come at Michael with his other hand that has a dagger. Laden lands a blow on Michaels exposed arm, before he could twist away. Michael draws his dagger to attack Laden. They go head to head, and Michael seems to always be the aggressor.

They exchange a couple more blows that amount to nothing before Michael manages to hit Laden. He hits Laden across the chest hard and cutting deep on his arm. All of the sudden light exploded up into the air in fireworks. Michael's name gets spelled out in the fireworks, after a minute it goes down. Michael gives Laden a hand up and they walk together going to the arch under Zar and Averia, they bow and exit.

The lion beast comes in again. *"Wasn't that exciting, now we go into our next stage in the game, but we shall have a five minute break. To allow everyone to stretch your legs before we get into the next stage in the games, the riding section."*

The beast disappears and I turn to Liam who sits next to me, while also running my hands through Flare's fur. "Why was there only one gladiator fight?"

"Those were three days ago they, most people spent the whole day here to watch, those two were to top contender." Liam hales one of the men walking through the crowd and he passes down two of their versions of a hot dog. Flare glances from his spot bellow us, *"uh hmm what about me?"* Liam chuckles and hales the vender once more, asking for ten hot dogs. Liam passes half the hot dogs to Flare and hands me a second before passing the rest out among our friends.

The lion creature reappears this time flapping his wings madly. *"In three, two, one, and begin."* At his word the portcullis's on seven arches lift and from each burst forth riders. The first is on Pegasus with a bow and arrow, in similar garb to the gladiators. The others are on bazar types of horses, including a shadow horse, a unicorn, a cannibal horse like Red Feather. One was something I hadn't seen before and is literally all spikes, instead of main and tail has quills and such, and the other just plain Jane horses.

The riders each have different weapons, but there is a difference from the gladiator's weapons, these are made out of magic. I watch as the warrior on the Pegasus shoots down a rider on one of the normal horse. The archer shoots down the other rider on the normal horse before the rider on the shadow horse throws his spear at him and hits him square in the chest and wraps around him making him out. The two that had been shot down by the archer had magic bands wrapped around them, making them out of the competition.

The other four faces off, but the spear thrower no longer has a weapon and a man on the porcupine horse cuts him down while he watches the others. The extra horses race out of the arena through the portcullis under Zar and Averia. The tree left in the arena surge forward to attack each other with their light swords. One surges forward tackling another from his mount to hit him in the face and stick his light sword in him while he was down. As the man looks around for his last opponent, only he doesn't see the person as they come from behind and use their light blade to cut the warrior down.

Lights go in the sky again, **Romona Fee,** the lion creature appears next to the… woman, as she raises her hands over her head and the crowd cheers for her.

*

The games take almost all day. We spend it losing our voices and enjoying the amenities of not having classes that work us to the bone. Liam and his friends stay for the after party, so Flare walks me home. We sneak back in through the garden gate that is hidden off the main path, unnoticeable unless you know what to look for. I follow Flare trusting him to guide me through the path in the dark.

I image if the coliseum in ancient Greece or Rome had still been going on it would've been a lot like that. I have never been to a sporting event that makes me get so involved that my heart skips a beat. It's also amazing to experience it with friends, being able to lean over and share in the energy. I personally don't know all the people participating but Flare somehow new and shared his thoughts. I don't know he has time to be so social and sill be doing well in his classes. I don't know what I would do without Flare or Raja they are both equally important.

As soon as the thought of life without Flare or Raja flashes by I know with a certainty that I wouldn't want to live, but I would for the other. Why am I even thinking this? He is my first bonded, he makes me okay with this world when a normal person would have just curled up and died.

The garden is peaceful and serein, except for the night animals coming out to enjoy the garden. *"Esper,"* I hear Cobalt call from just off the path, we turn to see Cobalt and Aurora cuddled up under a cherry tree. This tree is different than one on Earth. It has bigger blooms that look like pink lilies blooming all over set off with spear head shaped leaves. Breathtaking, the scent far beautiful then any flower I have ever seen before.

"How are you guys? I haven't seen you sense we got here a couple weeks ago." I kneel next to them, I can't help running my fingers through their fur, just so soft. Flare lets out a 'humph', so I run my other hands fingers through his fur. *"We have amazing news,"* Aurora pauses for effect. *"We have just talked to an enchanter, he has confirmed I am with*

a full litter of puppies, he says it could be six to eight puppies."
Cobalt looks so proud standing over his mate.

I squeal with delight and move back onto my heels, to clap excitedly. "Oh, can I have one, please." I know I can't, but I can't help but ask for one, be awesome, cute baby wolf. "I expect to be god mother to these pups." Cobalt gave me a wolf grin, and snuggles up closer to his mate. *"Esper, I think we should leave the couple to their celebrating."* I nod getting back to my feet to follow after Flare, who's already left the shade of the Lilly tree. "This is not over I do expect to be godmother." I call over my shoulder, running to catch up to Flare. I can't help picturing cute puppies with floppy ears and silver pelts mixed with a little black. If they are anything like their parents they shall be powerful little alphas.

"Hey you are supposed to wait, what kind of bonded doesn't wait for the other?" I throw my hands in the air, but he just chuckles and just keeps going, *"I'm no babysitter. Let us get to bed before we are useless tomorrow."* I throw myself onto his back letting him take my weight, "carry me." Flare gives a grunt but keeps walking with me draped half over his body. *"Esper you should really stop with the sweets, you are heavy."* I give a mock gasp of horror and slap the back of his big fuzzy head. "Over grown chia pet," I try to insult him but I feel his puzzlement over what a chia pet is.

Flare continues plodding on, and I watch feeling the blood rush to my head as we leave the garden into the entry way and through the office. We walk through the door on the left to the rooms. Barracks surround us with sleeping soldiers, who don't even crack their eyes open when we march through. At the back of the barracks is an archway that descends into the other rooms of the students that are littered through caves in the mountain. Even for it being nigh on lights out, the lanterns with balls of fire in them burn strong.

I snuggle into Flare's coat, a yawn splitting my face, as my eyes seem to get heavy and droop. "Hmm, Flare I think I shall sleep here." My speech slurs and I tug lightly on Flare trying to stay wake by focusing on the cave floor.

*

5 Days later…

Life marches on like it always does. My schedule brings about changes and such. Now as I progress in stealth, battle, and tactic those three classes are put to every second day and in their place I have music class, enchantments, and defense against magic. I enter for the first time into defense against magic, looking around at the people already seated. The room is set like a normal science class from on earth. I head for the middle, sitting at an empty bench an turn to the front, stopping short. Cara sat at the front lab bench, sitting on the top of the table. Her legs crossed making sure that the boys in the front bench and everyone else in the room's attention is singly on her.

Great...

Cara leans back throwing her long blond hair over her shoulder and gives such a fake laugh I grind my teeth. I see one of the guys in front of her is Jeremy, I can't believe he is falling for that fake. Cara catches sight of me and jumps off the lab to saunter over my way. I really don't like this girl. "So you finally made it, you're on my turf now. I am the master's assistant." She throws her hair over her shoulder and puts her hands on her hip. "Cara, I don't care I'm here to learn..." I feel like I'm swallowing a knife but I continue. "If you're good enough to be teachers assistant I can respect any advice you give me concerning this topic." I put on a poker face so I don't throw up in my mouth and ruin this fake truce I am trying for.

"Listen here princess. The only thing I will show you is the door." She leans in close her hair falling around us like a curtain, "you got that the only way we would ever be okay is if you are back in your own dimension." She turns throwing her hair over her shoulder, as she prances back to her drooling audience. Guys are so... predictable. Class gong goes off and the rest of the class rush to take their seat before the masters gets in, kind of like what goes on in an Earth high school.

Class starts out like any first day, roll call, class rules, and talking about the curriculum. When the time is up I know this class would have been a favorite but with Cara staring death into me, I have a feeling it won't be so nice.

*

Two days later…

Class starts no better, I mean what does this girl have against me besides I might have went on a date with her ex. So I was walking into class and knowing me I trip over my own feet and spill my water all down the front of me. I throw my hands in the air and try and dry my shirt as best as possible. My nemesis's cackle comes from the front lab bench, giving her oglers leave to laugh too. "Walk much?" What does that even mean?

Jeremy apparently wasn't completely hypnotized and even as she glared at him he comes over and helps me up. "You are such a klutz not like no one knows that. I'm surprised that you are any good at all this stuff." Cara calls from the lab, making a death sign at Jeremy and then turning her head away in a snub. "Ignore her, she wouldn't even bother to pick on you if she didn't see you as a threat." He wipes down my arms and looking at my soaked white shirt. What a day to choose to wear a thin white tank top. "You might want to send Flare for another top. In the mean time you might want to put your books up a bit." Jeremy always the gentleman advices, leading me away from the cackling group who laugh at my expense. I just want to die, no one like people laughing at them.

"Thanks, *you hear that Flare?*" I say the second half silently to my mind partners. "*Yeah, yeah, on my way, with all this tripping you do, I don't know how you aren't always in a cast.*" I see Flare ask for a pass from the teacher, and soon on his way to the dormitory.

I hear Cara's nerve grating laugh, uh so much for a truce I still want to strangle her. "How can you like her, she is so fake and easy. I'm sure that if you asked she would pull up her skirt for you." He snorts, I know it's petty but she shouldn't go out of the house naked if she didn't want the reputation. "*Meet me in by the door.*" Flare sends showing me the door to my class room, "Master Green may I go use the facilities?" I ask, sidling up next to him so only he can hear me. He looks up from his papers and waves me away before going back to grading.

Flare has the cloths folded neatly on his paws, and brushes against me before heading back to his own class. I go to the bathroom to change out of the top only to see the replacement isn't much of a top. It skin tight with slits across the sides and a low swooping neckline, in bright cherry red cut off at the midriff. *"Flare this is not a top, this is stooping to her level."*

I put it on over the wet tank top anyway; maybe two almost suitable shirts will make one wearable one. I walk back into the room, Master Green is explaining mermaids. Cara sits on the lab table with her tail out. It was a beautiful cherry red, which kind of pisses me off, and someone who's a bully shouldn't look so good. The cherry red tail has fins a thin gossamer webbing going down the back arch of the tail and merging into the big angelfish tail. The tail merges with her hips turning into her pretty skin turned slightly pink as they blend together.

She preens under the attention of the class, flicking her tail to and fro, while throwing her hair back. "Now, Merr people are often notoriously possessive and jealous, usually liking to stay under the water guarding their... belongings. Some of course are different," Master Green makes hand gestures to indicate not Cara. She notices at the last moment and scowls. I sneak over to my seat, the master giving me a nod. "Some Merr go bad and often try and sing sailors to their death by dazing them and pulling them from their boats, and drowning them, these Merr are called Banshees. Banshees are often thought of as a separate race, but are just Merr that have been corrupted by jealousy and as what Earth calls psychotic killers. There are not many but they are extremely hard to kill and blend in with the population of Mer."

Master Green moves to the board making an intense drawing of a Merr in one scene dazing a sailor and drowning him. The next in detail he draws the same Merr blending in to the population of Merr as armed Merr look for them. "Now you all know that usually each kingdom handles its own problems but with the killer aquatic we are not equipped usually to search, so the Merr king and Zar have a treaty. Now if you are ever in the water and you start to feel a daze coming over you, you are supposed to sing to block out the sound. Sing high and loud to block out the sound, while simultaneously finding things to plug your ears."

Master Green waves to Cara to put the tail away and she flaps her tail. The tail shimmers, slowly turning in on itself and splitting apart to reshape into her shapely legs. The typical guys you would see in the back of the class sleeping sat in the front mouth agape. I hate to admit it is impressive, and she knows it.

*

I meet Flare and Raja after classes in the paddock where all the dragons were trying to soak up the last of the summer sun as it slowly starts to sink into autumn. I lean back on my big dragon with a weary sigh, long day. The connection to these two means the world to me. "Esper, you know it's kind of weird to be sleeping in the middle of campus. Your stinking plan has us in trouble." The twins stand scowling in front of us. I can't help rubbing the sleep from my eyes. "What? How could you be in trouble?" I sit up, looking over at the twins whose usually laughing blue eyes are angry.

"You said we wouldn't get in trouble, did you lie? Lucan caught on." Dante pushes his hair from his eyes to glare better at me, making it seem kind of funny. "*How did you get in trouble?*" Raja insists getting curious about my scheming.

"Lucan caught on to what we were doing and laid a trap, making us prank Dean instead of him. He fed us false information which led to us almost being able to see our spines. If it wasn't for the teacher who gave Dean and us Detention we might have." Garrett heaves a sigh seeming to deflate, I can feel for him Dean is a huge mean kid older than me, with a temper to boot, but I need them.

"Boys this is just a minor setback. Now how dare Lucan do that to you, I mean doesn't it make you so mad." I move behind the twins talking in a low voice as I put my hands on their shoulders. "You will have to spend your night in detention while Lucan gets to go hang with Simone. I would be mad I mean who does he think he is you are the princes of pranks and mischief," I'm about to go on but they interrupt me.

"We are the Kings." They stand proud seeming angry over the slight to their honor in denouncing them to a lower rank. "Kings of course, and he thought he could dupe you guys, now if it was I, I would want pay back." I sow the seeds and see the light of revenge overcome them. Well that should keep Lucan away from his older crush.

"Now run along to detention before you get in trouble and get double." I squeeze the back of their necks before pushing them off towards the building designated to classes. I should feel bad, I know I shouldn't encourage it but hey a girl has needs and right now I need their evil minds.

"You are very devious, you know if they ever find out you manipulated them the revenge they heap on you will probably be very sticky and offal." Flare sits beside me content to stay out of my manipulations, "you know if I go down I'm taking you with me." I glance over, his head snaps up, *"there is no way they would believe I was a part of this! You wouldn't Esper, slime doesn't come out of the fur easy, I am forced to lick it off!"* Flare panics over the thought of the bath after but I just walk away shrugging to show that it means nothing, if I go down so do they.

"What do you mean 'they'? Esper, I do not want no part in this, I didn't say anything." Raja's shrill voice joins Flare,

"hey I told you if I go down I am taking you with me." I walk away blocking my humor from the bond so they can't tell that I'm laughing at them. I don't think that Dante and Garret will do anything. I mean just because they are getting revenge on Lucan for pranking them, they won't be mad I prodded them that way. Then again there was that time Yanni… I might be in big trouble if they find out.

*

A scream shatters the tranquility of the night waking everyone in the nearby vicinity. I roll off the pillow grabbing Saphique and head for the scream. The screams stop but I head for were most of the commotion is coming from, the reptilian bunks. People milled outside the cave entrances looking for what woke them suddenly in the middle of the night. "Who the hell put this in my bed, I want to know, right now!" Lucan's voice sounds angry as he demands answers. I walk in, and try to stifle my laughter, "you have a little problem Lucan?"

Lucan stands in the middle of the room with honey and synthetic feathers covering him from his spiked bleach blonde hair to his bare feet. His Hazel eyes spit fire around the room as he looks for the culprit for this feather disaster. I back up as my bare feet connect with something sticky on the ground; honey covers the ground and everything in the room along with so many feathers you would think we are in a pillow. The other occupants in the room are also similarly covered and none too happy about it. The snakes and other reptilian creatures seem none too happy with their new try to fly. I don't think feathers are their thing. Yeah he can never know I prodded the twins I don't need mad snakes in my bed.

Above in the top of the cave a giant bag had been extended, and a rope leading towards the door. I also take into account of the gigantic buckets stacked against the hall with residue honey. Yep, when the twins get revenge they aren't kidding they seem to have made their point not to screw with them mostly by not just getting the offender but those he has to live with. Those two evil geniuses' will be good at strategy when they get older.

"Esper did you have something to do with this? Where are those brats, I know this was them, they left their calling card!" Lucan looks wildly around only bothering to wipe the honey off his face before it reaches his eyes. He points to by the door a 2K, with a D and a G hanging from the letters. Well I must say those twins work fast and they sure worked hard, it must have taken them a lot of time pouring the honey over everything and everyone. I'm surprised they didn't wake anyone up when they poured the honey. This is also the first time I have heard anything about a calling card, interesting.

"I had nothing to do with this, did you do something to anger them…?" I can't help but hint, he looked so ridiculous, and I just want to rub it in. Lucan's eyes narrow and he glares at the calling card.

I turn away, leaving the reptilian bunkers to their plotting of revenge. I think I just started a war. I now know how puppet masters feel and it is quite a rush.

*

Eight days later…

The next few days prove entertaining, because of the attack on the reptilian bondeds they struck back at the bunk room Dante and Garrett are staying in. A counter attack was issued post haste between the reptilian bondeds and the eleven to twelve year olds. Soon pranks happen everywhere no matter which class all to get one member of the fraction, even if they didn't want to be a part of it. So far Dante and Garrett don't know I was a part of turning them against Lucan, so far I am safe.

*

Six months later….

The war between Lucan and his bunk mates against the twins and theirs has finally seemed to wind down. The prank war kept Lucan busy and left Simone and Dash to their romance making them happy as clams and going strong. Over the time Simone and I have become close, often double dating with some random guy on my side with a safe date. None of the guys seem to stick thou, and I just move along enjoying new friends that are easy to come by in droves here. Everyone is rather friendly both in campus and out in the city, waving and saying hello some even inviting us to try some food or over for dinner. I find myself hanging out with Ace a lot she knows all the places to be and those for a clean fun time.

But now the prank war has come to a truce, letting everyone give a sigh of relief and back to their studies. Life seems good my body finally seems to have adjusts to the work load and starts to feel good and like second nature. Stealth goes okay but I still trip a lot which is rather annoying. Magic defense is a drag who wants to spend every other day with Cara, I'm okay at it but far from the best. Everything else I do well just not worth going over, life goes into repetition, except on my off days I often go out on a hair brain adventure with Liam and his group.

Raja is a couple weeks from full growth, he finally stopped sprouting like a weed and now only grows a little, and he has made his own friends that seem to congregate around his vibe of power. Flare has reached full growth of the size of a fifteen hand horse with slightly extended canines then a normal leopard on Earth.

Today we have an outing to a far island. The plan is for dragons to drop us off at the island that is set up to have advanced training as an end of the year assessment. We get three days on the island to practice and survive as part of the end final and the final will be given, as a pass or a fail. The dragons have their own assessment along with the bondeds so the dragons will just drop us off before heading to their own finals.

We are allowed the option to bring rope, flint, and cloth, all not required but will give us better odds. Weapons not permitted, because it was a survival test using the skills we have learned. I have gymnastics, stealth, weapons training, hunting, tactics, and defense against magic, to use to find the scroll. On the scroll hidden on the island is what we are looking for. Whoever finds will become automatically graduated with honors, regardless your grades. They call it something else but can't remember. I just know that if you get the scroll and pass the assessment then you automatically get a bump in your profession.

The scroll is something that irritates the hell out of me. No one will tell me what's in the scroll, saying it's a rite of passage or something, cryptic much.

*

We load up on the dragons. I go to Raja planning on taking comfort from him until we get to the island. I feel naked, no sword or dagger, they literally searched us and had us hand over our clothing to check all stitching.

Our flight from the capital is rather short but we still travel out of sight of the city before we get to the four islands clustered in the middle of the ocean. Raja and the five other dragons circle over them before the others circle off into other directions. Raja fed with the directions from our advisor, a cheeky older fellow who says he is like six hundred years old, banks down to a soft sandy beach at the tip of the misshapen horse shoe island.

We all disembark and I size up what could be either my competition or my partners. Jeremy, in all his shaggy blonde hair and grey eyes… I don't really know his skills. I've never had a physical class with him. Simone jumps off which is typical that girl is like literally all legs. Simone brings brains, hunting, and stealth to the table. If we are to be enemies I would have to watch out she could be lethal if she ever gets over her sympathetic heart.

Asthenia is a nymph she isn't much to be worry about, she's too vain and sweet to be much of a threat, but she has a surprising ability to be able to stealth. I see Rav and Zed already on the beach taking in their surroundings. Zed is not human, I can tell from his snake Dred locks and gold glowing cat eyes. Zed's eyes are dark with slivers of yellow in them. He seems like a biker kind of guy.

Rav is all Merr more so then in looks then any I have seen so far. Rav has gills on the side of his neck and scales showing slightly up his arms, and on other places in random on his swimmer body. I think someone said that happens when you are born with a bit of another race in you it dilutes the ability to blend into both human and Merr. Both Rav and Zed are more brawns then brains, with muscular bodies, major amount of strength, skill with their respective weapons. They could be lethal but brains beats brawns, especially when I have a lesser but good amount of brawn to back it up.

Last but not least Eli floats down from Raja where he had been conserving his strength instead of flying himself. Eli has a lean mean fighting machine body, he's some species called the Argonians I have never heard about them before but apparently they are rare outside of the Slaver territory which use to be the Argonian's territory. Eli has big fluffy white wings, with the slightest dusting of gold on the feathers. Those feathers not only are on his wings, but also instead of hair he has black and red feathers going all the way to mid back, along with some on his arms up to his elbow.

I can scope him out well because he is wearing a red tank top with slits all the way down on the sides. Like the ones that were all the rage on earth. You can see all his muscles that literally look like they are stacked on top of the other, my guess from flight. I watch him during training fascinated by his uniqueness. He's good at stealth, gymnastics, strength, weapons, and just everything. He is going to be a major threat if I have to face him, he is not afraid to get dirty to get stuff done despite his quiet demeanor.

Our bag of bones advisor joins us on the ground. He doesn't seem to liking it very much as he gets sand in his gladiator sandals and stands there shaking them out and cursing. "Now your job is... blast this stupid sand!" Our advisor growls as he hops some more and we take pity and move up a deer path onto the rocky bluff.

"Your job is to find the scroll. It's been hidden somewhere on this island. You need to work together to get to the scroll first and locate it, however you go about it is your business, Liam will be overseeing and not to help. We will be watching, you are competing in five groups. The scroll will help you advance in your chosen profession farther in the beginning then you normally would. Use your strengths. You can do it however you want as long you do it together. That is the main objective but also you have to survive, no one has found the scroll in ten years so good luck. If no one finds it before the allotted week you will be taken home for evaluation on your grades." The advisor humps trying to think, turning to leave before thinking of something.

"Oh your clue is, 'where the Merr pray', being you have a Merr with you might help yea." The advisor leaves, hunched over as if all the wrinkles are pulling him down, and shambles down the beach followed by cursing over the "goddess damn sand." I can't help chuckle as I hear Zed making imitations of the old man.

I turn back to my new companions. They glance around as we unconsciously had formed into a circle. I glance up as Raja leaves for his own test on another island or something. *"Good luck."* I send I don't know if he heard me but I feel better for having said it. My attention turns back to the young warriors as they glance around sizing everyone up like I had.

I know what they will see when they look at me, auburn hair curling to below my waist, amethyst eyes that have taken to glowing apparently a sign of an attachment to two souls. I also have a slightly rounded face, with large lips, curvy with a bit of muscles, and topping at five foot five inches. I had dressed in a long sleeve corset that usually houses my daggers, finished with loose fitting breaches for fluid movements.

"I think we should appoint someone overall leader, so we have someone to make snap decisions." Simone looks around seeming to weigh everyone out. "Any candidates?"

Everyone looks from one another trying to see who would be better in the heat of the moment. "I nominate, Simone, Esper or Eli, I mean who would me or Rave. Be kidding we don't have the skills needed, he's too much of a pretty boy and so is Asthenia well…." Zed waves his arm down the front of himself, as if it explains it all. Eli starts shaking his head before Zed finishes, "I want none of that." I don't really want to either after all the awful decisions I had to make. But I have a bad feeling as Simone joins Eli in shaking her head.

"I do not want to be leader, just be the one to point out when they are wrong. That leaves you to Esper. We need ideas to the clue." Simone hands me a map the advisor gave her on the flight over. The map shows the island showing the forest, tidal pools, caves, and steam pools in 3D.

"So what you guys know about the Merr?" I turn to Rav who is the obvious choice, even for his entire pretty boy Merr-ness. "Well we… uh… spend seven tenths of our life in the water and the other third on land so the most likely chose for a prayer area would be on the ocean floor. But that would be obvious, for all we know they built a prayer circle in the middle of the island. All I really know is Merr use to live here like thousands of years ago. Don't know why they left or anything." Rav gives a big shrug, tussling his shaggy bleach blonde hair and his blue eyes dancing with excitement.

"Okay, well he wouldn't have given us the clue if it could be anything. Merr are about water so it's safe to say it's going to be near the water." I think out loud trying to filter information. "Well if you have ever been to their cities a lot of their structures are column based, I didn't see any columns when we approached the island." Simone calls in. I can see the whirling going on in Simone's eyes as she tries to think through the clue. "So it's most likely on land, what you think these red dots are?" She points out the dots one where we are, two more on this side of the island close by and others randomly around the edge of the island never near the tide pools or steam pools.

"I think this is us, and the others, my best bet is the prayer place will be somewhere over there. First off we need to think about food and weapons." I look around, "Well with the special rope I brought I can make a bow but I need to have something to carve it." Simone gives me a pained look but shrugs rather not liking having the answer. I lean down picking up a sharp rock, "this will have to do while we hunt down a bone. I remember lessons about how some Indians, used to use them as knives. I doubt there is very much to eat around here." With the entire bonded situation I am unclear on what is okay to eat. I glance over seeing Liam sitting on a log and studying us.

"I looked it up. The only things to eat are fish, boar, and curry." Asthenia quips she is unwilling to be unimportant. "Alright then, I'm going to leave you, to go and kill a curry or a boar with my bare hands. Eli and Zed you want to come?" The boy's perk up, seeming to like the idea. "What's a curry?" I ask looking at Zed, "Curry is a very furry long snouted creature, bigger than a man, with big claws and teeth. It likes to get on its back legs and attack." Zed tells me vividly enough I see the picture he is painting and sounds like a bear.

The best way I can see taking a bear down with no weapons would be using rope. Throw the rope around the bear until it can't move and capture it. I guess we could find a way to kill the bear then. I relay my thought to the guys. The guys exchange looks but nod slowly, unable to think of anything better. "Zed, anyway we can get you to get one of your snakes to bite it?" Zed pales at the suggestion but shrugs, always the brave one.

Well if I had to be thrown on an impossible dangerous island, I'm glad my groups brave. Twenty minutes later we come across a curry snuffling around a bush full of berries. The curry was large in stature and looks like a full grown grizzly. I see Zed pale farther from the corner of my eye.

"Eli, since I don't think any of us is good at lassoing. You are going to need to fly over and drop the lines around its neck and throw the lines to us we will tie them off and move to our next." Eli nods using his wings to get into the higher up branches of a tree above us.

Zed slinks off into the brush to head to his position while I watch and wait by my tree focusing on Eli. I can't see him anymore but I can see the ropes drop around the bear's front two paws. The beast snarls in confusion, but in the next fraction I have the end and begin tying it around the tree pulling it taunt and pulling its opposite leg out from under him. The other leg on my side goes out from under the bear/ curry, before he sprawls with his head in the dirt in utter confusion. On earth two ropes would be insufficient but in Pangaea some rope are enchanted to cause the person being tied momentary paralysis and are fortified.

We approach carefully none the less, the bear/curry struggling in vain to free his body. I motion Zed to the big beast. He pauses for a second before getting close enough to the beast for the bite. Zed crosses himself in a way I have often seen others do to ask forgiveness to their goddess. Before one of the largest snakes on his head leaned down and sank its dripping fangs into the captured creature. I force myself to watch the fangs sink deep seeming to penetrate the thick fur, we watch in sadness as the curry's struggles slow. After a bit his thrashing stops all together as the poison reaches his heart.

I bow my head in honor of the poor creature, thanking it for its use in our survival.

"Wont the poison that killed him kill us?" I muse, horror filling me at the thought of doing this again.

"Never has before, why do you think medusa's are the best hunters?" Zed calls.

"Get under the thing. We need to drag it back to the beach." I get under its shoulders. Eli unties the rope from the trees. Zed joins me taking part of the curry's weight, before Eli joins us getting the back end. We stumble off back to the rocks, making little progress with the bear like creature on our shoulders. Rav joins us taking some of our burden, letting us breathe a little more easily until we are able to drop it on the rocks above the beach. I have new appreciation for old time mountain men.

Simone sets to using a rock to bust open the skin and get to the meat and bones that we will need. I can't stomach watching this bloody and gruesome process so I pick my way down rocks to the beach where the surf beats at the sand. "I can't tell you a lot but I can say I think it was smart to get the curry." Liam drops onto the sand beside me. "Yeah, well after being here it's hard to eat anything that you have to kill. I think I have gone soft hearted." I sigh knowing I am being a little dramatic. Liam gives a snort at the comment. I shoot him a glare back for the slight.

"I just wanted to encourage you, and being chosen leader is a good sign, means they might be more willing to recruit you to a higher position when you join the army at the border." Liam encourages, throwing a rock into the frothing waves that are cast many colors from the setting sun. "I don't think I want that, I think I should still work my way up, not that I have a choice. I have a feeling I will just be going where Raja does and Flare shall follow. Not that I don't think if I couldn't stand war or this life Raja wouldn't give everything up for us, give up his kingdom." I sigh so much for a small insignificant life. Would I have been content with a small life? I have a feeling I would be hopelessly bored.

*

Simone seems to have stripped the curry of its meat in record time. As soon as she got a bone out that was usable to make into a weapon she gave them to the boys to start sharpening. They didn't look that bad, after being sharpened they would work about as good as a dull knife which will have to work in a scrape. We sleep the night on the beach before planning our next step in this test.

"I think that our best bet would be to go to the tide pools, investigate and if we don't find anything today there we shall move on to the steam pools." I glance around, also shoving all our meat and supplies we have collected into our sacks. "Esper I think our best bet is to actually to start with the steam pools, I won't bore you with the particulars but fact is that the prayer area will most likely be there." Rav speaks up, tying his pack onto his belt.

"Well sense you are the specialist on this, steam pools it is." I finish up and tie the bag to my own belt. Simone grabs the map and starts leading the way to the steam pools, "We should be there by lunch."

*

"Are we there yet," Asthenia repeats for the hundredth time sense we passed the tide pools. "We already passed some of those pool things, why aren't we there yet!" Zed turns and rails at her for the also hundredth time, "and we are here." Simone calls to get them to shut up and pay attention. I was feeling a migraine build on my brain, why can't they just shut up. The trees part showing pools randomly placed on craggy rocks with steam meandering up from the pools.

"Liam, do you miss the connection with Veevia?" I stand back of the group as everyone else goes to look into the closest pool. I turn to Liam who stands next to me thou. "Of course I miss it, this island has a field that numbs the bond, it is disconcerting but I knew that coming into this. She knows it too, I also know that this is only for three days, I don't think that I would be able to go about this much longer." Liam sighs, I know he is trying to word it the best he can. I don't blame him for not being able to say it right.

"Yeah I guess, I just feel it doubly so, I don't know what I would do or how I would go on if I had to feel this numbness for a long time. I wonder if this is what it would feel like to lose a bonded." I rub my hands over my neck, "I guess so, but I pray you never have to feel it." Liam pats my shoulder and leaves me to my thoughts as he goes to see what the others have uncovered. I head over to the group. Some are sticking their bare feet into the pools to feel the blissful heat from the hot springs.

"Rav, you willing to dive into these and see if one has no end? Simone you have any ideas how you guys are going to be able to breath under water." Simone walks to the side and sits with her feet in the water, enjoying the warmth as she loses herself into thought. Rav presses two fingers to his chest and then raise's them to us before diving into the steaming pool, his tail transforming in midair.

"Why do you turn to her, how do you know I don't know the answer?" Asthenia's indignant squawk sounds next to Liam. "Do you?" Zed asks, turning to her from his spot peering into the pool.

"As a matter of fact I do, there is a creature indigenous to this island that when you ingest the heart, you take on properties to the creature, one of which is surviving in water. I believe in earth some of the creatures actually existed and a culture made it common practice to take on their properties, before they went extinct." We gape at the apparently not so dense Barbie. She fluffs her hair and sits pretty.

"Well sense you are the expert on these things then you can take Zed with you to find them, you'll need enough for four. Hurry so that you will be back by the time we find the right hole." Asthenia pouts and looks longingly back towards a pool before trudging after Zed to find the creature.

"Why only four?" Simone comes up by my shoulder as we wait. "I can breathe under water sense Raja has the property for water, so does Veevia which means it passes to Liam so he can watch, and Rav is a Merr so we can all survive that just leaves you four sorry five in need of a means to survive." Simone nods for a second. I turn my attention from her and start stripping off my pants and my corset like top. "What are you doing?" Liam clears his throat and I see him turn his back from the corner of my eye.

My fingers untie the knot keeping the strings to the corset top in place, and I slide it over my head, letting it fall on top of my breaches. "I am going to go help but I don't feel like getting my only pair of cloths wet." Now standing in my lacy underwear I move to the adjacent hole. I should feel weird about undressing in front of the guys but after bathing in lakes with groups of friends they kind of shot my need for privacy out the window. "I know I can't ask you to help sense you are only an observer, and two people looking is a lot better than one. There are a lot of goddess damn holes to cover, if you need me send word down the hole." I joke sliding my legs into the water. I retie my long hair up to keep it so it won't get to matted, before sliding all the way into the water. I tread water long enough to give the Pangaea means of a salute and diver under the water.

I swim down farther even as my human lungs start to feel rather uncomfortable. I have to trust that it will work again. But what if it only works when I am in contact with Raja, this isn't exactly my ability. I miss simple life, no breathing under water, no searching for paper in water. I breathe the water in, letting my longs contract and I get the burning feeling that I got before. I really hope this works. I can't even feel the bond… I really hope that doesn't nullify the bond. I see darkness clinging to the edge of my vision. I blink rapidly to clear them until my eyes refocus to show the vivid scene hidden in the steam pool.

Bright florescent neon plant life clings to the rocks, some looks like they could be indigenous to Earth, but others look like some of the weird stuff that you see in fantasy movies now a days. My neck itches like I have fire ants climbing over me. I bring my hand up the itchy place trying to feel if I have a leach on me or something.

"Or something is correct." My neck is bumpy, but doesn't feel as if it is harboring some blood sucking creature, instead I feel muscle and scales where my once smooth neck used to be. I feel it out, either I'm delusional or I have gills on the side of my neck. I beat my feet a couple of times to keep moving only they feel strange. I glance down to see my feet look stretched out like a roller has gone over them and webbing on them. I could really use Raja or Flare right now to tell me what the hell is going on. Not that I can't guess I mean this is why I practically drowned myself.

I survey the cave I'm in, it's rather just a large tube, but there is a small whole leading somewhere outside of the cave tube. I swim over. It looks like I can fit through but if it doesn't go anywhere I am so totally screwed. I wiggle in anyways knowing the risks. I use my webbed hands to push my way through the narrow tubing that runs horizontal from the pools cave.

The tube goes on for several minutes before I finally come out into a lighter similar cave.

"Esper what are you doing in here? Did Simone figure out how to let you breathe under water? You look rather fetching as a half Merr." Rav calls from surveying the underwater cave. "Oh, no they are still looking. Raja gives me the property of being able to breathe under water. I was looking at another under water cave and it led me here, I guess we can check that one from the list." I ignore his comment on my looks pointedly. I have no clue what other changes have come about me, for all I know I have fangs and a nose that grows when I lie.

"This is good, but we probable want someone to mark off the pools we have looked over it wouldn't do for us to always be repeating all of them and the ones the other does." Rav runs his fingers though his hair, his big green tail lightly fanning the water. His tail is huge, a sea foam green with scales all over it. It has a common angel fish end, with the wide wispy… webbing like that of an angel fish.

Rav follows my gaze to his tail, "you like? It is considered rather strapping in my kingdom for size. the only better tail to have would be that of a wale or a shark, I researched your dimension." Rav explains while puffing up his bare chest in pride over both his accomplishment and his beautiful tail.

"It is beautiful, I haven't seen a lot of Merr tails but beautiful none the less. I must admit that Cara also had a pretty cherry red tail." Rav chuckles, but also seems to make a face at the mention of the big headed Merr.

"Red symbolizes a Merr most likely to turn Siren, she had the option to be watched over by our king's advisor for mental checkups or spend most of her time on land to get assessed up here, and she chose Pangaea. The kingdom did not always like letting others know that some of us are faultier then others." Rav signs, his tail beating the water harder. "I think we should go talk with Simone we do not have time for more chit chat before we lose all light." Rav grabs my arm, pulling my up with him. He pushes to the surface at a more rapid paces then I would have been able to have gone.

As of breaking the surface, my eyes go black again to readjust to the light. My skin gets the itchiness as my gills retract back to whence they came. Am I really mentally unstable in some hospital or something because this is all really farfetched, and perfect?

"Simone we need you to draw up a map of the pools so you can check them off." Simone nods, already using a stick to make the diagram, only glancing back at us once. "Eli went to go scout around, he said to tell you that almost every one of the groups are at the tide pools or searching the beaches and rocky places in pursuit of the cave. It won't be long before one shows up here, he's out watching them now." She turns away, biting her lip as she draws a diagram of our surrounding area. The other teams could be a problem, no telling if what they will do.

"Rav stay with her to mark the ones you have covered and the one I covered. I'm going over to that one." I point out the one close to the pool I had started in, but in the opposite direction of the tube I had followed. Rav nods pointing to four on the diagram, and Simone starts drawing an R and E on some of the pools with an X to show it was a no go.

I don't stand on ceremony I dive straight into the warm water, blinking before I hit the water. My vision clears fast and the itchy feeling is less intense and quicker, before I am back to as Rav put it my half Merr self.

This pool's cave goes only a little to the bottom. Which I follow down anyway, in hope of a tunnel or some sign that it once had one. After finding no opening or rubble of a past opening I swim back up, catching Simone's attention I make an X with my arms and move to the next one over, she waves me on instead to the one after that, I assume Rav is already in there so I move over another. She nods, but I stop again, Rav pops up giving Simone a double X before getting out and heading to the next. I move one forward to a higher part of pools that seem to go in rows like stairs. On a hunch I head all the way up.

"Esper what are you doing I thought you were going in rows?" Simone calls up, but I ignore her. At the top of the pyramid of steam pools are two pools, both looking exactly the same? "Rav you want to come give me a hand with this hunch of mine?" Rav comes quickly, seeming to clue in on my idea on the way. If I'm not that just means we cleared two more.

"You take this one, I'll take that one?" Rav nods and jumps into the one closest to the forest while I take the one closest to the sea. This water cave starts out like any other, with the exotic flowers and such, with a person size tunnel traveling down and towards the cave Rav was searching. I follow the cave through it slants down and around in a zig zag pattern until it opens up to a long downward tumble, the water seeming to have an air pocket that makes the water rush faster than normal. I'm pushed down and into Rav's waiting arms.

"Oh you all slick now... oh shut up." Rav gives me his cheeky smile, I can't stop the smile in reply, stupid handsome Merr. "I figured you were going to come out of there, you have to see this." Rav grabs my arm and pulls me down a big tunnel that was shaped in a Y, one being the way he had come, one I can see leading out into the ocean and another going far under the other steam pools.

"Why do I have a feeling you found it?" The tunnel is lined with more and more of those luminescent neon flowers lighting our way. The giant tunnel opens up into an even bigger room, filled with pillars and altars like an ancient temple that had been destroyed.

"I think we should go get the others." Floating over one of the alters is our prize a scroll encased in a bubble,

"Rav stay and guard it okay?" I push one of our bone daggers in his hand and push him to the scroll.

Rav's face goes serious and his body gets a ridged posture as he looks around. I swim for all I'm worth to the steam pool surface. Simone glances up as I burst from Rav's steam pool. "Have they returned yet? You need to see this. We need to get it as a team." Simone nods calling back into the woods, Zed, Eli, and Asthenia, coming out with odd lizard creatures slung over their shoulders.

"Come on eat your lunch and don't expect to get the twenty minute waiting time." I call down. Asthenia gives me a withering look, Zed already had his lizard cut up and its heart out. I watch with unwavering attention at the horrible image of Zed putting the lizard heart to his mouth and chewing slowly. His face contorts into a mask of dislike. Asthenia wasn't as quiet she puts the lizard in her mouth and starts making the whiny noises, trying to plug her nose, and talk about her gross meal all at the same time. Eli didn't seem even fazed he just ate it.

I missed Jeremy and Simone's reaction as my attention had been on the other three, when I did turn my gaze to them they had already hidden the lizard carcasses, and wait for the others to follow suit. My gills have receded but my webbed legs kicking back and forth so that I can stay above water. "Jeremy, you think you can keep up with me now?" Jeremy glances up briefly from his climb to me.

"I'm not worried about that, I think you shall be the one having a hard time keeping up." He gives me a cocky grin, coming to a halt standing over me.

"Uh guys, do you really think it is the best idea for me a person made to fly try and go into an underwater cave?" Eli glances down at the blue water that fades to black. "Not like you have a chose it is a group activity so I have a feeling we ALL have to be there to get the scroll." I put stress on all so that he knows there is no way out of it. Eli lets out a *humph,* but none the less jumps into the pool next to me, Jeremy joining right after.

"Guys come on I feel the need for a warm bed, just cause we have a couple more days to keep looking doesn't mean we have to use them." I splash my hands in the water, stirring it till a tiny whirl pool starts to form around my finger. I kind of lied, the water doesn't make me long for anything besides to maybe stay in it. After the last person hits the water I dive under waiting till I see everyone breathing and to let my own super power thing take effect, before I rocket down the tunnel I had come from. I'm not as fast as Rav but that's why I had him stay down there.

The others follow slower seeming to only have gills or whatever from the creature so they have to try and swim with hands and no webbing. Eli seeming to have the most trouble with his sodden feathers, I swim briskly back beside him. "Grab my arm," Eli gives me a small smile and takes my arm, and I pull him alongside the others, my speed reduced to theirs. I wish we could go faster I just have this anxious feeling at the pit of my stomach like if we don't hurry we will be too late.

Our slow progress doesn't bear fruit for a while, moving even slower as the ogle the vibrant flowers and foliage on the cave walls. I let out a sigh of relief when we reach the prayer temple of the Merr. "Took you long enough, uh Esper we have company." I look back to the corner of the room where a person floated, a spear aimed at Rav's heart. "I try to grab the scroll. I can't get my hand through the bubble." Rav keeps talking even as the person thrust his spear at him and warns him to stop talking.

Rav has his hands raised to the air, his bone dagger tucked into his belt. "Rav put your hands down, that spear or any thrown weapon down here is useless." I move to swim next to him by the scroll. The others make a ring around the scroll. "Grab the scroll when I say now, tell the others." I lean over slightly to whisper into Eli's ear, he in turn leans over to whisper into Simone's ear and on and on.

"You have no leg up in this situation," I call down to the boy-man, his long blonde hair swirling around his head. The boy-man scowls unhappy with me for calling his bluff swimming forward with his spear at his side. "Now we end this." I scream back as I rotate around thrusting my hand through the bubble the same time as the others. Our hands go through, I'm glad that my hunch paid off. My hand wraps around the scroll but I stop short off pulling it out, "Simone, we have a problem."

Simone nods, "I see it, um if it was impossible to take out they wouldn't have put it here, I think we just have to pull it through and hope its water charmed." I might seem like I am ignoring the boy-man but in actuality I make sure to keep one eye on him.

I pull my hand through with the scroll clutched in my white knuckles. Rav cries out, I look over my shoulder to see blood floating through the water like a halo around him.

"I thought you said that he was bluffing." Rav cries distracting me from the dry scroll I am holding me. "It must have been enchanted, how was I supposed to know? I got it lets go he no longer has a spear to throw at us." Rav picks up the spear that only grazed him and we advances to the man who looks rather awkward now he no longer has a spear to throw at us.

I don't allow my back to turn to the crazy spear throwing man, as my team swims out of the tunnel, to the steam pool. I notice Asthenia trying to swim out to the ocean instead of to the steam pools. I grab her arm pulling her back towards the rising path to the open steam pool. Bursting forth faster than I normally have shocks my system as my gills and fins transform back to my smooth skin no longer flattened.

Eli pushes past me jumping out of the pool in what can only be shear relief. He moves fast despite that sodden feathers covering his body. "You can move when you want to," I tease clutching the scroll as I lift myself out of the water and away so that I can make room for the others to get out. "Uh, I never want to do that again, I like the sky, water is not for me." Eli all but gets down on the ground and starts kissing it. I push him over so that he goes sprawl on the rocky ground.

"What does it say?" Simone pushes herself up beside me, looking at the dry scroll. "I don't know would you like to find out." I break the seal pulling it open, taking in the gibberish on the page for a second not even comprehending what it says. "Hey I think you have something of ours!" I glance up seeing another of group of our fellow class mates, "too late, Multa enim sunt, ut unum succedere." A shock zaps through the air rocking everyone backwards.

A dragon lands next to us on the rock. "So team five wins, that's nice... blah, blah, blah, an old man can't keep flying out here. There used to be a time that I had to give a big elaborate speech, thankfully I'm too old for them to yell at for not, now board the dang dragons. You have classes to take until you are placed in your new jobs or positions." Our advisor calls from on top of Quinavar, who just seems bored. He proves not to be, giving me a wink before settling down a little farther. Well talk about dramatic that winds down to nothing.

"Winning team allll a board," I climb on grabbing one of the silk ties that make up a harness the dragons use to carry people. "Quinavar, what did it mean on the scroll?" I poke him to get his attention, "Uh, in your world you call it Latin the rough translation is … uh, for the many to succeed they need to work as one, a quote that is something to live by. Not a hundred percent sure that the wording is all right you know it's not a common language in any dimension anymore. If you ask me I think they use it to be more dramatic." Quinavar chuckles, I can feel his chest vibrate under us.

*

13

Two months later...

Not much happens just concluding classes to finish our training. Raja has grown to full growth of a medium plus dragon, Zar says he will grow maybe a little more and be between medium and like giant heavy weight, roughly around the size of a very big one story house maybe one and half. Flare seems to have stopped growing at the size of a fifteen hand horse a nice size for a leopard apparently. Raja eats and sleeps so much in the time I don't know how he can even get in the air but apparently when I'm in gymnastics, battle classes, stealth, hunting, and flying fighting he manages.

Nothing interesting much happened between then and now except Liam and I become faster friends. Classes are interesting and we progress more and more rapidly, even though we have finished the basic courses. The history class I have first thing in the morning sounds so farfetched from what is believed on earth that it makes it all the more fascinating and easier to remember. Why couldn't earth classes be like these I have no clue but if they had I would've been out of school at like age five.

I haven't heard anything from Ray after that one date. it was like one moment he was into me and the next I don't exist. I know what they guys said, some super secret mission but come on a letter would be nice so instead I move on. To top it off I have to deal with his crazy ex trying to make my classes a living hell. When I mention Liam and I have become fast friends I'm talking about how it isn't uncommon for people to find Liam and Veevia asleep on our pillow. Raja seems to enjoy having some other dragon's sleep with him, kind of makes me wonder if dragons are herd bound. Lately thou Veevia can't sleep with us because Raja's size just won't allow it, she opted to go sleep elsewhere.

Veevia thou, has seemed to stop at the smaller medium dragon size, about one story, and I have a feeling she makes up her size with speed. If Raja could work it out thou he would have Remidus, Veevia, Apolala, and Grocin his four best friends sleeping with him at all times.

Raja is also hell bent to do something about it.

So at our next meal with Raja's parents, he brings it up, *"Father I know you are rather busy with running the kingdom and protecting us from those slave traders who lurk our border. But if I could have your ear for but a moment."* Zar looks curiously from his meal and nods, finding it weird that Raja is rambling so much. "*I would like you to get rid of the separate pillows in the dragon cave, I think we all but need Sithonium and heat under it and we can be just perfect. I know me and others who must sleep on separate pillows would much rather enjoy the shared sleeping area.*" Raja tries to act confident but I can feel the nervousness in his head. I have no clue what he is talking about an kind of afraid to ask while he is on a mission. I do get most though, I find it cute that he is trying to be the perfect son.

"*I think it's a grand idea but you will have to of course get the okay of each dragon first because some might not like to get rid of their pillow in exchange of a shared sleeping area.*" Zar looks proud of Raja for coming up with such a grand idea and licks the blood off his jaw from his meal. Wow, sometimes I forget I am surrounded by carnivorous dragons and predators bigger than me.

"*Of course, I wouldn't dream of it,*" Raja all but vibrates until the end of the meal and he can put his plan into action. I feel all the ideas in his mind pushing about in his need to go into action, it is quiet distracting.

"Raja you need to ask and not just tell because some might think it rude and automatically say no." I advise him soothing him by patting his side and move out of the way so he can go.

Raja jumps into the air with all due haste and wings his way towards the academy and the dragons who are there getting extra flying practice in. "Flare, I think we did something right raising that boy." I joke, threading my fingers through the big leopard's fur as we make our way back at to the academy at a more sedate pace.

The market is turning in for the day, the shop owners putting down their steel shutters that can withstand anything and doing likewise to the serpent holes. The few shop owners wave as we walk by and call a sleepy greeting before shuffling into their houses. Some children who refuse to go to bed run down the street with their mothers calling after, be it human or a type of creature.

We have only made it to the gate of the academy when Raja and every single dragon that is staying at the academy take flight over me to go the palace.

"Looks like he got those 'Okays' he was looking for," Flare just purrs and heads towards the sleeping area which I have a feeling would get very social really fast. "Hey wait up, ungrateful house cat." I mutter to myself, following after the uncaring feline, a smile pasted on my face.

*

Everything is rather fun sleeping between Raja and Flare toasty warm for all the other dragons draped over them. It is rather good their tails are armored because when I got up in the morning it is impossible not to step

343

on one. Then we go to breakfast, classes, and then dinner, then sleep or off to spend time off campus like at a shop in the market.

We have been invited to a dinner that Zar has called to celebrate the birth of Raja's egg and the egg bonding between of us, he has invited lots of people, including all their friends and ours.

I sit at the high table, in a beautiful ankle length gown that has the same design as the one I wore on that date with Ray. This one is royal blue and fades to black on the bottom. I enjoy the conversation of Zar and Raja because it just makes him so happy. "Can we get a muzzle over here? Come on it was an honest mistake why did you have to bring Ceribi into this!" Garret whines. They had gotten in trouble again, this time they had given their teacher an exploding book, saying it was the wrong book that they meant to give it to Lucan.

I gave them that look and then grin when Ceribi keeps chattering on about how they have tried to fly when they were a pup but found out the hard way they didn't have wings or magical hovering powers.

"Come on E, dance with me!" Liam grabs my hand and twirls me onto the dance floor with a laugh. While we have our dances so did each type of creature. Some are more successful than others. The dragons opt to keep their dancing for the skies.

Liam twirls me to break me out of my musings. "You aren't paying attention to me," he pouts, "no one ever pays attention to me!" I laugh as he twirls me around and an exaggerated dip. "I seriously doubt that. I think you get lots and lots of attention. Especially when you smile or look towards the ladies, sometimes even when you aren't looking." I tease.

Liam chuckles and dips me, "well you don't pay attention so much." Liam picks me up and twirls us around that I couldn't help but squeal. "Oh well I think you get plenty of it why do you need another fawning fan? I'm not that type, I like to think myself the supportive fan." Liam puts me down as the song changed to the waltz and we take position. "May I cut in?" A voice I haven't heard in a while sounds behind Liam.

"Of course but I claim the next one, who else am I going to get a laugh from?" Liam bows to me and heads to some of said fawning ladies to invite one to dance, typical for him he heads for the pretty blonde. "Hello Esper?" I turn to Ray who looks all strapping in his tux, just not fair. I don't say a word.

"Well I didn't expect a warm greeting but this is just down right frigid." Ray pretends to shiver and holds his hand towards me as the song plays. We are already behind the others. I can't help the reluctance I feel to accept, I mean he did not show his face for over eight months after our date. I may be totally guessing on the number but hey I have that right. It's weird that it is only at the end of what we would call autumn.

"I wanted to apologize I really enjoyed our date but I was called away to help protect the borders. It would seem the slavers are trying to invade from under sea but we have more of an advantage and we need to scare them away from ever trying to use that route again." Ray whispers against my ear as we go through the steps of the waltz.

"I know but you could've sent word…" I mumble.

"Well you have every right I should have sent word that I would have been gone for a while…. I see you and Liam are far closer now. It's my fault. If I had staked my claim you wouldn't be falling for him!" He rambles, even stuttering in his steps and stepping on my foot, "CRAP! I'M SOO SORRY!" He sounds so embarrassed I can't help laugh even thou I was slightly angry over the mention of 'claim'. Who does he think he is even if it's kind of cute. Relationship politics are far more gruesome and confusing then political politics.

"First of all I am fine and secondly no one is going to stake their claim on me I am not a piece of property. Also Liam and I are friends if he wanted to be more he had better clue me in, but in the end it will still be my choice. I think I am going to go sit with Raja." I leave him standing on the edge of the dance floor to go sit next to

Raja who is now talking to his friends who are chattering away talking about the war down on the border that is happening against the slave traders.

I look around surveying each of Raja's close friends. There is Apolala, known as Api the only female dragon in Raja's circle. Api is crimson with a black fade on each limb, she also has a few streaks of gold sporadically over her body. She is a mix of the heavily armored dragon and a sleek flier, and she is the smallest in the group at about the size of an elephant and some extra.

Remidus the dragon who is for sure Raja's favorite, has grown bigger than Raja, he is still white with his black fade and speckles but now he has grown into all his limbs and doesn't seemed inclined to stop growing anytime soon, he is about two thirds the size of a heavy dragon at the moment. Remidus will probably end up being abnormally wide and tall enough that he will be in two stories or more.

Then there is Grocin, he is all sleek and preparing to be an amazing flyer and spy, he is tones and shades of grey that seem when he stands against rocks to blend into them. But he also has a bad case of spitting out everything he is thinking with no forethought, not so good in a spy.

"I hear that Dran will be coming soon, he is going to look over the newest dragons to take to the front, and apparently the slavers have found a new supplier in getting them dragon eggs. Also new means in catching dragons and keeping them,

who could do such a thing I have no clue." Remidus growls in agitation. He twitches his tail so much so that he nearly took the head off a passing cougar.

"*What if we get killed? Or worse captured while we are there, but would the worse fate be not getting chosen to go, we would be the laughing stalk of dragons.*" Grocin worries on as usual, nothing new there. "*Oh my goddess what if they steal my cake!*"

"*Grocin you know you are not supposed to even be eating cake it gives you gas! We are the ones who have to sleep next to you!*" Apolala groans and shifting her weight away from him, Api rather likes to tease Grocin good naturedly without end.

"*Well how else are we going to prove ourselves, I have talked to father and he has told me that I will be starting with you and no advancement is assured, so I will have to work my way up like anyone else. I find comfort in it knowing that. I don't want to rule my people by having to accept handouts or have someone basically rule for me because I don't know the way of my own military.*" Raja looks rather pleased until Grocin decides to voice his concern.

"*Dran is your older brother right? What if he hates you because you took his spot at heir to the throne, I mean he is already one hundred years old and to know that your birth right was given to someone else... why did they give it to you?*" Raja visible deflates, shrugging his shoulders.

Dran's disinheritance is a well-kept secret that we only hear because we are friends with someone who overheard it.

"*SHUT UP, GROCIN!*" Api yelled, she even launching herself at him even thou he is bigger and she holds his muzzle shut. I can't say I blame her it also gave Raja leave from having to answer and possible lie to keep the shameful secret of his brother.

"Raja, I am sure you, Flare, and I will pass the test and be taken to the front line… and if your brother doesn't love you now, he must love you when he gets to know you!" I look back around, to see almost everyone looking curiously at Api still sitting on top of her flier friend. "Api, get off Grocin." The young female did with a final growl at Grocin. Grocin could have pushed her off but I have a feeling he doesn't because, he one part likes her and the other part is scared of her.

"*Let everyone go take to their seats now, because dinner is to be served in a few minutes.*" Zar's voice booms over the crowd.

I am seated between Raja and Flare, I can see everyone else because Zar has made the seating as best as he could into a circle, but of course in special cases are rather accommodating, like placing a table on top of the water for the aquatic animals that can't leave the water.

Half way through the meal someone throws open the doors bringing a gust of cold wind and rain in with them.

A dragon of white gold with a gold ruff that seems to be translucent stands ominously in the doorway. He has bejeweled talon sheaths that clink as he walks. The sheaths seem also to have dried blood caked on the points. The dragon is mostly sleek but also seems to have very few spikes. But it would seem no spikes on his tail for he has another modified sheath on it to add spikes and other things such as jewels. The tail sheath contraption looks extremely grim, I can see that what is holding it on are their 'version' of steal, gouged into his tail, his tail's skin and scales grown around it.

Zar stands but instead of acting as if this dragon is there to kill them he welcomes him, but more like welcomes in a sarcastic I'm thinking anything but in a kind of way. *"Dran, my eldest son has returned."* Zar's speech sends everyone into the hall in a moderate cheer to welcome the eldest son home, seems as enthusiastic as you would be about a heart attack or dog mauling.

"Well isn't this nice, the happy little family who cannot be bothered with the war that they are supposed to be waging. I hope we are not forgotten, while we are out there fighting for cause that you put us on!" Dran drawls, I know I did not like this dragon, Raja's brother or not. *"Son we are working on it but all things take time, the dragons you are here to look over to take to the front are barely a year old, they must be trained five times as hard as what everyone else has had to*

do because of our need for them so bad. I think I can say a hundred present sure that if we didn't need to fight this war, then we wouldn't be." Zar's voice comes out harsh and as a rebuke to this crude savage looking prince.

Dran snorts, and turns around, *"I will be expecting all the dragons able to fight, lined up at dawn for inspection."* Dran exits, leaving everyone in his wake cold like the cold air that has brought him.

Morning comes all too swiftly, with the dawn brings the dragons awake from nerves. It is all I could do not to get trampled as they all try to get ready. Thankfully I have had the foresight to get ready early. Raja, Flare, and I are able to escape unscathed. Not long after Remidus comes clutching Lolane in his claws, she has only one part of her hair brushed the other is a rats nest in wild disarray. Api and Grocin soon follow but they seem to have let their assigned get dressed, William and Laurence, still don't seem happy about it thou, muttering oaths about pushy dragons.

Raja hurries us to the field with so much speed if my legs weren't strapped in I would have gone right off. Of course with all our rushing Dran still isn't here, we wait for about an hour, giving all the dragons time to get here and wait before the 'great' Dran 'honors' us with his presence.

"So this is all I have got to work with, a bunch of whelps an a few strikers? Pathetic," Dran stops for a second to look at Veevia who is rather small for a dragon fighter. But

she is larger than most strikers, she grumbles reading his look, I can just imagine Liam patting her noise to sooth her ruffled feelings.

"*The first test will be if you can keep up with the march, so I am going to set a pace and we are going to fly for several hours... just be happy it's not days, any who fall behind or cannot keep going are to return and think themselves no longer eligible this year.*" Dran doesn't give us time to fret he jumps into the air, and everyone rushes to follow suit. Flare has his own harness for Raja, it is almost like a locked basket that he revolts, but can get out of if he tries hard enough.

Raja follows close on Dran's draft, "*it is the smartest way, this way he sucks me forward I save my energy and the person behind me can follow in my current.*" Raja seems to have told everyone to do just that and everyone follows in a straight line. I settle in for a long boring march, Raja keeps up just fine with that extremely fast speed.

*

We finally land but not in a city we are somewhere out in the woods far, far from the capital. From what Dran said we are not far from Ladano Lake. "*So looks like everyone kept up, from now on we will be winging our way to the front and if you fail just go back to the capital or I will run you back. In the evenings we will do the other trials. Tonight you*

shall each fight two people, you must at least win one of the
battles, if not you are of no use to me and will leave."

"*Esper, I hear something funny, I think we should go
check it out.*" Flare leaps up from his sitting spot and heads
for the woods giving me no time to think just follow. "You
know Flare I was planning on watching the fight! What if
Raja gets hurt or someone else does?" It is second nature
now to put to use those skills that have been pounded over
and over into me in these classes. "*Don't be ridiculous, You
will tell if he is in trouble and it is not like you will be able
to help if anything does happen to someone else.*" I growl, but
keep following. I really need to stop hanging out with
animals.

We slink through the woods, careful not to step on
twigs that can make popping noises, in search of the noise
Flare has heard.

Clang. Clash. Clang.

What I hear comes from a head of us. I tense trying to
hear more, and then it comes again, like chains.

"*Esper I won!*" Raja crows and I don't have the heart
to tell him to shut up.

"You idiot pull those chains up, do you want to alert
the whole kingdom we are here." I hear faint voices hiss to
each other. "Flare you need to go see what it is I can't get
to close or they will notice me." Flare doesn't reply he just
jumps into the tree and disappears.

Something just seems not right almost spooky, I usually feel relaxed in the woods but it just feels bad here.

I wait with abated breath for Flare's return. I hear another rustle and all but fall over with relief. "Flare, about time I thought something had happened." I suppress a shiver from the cold air. I hear another rustle and no reply, I lean against the tree trying to survey the area, over and over looking for a flash of his tawny and black speckled fur. Unease travels up my spine when I don't see him, I back up looking wildly.

Then someone turns out the lights.

I am stunned as the light disappears and I feel the rope tighten around my neck. "What the hell!" I twist trying to rip the bag off my head, but someone grabs my hands binding them in their stronger larger ones. I try to wrestle them away but to no avail, I feel someone knock something into my shoulder blades and I fall face first onto the ground.

Unfortunately they don't release their hold on my hands, so my shoulders nearly pop out of their socket. "She was calling out to someone else so we should look for the second person." The person behind me calls to someone else that I can't see. I hear someone shuffling off and the clang of chains as someone approaches.

"Raja.... Help .... Crazy people chains, snuck over border. Flare's off somewhere, they caught me unaware. Need

help." For once I finally send it telepathic without speaking it aloud. I don't want those men to hear that I have help on the way. I can feel Raja's worry as he rallies the other dragons. Flare listens in, I can feel him it is like a soothing presence, along with the even more soothing feeling of a like who-knows-how-many tons dragon listening on his way. I hear a shriek from off in the distance, cursing close by, and then another shriek.

"From those shrieks I think her partner is searching for her. Let's get her bonded before he alerts someone else." The man behind me barks orders as I feel a man start to put big heavy chains on my wrists, their weight making my hands sink he doesn't lock them yet but calls out to someone else. I have to act because if he got those manacles locked it would mean when help arrives I will be a sitting duck.

While the man behind me barks orders I bring my body weight backwards making us both topple over. I rip my hands away and start on the strings holding the hood on my head. The man curses behind me, I can tell he has regained his footing and he will be on me in seconds if I don't get this damn hood off.

A earth shattering roar sounds dimming the echo of an angry feline yowl. Help has come, and it is about time. I finally get my hands to undo the knot and rip at the hood. It is a mad house. Dragons have ripped up trees by the roots to get a space big enough for them to get at the slavers. The men who want to enslave everyone run like the rats they are, but can't because the dragons have already cleared a large clearing while others swoop in as a unit and grab the shrieking men... no women are among them willingly. The only women here are the ones in chains.

The men who haven't been snatched up by the dragons are being corralled into a circle in the center of the dragon made clearing. Raja lands next to me, running anxious eyes over my body, trying to reassure himself I am alright. Some of the dragon bondeds help the women, children, and couple of men out of their chains. I can hear the faint clanging and sobbing as they are relieved of their chains.

A tiny woman who probably doesn't top five foot, with flaxen hair, and big blue eyes, shakes off the men holding her, and charges at another man standing with the people willingly here. But she heads for the biggest brute in the front in particular. The tiny woman punches him with such force it wipes the smirk off his face and everyone else's.

"You filthy pig I hope that they feed you to the dragons, then again with how rotten you are the poor dragon would probably not be able to swallow you." The man just scowls ignoring her like she is nothing looking off at the dragons who line the clearing trying to find anywhere big enough to perch.

"What you have nothing to say to me? Once a long time ago you used to love me, before you went to fight that damn war. I wish you had died there, and then maybe you wouldn't have been captured and traded your family to these animals." The little pixie of a woman looks about to punch him again or burst into tears, personally I was rooting for the first. She chooses to do both, he doesn't stop her or anything just looks away, and whispers more to himself then to her, "all have their place." An older woman who greatly resembles the man glares at what I am assuming is her son as she draws his wife away to stand with the other freed captives letting the woman weep into her shoulder.

I can't believe it, if what the small women said is true then something the slavers have done to this captured soldier had turned him against his own family and the kingdom. *"Raja what did they do to him? Are these other men like him? Did they turn in their families too?"* Raja lets out a low rumble pulling me farther away from the men with his big giant claws. *"Change of plans, Recruits, it looks like we will be flying to Claret before we head to the front."* Dran drawls looking over the men, *"We can be eating great for a long while with the reward we will get from these. Pick them up."*

Dran doesn't pick up any of the people. Instead he looks on as every other dragon takes up a person either a slaver or a freed captive. We end up carrying the pixie like women and her son. The boy is none to discreet about his enthusiasm about being carried by dragons. It is the coolest thing to ever happen to the boy. "Did the slavers say why they would travel into the kingdom to get you guys, or how they even brain washed your... you know." I feel kind of bad to rub it into her face that her husband has betrayed her and just can't call him her husband without feeling awful.

"He said that his unit was ambushed, and most were captured or killed. None escaped, including his bonded Axis. Then he said that they had to shamefully spend weeks trying to 'show him the light'. He said that it was shameful that he didn't see it sooner, he didn't mention anything about where his bonded was. Their last test to show they were committed to the order and "the light" was to turn over any and all loved ones, to show total commitment. So that they too could take their rightful place, the places we were meant to. He even bragged that after a few years of service to their cause and new leader that he would be considered free and eventually buy his own slave to make strong *loyal* children if we couldn't be saved."

The woman lets out a hiccup sob but wipes her tears and keeps going, seeming to try and save face by being as brave as possible. "They said their sons would be shown the light also, the elders would become servants and eventually put down to make room for the new. The women would know their rightful place, as total submissive to their owner as long as they aren't given freedom!"

Her son wraps his arms around his mother to comfort her. He looks like about ten and like he could hurt anyone who makes a move against her, including his father who has done this, caused her tears. "My husband was a good man before he was captured, he was very attentive and loving he wouldn't in a million years believe that stuff. If it hadn't come out of his mouth with such conviction I would think it a lie." The little pixie of a woman falls silent and hugs her son closer as if he is the only thing keeping her going, her life line.

"*What did they do to him?*" Horror fills me, if we hadn't stumbled on this group no doubt these innocent people would also soon have found themselves likewise brainwashed and put to work as slaves. To think that the slavers think it right, enough so they are going to war to conquer Pangaea. I will die before I ever let myself be brain washed.

15

Three days later...

The flight to Claret is long, and slightly chilled, and makes me crave an even longer hot shower. With all the inexperienced dragon flying passengers we have to stop about five times a day. I know we can't expect an old lady or a small child to hold it, and the dragons wouldn't appreciate being peed on, but really!

Lately I can't sleep, just thinking forbidding thoughts about the war against the slavers and what will happen to our family, knowing that right now I should be thinking more about myself and my bondeds but unable to. Were the others from earth going to be in the war eventually? "Flare do you know what age they draft people into the army?" I whisper as to not wake all the sleeping dragons and people, my eyes spacing out to gaze at the sky so like Earth's except for the six moons. So I guess it's not a lot like Earth's.

"Do not worry Esper, they only draft people with fighting bondeds usually. The other breeds usually are more docile

people and have no wish for war. But if you truly have no skill or do not want to go you can bow out so long as you help out in another way. There are rare cases though that some more docile bonded pairs will chose to join, the youngest they will allow is sixteen, they prefer about seventeen thou.." Flare purrs and moves closer to let me enjoy his heat. I tunnel my hands in his soft fur, stroking unconsciously, and thinking over what he has said though.

"That isn't helpful, Pegasus are somewhat docile but I hear about them leaving for war all the time to be like a special unit. Lucan is also bonded to a snake, and Toni is bonded to a bloody wolf!" I glance from the sky giving him more of my attention as I get worked up a bit more.

"Oh, well then it is their decision, if they complete their classes and they so choose, which sadly knowing them they will they shall join. E, it's not like you can march on home and forbid them, nor if they do come can you walk them home, not without shaming yourself, Raja, and anyone associated with you or them." Flare sighs settling a bit different as to get comfortable. I go quiet for a while to think this over.

"The night sky is so much more spectacular here then on Earth with the six moons it is six times more beautiful." The air is rather frigid for what I have known Pangaea to be. What earth calls "winter" is now, except it would seem that Pangaea's winters shall be six time more cold than an average winter on Earth at least from what I am use to.

I'm told that when winter is in full swing it will be so cold no one will be leaving the warmth or moving from under a blanket for the duration.

"*You should get some rest, Mya and her son will be riding with Api and we will be carrying her … estranged husband and another of the slavers.*" Flare grabs my blanket with his teeth and pulls farther up and better around me, I snuggle back into him, "Well apparently I have to look forward to being a jailor for tomorrow." A yawn splits my mouth open wide and I snuggle in closer to his soft fur, and let sleep take me.

*

Claret turns out to be more of a military base than a town. Apparently it is where a lot of the people who want to be closer to their loved ones who are fighting live. I see some men from leave are partying at some clubs. Some soldiers looking like they are on the clock, they are in uniforms and marching. They only glance briefly at the many dragons swooping down on the base.

A tiger about the size of a Clydesdale comes stalking out of a building heading for Dran. "*I thought you would be heading towards the front with the new charges, instead of here*" The tiger survey the young dragons. "*They will do for now but they are not much right now, they look still so young,"* Dran snorts, *"they will do I guess. What are you up to, Karsh?"* Karsh just flicks his tail, an arches his kitty brow in curiosity when we start unloading the people and prisoners from the dragons. *"Fine, fine, I would take it your trip here was rather fun, what happened?"* Karsh strolls over to the prisoners, and I can see recognition in his gaze when he looks over a couple of the men. *"My brother's bonded found them. Managed to get herself caught, but seems that these men have been brainwashed."*

Dran drawls as Karsh walks up closer to certain prisoners, *"Flash is that you?"* The man Karsh speaks to stands next to Mya's husband. He won't look Karsh in the eye… even though the tiger is way bigger than he is. The man mutinously sticks up his chin and doesn't answer. Karsh sighs, shakes his head, and moves away from the man to look over the other prisoners.

"Almost all these men have been missing in action or believed dead. Only two of them I do not recognize I believe they are the original slavers. We have had information from sources that they have found a way to torture someone to extract information while simultaneously turning them into what they themselves are, and so goes the cycle," Karsh growls sounding immensely angry. I'm unsure if he's anger directed at what he assumes are the weakness in his men. *"We are, as we speak, trying to reverse the effects."* He sounds

so dedicated like it will be over his dead body that they will fail.

"*Take the men Karsh, we need to make it back to the front, just credit the points towards me and I shall see it distributed on pay day.*" Dran doesn't give him another word, just jumps to the air while everyone else scrambles to accommodate him. Smaller green white and black dragons rise with us, each carrying a pouch full of scrolls and a few are loaded down with supplies.

"*We shall be slowing down to accommodate the supply train we will be escorting to the front.*" Dran thinks to give us a heads up, everyone gives a giant sigh.

"*Remidus, what do you think the army is going to look like? What will we be doing? Are we going to live! What if the army has no cake?*" Grocin worries endlessly, trying unsuccessfully to get answers that no one has. "*Maybe when we get there, someone there will throw us a party with cake.*" Api calls trying to appease the worried dragon.

"*But I would have to share!*" Grocin whines, "*I might only get a bite! What would happen then? I could waste away or worse I could be open to turning rogue for another bite.*" Api snorts, "*Dude if that's all it takes to make you a slave I do not want you on my side! Also, you over grown eating machine, your parents didn't teach you right. They were supposed to teach you sharing is good!*" Api teasingly slaps

Grocin with her spiked tail, only grazing him though, her tail swinging back and forth to only a melody she can hear. *"Hey don't go pushing your morals onto me, we had ours... sharing leaves you hungry and weak."* Grocin tries in vain to come up with a motto but doesn't seem to get one he likes. *"Sharing is caring,"* Api mocks in a sing song voice back.

"Raja, you agree with me don't you?" Grocin glances over trying to convince Raja with his eyes. *"Sorry Grocin, but Api is the one with the actual known motto, I think yours is just in your head."* Grocin starts getting huffy to a point I think he is going to blow himself out of the sky.

"We really shouldn't tease him," Raja says in one breath, while laughing in another. *"But if we didn't the world would stop spinning!"* Api may be a dragon but she can express herself better than a human.

"Maybe instead Remidus will give us one of his impressions?" Api grins a malevolent grin as Remidus starts an impression, *"I am so mean that I make this spike through my tail look nice, why who cares about fun you want fun take a forty mile run! Can you tell who I am?"* Remidus flips his tail and tries to imitate Dran's.... unique voice. At first the others laugh... that is until Dran happens to appear behind Remidus. Remidus looks puzzled... until he hears a clearing of a throat behind

him. *"Oh, he's right behind me isn't he?"* Remidus whips around. *"Oh, uh, you're excellency we were just saying how you are all knowing."*

"Laying it on thick aren't we, Remidus? Do I even want to know what you were saying?"

"No....." Remidus whispers.

"What were you saying? Quench my curiosity," Dran drawls laying it on thick, seeming to like to play cat and mouse with the poor Remidus.

"I was saying words that had meanings..." Remidus evades, acting like the kid caught with his hand in the cookie jar.

"Would I be very happy at the meaning of these words, in the order you used them in?" Dran asks again going into specifics to not let him off so easy.

"NO."

"Then do not utter said words again," Dran growls, flying back to the front of the convoy.

"Way to go, Remidus, you should know he has like a homing beacon on his name." Api mocks flying faster. *"How would I know, was there some lesson I didn't attend telling us what not to say to get in trouble with that warden? A book?"* Remidus cries. Trying to fly after her, but she is quite faster then him.

I just laugh away listening to all of this, glad I hadn't said it. That dragon would have swallowed the twins within two seconds of meeting them.

Because Raja and his friends are afraid of speaking after being chastised, they fly to the front, settling in for it to be long and quiet.

16

We come upon the camp suddenly, but apparently we've already been spotted. A griffin streaks from the side to take a running stop in front of a tent in the middle of the miles wide camp. The camp has tents of all size, with cook fires beside each one. The camp itself extends as far as the eye could see in all directions, and is hidden by mountains and the enormous trees. I image it must be what a real army somewhat medieval would look like.

Pegasus's do formation with other winged creatures, most with a person armed on their backs. Unlike in medieval times I have found out that the armor we are to wear is enchanted to be light weight and impossible to penetrate. Unless done so with an enchanted blade, but isn't that the exception to everything. One thing I notice is among the eagles and hawks that leave to and from the camp not one is a phoenix. I guess Delan and Radiva are special. I honestly haven't thought about him a lot since he went off to join the army over a month ago.

"*Flare, why does Delan have a phoenix and none of these others do?*" This not knowing everything is getting old. I can't wait till the day I don't have to constantly ask someone everything, and I can be the person to be all "I know that". My thoughts straying to Delan at the lack of the majestic phoenixes, I do believe that Delan is in another base of the army.

"*Phoenixes only nest in the Phoenix Mountains, only a handful are ever hatched, the ones that do live tend to get stolen when they are still an egg, and things go bad. That was actually how Delan came about Radiva. A poacher stole her from the mountains but when was unable to find someone to trade her with who could bond with her they cast her away to die. And Delan found her, as we know the rest is history.*" Flare purrs through the basket rather happy seeing an end to the basket rides.

Raja touches down on Dran's right side, enjoying the gawks of the soldiers. Dragons that have been sleeping lift their giant heads over tents to see the new recruits. There are new types of dragons here. Some have no spikes, tiger stripes, goat horns, and some with extra limbs. An odder one comes up to greet Dran, "*Dran we all awaited with bated breath to see if the rumor were actually true and the young heir has finally decided to make his way into this world and bring the next generation with him!*" The dragon – if you can even call him that - who speaks reminds me of a praying mantis with gigantic wings…. Actually it is a very good description for him since he is a dark shade of green, and creeps me out with his bug eyes.

"Yes, yes, this is a miracle, blah, blah, blah, not to burst your bubble but we have a war to fight. Now how has the war been going?" Dran mocks, pulling the praying mantis away and towards the gigantic middle tent. I could definitely tell he was not happy at the worshiping tone of the praying mantis about his brother. *"Sir, something horrible has occurred!"* The praying mantis squeaks, before he they get into the tent and it falls closed around them blocking the news that is so horrible.

Oddly enough you can't hear their loud voices. *"It is enchanted,"* another voice rumbled, behind us. I turn to see a head twice as large as Raja's looming above us. He is a cold grey with black stripes faintly crisscrossing his scales. He also has gaps in his scales that are red and swollen, some even oozing blood and white stuff. I can't stop looking at two slightly blood covered fangs that extend from his upper lip. I bet if someone was high and found themselves in Pangaea they would need to be put in a mental institution.

"All of the tents are enchanted. Trade a favor from a warlock he or she will enchant anything with other properties, right now the basic is sound blockage and heating. I by the way am Casca, and this is Clara." The giant dragon looks

around for his bonded that apparently seems to have run off.

"*Well Clara should be around somewhere. She is most likely at the training area.*" He chuckles lifting his head to see and nods as if seeing her. "*You seem to be standing around like you are lost, has no one shown you to you the armory and stores?*" I look around trying to locate the voice and come face to face with a pair of fangs. I'm pretty sure my eyes are about to pop out of my head. I look higher to see a lion as big as Flare and I'm pretty sure those fangs are almost the length of my forearm. Her pelt is tawny and she has wings of black and dark feather shades attaching to her shoulders and half way down her back. She also has feathers trailing down her back to end with tiny miniature feathers at the top of her tail. I also notice that instead of tuff of fur at the end of her tail, she has feathers.

"*I am Roxana. I will be your guide around camp. If you would follow me I will show you to the equipment tent.*" Roxana turns, with Flare hard on her heels, I think I can see his tongue collecting dirt as it drags. "*So my fair beautiful enigma what brings you to the army?*" Flare pants after her like she is the only female he has ever seen. "Flare I think you left your tongue on the ground back there." I jab him in his ribs. He doesn't even look away, just moves closer to Roxana brushing up against her hanging on her every word as she describes how life in the camp works. I think Flare just found his soul mate.

"So what are you, Roxana, you look like a saber tooth tiger and griffin mix?" Laurence calls, hurrying as best as he can so he doesn't have a dragon stepping on the back of his heels. Raja's head swivels around to take in the many faces and awe inspiring army. I feel his awe and his discomfort about the staring. "*You are beautiful, Raja, all they will see is a extremely handsome dragon.*" I consul he gives a rather toothy grin in reply.

"*Because that is what I am, both griffin and saber,*" Roxana flutters her wings so they brush Flare. She also throws her head to the side giving us a Cheshire grin. "*So this is the equipment tent grab some tents, one per bond and the stores for food are next to it so you can each get rations, we are fighting a war. Cookie distributes food so just ask Cookie. Cookie is usually a very understanding person and I know the cliché of a cook named Cookie. The armory is a couple tents down. Those with superior skills will be asked to work in the armory repairing armor and weapons. You ever need anything patched up that's where you take it.*" Roxana leans forwards towards Flare and me mischievously, "*Word is John is selling goods, under the books.*" She weaves through the tents once more, we follow like lost puppies. She heads to a patch of open grounds.

"You can set up your tents. I will be nice and start the cook fires so you can make yourselves some dinner." Roxana purrs flicking her tail across Flare's chin. *"I'll help you with that,"* Flare purrs back his eyes almost glazing over. Gag me the images going through his mind, I did not need to know this much about Flare.

"I think Flare is in love" I extended the E on love for more mocking effect. Raja laughs, starting to unfold the big tent, taking the polls following the others as they put their tent up. I feel kind of useless I mean I want to help but, I'm only five foot five and the tents are two dragons high. "I think I'm go get some food from Cookie." I call up, with a wave.

On the way I feel my thought drifting back to my normal dilemma. Would they allow Toni or Dash to join? Knowing those two if they had a choice then they would be here in a heartbeat. Now that I am thinking about it what was I thinking? I didn't even say good bye to my family. Maybe the army will have something I could use to get in touch with them. Convince Dash and Toni to stay there to not do anything rash and become a part of this war.

Most people walk into doors when they are thinking, me I walk into a person who happens to be swinging a sword at someone else.

I smack my head against a leather covered back, literally bouncing off him. I fall to the ground and see stars. I can hear a whistle sound over my head as if metal was cutting through the air really fast. "Crap, are you alright! What were you thinking? Don't you know that I could have taken your head off?" A handsome face looks down at me, while also taking his sword that he nearly took my head off with and sheathing it.

The guys is about twenty Earth time with chocolate brown hair that goes around his face into a beard and a slight mustache, his eyes seem to sparkling green grey in the sunlight. He looks to be a couple years older than me but I can never tell, and sort of rugged with a silver stud in his ear. His leather padding/ armor looks as if it has been poured around his bulging muscles, he also has tight cotton leggings with a Greek belt and about anywhere he could have put one I can see a hilt or blade. To top it off he has combat boots and a thick silver chain with a moon and sun pendant attached.

"It's fine. I should have been paying attention where I walk, especially who I walk into." He extends his hand, smiling down at me, humor lighting his eyes up and showing slight dimples and laugh lines. I grab his forearm and he pulls me up.

"So what has you so deep into thought?" The man who is a perfect example for a pirate asks curiosity making him look even more rakish. "Oh just wondering what my family will be think with my sudden departure. I'm just glad I didn't depart some place further that I wouldn't be able to come back from, not that there isn't a chance I won't return from here." For some reason I feel shy, I can't stop myself from brushing back my hair and fiddling with my clothes trying to get all the dirt off which is a useless thing to do. For some reason I just can't stop the girly motions, messing with my hair, fidgeting.

"I was going to get food from Cookie, I came in with the new recruits and I wasn't much help with all the tents and stuff." I look up from my babbling, finding his eyes, he has to be like a few inches short of six foot, maybe five feet nine inches. "I'm Esper by the way," I reach for his hand again, it is warm… "Michael." I can't help but smile - and god help me I actually blush what the hell is happening - he is gorgeous in a rough rugged way.

"So how about I escort you to Cookie, I would not want you to run into anymore unsuspecting volatile men." Michael winks, "you know there is a good chance that I might want to ask you t—" Michael doesn't get a chance to finish. A tired fully armored man stumbles into the training yard, having staggered from the woods, screaming, "Ambush, we're under attack, TO ARMS!" The warriors in the practice area bring their weapons up instantaneously, while the people by their tents lunge for their own weapons. Dragons roar a warning as an army descends upon us.

Michael unsheathes his weapon and runs to a tent with a pale sleeping griffin in it. He grabs a shield and shakes awake the griffin. I feel my heart beat accelerate with the commotion, and I too reach for my weapons.

A clatter sounds behind me and I glance back to see Raja leaping over tents and people, I don't get a chance to do much of anything, before he picks me up and sets me on his back. As soon as I get the straps on Raja leaps for the sky with a war cry that echoes from dragon to dragon. The ground is also a buzz as the grounds creatures prepare protect their temporary homes by any means necessary.

The horde descends coming from air to ground. This is going to be a confusing battle. The only way to know who the enemy is, is when they attack you.

I am shocked out of my thoughts as Raja dodges a deadly swipe that would have taken off a good portion of his neck. I grab the dragon spear that is strapped onto his saddle, as a huge dragon barrels down on us. The dragon, while huge, has wounds on his wings as if something has punctured them numerous times and hadn't been taken out with care each time.

Raja is smaller and moves more quickly and uses that speed to keep out of range of or avoid the swipes of the other dragon. The dragons ghastly damaged wings make it impossible for the huge dragon to land a blow against Raja. A griffin comes in behind Raja on the soft part of his stomach. I swing on instinct, throwing the dragon spear.

The spear sails through the air, imbedding itself in the griffin's wing as he tries to wing backwards. With the spear embedded in his wing he drops out of the sky, grounded. The griffin forced to fight for his life without the advantage of the skies to protect him. I see a snow leopard the size of a sixteen or seventeen hand horse jump at the griffon, taking him under and I lose sight of them, I whip my head around to block out what comes next. I need to concentrate and stop thinking about death of a creature that might have once been a friendly or a victim… There I go again, I need to tone it out, it will get me nowhere.

Raja roars a challenge at the bigger dragon brings me back to the now. I unclip myself from the harness, but still keep myself strapped in. I cautiously lean over to check the damage the griffin has done. His side and soft tummy have long thin slashes about a thumb wide. They aren't so deep but they probably sting. I feel his pain and to me that is just unacceptable and any remorse I felt for that griffin withers.

"I'll be fine, but you need to strap back in, I can't keep trying to stay vertical to avoid him." I can feel he hasn't hurt the other dragon, and he doesn't want too. The dragon is just a puppet, and he wishes to cut the strings. "Raja you

have to fight back. I know it's not right but we have to. If we don't then they will just use these people to make everyone else slaves." Raja seems sad but he finally stops trying to avoid hurting the other dragon. Raja darts in coming up under the dragon's lunge, to rake his claws across the other dragon's colossal belly.

The dragon gives a cry, lunging after Raja's retreating form but stops giving a mighty bellow when the movement rips his wound open more. The dragon turns without another pass and heads back where he came from.

"…..Raja what if you spoke to the dragon, see if there is any way we can free them." An outlandish idea forms in my head, a way ward plan. If the slavers can steal people from us maybe we can steal them back. *"Look out!"* Raja turns nearly falling out of the sky. A beam of light passes by close enough all my hair stands on end. It crashes into a flying serpent on their side. Grey rapidly takes over the serpent until he is completely encased in stone. The serpent falls to earth, and shatters on contact.

"Look out!" Michael calls, just before he jumps over my head pushing off Raja's large back and catapulting himself onto a different type of griffin. Instead of a lion body it has eagle talons for its front legs with a shackle wrapped around its legs, and horse's hind quarters. The bird horse gives a snort and tries to throw him, Michael plunges his sword into the creature's spine and it seems to cave in on itself falling from the sky.

Michael leaps from the creature only to land on the griffin that he started on, flying him away with another war cry. I feel immense awe over him, who could just leap from creature to creature. All the withering bodies it seems like a death trap to me.

"That could've been us," Raja cries out of breath, snapping me from my intent watching of the warrior I had run into, and back to the crumpled stone serpent. Another dragon charges us. *"Friend, stop! How can I help you?"* Raja tries to reach him but he only chanted back, *"It is our place, our masters over all."* Raja snaps at his neck tearing into it a bit and swings around nearly taking the head off the slaver, too bad he didn't.

The pain momentarily stops the dragons chant, *"It's too late for me, but there are others at the base, who haven't submitted, seek them."* He let loose a cry and shakes his head trying to snap out of whatever the slaver's magic did to him only to revert back to his other state. The dragon charges us, Raja drops to let the dragon shoot past and comes up under to rip at his body, the dragon shakes his head again. Seems the pain helps him clear the clutter in his head, but it also makes him submit, a slippery slope. Raja gets another swipe.

"*They use our bondeds to get to us, and sending them off. Masters over all. You won't find their bonded's, focus on the unbondeds. They are kept in line by a shackle on their ar—it is our place, our masters over all.*" The dragon gives one last pleading look before he once again goes under. "Raja you know what to do." My voice is barely over a whisper.

"*But he can be saved if only-.*" I interrupt Raja. "Raja he's brain washed and so is his bonded, so long as his bonded is in their hands he's gone, and no one can retrieve them from in the heart of the slavers." Raja nods reluctantly, and lunges for the apex between the dragon's wings and neck where the slaver sits.

Raja rips the man into pieces with his teeth and claw in seconds, and reels back as the dragon goes crazy. "Raja," I whisper hating that I have to egg him on, into this horrible act. Raja lunges again feinting one way and going another. Raja tears at the dragon's throat, blood streaking his muzzle and a giant hole in the slave dragon's throat is left in his wake. The dragon gives out a gurgle as he falls from the sky and whispers, "*Thank you.*" He is dead before he hits the ground.

Our hearts break for the poor dragon, I know tears streak down my face but the dragon deserves someone to mourn for him. If he could have been saved nothing could've stopped us.... But something had, my brain argues, distance and a bigger enemy than I myself could go against. Raja stays hovering in place for a minute starring at the broken body on the ground of the now freed dragon, a freedom he had gotten in death.

"Raja there still is a battle being fought and we are missing it, we can still help some deaths, break the shackles bound on their wrist." Raja lets out an anguished cry charging a fighting pair, shocking them when he throws himself at the dragon's arm, using his teeth to rip the shackle off. The sounding of his teeth scraping against mettle is deafening and one I do not want to relive.

At first the dragon tries to shake him off, but as Raja makes more head way prying the spikes out of the dragon's scales the dragon slows his thrashing. As the shackle comes completely off and out of his hide the dragon let out a sigh and looks around as if in confusion. The two griffins that had been fighting him hover in confusion, not knowing what to make of this.

"Take this shackle to Dran and the now free dragon to the infirmary." I am hoping they won't question what right I have, which I actually have zero of. One griffin looks at his buddy and shrugs they pick up the evil contraption from Raja's talons and the freed dragon follows them.

"What did you do?" Michael calls astride the pale griffin again. "No time to explain, take off the shackles. Pass the word to everyone, some can be saved." Raja growls and flies once again at a fighting dragon with a shackle on her wrist.

*

We repeat this several times and it seems as if the tide of the battle is changing our way as more of our side frees the people on the other. We are on to helping another dragon but as the dragon is going through the confusion, she cries out, folding in on herself. She is the first female dragon we had seen on the slavers side. Raja darts under her and we see too late a slaver hidden between her wings. The slaver holds a bloody knife, and seems to have stabbed the dragon over and over. Raja relays this to me craning his neck up to see the problem.

I watch through Raja's eyes as the slaver jumps up slashing Raja with his blade, and leaps onto his neck while Raja reels back. Not to let this man hurt Raja like he did the slaved dragon I draw Saphique and slash at him. The slaver leans back letting the sword pass by harmlessly.

I bring my foot around in a second strike kicking the slaver's feet out from under him. He goes over Raja's side but stabs his knife between Raja's scales to keep from falling. Raja shudders, dropping about five feet, nearly losing the smaller the dragon that is sprawled across his back.

With due haste I move over to lean over where the slaver has his knife jammed into Raja and is dangling from! I awkwardly bring Saphique down on the slaver's wrist. The blade goes halfway through but being an awkward angle doesn't go all the way through. I bring it down once again going farther through his wrist. I ignore his cries and curses for me to stop, right now this douche monkey is hurting my bonded.

The man screams as eventually losing control of his hand as it contracts and releases his hold on the knife. The man falls to earth with a splat, my mind adding sound for effect. I jerk the knife out and begin to put pressure on Raja's side.

I shouldn't stay here and Raja is vulnerable. "Head to the infirmary," I call up, my clothes already half soaked through. "*Esper, watch out!*" Raja warns as he tries to head to the infirmary. I sheath Saphique so if we got jostled I won't stab him. I look up to see a hydra's malevolent face, just before it swipes me with its head trying to knock me off Raja, but it ends up stabbing me in the shoulder and ripping it open to jerk its horn out. I feel a pain like no other that cannot even go into description but soon goes numb as Flare does something through the bond.

Raja gives a cry of pain and anger but is unable to do anything with the other wounded dragon on him.

The hydra's other head hit sme, succeeding where the other had not and pushes me into a free fall.

I'm pretty sure I am screaming......but I can't hear anything over the rushing sound of the air, my cloths flapping, and dragons roaring challenges.

Reaching out I try to grab onto something, anything, why the hell can't I grab onto anything. Who would think in the sky, way up, during a dragon battle there wouldn't be anything to grab onto.

I reach again wildly as I try to grab a creature or really anything, in a hope I won't be the next person to go splat. I finally feel a scaly thing in my hands almost whipping by my hand, I grab with all my might and tried to hold on to it as I look it seems to be a scaled tail. My first grip is enough for me to wrap my arms and legs around him. I can feel whiplash starting to come on from the constant jerking as the dragon flies, along with the jerk from free fall. I can't die this way. I still have a full life. I still need to know if I'm crazy or not. I guess this would be one way to find out, falling to my death.

"Raja it might behoove you to hurry!" I scream just to be clear he heard. *"Esper I'm sending up Roxana."* Flare calls I can feel him as he watches me and also rips at the enemy. Trying whenever possible to get the shackles off. I feel his displeasure of the metal against his teeth.

The tail jerks again this time harder, as if he notices the new weight on his tail. The tail jerks became more rapid. Come on I just need a few more minutes, come on Roxana. "Might want to tell her to hurry, losing my grip here!" The dragon tries again, I feel my hands get sweaty, then slip, losing my grip, and he sends me flying far off his tail.

Being back in a free fall isn't fun, and then a building hits me, or something that sure feels like one. "*You scream like a girl.*" Roxana teases, "you would too if you didn't have wings!" I quip. She laughs dodging the beam of light that turns things into stone. Roxana lands in a hurry turning me over to Flare, as she goes to guard some of the dragons saving the slaved dragons.

Flare lets me climb onto his back as he bounds back to the fighting. I climb down and once again draw Saphique. I cut down any one not on our side who doesn't have a shackle or band marking them as a savable slave, letting myself focus completely on the battle and killing. I know I'm losing blood and its stupid but sometimes every person needs to help and thanks to Flare if I favor one arm I can just ignore the other. He will let me know when I become too close to gone.

*

The battle gradually winds down until I am left standing, chest heaving, looking for my next opponent. *"It's over Esper, they have retreated."* Flare purrs, nudging up against me, "I know. I was just in the zone. That was a new way to start a first day," I whisper trying to crack a joke, hoarse from lack of water and constantly uttering my war cry. I grab Flare's scruff hoisting myself onto his back, and we set off for the infirmary to see Raja and have our wounds tend to. Raja is curled in on himself by the freed dragons, only looking up when he feels our thought waves. My thoughts feel jumbled and my mouth thick.

"You okay?" I call ahead, Raja just nods sullenly, wrapping protectively around something. *"Just a little sad that all this was necessary, they made babies fight."* Raja uncurls to show us a baby griffin as big as a medium sized dog, the griffin is covered in blood, and his fur and feathers are so matted and covered in blood you would never be able to see what color he is. "Poor thing, has the doctor looked him over?" Liam calls walking over to stare sadly at the baby, motioning a surgeon over to look at my shoulder in the next breath.

Liam then calls some squires to clean the bloody baby griffin. Slowly I can finally see the griffin under the blood with each swipe of the wash cloths. The griffin is fuzzy but the black and brown feathers of a golden eagle are coming in. I guess he is golden eagle because of the regal shape of his head. At the moment though, he has a big fuzzy head with a black and chocolate brown lion's body.

He is near the cutest thing I have ever seen when cleaned off, having been cleaned the baby is sapped of all energy and all but collapses in a tired heap. "Raja at this rate we are going to start tripping over all the people in our group! Let me guess your next words are, 'can we keep him.'" I have every intent to say no. but as I open my mouth to say it, Raja gives me a pleading look that melts me to my toes. I look from him to the young griffin who is probably orphaned, I am hopeless and helpless. Flare might as well start burying my whole, because if I can't say no I am bound to wind up in one. Who am I kidding if he hadn't suggested keeping him I would have?

"Fine, but he is your responsibility!" Flare snorts and I shoot him a glare. "*You are such a push over didn't we learn anything when we took in the ever growing lizard!*" But none the less Flare plods over, picks the griffin up by his scruff and starts heading towards our tent, Raja hopping after, overcome with excitement.

Meanwhile I am being held by an overzealous doctor stitching me back up like a patchwork doll. "You did great in the battle." Michael joins me with a pale female griffin on his heals who sort of is eyeing me like a curious object. "I got hurt I wouldn't call that even good I would call that sloppy. I am spending the night after being stitched together again." I can't suppress the scowl, put out I am spending the night getting put back together like Humpty Dumpty.

"Well a lot of good soldiers who were skilled are spending their night having their last rights read over them before they're bodies give back to the earth. Didn't mean that they were mortally injured because they were unskilled, it just meant that the other man was better or got lucky. Our overall loses were thirteen dragons alone to the magic thing that turned them to stone, ten dragons by other means, fourteen griffins, six Pegasus, two winged serpents, and those are just our winged creatures. Our ground ones, one hundred and seventy seven men, twenty three leopards, panthers, lions, tigers, and many more all dead. I just won't depress you more to have to listen to how each species suffered a loss.

"I call you lucky, you not only did your part and stayed alive and also saved a bunch of people in the process, including taking in a baby griffin with a whole future ahead of him. Zoe wanted to thank you for that kindness." Michael shrugs. Setting his shield down beside him, it has a checkered border sort of like a soccer ball and some weird language written in the middle. My attention wanders back to Zoe as she bows, leaning back on her haunches and resting her noble bald eagle head to the ground. I stroke her head to show her I accept her thanks and allegiance and can't help but marvel over how soft her feathers are.

She should have been intimidating but she looks fairly young. She looks like she has probable just gotten her adult feathers, twin pale cat ears poking out of her feathers. She has pale tawny lion body that is just a couple shades above white, capped with amber eyes. She is fairly small next to other griffin's just barely reaching Michaels chest, and evidently just big enough to fly with.

"How long have you been bonded?" I ask stroking her velvet soft head. "About eight years earlier than most but yeah she's only half her true height. Griffin's grow at a very slow rate, she usually doesn't go into battle but we make exceptions if they have training or can carry and we are ambushed. I would have loved to see someone try and keep her back." Zoe snorts and hops onto the bench beside me laying her head in my lap to let me continue to stroke her soft white head.

"So how did you end up bonded eight years before people usually?" I lean back relaxing a little so the healer can stitch my shoulder up better.

"My family took me to see the newly hatched cubs when I was six, of course it was already been two month so they weren't too new, you do not want to go visit a mom right after birth, she can be very protective. Zoe was one of seven cubs and the only pale one of the lot, it is usually very rare to have a pale griffin. I was playing with her litter mates when she fell from the sky. She had climbed up high in order for a sneak attack and something jumped out at her startling her and she leapt blindly landing on the hanging light and slipped off falling practically in my lap, of course she came up hissing before things clicked. After that she stayed with her mom till she was no longer in need of her milk and spent her free time following me around and she came to stay with my family."

Michael chuckles as the surgeon grunts from behind me. He moves over to sit down on the other side of Zoe he moves her haunches onto his lap and her fur affectionately. "Normal I would ask about yours, but well your story has been broadcasted everywhere."

Zoe lets out a purr enjoying a scratch behind the ear, *"you human and your pleasantries you don't see griffin's having uninteresting small talk. By now if we found someone we liked we would just skip to the grooming and such. I mean take you. I like you and guess what you doing after seconds of meeting me."* Zoe brags stretching out and moving so her body is also draped more so over Michael's lap.

"So how come your so fearless when you are in the sky I mean you were hopping dragons and griffins like they were stepping stones over a little stream, instead of like creatures that move and possible enemies and you could fall to your death?" Thinking back to his kill of the horse

bird, similar to the magic book that everyone loves......
gosh I cannot seem to remember anything it's almost like
most of the inconsequential things from my Earth life
just fade.

"I trust Zoe." He says it like it will make everything
better. "But what's that got to do with wing jumping?" Zoe
snorts again all but asleep in my lap her head nuzzling into
my leather padding. "I trust her that if I fall I won't fall far
because she will catch me. Eventually you will have that
faith in Raja and Flare.... If you would like I could teach
you to wing jump. The hardest part is the nerve to actually
jump." Michael seems a little timid with asking but once
he gets it out there, he starts telling me in-depth.

"The jumping you got to calculate the distance and of
course practice jumping long distance. You have to know
how far you can jump, also helps that you aware that they
might catch on and try and hit you in midair..."

"Sounds perfect, how about we start tomorrow?" I
interrupt. The doctor has just finished and I am about
dead on my feet, I don't even know what is pushing him
on to not pass out.

"Sounds perfect see you tomorrow, come Zoe let us
leave the poor girl before we over stay our welcome." Zoe
grumbles but gets up, shaking out her white wings. *"Look
forward to dropping you tomorrow... I mean catching you."*
Zoe gives an evil chuckle before leaving with Michael,

every once in a while tripping him with her gigantic wings.
I know she was just messing with me but it doesn't install
confidence… I think she was joking.

My muscles have stiffened, that is going to be a pain in
the morning, and dummy I am I agreed to do free falling
and sky jumping tomorrow. The walk to out tent is like
a death march for me my feet dragging so much I don't
think they ever left the ground anywhere. Even with the
magic stitches or whatever they used on me to accelerate
the healing I don't think the doctor would be eager for me
to start wing jumping.

"Hey, Casca, what's the matter, where's Clara?" The
giant grey striped dragon from earlier lays in the middle of
the clearing, looking off into empty space. He just seems
off, off enough to make me take notice even when half
asleep.

Casca's eyes don't seem to focus just keep staring out
into space, mumbling, "*she's at the training ground be back
very soon.*" I feel a hand on my shoulder. I turn to Ace, one
of Liam's friends. Ace's face is pained as he draws me away
from the hazed out dragon.

"Esper, Casca is going home, he is no longer mentally
sound… Clara perished in the battle. He just can't seem
to accept she isn't going to be coming back, so he likes
to think she will be back any second." Ace squeezes my
shoulder as I glance over my shoulder again to see the

poor lost dragon. It hurts my heart to, but I have a feeling that dragon will be forever expecting his bonded to return from training. "Do you think he will be willing to leave the camp if he thinks Clare will just be returning from the training yard?" I whisper softly even though I doubt Casca would hear me.

"The sorcerers will find a way." Ace shrugs seeming unsettled about what the sorcerers are going to have to do. All the sudden I don't want to know more I just want to forget that I am fighting a war and just curl up with my bondeds.

"I got to go, how about we catch up some other time?" I shrug out of his comforting arm, a need to be with my bondeds to be wrapped up in fur and scales.

"Yea," Ace also glances back at Casca but leaves in another direction, I once more head back to my tent feeling like my heart is going to plummet to my feet.

"*You didn't have to stay fighting so long, the reinforcements had come you could've fallen back and rested.*" Raja admonishes picking me up like a child and places me next to the fuzzy little griffin and the furry leopard.

I am out before he is fully done situating me.

*

Michael dumps water on me at noon having let me sleep in a while. He had recruited help from a griffin and a Levicious. Levicious's are the creature with a bird head, wings, and a horse body. He takes me to a clearing where they wait, motioning to take up onto one.

I rotate my shoulders a few times feeling a bit stiff but don't show any other signs that they were almost disconnected from my body. I survey the group some more, people on Pangaea are just so energetic, it is rather tiring.

I settle on the Levicious, "So horse bird up, up, and away." I can't help but tease. "I am not a bird horse, I am a Levicious, you hairless monkey, and the name is Cleric." He seems rather grumpy about it. Maybe it's a touchy subject, or maybe he didn't get his coffee this morning.

"Okay, Esper, I tried to wake Raja but all I got was almost crushed by his huge tail fin. So Roxy has volunteered to stand in for him, so do you trust her? It won't work unless you trust her to catch you when you fall?" Michael asks leaping onto Zoe, she seems rather weighed down. "Yeah I do, partially because Flare does," Roxy's chest puffs up. "Well if you miss it's her job to catch you. So I hope you are right. Take to the skies!"

Cleric jumps up, spreading his huge speckled wings and beats for the sky. "Now we will start with just getting over the jumping into midair, you need to get over it first or things might go wrong… absorb the shock, find your balance and you must keep that balance even in the hardest conditions. Now stand." Michael stands on Zoe demonstrating what he expects of me.

"You sure about this as you said I did fine doing it the normal way, you know like just sitting, no standing and jumping needed!" I feel my nerve slip away as I stand on Cleric's back, and look out over the tiny little camp that is oh so far down. "You want to be okay warrior or you want to be great? Now jump," I do try, I lean forward a tiny bit looking more, my joints freeze and I can't bring myself to take the final plunge. I feel like I am in my own bubble except only broken from Cleric's steady wing beat, and occasional gliding.

"Cleric you know your part." Michael calls over, his face stretching into an evil grin, "What are you planning, I don't think I like this!" I scream feeling the horse muscles move under me move and roll, sending me off his back and into a free fall.

I feel myself scream over and over, my screams cut short by Roxy gliding up and under me. Roxy grunts, *"You know if you are going to fall on me you can at least do it quietly, or you shall alert even the dead to your location."*

"What did that accomplish besides making me not trust you!" I scream to Michael, holding even tighter to Roxy.

"Okay, Esper let's try this again quieter now, and without the forced eviction. Now just jump over to Cleric."

"Go or I will throw you." Roxy threatens, when I just wrap my hands further into her soft pelt.

Not trusting Roxana to not throw me also, I gather myself up, prepping for the jump. Standing on her is not much different from standing on the Levicious, they are both the size of a big horse.

ONE Mississippi

TWO Mississippi

THREE Mississippi

I need to jump now!

FOUR Mississippi

FIVE Mississippi

Roxy's muscles began to bunch, so I leap for Cleric's back, who hovers nearby. I prepare for impact…. Only to miss, my hand grabbing his wing, startling him out of his steady beat, both of us drop. "Let go!" Michael bellows from adjacent. I release the wing knowing I'll fall but I don't want to take Cleric down with me, Cleric scrambles his wings swinging around hitting me in the face. I land on Roxy again, she grunts but keeps flying. *"Can't you be more graceful? You don't see me landing on people so hard."* I just grunt put out that my first jump and I can't even make it. That failure took me a matter of seconds but I don't doubt I will remember it for a lifetime.

"Try again," Michael calls again. "You know this is totally making me see you in another light! More brutish," I call back but once again standing on Roxanna, this time another larger griffin hovers nearby. Why me! I can't believe I asked for this!

ONE Mississippi
TWO Mississippi
THREE Mississippi
I jump.

This time I launch myself half onto his back, my legs dangling over the side, "nice you made it this time." Michael quips making my want to punch him, as my muscles scream in protest. Zoe nudges me up all the way. Michael makes me do this twenty more times before he lets us move on. That being when I can land standing on the mark.

Michael makes a jump over me, using the griffin I am on as a spring board to land on a Levicious on my griffin's other side. "Okay how about you try jumping like I just did, in a battle people aren't going to conveniently move." I stand once more, marking the distance between. I push off the griffin jumping to the Levicious springing from him, making the second jump to Zoe. I land hunched on her back, "nice that's a little easier when you have momentum, less thought helps, trust yourself, you should instinctually feel the momentum to jump between." He pauses for breath thinking how to describe it to me.

"When you are going a jump kill like that you stab at base of spine as soon as you feel them give you jump clear, Raja or your back up should be there waiting below." Michael instructs, "let's try it again......"

1 month later...

A month is spent quietly, practicing our skills, and air jumping. Raja spends a lot of time with Quinn – the baby griffin, who still looks like a fuzz ball but sort of cute. The baby has dark chocolate almost jet back lion fur and chocolate eyes but his eagle head is still fuzzy with youth, when he begins to molt it is going to be a nightmare.

Raja enjoys molding the mind of the young griffin. Api and Remidus are always not far, helping with Quinn all day but by the end of the day it is Flare, Quinn, and me snuggling at night, at least with Raja wrapped around us. Winter is in full swing, and Raja has come into his full growth of an in-between, as in between middle weight and heavy weight like his father, also retaining his quickness, thankfully.

With snow waist deep for us human and less furry creatures staying inside the enchanted tents is the only option. Or we venture out to go ice skating and build things in the snow never spending too much time out thou unless on patrol. Being at war it is given we have a few attacks but not a lot, the slaver's are as unwilling to go out into the snow as we are.

My practice sessions with Michael and Zoe are less frequent with the cold but we have them every once in a blue moon. He says I am making progress but next to him I feel like an ungraceful cow.

One day I was going by the command tent, trying to blow off my hyper mood with very few outlets. A Kurama - the nine tailed fox - walks past heading for a tent that many people visit, but I personally haven't been in. Curious I follow. Inside the tent is a space filled with drapery and pillows on the ground… well actually one pillow, in front of the shrine. Creatures of all kinds mill about either off to the side of the shrine lighting candles or in front bowing as they pray.

The shrine is a beautiful lady with flowing hair that turns to mist and eyes the color of the stars. Her dress is made of leaves and branches that have extended and woven to make her a strappy dress with a branch belt under her breasts then the dress falls to the ground in waves of green.

The lady has her hands extended and a simple bowl in her hands. The statue must have had magic on her or something because her eyes glow, her skin seems alive, the stone animals at her legs jump and frolicked playfully around her. As I watch the lady reaches down and touches the praying wolf a smiled lighting her face before going into her original pose.

"*Raja what is this place?*" I telepathically send to avoid disturbing the peace, amazed at this beautiful display. "*That is the shrine to the earth mother, if you go to her with a selfless prayer then she will reach down and tell you something to help you achieve it, but if it is selfish she will yell and shame you. It doesn't happen so often but she listens to all,*" I watch as the wolf leaves and another takes her place. "*Every seven months she visits at the moons peak and bestow a gift on someone worthy, that will save others one day, but without the gift would parish. I know what you are thinking yes she appears to everyone at the same time all over Pangaea. From what I have heard she does not appear to the slavers, for they reject her and live off others for selfish reasons.*"

Raja drowses with his head on Api and Quinn on his back in the hollow I sit in. I can use a lot of help… I am in a war, not like it would hurt me none to talk to her. I still don't feel exactly comfortable, so I creep a little closer, it is almost as if I can feel the presence of the goddess's lean closer. She sets the cup aside as I take a knee before her.

'*I know I am not a part of your faith, but if I could get some guidance on how to help these enslaved creatures whose bonded's have been captured? Is there any way I can help Yanni or Jenni, are they safe?...Also might be nice to know how to help the twins not grow into delinquents, since I'm asking.'* I throw the second crack about the twins, cause what can it hurt?

I sat in that bowed position waiting, a cramp working in my back, just waiting…. And waiting. Uh this is stupid, I must look like an idiot, I'm not even part of her faith.

After a while I feel a hand stroking my hair, before lifting my chin. I look up, and up into the face of the life like statue. *'Your heart is there, worry not for them, your time to help will come, draw strength when you have none from those around. Not everyone can stand alone but sometimes even those who can, need not. Pick your moments wisely and prepare. Not everyone is as they seem, here is a gift and reminder of who you are.'* The statue of mother earth grabs my upper arm, I feel a sharp pain before she let's go, strokes my head and reverts back to her old pose.

I look to my arm unsure what I will find, images of a ghastly scar will be on my arm but instead I find a silver band woven intricately around my arm, like vines. On the side of the band is a dragon and a leopard woven in but still sticking out. As I watch the leopard and dragon leap from my arm and onto my skin running and playing, leaving fading foot prints after. They resemble Raja and Flare.

My fingers on their own accord trace the running figures, the tattoos look up, both letting out sounds of pleasure before continuing on their frolic. *"Ahm, if you don't mind others would like to talk to the goddess."* An eagle calls perching upon a mini fountain, "sorry."

I move away quickly grabbing my coat and pushing back into the snow.

Flare is waiting for me outside our tent, having watched what happened through me, he isn't surprised when I take my coat off again in the tent. *"The goddess's harvest is tomorrow night, I never heard of her bestowing a gift early."* Flare sniffs the dragon on the band. The dragon leans towards him and smacks him on his nose, then reverts back to its original pose. *"Cheeky little thing."* He grumbles heading back to his resting place, I follow suit.

*

The next day is spent preparing for the feast and revelry for the goddess's visit. I made the mistake of trying to get breakfast from Cookie and was drafted into cooking. So me and some likewise unlucky individuals cook up a storm until the sun started to sink, he then releases us when the final piece of bread is put into the large ovens. "I'm going to get to the bath house first!"

Simone laughs running after me, she had arrived at camp a couple days ago, "Esper, you had a head start that's cheating." Out of breath when she finally made it to the bath house, "you know the saying cheaters never win is only figurative they do usually win physically." She hits me in the shoulder before we depart into our stalls to shower.

My shower starts out nice, soaping my hair humming under my breath the rock songs I can barely remember anymore, when I hear the outer door hinges creak. "Simone is that you?" Turning the water off I cover up as best as I can and peek around the shower curtain. Before it is fully open the curtain is yanked away, I startle coming face to face with the camp terror, Kyle, and his picture wand.

The flash goes off as I lunge for the wand knowing it can be bad if people saw those. "Nice body!" He yells as he bolts out the stall door inches before my grasping fingers. "Get back here and give me that wand! *Flare, we have a problem…* I'll get you back Kyle…" I vow silently, climbing back into the shower to get the soap out of my long hair, otherwise I shall be itching all day.

My instincts scream for me to run after him to get the wand but I can't exactly go streaking around without it being worse than those pictures seeing light.

*

One long weary shower later I no longer have batter under my nails, flour in my hair, and am dressed for the feast. I found out the hard way the arm band doesn't come off, just shifts up or down, expanding and contracting to accommodate which way I want to move it, but never all the way off.

I actually am going wear a women's white toga sort of like the goddess statue, with ballet slippers and my auburn hair curled in small ringlets. Raja has spent the day with the other dragons at the lake taking a bath, but he is already at the tent when I finish. Everything all normal as Flare mocks him from the side.

"How do I look?" I call ahead, even giving a little twirl. *"Good, maybe we should paint you thou to have scales?"* Raja cranes his head around seeing me from every angle. *"Or fur,"* flare chirps, "Thanks but I'm not interested in a cat or furry creature or even a scaly one, I'll stick to mainly hairless," I quip back smoothing out the dress, *"Suit yourself,"* they chorus.

The middle of the camp has been cleared away - including the snow - a big bonfire put in the middle and area cleared for dancing to the side and around it, and tables of all sizes put out. Raja and Flare immediately abandon me for the company of Api and Roxanna. Unlucky for him the first person I see is Kyle hitting on Simone, while Laurence laughs at every cheesy come on line he overhears. "Hey Kyle I want a word with you." Kyle's beady eyes rake over me knowingly. I can feel my face get red with anger, the annoying twerp is asking for me to slug him.

"What you want, doll face? I was going to post those pictures to everyone's wands in the morning." He snickers, with a superior grin. "You can delete those now or I can later after I pay you back for the invasion on my privacy." I growl my best imitation of Raja, "not on your life." Another arrogant smile another tooth I want to punch out.

I feel my patience snap, I grab his tux lapels and bring him to my face, "I've warned you, now if I were you I'd sleep with one eye open," another snarl forms. "Hey, everything okay over here, Esper?" Laurence, Liam, and Michael ask all looking strapping in their tuxes but massive with wide shoulders and tapered waists. "Yeah, just making a point, I hope he got the point and would like to go get what he took and return it." I say with added sugar, "Not even in your dreams." He chuckles evilly obviously thinking I am bluffing.

"Well than I can't stop what's going to happen!" I bat my eye lashes, "enjoy." I Laugh as he glares and stumbles away. *"Flare follow him please I have a feeling he is going to check on those pictures, you know what to do when you find them."*

"Well that was vague and overly suspicious. So what's going on?" Liam asks throwing his arm over my shoulder and leading me farther away. "Not going to say, plausible deniability." They laugh, letting me get away with it, "may I have this dance?" Michael doesn't wait for an answer just grabs my hand and twirls me out onto the dance area. I laugh feeling the rush as he dips me and twirls me again and again, more than everyone else is just because I can't stop laughing and smiling.

Our song is almost over, when a giant rain drop smacks me in the cheek. Someone yells out, we watch as the spell casters draw their wands, blue light beams up making a dome around the camp so the whole thing won't have to be scrapped. The party goers go back to their revelries forgetting that rain had almost ruined the whole thing. "Shall we continue our dance? Show these chumps how they supposed to treat their women?" I placed my hand in his larger one and he twirls me off.

*

We return when both our feet start to hurt, I come to a dizzy stop next to Liam and lean against him for support as the world goes normal again. "I think my feelings have been hurt, that was our thing." Liam pouts holding his heart as though mortally wounded, "well we liked the waltz's more remember? If it means that much to you, lead away."

I hold out my hand, my breathing finally getting under control, and my skin cooling off from the close exposure to the bonfire while dancing. Liam gives me a wicked look and pulls me into the crowd once again, laughter following us. I don't think I have ever had this many friends, let alone ones I know would take a knife for me. People on Earth have been conditions so much to look after themselves first. Janie twirls into view bumping her hip into Liam to push him out of the way. "Girl time," Janie giggles as Simone joins us. Fiona and Amanda soon join. There aren't that many girls at camp, at least of the two legged none furry, human variety. So consequently we band together, girl power all the way.

*

The moons start to rise, bringing everyone huddled around the bonfire to watch and wait for mother earth. The final moon appears casting its rays on the bonfire. The wind picks up fanning the flames. The bonfire whooshes bigger, making several people jump back to avoid losing some eyebrows.

A spitting image of the statue in the goddess shrine steps out of the flames. The true goddess is far more beautiful than the statue. She has a glow around her with giant white wings, patches of her skin on her neck and body has scales, and what looked to be gills along her neck. Instead of fingers she has eagle talons and a braid draped over the shoulder with pink feelers at the end.

The goddess looks around before moving around the circle of a bomb fire looking at everyone, sometimes stopping to talk to someone before moving on. She stops at Dran though… she doesn't look happy. She balls her fists and screams at him like a banshee. Even with Dran being a giant dragon he flies backwards knocking into tent after tent even taking an unlucky dragon that got caught behind him down with him. She growls after him before moving on, I watch in the back, the band on my arm tingling.

'Esper' she calls back with thought, *'I forgot to tell you, your brothers shall be fine. Trust in Zar, he has raised a kingdom. he may not like it but his fate will be to influence them, they shall be great.'* The goddess gazes around chucking sadly as she passes over someone. After a minute thou she stops walking and heads back our way, the crowd parts like the sands of time. She stops in front of Michael, *'you will need these.'* She reaches into a fold in her gown pulling out two twin assassin blades. As we watch the daggers harden and solidify into daggers of beauty with cobalt veins running through them.

'Necrosis and Misery, Necrosis will kill instantly as soon as drawn blood, Misery shall paralyze for twelve hours, if you put the hilts together something… amazing shall happen.' The goddess places the assassin blades in Michael's trembling fingers, before placing her fingers to his forehead for luck. *'Best of luck to the righteous and even if you die tomorrow or*

five hundred years from now die with honor!' The goddess grabs the edge of her dress twirling around and around in a whirl of motion and color she disappears, leaving behind thousands of butterflies.

"It's beautiful, Michael!" I want to like just ogle them. They are twin blades, the blades themselves only a foot or longer.

The daggers each have their name intricately etched into the top part of the blade, and have Michael's name etched in the extended leafs above the hilt. A hand guard is rather simple, with just three prongs crossing.

"Thanks Esper…. I don't think I shall ever take them off. She saw my death without them and mine leading to more." The cobalt strands in them glint in the fire light, as everyone close leans closer to stare in amazement.

Zoe sniffed, "it's only nice to give the bonded something too, talon sheaths, jewelry… it was very discourteous of her not to."

"Zoe, I would assume that would go under a selfish want," Michael says not shocked enough to not quip with her, while clutching the blades to his chest. "Still," her sigh is full with longing, but seconds later the air pops in front of Zoe, and synthetic rabbit formed at her feet. She falls on it with enthusiasm.

Festivities increase once again, but in even more merriment.

"Michael, would you like to go grab a couple sheaths to fit these puppies? Must be careful with those, those slaver's might decide they want to kill you more for those blades. You know how they don't know when to say no." I grab his hand. Trying not to notice how warm and callused they are, as I pull him out of the party for the armory.

Because of the goddess's celebration I am not expecting anyone at the forges, but John is working away, his small dog size jade dragon curled up on a pillow sound asleep. "What you doing working, John? Why aren't you at the party?" He looks up briefly before once again looking down at the sword he is writing hieroglyphs on as it glows red of hot bendable metal.

"Uh, we wanted to get a sheath fit for a these daggers?" I lean on Michael's large arms to encourage him to show his new daggers, and nudge him in the side a couple times. Michael brings them up to the best he can to show casing them to their fullest advantage in the fire light from the forge.

"The free ones are over there, but..." He leans closer, "the ones with more detail and quality... such as ones taken off slavers, are going to cost you rations. Cliché is with eggs and will be eating more than her share." John finishes up the sword looking at Michael's daggers. "I want a better. It would be disrespectful to get a plane offal one for the goddess's gifts."

I can hear his reluctance; he is trying already to feed a growing griffin and himself. "I'll donate the rations." Before Michael can argue I interrupt again. "They already over feed us, with Raja, Flare, and Quinn they act like we are kings…. Then again Raja will be king, I honestly need them to stop eating, and you would be helping me out. If they eat more they will never be able to go into battle." Michael shoots me a look but swallows his pride. "This way then….."

18

The store room John leads us to, is full to the brim with sheaths that are haphazardly cast about in piles like treasure. "Pick your fancy." John leaves us to it without another word, just sighs as he glances around. "What about this," I show Michael a dark chocolate sheath with hieroglyphs allowing it to be split in two, able to fit the two daggers, increase strength of the blade, hygiene, and rust protection. Hygiene keeping the sheath clean of blood and other things, magically.

"Esper, No, the hygiene with the rust protection turns the blades purple." We continue searching through more till I find one in the back. The sheath is enchanted like the other to split in two and take the shape of the blade. The sheath itself was dark brown almost black, with hieroglyphs for identification, rust protection, and to keep the blade strong. There is also an enchanted story on the side, imprinting the sheaths memorable moments.

It starts sucking me into the story, bringing me to a scene like a bird in the sky to a vivid scene that has a sort of fade at the edges.

A man in his early hundreds looking twenty five though of average looks, blonde six foot, nothing really memorable about him. He is hunting in the woods when he found a wounded dragon that had taken to sickness. The man takes the dragon in, caring for him. Everything was fine till he gets the idea to keep the dragon by his treasure in the bank as a way to guard it from theft. For everyone's 'safety' in the dragon-less society he chained the dragon up. The dragon having gone insane from loneliness of the soul and his illness would go ballistic on others except on the man. The dragon in one of his rages killed a man who got to close.

The man who saved him was a merchant and he had a long standing rivalry between him and another merchant for spaces and customers. One day one played a trick on the man, so the man went into a rage and fed the other merchant to the dragon. Giving the man a idea, a bloody despicable idea. To use the dragon as his own personal killing machine that only he could control.

The sheath pauses, changing scenes again.

The man sought out a wizard, seeking a way to control the dragon's fractured mind for his own gain. The man soon learned more ways to control creatures, being so far from society he got the town or most of them into his way of living off others. Leading the town and soon the surrounding villages into a life living off the backs of those they enslaved.

The sheath shows the spread of slavery like an infestation, or one of those plagues maps. Then the sheath switches back to the man.

Some of the scenes to show the spread of slavery: *some just about catching their victims and then being chained and worked and showing more and more joining the first.*

The man sits pampered like a king in a house built like a palace built from the slave dragon, and other creatures he had enslaved. The man had been taking bribes from others, teaching them in exchange on how to control the mind, to fund his little palace. He never revealed all the secrets of the craft, so the buyers would have to come back when something went wrong with their spell eventually.

A slave, who hadn't been completely taken over, snuck into the man's room as he sleeps, easy for the slaver was cocky over his control on his slaves. The slave slit his throat from the knife in the evil greedy man's sheath. Taking the weapon the slave ran for it, not having the heart to leave all of the other slaves. He escaped on the back of a dragon, heading for the capital. Once to the capital to warn them, he cast away his ex-masters blade vowing to never rest while others were enslaved, but never to do it with the tainted blade.

The story that has sucked me into the flash sinks back into the skin of the sheath in a thin smog. "Michael, how about this sheath it was there at the start of the war, so it would be perfect for it to be at the end? The Sheath seems charmed to show its history. What better way to tell the ending?" Michael glances at the dark chocolate sheath, with its gems sown on the side and intricate designs. "Isn't it a bit ostentatious?" His face contemplating, "well you can pry off some of the gems, and sell them for extra food for Zoe."

"I guess without all the gems it will work perfectly okay." Michael reaches for it, feeling along the edge and inside.

"Well you have turned your nose up at everything else. At this rate you will have to carry them in a paper sack!" I argue, we have been here for what feels like hours, and he has turned up his nose at every one of them, some perfectly good sheaths. "They didn't feel right! I'm not going to put them in an inferior case." Michael defends, clutching the daggers closer to his chest, I'm surprised he doesn't start rocking them, and cooing like they are a baby.

"Okay, Cujo, let's just go now, we have a sheath that will work." Michael nods pulling the sheath into two and slowly putting the daggers in so the sheath will have time to adjust and change shape. We exit the forge waving good bye to John. The moons have almost gone all the way down, it will be dawn soon. A bird's strangled cry sounds close by. I snap my head up looking wildly for the wounded voice.

"What you think that was? Maybe we should go check it out?" I pull on Michael's hand leading him to the edge of the camp. "It's probable nothing," none the less he pulls out Necrosis and Misery, making sure he is ready for anything.

"Ugh!"

A strangled, surprised moan sound but ends short in a gurgle. I let go of Michael's hand, raising two fingers pointing to him, then right, and me to the left. He nods practically turning into shadows.

I hike my dress up, but it restricts movement so with a heavy heart. I rip my dress on one side from hip to ankle. I move on light feet channeling the stealth of Flare along with his increased hearing. I move warily around trees and brush, looking for the source of the cries.

I haven't gone more than three hundred yards before I land face first next to something soft and squishy that has tripped me. I have a bad feeling I don't want to see what's under me. This will probable give me nightmare I shouldn't look, I shouldn't, I'm not going to look… I look. I stare into the face of the night watchman, Van, his throat slit, a look of stricken grief stretched over his face. Beside the man is his bonded, a giant hawk, she has an arrow sticking out of her chest.

I lay next to them for what feels as if an eternity with my heart pounding in my ears. I just lay on the ground staring at the face of a man I know and his quick painful death, listening for sounds of his killer. I jump up looking for the people responsible they can't have gotten far. "Stop her, before she gives us away!"

An arrow thuds into a tree near inches from my face, I decide not to stick around. "Raja, warn the camp now! We are under attack!" I run for it weaving like the hounds of hell are right on my heels, the more intimidating ones then Ceribi. Most likely I have a few chasing me but I'm just not willing to check. I am definitely to nosy for my own good, I don't see Simone always getting chased or shot at.

Another arrow thuds into a tree closer than I like, more arrows follow, if they get any closer I won't make it out of these woods alive. "*Now might be nice for backup!*" I run faster calling on Flare's leopard speed. "*Hold on!*" Flare growls, I can sense him closer, charging forward with all his might, Roxy hard on his heels. There is some dumb stuff to do when running for your life, one just happens to be tripping, and of course that is what I do. I hear another arrow this time it sails past where my head use to be, imbedding itself inches into a giant tree instead. I can hear them closing in their breathing labored, and many, many footstep. I roll to the side grabbing first tree I can, it being four feet wide.

I climb up, with muscles I didn't even know I had when I was on earth, using all the branches and holes I can find. I tear my dress some more, even staining it. I climb higher and higher, until the people hunting me are harder to discern, and then I climb down enough so I can see them. There are thousands of creatures all surging toward the camp, no longer bothering to be discreet, the forest echoes with their war cries and thousands of feet.

"Raja I think their whole army is here, tell Roxy to come get me from the tree, before they notice me. Also contact Zoe, see if Michael's okay." I look down at my beautiful gown ruined, and one of my slippers lost to goddess knows where.

"Did someone call for a ride? Flare told me about your world as he put it I should be getting stuff for being your... taxi." Roxy grumbles fluttering her wings, ready to be gone from this place. I don't take my time. I just jump for her back and hold on tight, as the winged saber tooth tiger jumps from branch to branch higher and higher, to get up into the air without being shot down.

From Roxy's back at the top of the tree I can see Raja in battle with a Cyclops. First Cyclops I have ever seen. The Cyclops tries to bludgeon Raja as Raja looks in vain for a band controlling him. *"Raja he is either willingly helping them or they have his bonded,"* either way, we can't help him. "Roxy take me down by my tent, I like a dummy forgot Saphique and I need some padding." Roxy doesn't say anything just banks left.

We drop, she runs to a halt, next to our large tent. *"You need me or you good?"* Roxy hops from foot to foot with impatience. "No, go help Flare, he is outnumbered and some are ganging up on him." I push down my own panic for him knowing I can't do anything for him but she can. It's best to send Roxy fast from what I can sense.

Roxy doesn't need more prodding. She jumps to the sky, and gone in seconds, streaking off in a flash of tawny fur. Now I think, her teeth don't seem to scare me anymore. she and Flare are going to have cute cubs. I know they haven't said anything but I know they snuck out a lot while she was in heat, and they always mushy together and I am his bonded I don't need confirmation when I can spy in his mind. Wow, where your mind strays when waiting.

I hurry inside, going through the familiar motions of putting on my impenetrable leather chest padding and wrist guards. I don't bother removing the dress, it is already ruined. I belt on Saphique and my many daggers, and some gloves, for good measure. I finish up my mental check list. As I lace up my combat boots.

I check twice more, 'what am I missing…. I know there's something….' "Flare at the rate you are going through them you going to finish this war without me." I unsheathe Saphique as I exit the tent, I don't knows who's walking out here. I honestly don't mind if he killed them all before I got there I would rather not kill. I kill for my friends, my family, my bonded, and all those that can't fight.

"Found Zoe, Michael's is with her. He managed to go unseen." Raja reassures, sounding a little put out with me thou. Raja has already finished off the Cyclops and is now trying to catch a griffin while avoiding the thing that is shooting rays that turned creatures to stone around him. *"Thanks."*

I hear a cry as someone gets injured up ahead. I peak around the corner of a tent, seeing Simone unarmed kneeling before a slaver. She is about to be beheaded, blood at the side of her mouth and bleeding from multiple wounds.

"Hey!" I scream at the slaver, trying to distract him from his death blow he is about to deliver. The man has already swung and instead jerks his blade down burying the blade into her right shoulder, awfully deep. The man tries to jerk the weapon out of her, but finding he doesn't have enough time, as I lob off his own head. His warm blood splatters across me as he falls at my feet. I ignore it thou to fall beside Simone. "Simone, oh goddess, we need to get you to the healer's like yesterday!" I'm afraid to touch her, but the blade must come out.

I move a little to the side grabbing the hilt. "I'm sorry, this is going to hurt!" I close my eyes, counting to ten.

I grip the hilt harder, pulling it out little by little, knowing it is torture for her but, if I go faster it might not come out so clean.

She cries out clutching her hands to my legs, whispering my name, her voice so week. I stand so I can get better leverage to pull it up. Simone moans as the blade springs free and she collapses at my feet. I kneel beside her, putting pressure on the wound. "Simone I have to go get someone, I can't move you by myself."

I squeeze her hand, before getting to my feet. I run towards the sound of battle to find someone to help her. I find an assistant helper to the healers around the corner in trouble. Also he happens to be an elephant. The elephant is being attacked by wolves with bands above their paws.

I don't give them a time to notice me, I spring for the wolf at it leaps for the elephant. I bring my blade up to smash into the anklet, shattering it, and slightly bending Saphique. The elephant catches the wolf that seems to have gone limp after the shackle broke. The second wolf jumps towards me in a frenzy, snarling and practically foaming at the mouth.

The wolf gets knocked out of the air by the elephant's trunk. While she is stunned I creep forward, unsure if she is just faking or not. The wolf isn't moving so I bring

Saphique around. Instead of hitting the shackle I hit the ground. The wolf rolls away, jumping towards my face while I'm collecting myself again.

The elephant pushes me away, sending me summersaulting away from my almost certain death. The wolf lands where I had been and turns only to get hit by the assistant healer's trunk. The wolf sails through the air to land at my feet, I bring Saphique down while she is stunned, and break the shackle in a hacking blow. The wolf face that had been forming a snarl smooth's out into confusion and making her appear like a lost puppy.

"I need your help for my friend she was hurt bad, she took a sword to her shoulder. I got it out, but now she won't stop bleeding you have to help her or take her to someone who will." I know I'm babbling but I also know I can't stop, Simone and I had become good friends, I don't want her to die. I run up to the elephant, grabbing his trunk to pull him back the way I had come. He trots after, with two lost looking wolves wandering behind like baby ducks following their mama.

"Help her, please help her." I run ahead to the prone figure lying in a pool of blood. I step over the slavers body to take a knee beside my friend, urgently motioning them closer. The elephant daintily steps over the slaver to look down over Simone. "*Probable best if we get her to the healer post haste.*"

The elephant wraps his trunk around Simone lifting her up. Simone's spine bends, her head falling back, and her hands hanging below her. "Be careful. Be careful, she's hurt bad." I mutter fretting around them, the wolves warily watching every bend for possible threats as we make our way to the infirmary. My brother Dash will kill me if I let something happen to his girlfriend.

The infirmary has moved closer to the fighting then they are normally situated, so they can be of more help. Dragons and larger animals are off to the side so they won't be in the way or get caught up in the tents. Warriors guard the area as doctor's work on people, the worse off first.

"We need help over here, she was stabbed." I hover over her, as a doctor rushes over. I look over as he lightly pulls her clothing away from her blood soaked shoulder, to examine the long laceration on her right shoulder. "Get her out of here," the doctor calls, and a man pushes me away so I won't be left staring at the injury as the doctor attempts to save her life.

"Esper, Zoe says that Raja looks to be in some trouble and needs some help he is east of your position, under heavy attack. You are closer." Flare sends the urgent message while running for all he's worth towards the location he mentally shows me. I see Raja with chains from all directions, some over his wings to keep him from flying.

He fights for all he's worth. I can see groups of trees off to the side, almost surrounding them. Also he is in a crater as if he had fallen to earth. I don't even take in all the information that Flare gives me, I run for all I'm worth towards the mental connection of Raja. I even poor in some of Flare's swiftness, and Raja's strength to reach grater speeds.

Now that I am focusing on him I can feel him holding back his thoughts as to let me focus on Simone and not make me worry about him. I run through trees, like the wind (praying I don't trip, I can't always be clumsy).

I burst out of the trees to the clearing where things have gotten worse for Raja. Now along with chains he has a netting throne over him. A dragon sits perched on a giant tree overseeing as the slavers are on the tail end of securing him.

I don't think. I rush forward bashing the nearest man over the head with the butt of Saphique. As the man crumples to the ground I put Saphique in her sheath not willing to use my sword when it is in a bad state. I pick up the fallen man's sword, and rush the other man holding the rope who hasn't noticed me, somehow. I run him through, ignoring him after he is no longer of consequence. I place the stolen sword between the links in the chain using my body to try and lever it open. The chain jingles but holds.

The men holding the other chain finally notice me. They rush me as my weapon is still caught up on the chain.

The man's sword comes up, I twirl away and the blade lands against the heavy chains in a shower of sparks. I have sacrificed my stolen sword in a means to prevent being cut in half, so I grab two of my simple daggers and bring them up to block the slavers next rushed blow. I use the smaller daggers to push them away. The man goes off balance and leans to the side with his sword. I lunge forward burying my dagger into his heart. The man drops, soon another slaver takes his place and we start all over again.

Raja beats against the chains and heavy mesh that's thrown over him. With all the slavers attention on me, Raja soon manages to pull out a couple of the spikes that keep the mesh in place. As the second spike breaks free the slavers who still live cry out to the dragon who watches from the tree. Raja increases his resistance, the chains making marks on his body with the increase rubbing.

Raja gets another free, only four more holding the Mesh and chains in place, evidently not enough because with Raja's strength against the four they slowly start to come up. The black dragon in the tree lets out a roar in furry, leaping from the tree to attack Raja. Meanwhile I keep the slavers busy.

The dual battles don't last long. With two dragons fighting on the ground, it leaves no room for us smaller creatures to fight. We all soon give up in way of hiding in the trees to keep from getting crushed. Raja has managed to throw away most of the chains but some still tangle around his limbs as the smaller dragon tries to break through Raja's tougher outer scales. Raja extends his wings thrusting in a way to push off the rest of the chains.

The small black dragon roars raking his claws over Rajas softer belly, finally managing to break the skin and open up a small gash. Raja roars his hurt back, not happy to be injured. I can feel the claws as if they had raked through my own stomach. A cry leaves my lips in worry and sympathy for my bonded. Raja lunges forward getting a grip on the smaller dragons shoulder, his claws extending to gouge into the smaller dragon. Raja leans forward as the smaller dragon fights to break his grip, *"Raja, try and break their hold."*

I cry too late as Raja takes one of his paws and pushes the dragons head to the ground ignoring the injury the other dragon inflicted on Raja's body by means of his back feet and strikes. Raja rips into the dragon's throat tearing it out and mortally wounding him. *"He doesn't have a band and he told me he is working with them on purpose, he chose to help them to enslave his own kind."* Raja's voice is low and brutal as he passes judgment onto the other dragon, his teeth still buried in his throat clenching harder until the smaller dragon slowly stops fighting and finally stops moving at all.

I watch in morbid curiosity as the dragon's arms and legs go limp, his talons covered in Raja's blood. I run to Raja, always aware of the slavers who flee around me. Raja slumps, his adrenaline leaving him, I can hear him take check his injuries. Multiple gashes on his belly and arms from the dragon's last flailing attempts to live, his wings from his fall and the chain, are also injured beyond flight.

"Let's get you to healers. I am very upset with you for blocking me, while you were in clear need of help." I glare holes into him as he pointedly ignores it and keeps trudging on through the trees. I sense Flare turning around to rejoin the fighting, promising to take a break in a bit.

"I promise to get help next time but I thought I had it or would be able to handle it that was until the slavers ambushed me after the dragon knocked me to the ground, injuring my wings." Raja seems so tired, his tail dragging in the dirt, I can feel he just doesn't have the energy to pick it up. The battle winds down around us, we having seemed to have fought back almost all of enemy fighters. I wish he was smaller or I was bigger so I could let my big marshmallow have me to lean on.

Leaving Raja at the medical center, I head off to find Zoe and Michael knowing they would be in the thick of what is left of things. I find them as I suspect in the middle, running off some slavers. It doesn't look like they need me so I lean back against a tent watching them do aerial maneuvers to get rid of the last of the enemy.

"I think you are getting slow, Michael, that took you longer than usual." I call over to them, as they descend down to land beside me. "What by about five seconds, pshh, maybe you are just getting better and showing up earlier." Michael hops off Zoe, wiping sweet off his brow. "Well I would love to think that, but that might just be wishful thinking." I hug him needing the comfort after nearly losing both Raja and Simone. He wraps his arms around me.

Michael rubs my back in reassurance, before I move back. "Yeah well Super Star, how about we go get ourselves cleaned up? Maybe go get some food?" I suggest Michael nods, "how about we just go to the lake get clean that way. I think the bathrooms might be out of order for a while I pretty sure I saw a Cyclops step all over it before he died on top of them."

I laugh wondering how this guy could make me laugh after a bloody long battle. "I'm sure Roxy wouldn't mind carrying me if it meant she could get clean. But honestly I am not made for a polar bear dip so how about a warmed water that's enchanted?" I link arms with Super Star and pull him off to find Roxy, "Zoe says she is going to wait for us in the ruins of the bathrooms." Michael whispers it into my ear, as we pass by a tent that has soft snoring coming from the crack of the tent flap, I giggle from the feel of the air tickling my ear.

*

We ended up stopping at my to let me get dressed before we head to the medic area to check on Simone and Raja. I think I would probable give Raja's nightmares if I showed up in my now ruby red gown. I sometimes think Raja would be much better if he didn't have to have anything to do with the war, it troubles him. Michael and me had convinced a sorcerer to warm up some water and make a miniature biohazard shower for us. Honestly sometimes I think I need a hazard team from Earth to work me over just to feel clean again.

Raja is off to the back having been treated adn now just needing to sleep it off. Simone is in the main tent with a enchanter whispering over her as she fights for her life.

I kneel down beside her bed taking her clammy hand into mine, "How you doing girl? You gave us a scare. On my world, we believe that if you talk to someone when they are sick they will get better, and you are going to get better, you have no other options. Not after all but pushing me into being you friend." I laugh through my tears, looking up when the Enchanter clears his throat.

"A few more hours of healing she just might be able to recover on her own." I nod giving him a watery smile in thanks. I just have to say it's hard on the soul watching a friend almost die.

"Raja will be fine also, he just needs strict rest." He continues making hand gestures off towards Raja. I nod some more not so worried he is big and strong, Simone is like wafer small, she doesn't got a lot to cut up and the slaver sure was trying.

19

Three days later....

The next few days are spend repairing the camp and caring for our wounded, even giving last rights to the slavers. Pangaea's last rights are very beautiful ceremony. A siren sings in her beautiful voice that makes your heart ache, she sings to and for the dead wishing them peace. She sings to the mother seeking entrance for these poor spirits and their bodies into her skin, to welcome them once more. As the siren sings to both the earth and the dead the earth moves taking in the bodies, by the end of the ceremony all the bodies are gone, and on a rock or tree nearby names form of those deceased. Also its probable confusing when I say siren, cause there is the evil Merr siren and there is the beautiful sexual siren. On is a turned evil person and the other is born that way. These kinds of sirens are beautiful people with the most beautiful voices that are not of this world. It might sound cheesy but you don't listen to a siren with your ears you listen with your soul. That's as good as description as it gets.

The siren people don't fight they are healers and basically the priests who perform Pangaea's last rights, and yet completely different. If a siren joined either side on a killing capacity they could decimate swaths of the army, anyone within their power range. The army would all just die or just give up and never be able to pick themselves up. The toll to the siren though would be as bad the siren would self-combust from power like a suicide bomber, kind of. I know because I asked.

After about three days though things go back to normal with the exception that Simone and Raja are both put on strict bed rest, even with all their grumbling neither argue with it, too exhausting. Soon trade resumed like nothing has ever happened. New recruits pour in by the day to fill in the great losses that we sustained during both ambushes and the minor attacks in the last month.

I hail down the messenger about to leave for Claret, "Hey, can you do me a favor? When you are in Claret I need you to pick me up something." I draw him away from his audience, who want to give him mail and what not to send with him. The messenger is a small dragon about the size of a horse, as I slowly look him over. I realize why he looks so familiar.

"Xavier, it's been awhile, remember we met in the town Anasazi or Gizmo I can't remember which. I need you to buy something for me while you are in town..." After I finish telling Xavier what I need him to buy for me he goes back to his crowd collects the rest of the mail before leaving off with some gold coins for my item and a few extra for him. "So what did you ask him to get for you?" I jump as Michael sneaks up behind me, I twirl around hitting him in the gut with a hard right. "Stupid moron if I had Saphique with me you would be dead." I growl mainly for how hard my heart is racing.

"Psh, you could never hurt me that was like a reverse of our meeting you spacing out getting startled, but this time I'm the one who almost gets hurt, maybe not reverse but jumbled. By the way where is that weapon of yours? You finally get sick of it? Decide you want to join the new fad about wielding two daggers like me? I don't mind if you want to be like me, who doesn't." He falls into step beside me, looking all strapping in what should've been a loose shirt but is now fabulously tight and Pangaea's version of jean pants.

"It got bent in the fighting I made the mistake of thinking she could cut through those slave bands at a weird angle." I head for the cooks tent rather wanting a snack. "Well how about we swing by your tentm, get the sword, drop it off at the forges and then get your snack. That way if you need it you shall have it." I fake sigh pretending like I'm just giving in and that it wasn't the best idea.

We head to the tent I share with Raja, Quinn, and Flare, and I go to my little nook where I keep all my armor and supplies. Quinn lounges on top of Raja who is sound asleep. Due to Raja's fall he has severely injured his wings and the healers say he will be unable to fly for at least two weeks.

I grab Saphique feeling sad that my stunning sword is now slightly misshapen. "Come on Super Star, I got it, Quinn would you like to go with us? We are going to stop for a snack after we stop at the forges." Quinn pokes up his slightly still fuzzy head, "*Sure.*" Quinn stumbles off Raja, who just gives a grunt and resettles. The little griffin falls off the dragon to the ground. He falls into step with us as we leave the tent. "Quinn how is your classes coming, is my big lug of a dragon treating you alright?"

The little griffin is looking more awkward than he did when he first came to us. His fuzzy feathers are starting to fall out and he's starting to get his grown up feathers. He is the size of a big dog now, "You say griffins take a long time to mature but he seems to be growing rather nicely." I look over at the little griffin again, but pose my statement to Michael.

"Yeah, Zoe grew like a weed for a while but when she got to just about chest height she stopped growing so fast. I think though she is going to be on the small side. Him I see getting as big as well bigger then you or me." Quinn listens in rapt attention, "from the feathers coming in I would say he is going to be a mighty handsome fellow."

Quinn puffs himself up so big I think he is going to trip, because he can't see his feat. I take an abrupt right into the forge, the little griffin doesn't expect it so he goes off balance and collapses into Michael sending them both sprawled. "Okay wasn't exactly planning that out especially but that was just an added bonus." I cackle from a safe distance.

I head deeper into the forge and finding John as usually working, he was smelting down a couple blades. "Hey John, I need some work down, Saphique got bent." I hold her up for him to see the damage, a long whistle coming from John. "One bronze coin and maybe four days, I have a lot of work to do before I can even get to it." He moves back to his project taking the blade and burning it down, "come on John you can do better than that," I cajole moving around his work bench so I can face him.

"It's the best I can do Esper take it or leave it." He keeps right on working. I feel a light sweat forming from the heat of the forge. "What am I supposed to do for four days without my main weapon?" He sighs putting down the liquid metal as soon as he looks over I give him a sappy look with my purple eyes. "You got daggers don't you? They say the big counter attack won't be for at least two and a half weeks so you will be fine. Word is we are even moving the camp to somewhere new so they can't find us so easy, talking major warding." I sigh knowing I am not going to be getting any sympathy or the date moved up. "Fine, see you bright and early in four days' time. Go ahead and grab a spare if you wish." He thrust one of the slavers blades at me that he hadn't smelted yet.

I stalk out none too happy, collect Michael and Quinn, and head off to our awaiting snacks.

"So how long is it going to take?" Michael grabs a tray and we head through the mess hall line. "Four days at the earliest, did hear something interesting though. Apparently soon we are moving the camp and in over two weeks we are going to make a counter move against the slavers." Michael looks up from cramming a slice of what looks like pizza, "well that is interesting. Wonder why it's so hush, hush, unless they think there is a spy among us."

"I don't even try to assume I know how those commanders think. Let them think and I will think how I think and hope I don't get blown away because theirs is faulty." We continue eating in silence until Quinn gets bored with the not talking, and starts talking about everything under the moon.

*

"MICHAEL, MICHAEL, MICHAEL!" I run towards his tent, bursting in without being asked. "It's here, come see." I draw the words out for effect but stop short as I see a rumpled Michael wiping sleep from his eyes, his chest bare looking like his sculpted leather armor. "Oh I'm sorry I didn't mean… well I meant to wake you… but I assumed you would have a shirt on. I'll wait outside." I hurry out before he can say anything, standing outside the tent though to wait enjoying the crisp cold wind.

"What was that all about, you have seen me without my shirt, gosh, Esper you are acting strange?" He laughs, pushing back the tent flap. "Look, your surprise is in!" I hand him the light box kept closed by ribbon, ignoring his comment on my strangeness. Michael pulls off the purple ribbon to get to the grey box, lifting the lid he pulls free the red and black cloak. He lets the box fall to the floor and shakes out the cloak; it starts a dark red up at the top and as it goes to the bottom turns black. "Oh, my, goddess, you didn't have to do this it's so beautiful, I don't think I ever want to let it out of my sight." Michael sounds so happy like a giddy little kid, swinging his new cloak around in a swirl of red and black, tying it around his shoulders with the gold chain meant for the task.

"How do I look, strapping?" He sticks out his chest and lowers his voice a bit.

"Well you sure look… interesting." I hide my smile behind my hand, he sort of reminds me of Superman.

"Haha, I think I look good, Zoe thinks so too." Zoe opens one of her big gold eyes to look over at him, but closes it a second later. "You just jealous you didn't think to get one for yourself." I nod all solemn like that is actually what I am thinking. "I have to admit it does look strapping on you." I actually mean it though, not many could pull it off but with his broad shoulders he pulls it off. I pull at the lapels of my trench coat, "if I take up a cloak then who would pull off the trench coat? You have got to admit I look good?" I twirl around for him to see.

"Yeah I see that," Michael swoops on the twirl over taking my hands and starting us dancing, "Super Star, why are we dancing there is no music?" As if on cue music starts playing softly from his tent. "Zoe?" he smiles and nods, "hey have to make everything romantic for when I ask you something very important." He twirls me. I ignore the people glancing our way, basically not even noticing them.

"Oh and what would that be?" I giggle some more as he spins me around and around, I love the feel of being twirled. "Would you go on a date with me? As more then friends?" He has a nervous smile on his face. I can't keep the grin from forming on my own, "Yes!" I hug him, "shouldn't we hold that off till we manage to get to a town?" my smile dimming a little at the thought of how long that will take.

"Now just leave that to me." I smile again, my mind trying to come up with possibilities, like horseback riding, or what a trip to the mess hall. "I'll trust you on this." He smiles twirling me again and again till I laugh harder. "I will pick you up at three tomorrow." He smiles kissing me on the cheek. "Well then I have some planning to do before then, I will see you tomorrow at three, dress nice, I'll pick you up at your tent." Michael lets me go on a spin sending me spinning on my own, as I slowly stop spinning I see him every five seconds running towards some unknown place.

I walk off a little dizzy and on a bubble of happiness. "*Esper, you need might want to see this.*" Flare mentally calls, not letting me see through his eyes, forcing me to in person come see. I weave around tents following Flare's directions, seeming to be taking me to the area the new recruits are setting up their camps.

I round the bend seeing wolves, lots of wolves and different types of wild cats. Off to the side are Pegasuses and other type of horses, along with Valla, Red, and Sheena. I also notice a certain brother of mine standing near them talking to another man, Dash. Well this is going to get interesting. I feel Flare off to the side hiding in a tree that has a vantage point over the clearing. I walk behind my brother Dash tapping him on his shoulder.

Dash turns his big brown eyes widening at the sight of me here, "Esper... I was hoping to put this off for a while longer." Dash runs his hands over his face, not having much hair to run his hands through in agitation. "Before you say anything I'm not the only one who's here. Toni is here and well so would be Lucan but Zar convinced him to wait for another year." Dash looks around bringing his foot back to kick Sheena above the hoof to get her attention.

Sheena dejectedly turns, I still don't say anything just imagine my amethyst eyes drilling holes into their heads. Dash shifts awkwardly, changing tactics. "Did you realize that if we were on earth it you would be eighteen or nineteen, I would be like seventeen or eighteen." I don't know how I should feel... "You have all your weapons? Finished your training? Gotten Sheena her equipment?" I finally break my silence to mother hen over them. "Yeah, yeah, Esper, we got all that this wasn't just a spur of the moment decision. Esper, you," He sweeps his hands to encompass the whole camp, "they need us." I don't argue and just nod. I have to let him decide for himself at some point.

"So you say Toni joined, where is he?" I look around for him but seeing no sign of him or his silver wolf. "He's back at Claret with Cobalt and Aurora. He got his shipment extended so Cobalt can be with Aurora for when their pups get here, Cobalt won't be here for nine months, but Toni will be in a month or two, with the option to visit every couple of weeks. He pulled that off by making pals with Averia, and so did Aurora. Averia has her husband by the gonads when she wants something." Dash chuckles apparently thinking back to the scene where Averia got her way, I smile picturing the images he paints for me. Of her getting her way not the gonad thing.

"Well I'm happy for him, and he had better know I am going to ask for time off to come visit them, I expect to be like god mother of them!" He smiles, "I think he already knew that." Dash flashes me a smile, "he better have."

"Esper, Flare, you are wanted at the command tent." A big black man bellows, in a low deep voice, making him sound rather ominous. Flare instantaneously appears at my side, as the man motions us over.

We move towards the massive man. He looks down his nose at us seeming to make a judgment, and finds us lacking. The big black man turns heading for the command tent, his shoulder about twice my size, maybe twice Michael... He kind of looks like Michael Clarke Duncan.

The big bear of a man seems pretty nimble because he practically dances around obstacles that should've tripped him up. We make it to the command tent in one piece, barely.

The tent is twice as big as any of the dragon tent, big and black, with an emblem I had seen around the capital on the top. The big burly man pulls back a flap to the tent to let us inside. Inside the tent it is pleasantly warm after the outsides nippiness, Dran sits to one side overlooking a giant table with charts and maps strewn across it. Other men and creatures fill the tent, arguing loudly to one another, all of the arguing comes to a screeching halt as we enter thou and move to the side.

"Ah, yes, finally here, about time." Dran drawls thumping his tail down for emphasis, *"can we have a second."* He doesn't make it a question, but a demand for the other people in the tent to leave. The others collect their things an scurry out, some quite literally scurry, leaving me alone with Dran, Flare, the big black man, and three other non-descript soldiers.

"I have a job for you," Dran moves towards the maps, motioning us to come have a look. *"I have chosen you for a mission to scout out locations for our new camp. You will be leaving at midnight tonight to travel down the Slaver's border for a location big enough to hold the whole army. I want it far enough from here to not be obvious and I want it easy flying from Claret."* He shows us on the map where he wants most likely area to be.

"Now of course while you are out it might behoove you to also look around for the slavers or possible battle grounds. Esper, Flare you may go. The rest I need to talk to you," Dran waves us off, the other men all but pushing us out of the tent before turning back into the tent themselves.

"What you think that is about?" I whisper down to Flare as the giant back man glares at us as he pulls the flap down to block us from whatever is going on in the tent. A blue shimmer goes around the black tent, before it goes normal again, not a word to be heard from inside the tent.

"Might want to go get ready, you might want to go reschedule with Michael, so he doesn't think you stood him up." Flare nudges my shoulder towards the direction of Michael's tent, before heading in the opposite direction. I shuffle off to where I can hear Michael humming and practicing with his daggers.

I turn the last corner to find him whacking at a holographic opponent with his twin blades, Necrosis and Misery. His form in perfect order as he starts too sweat through a thin no sleeves T-shirt, only once in a while the holographic warrior would land a blow that would flow right through him, usually though followed with much cursing.

"Michael we need to talk." I walk up beside him. He stumbles a bit from my appearance but regains his footing. "Voice command pause," Michael calls to the holograph that stops in midstride. "Yeah, Esper, what's going on?" His chest heaves more from the shock then from his workout, now I think about it I never see this man just propping up his feet.

"I have to reschedule our date from tomorrow to sometime in the next couple days." My shoulders sag hoping he won't just cancel it all together.

"Why?" Michael grabs a towel from a sword rack next to his tent, drying his neck, and slings it over the holographic warrior. "Dran asked me to go out for scouting very hush, hush, but I don't know when I will be back so we need to reschedule." He nods not seeming put out, but okay with the change in plans. Thank the goddess.

20

Midnight rolls around much too soon, Flare and I, stand waiting at the edge of camp on foot. I'm kind of unsure how we are going to cover a good distance just walking. The nocturnal bondeds could be heard from here, with a resonance, which is rather eerie at the clarity like the animal is right beside me.

A voice calls from the dark, as if reading my thoughts, "Well you can walk if you want girl, but I plan on personally hitching a ride."

The giant black man makes his way out of the darkness, two black horses following behind hard to differentiate from the shadows. Valla trots over to nudge me welcome after such a long time apart. The other men who were in the debriefing also appear out of the shadows unsettling me at the ease they had snuck up on us.

Flare growls lightly at the sneaking appearance of the other men. But instead shrugs and heads for the woods, realizing that it would take him nowhere to continue on with the slight. I swing onto Valla, enjoying being back in the saddle, once again, and head off ahead of the others to follow my other bonded. It's kind of nice not to be riding on a truck size dragon that you basically have to learn to do the splits to ride.

The woods seem alive in a different way, making weird noises that you wouldn't hear in the day time, like owls and wolves howling at the many moons. Normal people would be afraid but knowing they are as smart as or smarter than me, not so much.

"See you when I get back Raja make sure you rest up those wings I want to be flying soon." I send to my bonded getting a slight hum back through the bond as a reply, *"Yup the basket riding it starting to grow on me."* Flare sends also to Raja, imagining the basket open and the wind flying through his fur, to him a very good image... kind of like a dog he is.

*

Dawn can't have come soon enough for me, I may love the forest, but apparently I have forgotten how the dark here creeps me out a little. Dawn comes on the backs of the birds who coo to the morning sun and shock us back into awareness with their sudden flight to the sky. The forest I love welcomes me as an old friend as Valla runs across its spongy floor, jumping giant trees that get in our way.

"*A large clearing up ahead might work for our needs, come check it out.*" Flare sends from up ahead. "Guys, Flare thinks he might have found a good location." I turn in my saddle to look back at the not to chatty group behind me. The giant black man, Marise, is the seeming leader of them, just nods and shares a look with the others. That look doesn't sit with me right, like they know something I don't. At the edge of the clearing we dismount, leaving the horses there so we may check out the clearing and give the horses a rest to graze and drink from the small pool off to the side.

"Not bad Flare it's huge." I look around an enormous clearing, surrounded by tall huge trees. The lowest branches hanging over well taller than our biggest tents, they hang over most of the camp like a canopy with an occasional tree to produce more canopy coverage. The sun streams through playing shadows over the soft flooring. The place was perfect.

"No matter how long I am here I can never get over how beautiful Pangaea is with is gigantic forests and vivid flowers… I wonder what would happen if they were taken to earth."

"It's perfect, that's why we found it a week ago," Marise growls behind us, I hear a startled howl from Flare behind me. I turn around in confusion, "what you mean you—" I cut off with a strangled gasp. Agony rips through my body and soul. I know how people will say that but I can say for a fact I feel my heart about to burst from the heartbreak its causing me. I might be dramatic but this is unlike anything you could imagine a human could endure.

I fall to my knees, crawling around to see Flare on the ground bleeding. He isn't moving... I reach mentally to him, shying away as I feel the mortal pain emanating all through his brain. I want to pull away from the pain, but I won't leave him alone, not in that kind of pain.

I embrace the pain in him pulling it into myself so he may be free of the pain. I can feel his soul slipping away from me, too tired to keep going for long. *"You can't die, you have to stay with me"* My knees give out, I start using my arms to pull myself forward towards my dying soul partner. "You thought you were part of the mission."

I ignore him keeping my focus on Flare, *"Come on Flare, remember how we made plans for after this war, we would be sitting pretty, just growing old and fat together. Us having milk by the fire as Raja talks about his hardship keeping the kingdom running, your grand-kits running around the room. They being little hellions like their grandpa, our mates sitting next to us, one big happy family. Don't make Roxy raise your kits alone."* I will him to live, he is my first bonded, loved beyond belief, and sharing his own part of my heart with Raja. I learned about Pangaea with Flare I decided to stay because of him, I can't imagine a life anywhere without him and Raja, I didn't need him to just live for himself I needed him to live for me and Raja and us.

Marise chuckles at our stupidity, "You were in a way, more the mission in general though. A peace offering to some needed allies, so to speak. What better way to get rid of his pathetic younger brothers will to live, let alone rule." Marise stands over me, a look of contempt on his face. I reach my hand out weaving my fingers through Flare's fur. I try calling to Raja but all I get is white noise like interference.

Flare lets out a sigh turning his head to look me in the eye. I hear a scraping noise, turning my head in time to see the sword before he shoves it through my back. I gasp losing the handle I have on Flare's pain. I turn back to him without thought of the wound that may be mortal or the lunatic standing over me. Tears stream over my face as I make eye contact again with Flare once more. *"Sorry…"* he's slipping so fast… and I know. *"You can go, Roxy will never be alone. You don't need to be in pain anymore."* Tears flow faster and harder, I don't care let them come.

I watch with horror and anguish as the light of life empties out of him, sounding weird but I can literally see the sparkle that has always been in his eyes drain away. I reach for him in our minds crying out to him as I come up with empty space.

Flare's just gone.

Tears quickly turn to anger. I turn my head to glare murder up at Marise and his minions who blindly follow a man who also blindly follows another corrupted soul. I have no doubt that Dran is behind this and even if I have to haunt him Flare will get his justice. Dran was the one who wanted us to look for this camp. Dran also was the one who has every reason to want us dead, those reasons being very few people know what he did to his sister. If Raja had no more will to live then the people would demand Dran to rule. I know most people won't put two and two together.

Marise kicks me in my wound, "let's get the offerings ready they will be here soon." I see black for a while laying still to bring no more punishment on myself. A man from our group moves over me chanting. As he leans over me he pulls a silver band from his pocket.

I dig my hand further into Flare's fur to clear my muddled thoughts and the black spots in my vision. The man grabs my arm attaching the silver band onto the already attached one. The leopard on the band is curled up eyes closed and completely still for the first time ever. The dragon seems in a tizzy not liking the added silver or anything.

He holds my arm and chants. The band goes liquid and moves to cover over my skin seeping like a parasite into my skin. I watch in abject horror as the silver substance moves through my skin spreading everywhere to cover me. I have no energy to fight it but I wish I could.

The substance seems to shimmer and seep into my eyes, I feel spasms going through my body, and my vision goes black. I draw my knees up to my chest trying to ward off the new pain. I cry out as my skin ripples and my bones break and move. Then everything stops except the wound that steadily pulses from my stomach.

I slowly regain my eye sight having to blink away the giant black splotches. I reach out to Flare once more… except my arms wont stretch as far, and something is wrapped around me, everything feels different. I open my mouth to scream at them to ask what's going on but all that comes out are confused snarls.

When did they tie me up? My skin has been crawling so much they could've, I'm not even sure I would've felt it. I struggle to my feet… on all four of them… I look down seeing black fur instead of my smooth skin. Marise chuckles, "they have a taste for cat more than human, we aim to please." He kicks me in my stomach, aggravating the wound so I fall down again with oomph. "*You won't get away with this,*" I send telepathically like I would to Flare, seeming how I can't scream it at him vocally, to haunt him for the rest of his miserable life.

"Ah, they are here, bye, bye kitty." Marise chuckles to himself and waves in an exaggerated movement. Something picks the thing weighing me down off of me, and then I feel the familiar feel of claws closing around my stomach none to nicely.

He's gone…

The claws lift me into the air and away from Marise who grins evilly from below. My head swivels to see Flare in another set of claws, long gone from this world. The creature that carries us shakes me roughly hurting my wound. Sending my mind into darkness, only thing to keep me going are the words, '*I will get revenge,*' and '*I will get back to Raja.*'

*

To be continued

MAIN CHARACTER LIST

Esper Colette- 17+ years old, long auburn hair, violet eyes, five feet four inches, curvy. Carries an ancient sword named Saphique, Bonded to Flare, and Raja, rides **Vala** a black fire horse.

Flare- Young Leopard, Esper's and Raja's bonded,

Raja- Dragon, black tinted purple and blue, water and sky dragon. Long leather wings, five fingers and toes, his tail ends in a fin with seven webbings attached to spikes, two spikes at the base of his tail. Golden slit pupil eyes and lots of scales. Esper's and Flare's bonded.

Garrett and Dante Virose- identical twins, 10+ years old, shaggy black hair and blue eyes, fight with slingshot. Riding twin water hoses **Arachnid, Navi** white dappled grey and blue water horse.

Toni Daylagos- 16+ years old, brown hair, brown eyes, chiseled face, and gangly body. Loves sports and fights with a long sword. Bonded Cobalt, rides **Philip** a blue roan thoroughbred.

Cobalt- a young wolf, waist high, silver fur, cobalt on his ears, and alpha. Mated to **Aurora** a silver wolf, bonded to Toni.

Dash Stay- 16+ years old, handsome mocha/Carmel skin and full lips, black hair and big brown calf eyes; Bonded to Sheena.

Sheena- pure white Pegasus tinted blue a little, stubborn and sarcastic, loves food especially sweets. Bonded to Michael.

Lucan Ren- 15+ years old, Raven's fraternal twin, hazel eyes, with bleach blonde hair cropped short, and a lean body. Fights with double short swords, bonded to Shar and rides **Davidia** a shadow horse.

Shar- Male, young, under three feet green and black python, loves mice.

Raven Ren- 15+ year old, black hair, grey eyes, all about makeup and fashion, and slim, with a crush on Michael.

Bonded to Verico, rides a white and rainbow unicorn named Dalia.

Verico- a black and white climber monkey baby, shifty, sneaky, hates water, and quick; bonded to Raven.

Yanni –14+ years old, came from Earth, German with sandy blonde hair, all limbs, and blue eyes. Rides **Red**

Jenni- 4+ years old, has long curly red hair, rounded face, beautiful green eyes, and a great personality.

Dragos- An older man who teaches kids to fight, scruffy looking, and has a crush on **Carmen** the inn keeper.

Delan- Unknown age, six foot tall or taller, dark chocolate hair, ice blue eyes, built big.

Zar- King of the dragons, Raja's dad, gold body, bigger than most of the dragons. Zar is mated to **Averia**, who is queen of the dragons, water dragon herself, with blue green coloring, and is her mates life. They had three children, Dran the older, Joan of Arc (tittle given for a heroic dead), and Raja.

Dran- White gold dragon with a gold translucent ruff, bejeweled talon sheaths, and his tail modified to have spikes protruding from them, and sleek body.

Michael- golden brown skin, brown hair, green grey eyes, and silver earing, muscular body, five foot ten inches. He uses a bow that produces daggers at both ends and dual daggers named Necrosis and Misery. Bonded to **Zoe** a pale Griffin, bald eagle head and albino lion body with amber eyes.

Remidus- Raja's friend, battle dragon, he is white with a black fade, and speckles of color, assigned flying partner **Lolane**.

Apolala – Raja's friend, crimson with a black fade with streaks of gold, assigned to **Laurence.**

Grocin- Raja's friend big flier, a solid silver grey, assigned to **William**.

Quinn- A baby griffin with dark a body and molting fuzzy golden eagle head. Quinn is a former slave captive and newest member of Esper's Family.